THE
NEVER
HERO

THE CHRONICLES OF JONATHAN TIBBS

T. ELLERY HODGES

Cover design by Damon Za

www.damonza.com

Library of Congress Control Number: 2016910549

Foggy Night Publishing, Seattle, WA

ISBN-13: 978-0-9907746-2-4

ISBN-10: 0-9907746-2-7

Dedicated to all who wondered where their Mr. Miyagi was while life was beating them down

PROLOGUE

SEPTEMBER 2003

IT WAS COLD in the elevator shaft. The surfaces of the building's inner structure, where only maintenance men ever visited, were sheathed in years of built up dust. It was silent by nature—the only noise that found its way into the dark passage was the occasional passing of the elevator car. A button would be pressed and the hoist would come to life, taking the lift from one floor to another. The doorway would open, the passenger would exit, and the shaft would return to its hibernation.

Somewhere on the building's upper levels, a powerful impact broke the silence, ripping the steel doors off their mounts and shooting two enemies into the shaft. Light burst into the passage as the figures struck the adjacent wall. They began to fall, each struggling to gain the advantage over the other, grappling with limbs, trying to maneuver so that one would find himself on top when they hit the ground.

Peter's hair whipped past his face as he plunged out of the light and into the darkness below. He grunted as the beast pushed him into one of the I-beams lining the shaft's corridor.

The enemy always had an edge in tight spaces. They had more mass to use against him. This, and the darkness, was putting him at a considerable disadvantage.

He'd been outclassed since the fight began, unable to find a vulnerability. Now, as he fell deeper into the dark, he knew that if he didn't land on top, it would be the end. It wouldn't kill the beast to take the brunt of the fall, but it might hurt the bastard enough to turn the tables.

He could only imagine the ground rushing towards them. He couldn't see in the blackness, but knew his enemy could. He felt another impact, sensed their momentum slow, and knew the beast had taken a hit against one of the beams just as he had a moment earlier.

I hope it hurts, he thought.

They slammed back and forth violently, beam to beam, until their bodies dropped into free fall down the shaft's center. Despite Peter's efforts, it had little effect on the uncontrollable spin into the dark. They crashed hard into the basement floor. The cement cracked beneath them as it absorbed their fall. The lower floors of the building rumbled as the vibrations from the impact shook its foundation.

The beast's weight on top of him made the sudden stop feel like being crushed between two walls. Ribs broke. A lung collapsed. The air rushed out of him and he nearly lost his grasp on consciousness. On the ground floor, he desperately attempted to breathe, but only coughed on mouthfuls of agitated dust. He knew he'd lost.

The beast, hurt but not injured, rose to its feet over him, its massive shoulders and head only an outline as the light from above kept its features in shadow. It seemed to be waiting, hoping Peter would get to his feet and fight back. In his panic, it was all he could do to focus on breathing. Forcing his broken body to stand was no longer possible.

Peter searched for the zipper holding his jacket shut. His fingers fumbled through gloved hands as he tried to get a grip, desperate to make his breathing easier. Finally grasping the pull tab, he drew the jacket open. A soft orange glow from beneath his T-shirt illuminated the passage. The light, like a candle in a cave, brought his enemy's face into view. It flinched as its eyes adjusted.

Breathing painfully, he met the monster's gaze. He'd never seen one of them hold still this long, never looked into their empty white eyes. This was the first time he'd been this helpless in front of one. His enemy could see he no longer presented a threat.

Its large hand reached down, grasping him by the jacket, and raised his body out of the small crater they'd punched into the floor. The movement was agony. He could feel his ribs, loose within his torso, moving unnaturally under his muscles, and he cried out. The beast pressed his back against the wall of the shaft, his feet dangling a foot from the floor, his head at eye level with the monster. Peter let his hands fall to his sides, all his energy going into the effort to breathe, to keeping his head up.

"Go to Hell," he whispered. If he'd had the strength, he'd have spit the blood now pooling in his throat into the thing's face.

Its head tilted.

The beast had heard the words, but did not seem to comprehend. Peter could guess at its confusion—it didn't know what the term meant. There was no word like *Hell* in the damn thing's language.

It didn't seem to concern itself for long with comprehension. It said nothing, and Peter saw that its neck was contracting, bulging up around its jaw line. He looked away, letting his head come to rest on his chest.

Better to close your eyes, he thought.

He tried to think of his parents, his brother and sister. He heard the monster's mouth opening, heard it growling, felt the heat of its breath. He thought about the damn blond man, how he had asked Peter to fight. When the teeth sunk into his neck, he cried out again, clenching his eyes shut as the blood ran. The beast's head jerked back and forth mercilessly as it ripped the flesh from him. He wailed as the skin and muscle tore free, heard the beast spitting out parts of him to the shaft's floor.

Peter remembered the blond man had asked, "Will you help us stand against them?" It was the last thing that crossed his thoughts before they stopped forever.

The light in his chest began to flicker and fade as his heart struggled to push less and less blood through his body. Eventually, the glow died out entirely and the creature was returned to darkness. It frothed from its jaws, its saliva becoming thick with a waxy purple excretion. The process was short lived, interrupted by the arrival of the gate as it surrounded the beast and Peter's body. For a moment, the shaft was filled with the gateway's bright red light. Then there was a sudden flash of white.

The passage was dark; no light from above, no imploded doors, no damaged walls, and no crater in the flooring. Somewhere in the upper floors, a passenger called the lift. The elevator came, the doorway opened, and the passenger boarded. The car lowered, stopped, and delivered its occupant. The shaft returned to silence, a place no one ever went, waiting for its next passenger, hibernating.

DECEMBER 1996

SEVEN YEARS EARLIER

CHAPTER ONE

DECEMBER 1996 | SEVEN YEARS EARLIER

HIS HAND GLIDED over the mahogany, lingering on the table's smooth surface, cool to the touch as he moved his fingertips slowly from one picture frame to the next. The table with the photos stood out against the gray walls and white trim. Jonathan had chosen those colors. His father had let him pick out the paint when they had refinished the hallway, under the condition that he chose something tasteful.

"Be nice if it matches the furniture, too," his father had said.

Getting to pick the paint had made Jonathan more interested in helping to do the work, as its success or failure then hinged on one of his decisions. He'd only realized later that Douglas, his father, had planned it that way, to give him a stake in the outcome.

That memory was far away now as he stood there in his black suit and tie, his brown hair combed neatly; a thirteen-year-old boy without a father.

When Jonathan's grandfather had passed, he'd put up a fuss about wearing the suit. He'd asked his father why it mattered. What was a pair of slacks over a pair of jeans? How was an uncomfortable collar or a tie relevant to showing respect? If they had to be grieving, couldn't they at least do it in comfortable clothes?

He'd been eleven then and his father, patience wearing thin from grief, had let out a tired sigh as he knelt in front of Jonathan to help him with his tie.

"Traditions get passed down; they become the rules. Some make sense, some seem pointless, but others," Douglas said, "others only show their value when you don't obey them."

"This one seems stupid," Jonathan responded, squirming in his tight collar as his father finished.

"Well," Douglas said, standing and turning to the mirror to put on his own tie, "I don't think today is the day that we test the rules."

Jonathan had started to press his case. He'd never liked following rules. He wanted to know the reasons behind things, but his father had cut him off.

"Jonathan, your grandfather followed this rule, and he would appreciate it if you followed it for him. It's literally," he paused, "the last thing you'll ever have to do for him."

Douglas looked cross at first, but even at eleven, Jonathan could see it wasn't anger. After all, his father had just lost his own father, and Douglas' own words, *The last thing you'll ever have to do for him,"* had caught him unprepared. They brought the kind of outpouring of emotion that even a grown man was hard-pressed to hide, and a tear emerged from his father's eye.

It was the only time Jonathan had ever seen him cry, and a wave of guilt washed over him. Immediately, he felt ashamed of himself for worrying about a thing like comfortable clothes on the day of a funeral. Even at eleven, that guilt had brought his father's grief into clarity.

"Yes, sir," he said, staring down at his shoes. "I'm sorry, Dad."

Now, only two years later, in a suit and tie again, staring at the photos of his own father in the hallway, Jonathan understood. His mother hadn't had to fight with him to put the suit on. It wasn't a rule he cared to challenge. If his father had wanted it, it didn't matter if it made sense.

It was one of the last things he could do for his own father now, and it wasn't enough.

The photos of Douglas had been set out for the wake. They were all taken long before Jonathan was born. He picked up one of the black frames from the table. The picture was of Douglas with four other men from the Army, none of whom Jonathan recognized. A notation under-neath was put out for the guests. It read *Staff Sergeant Douglas Tibbs with the surviving members of his Army Ranger Strike Team, Libya, 1984.* The men in the picture looked solemn, sad. Jonathan had to assume that the keyword from the photo was "surviving." Perhaps this photo was taken after one of the team had been lost. There was a lot his father had never gotten the chance to tell him.

Jonathan set the frame back down carefully and walked away, mak-ing his way through the friends and relatives in his living room. He was hoping to get away before he was drawn into another outpouring of a vis-itor's condolences. A man he didn't recognize put his hand on Jonathan's shoulder before he could make his way out of the room. Jonathan halted politely, looking up at him.

"I just wanted to tell you, Jonathan," the man said, "you were well-spoken today. The words you said at the funeral were heartfelt. Your dad would have been moved to hear them."

Jonathan nodded politely, thanking the man for the compliment.

He'd been told this a number of times today, and didn't know what else to say outside of "thank you." He didn't understand why they felt the need to tell him this. Perhaps, having never met Jonathan outside the funeral, it was all they knew of him to comment on. If Jonathan was supposed to find some pride in his speech, he couldn't feel it through his grief. That, and didn't they see he hadn't said a word of his own? All he'd done was written down his father's own thoughts as he remembered them, putting the words together in a speech. His dad had always had a way of saying things. He'd have been a fraud taking credit for them.

He left the man and walked into his father's garage. It was the only place in the house that wasn't made immaculate for the wake and the closest thing Douglas had had to an office. The garage had a cement floor. It was cold and dusty, having seen years of cars being torn down and rebuilt. There were oil stains that had absorbed the grime of the floor, metal shavings, loose bolts. The work bench was exactly how Douglas had left it. His tools were still out. A rag where he'd wiped grease from his hands sat on a vise grip bolted to the work bench. His father's stool was empty.

Taking up most of the garage space was an old truck. Jonathan didn't know where his dad had found these projects, or what moved him to work on them. The thing looked like it belonged a hundred miles away on a farm. It was the color of rust, if it wasn't just simply rusted; Jonathan couldn't tell. Douglas had still been in the middle of repairing it, but Jonathan couldn't imagine what was wrong with the thing. He'd never asked because he wouldn't have understood the answer.

Heavy chains attached to a hoist had the truck's engine suspended out of the vehicle. Jonathan gripped the links with his hands. The chain was cold, tough, so strong it held gravity at bay. The metal was clean and new, in stark contrast to the dirty engine that it supported.

When he released the chain, he sat on his father's stool, his feet not yet able to reach the floor, and pondered the engine. He thought he should try to finish the project—a symbolic effort to his father's memory—but it seemed too complicated. Without his dad, he wouldn't know how to start, and he felt defeat before he'd even begun. For a fleeting moment, finishing what his father had started seemed worth the effort to learn.

"He'd never see it," Jonathan said to himself, the statement crushing his drive to carry out the sentimental gesture as soon as he'd said it.

When his mother had told him his father was gone, when what she was saying had truly sunk in, he'd been ashamed at his initial reaction. It hadn't been grief, although that had come later. It had been a suffocating fear. Jonathan had known, quite suddenly, that the shield between him and the world, the force that had defied reality to keep him sheltered, was suddenly gone, and he was afraid—afraid that he wasn't ready to rely on himself.

Remembering it now, he began to sob. Was he so selfish? Was his first reaction to the death of his father no more than fear for himself? The self-defeating thoughts made him want to lie on the floor and cradle his knees against his chest. He couldn't though, not here. He wasn't going to lie on the filthy floor. Not in the clothes he wore out of respect for his father.

The garage door creaked open and Jonathan turned away to face the wall. He didn't want to be seen sitting in this depressing garage sobbing.

He hoped whoever it was would find that they'd opened the wrong door and leave him. Instead, he heard footsteps, and when a hand rested on his shoulder, he was forced to look up through his reddened eyes and see who was interrupting him despite his obvious wish for solitude.

He was relieved to see his mother, Evelyn. There was no shame crying in front of her; there never had been. They'd had their bouts with tears since the news had come, and this wouldn't be the last of it. Still, his mother seemed to have more control over the emotions. It wasn't that she loved Douglas any less than Jonathan did, or that she wasn't assaulted by unwanted pain. It was more that she seemed to have accepted the reality of the loss.

She didn't have the same luxury of a thirteen-year-old boy. After all, she was a mother, and still had Jonathan to keep herself together for. Evelyn was more practiced with grief. She'd already endured the loss of her own parents as well as her father-in-law just two years earlier. She knew the terrain of this pain, whereas Jonathan walked it now for the first time.

"Gonna be okay?" his mother asked.

Jonathan shook his head, wiping the tears from his cheeks. She hugged his head to her and began to rock. Some time passed, neither speaking as they swayed. Eventually, Jonathan broke the silence.

"When do we feel normal again?" he asked.

Evelyn sighed.

"Never, really," she said softly. "Tomorrow we'll get up, and what we thought was normal will just be a memory we took for granted. So we'll try to find a new normal, and eventually, wherever that is, we will start to feel okay again. Until—"

She'd cut herself off, but it didn't matter. Jonathan had already known where her thoughts had been headed.

Until something else happens and takes it away again, he thought.

JUNE 2005

NINE YEARS LATER

CHAPTER TWO

JUNE 03, 2005 | 7:30 PM – 9 YEARS LATER

IN A POORLY lit room, a man sat at a desk in front of a computer. The office was simple; old linoleum flooring that had once been white, cinder block walls, one metal door, one power outlet, a desk, a phone, and a filing cabinet. The man was studying images as they downloaded onto the screen. The pictures were from various cities around the globe. The only thing every photo had in common was a tall man with blond hair down to his chin, wearing a black woolen trench coat and a fedora. The phone rang.

"Yes?" answered the man at the desk.

"Have you received the files?" asked a voice, masked by a speech modulator.

"I'm reviewing them," the man said. "Have you found a pattern in his movements?"

"Most of his recent U.S. destinations have been in the Northwest. Seattle, specifically," said the caller.

"Should we expect an incident?" the man asked.

"It fits with previous patterns," the caller replied.

"Have these appearances been confined to a sector of the city?"

"Yes, a university campus."

The man at the desk didn't respond immediately. He seemed to be mulling the answer over.

"That doesn't fit any previous pattern," he finally said.

There was a delay on the other side of the phone; finally, the disguised voice responded.

"No, it doesn't."

"Any theories?" asked the man.

"Still in progress. Will you be dispatching a team to investigate?" asked the voice.

"Yes. Two: one through standard channels, the other through the private sector. Solid work as usual," the man at the desk said, hanging up.

He saved the images and reports, encrypting the files as he attached them to two identical emails. All that was typed in the first email was, *Seattle, WA. Secondary protocol. Dispatch ASAP. In* the second email, he wrote the same instruction and then stopped. After thinking for a moment, he added the words *Should be safe* and sent off the messages.

The man reclined in his chair and let out a frustrated sigh as he stared at the images of the man in the dark hat.

"What the hell are you doing on a college campus?"

CHAPTER THREE

FRIDAY | JUNE 17, 2005 | 8:00 PM | SEATTLE

"WHAT THE HELL just happened?" Collin asked, as if on cue.

Jonathan stood over the half-dismantled motorcycle, considering just how annoying the slip of his wrench was going to prove. It would slow their progress, of course, but more, it guaranteed him crap from Collin.

"Tibbs! You think I'll ever let you ride Jenny again if you're this clumsy?" Collin added.

Collin had a habit of calling Jonathan by his last name when he was about to say something condescending. The two stood in the driveway of the house they shared with the rest of their college roommates. It was an older house, located on Capitol Hill, an inner city neighborhood of Seattle. Living there, Jonathan sometimes got the feeling he was in the woods and not the city at all. The illusion was due to their driveway being sunken into a dense grouping of trees and bushes that blocked the view of the street from the front yard.

Less than half an hour ago, having returned home from school, Collin had stopped Jonathan on his way into the house under the pretext that he needed help with some maintenance on the motorcycle, which he'd endearingly named Jenny. Collin didn't admit it, but he was trying to get Jonathan to take an interest in the hobby. He'd managed to get Jonathan to an empty parking lot on a couple of weekends so he could learn to drive the thing. He seemed to hope getting Jonathan to do some of the upkeep would get him more excited about *guy stuff*, as Collin referred to it.

With Jenny's gas tank lying next to them on the pavement, Tibbs had clumsily dropped the bolt he'd unscrewed into her air intake system and couldn't see where it had gone. Now, he looked at their front door, deliberating on how long it would be before he could get back to work on the half-finished paper he needed to complete by Monday for his Phylogeny class. He didn't hate working on the bike, but he'd put a lot of work in this quarter to keep his grade in B minus territory. It was only Friday, so he tried to remind himself to relax.

Jonathan set down the wrench and headed toward the garage in search of a flashlight.

"Jenny doesn't mind," he said, grinning over his shoulder at Collin. "She says it's all foreplay."

Collin gave the motorcycle a disapproving look.

"Do not flirt with this man; you do him no service leading him on."

The owner of the house had been renting to college kids for over a decade now, as its layout and location were suited to low income students. Meaning it had four bedrooms so the rent was split four ways, it was close to campus, and more important, it was close to the bars. Both Collin and Jonathan attended the University of Washington, as did their other roommates, Hayden and Paige. Collin and Hayden had been friends since high school, but the rest had only met when they moved in together for school.

In the garage, Jonathan fumbled through the tool box to find the small flashlight. When he returned, he saw Paige walking down the driveway. She wore her dark hair short, and her skin was remarkably pale for how much time she spent out in the sun. Urban Agriculture and the Environmental Sciences, her majors, tended to put her out in the campus greenhouses a lot, working on her green thumb. Her eyes were up in the trees and she was smiling. The past week she'd been in such a good mood it bordered on irritating.

Jonathan watched as her eyes speculated on the scene in the driveway. First, the dismantled bike parts on the pavement, then Collin bent over the frame, staring intently down into where the gas tank should have been, then to Jonathan, hands covered in grime and holding the flashlight. Her smile widened as she raised an eyebrow.

"Oh dear, Tibbs, what have you done to Jenny?" she asked.

"Foreplay," Collin replied before Jonathan could speak.

"I thought she was a classier gal than that," Paige said.

"Burn," Collin said.

Jonathan shrugged it off.

"What's with you?" Collin said to Paige. "You've looked stupid-happy for days now."

Paige considered the two, weighing if she should tell them. They watched the desire to keep a secret dissolve as she gave in to the stronger urge to share it.

"You guys remember Grant?" she asked.

Collin and Jonathan looked from one to the other blankly before Collin spoke for both of them, "I'm going with no."

"The Army guy who bought me a drink at the bar a week back," she said.

Collin and Jonathan shared the same blank look again. The two weren't being purposely obtuse. A lot of men approached Paige offering to buy her a drink.

She looked at Collin. "The one you referred to as Meathead for the rest of the night."

Clarity surfaced on Collin's face.

"Right. Meathead," he said, then asked, "Meathead was in the Army?"

"Well, *Grant*," she said, ignoring his question, "called a minute ago. He's in Seattle. I invited him to join us tonight."

"Great!" Collin said.

Only Jonathan caught the false enthusiasm. It was harmless, but not the first time he'd seen Collin turn passive-aggressive when Paige talked about dating. He'd chosen to suppress his feelings for her; not just because they lived together, but because of Paige's blatant attraction to macho males. Dark, muscular, military sorts, like this Grant fellow, always seemed to be the ones she got excited about. Collin was blond, pale, and no more muscular than Jonathan, who probably couldn't do a pull up if he were hanging off the edge of a cliff. It didn't help Collin's physique or complexion that he was a Graphic Arts major and spent large amounts of his time glued to a chair in front of a computer screen.

"Speaking of, finish with the motorcycle later. We were supposed to meet Hayden ten minutes ago," Paige said, looking hurried as she headed into the house. "He could go off on one of his rants in front of Grant if we leave him unsupervised."

"Does that make us the less-embarrassing roommates?" Collin asked as she disappeared into the house.

Jonathan, thinking about it, didn't remember ever agreeing to go out this evening.

"So then you're joining us tonight, Tibbs?" Collin asked, looking needy.

He wanted to decline. On top of the paper he needed to find time for, Jonathan had to work part-time at a hardware store to supplement his student loans, and was opening tomorrow. His boss, Mr. Fletcher, was an old veteran who had an uncanny ability to detect a hangover on sight, a skill he obtained from years of experience commanding men in the military. Mr. Fletcher would never mention he suspected it; Jonathan would just slowly find he was being tortured by every task he was given. Regardless, trying to work after a night with his roommates was always a lesson in regret.

He could already feel Collin's needy facial expression breaking his resolve on that matter, and Paige seemed to have assumed he was coming.

"Okay, but I'll probably leave early," Jonathan said.

"Yes, of course, definitely," Collin said. A moment later, as he made his way in to the house, he added, "Maybe."

Jonathan pretended not to hear.

The bar was a dive. The booths, square and uncomfortable, looked like they had been built by the owner. It was poorly lit, with dark brown stain on all the furniture and a floor of polished cement. The only light was over the pool table in the back, and the entire place smelled like spilled beer had permeated every inch of wood to be found. Jonathan's roommates were drawn here regularly more because of its proximity to their house than by the atmosphere.

Grant was indeed military; short cropped hair, built, and competitive. He had systematically destroyed Collin and Hayden at the pool table. When he'd picked up on Collin's lack of enthusiasm about his presence, it hadn't fazed him, just made him more pleased with himself when he won.

"Want to play for the championship?" Grant asked Jonathan when he'd finished with his roommates.

"No thanks," Jonathan said. "I don't play. I'm sure you'd mop the floor with me."

Grant seemed disappointed he hadn't risen to the challenge.

After pool, they had shared a table for most of the evening, until it appeared that Grant lost interest in the roommates' discussion and asked Paige to join him in a separate booth.

She and Grant were now staring at each other intently. Jonathan didn't have to hear the words to get the context. He figured he would either be seeing Grant tomorrow morning or Paige wasn't coming home with them tonight.

As the hour grew late, Jonathan had nearly left, but he got caught up in an argument that Collin and Hayden were having.

"It's the same story!" Collin reiterated to Hayden.

Hayden was a larger man, overweight but not obesely so. He wore glasses and kept his brown hair short with a well-groomed beard. The beard was new, and he hadn't yet broken the habit of rubbing the hair around his mouth with his fingertips whenever he was thinking intensely. He was rubbing it now.

The argument had started over the question of whether or not the stories of Superman and the Biblical Jesus were thematically similar. Hayden, being a practicing Roman Catholic, wasn't initially very enthusiastic about the comparison.

"What have we got so far?" Collin asked, rubbing in his earlier victories. "Superhuman abilities, sent to earth as an orphan by his father who happened to be the leader of a spiritually and technologically superior race, adopted by human parents, and put here to inspire mankind to rise above their less-admirable natures."

"That's crap," Hayden replied. "It's similar on a superficial level at best."

"Oh come on, there isn't any defeat in admitting it," Collin said. "Hey, I just thought of another point. In the early nineties, Superman died to save mankind. Hey, Jonathan, can you guess what happened after that?"

"Please don't involve me," Jonathan replied.

"That's right! He was…." Collin paused for dramatic effect. "Resurrected."

Jonathan would have thought Collin was being a jerk, but the truth was, the two friends bickered like this all the time; that, and Collin hadn't actually started this debate. Collin had mentioned that he was thinking of getting the Superman shield tattooed on his arm. Jonathan had thought it was a misguided, booze-induced boast. Unfortunately, Hayden, not at the top of his game, hadn't seen it for the unlit fuse that it was.

"Sad, stupid cliché of a thing to get a tattoo of," Hayden had said.

"No sadder than a crucifix would be," Collin had replied.

Grant and Paige had gone off by themselves shortly after that. Jonathan had lost track of time listening.

"It's not the same," Hayden said. "Superman isn't based on any historical facts; it's a work of fiction."

"Hayden, come on. Ask an Atheist if the Bible is a work of fiction. They'd hold it with the same esteem they do legends of Zeus and Hercules, which, I might add, are both also comic book characters," Collin argued. "If I get a Superman tattoo on my arm, it would be a symbol of values that I happen to find inspiring, just like a crucifix would be on your arm."

"A crucifix isn't just a symbol. It's not based on a work of fiction!" Hayden said.

The two were going to circle around this more than once. Neither was going to sway the other, as was their way, but they enjoyed the bickering nonetheless. As the night moved on and they consumed more drinks, the debate devolved into the apparent differences in the storylines, in which both of them were now actively engaged.

"Superman will resort to violence," Collin said, starting to slur, "but Jesus was a pacifist."

"Jesus didn't have a secret identity," Hayden said, his eyes looking drowsy.

Jonathan was getting up to leave as it was approaching one in the morning and he still needed to be half-competent at work the next day. He said goodbye to Collin and Hayden, waving across the bar to Grant and Paige.

As he was putting his coat on, Hayden turned to him.

"Jonathan, if you had to pick between Superman or Jesus, which would it be?" Hayden asked.

"For a tattoo?" he asked.

Hayden shrugged, as if to say, Take the question however you want.

Jonathan thought about it as he zipped his coat up.

"Neither," he said. "Yeah, definitely neither."

Hayden frowned at him as he made for the door, obviously feeling like the answer had been a cop-out. He turned back to Collin.

"This might be blasphemous, but I think we should reboot the New Testament as a graphic novel and present Jesus as a parody of Superman. I bet it would be hysterical."

The last thing Jonathan heard as the door shut behind him was Collin saying, "You had me at blasphemous."

At the end of the bar, a tall blond man in a long black coat rose to his feet. Placing a black fedora on his head, he followed Jonathan out the door.

CHAPTER FOUR

SATURDAY | JUNE 18, 2005 | 1:15 AM

AFTER SO LONG in the bar, the smell of alcohol and secondhand smoke was heavy on him and the street was crowded with others who smelled the same.

Laundry day tomorrow, he thought, recoiling from his T-shirt. On second thought, he considered throwing the shirt away entirely.

As he began to walk away, the bar door opened again behind him. He turned to look, thinking Collin and Hayden might have decided to head home with him. Instead, a tall blond man stepped out of the door way and turned in his direction.

"Excuse me," the man said as he passed, never really looking Jonathan in the eye.

The sight of the man gave Jonathan pause, like he'd seen the relative of someone he may have known once, but the association was too distant to grasp. His eyes watched the man's back as he walked away, and he felt a chill. It wasn't that it was disturbing, just that the man shouldn't be there, but Jonathan didn't know why.

He'd never been a fan of intuition. He didn't like getting a notion and not knowing its source any more than he liked following a rule without understanding the reason behind it. Intuition was like bringing a new lover home for the first time and having your dog get overly upset at the sight of her. It forced him to speculate on what the animal's instincts might see that he could not, and it was irritating. If his animal brain knew something, he'd prefer it explain itself.

If the man had seemed out of place, it was something not easily achieved given the surroundings. Standing on a street corner on Capitol Hill was like being bombarded with what might otherwise be called the "*out of place.*"

This region of the city was diverse; a mixture of overpasses, hills, and parks. Old brick buildings resided next to modern condos, upscale coffee shop chains sat next to stores owned by spiritual gurus selling Buddhist and Indian knick-knacks. Expensive restaurants were across the street from adult toy stores. The union of unlikely neighbors was a reflection of the community itself. College students, all shades of the LGBT, goths, hippies, and hipsters were all thrown together here.

Sticking out in this crowd took a lot more than a ridiculous fedora. Why should a stranger, in a street full of strangers who were all more noticeable, stand out to him? Why would he evoke such a peculiar reaction?

Standing there looking troubled, he started to realize he was being ridiculous. After all, he'd been drinking, and though it was odd, it wasn't the first time that alcohol had swayed his emotions in a strange direction. He turned away and headed home, plunging into the moving crowds on the sidewalk. He looked over his shoulder once more, but the tall man was now lost in the flock.

He soon found that his instincts weren't so easy to shake off. His mind wouldn't let go of the unexplained anomaly he'd sensed at seeing the man's face. It became worse when he walked past his reflection in a window and thought he'd spotted the man behind him only to look again and see it was some other stranger walking amongst the crowd. He tried to laugh at himself, turn his thoughts over to other distractions, yet suspicion lingered, and he didn't feel safe.

Stop being paranoid.

Still, he found himself walking faster, his eyes scanning the crowd with uncertainty. The feeling didn't seem to alleviate until he was within sight of home.

He entered through the side door of the garage. The larger car door was down now as Jenny still laid in pieces on the cement floor, surrounded by the tools that he and Collin hadn't had time to put away. The four of them didn't use the place for anything but Collin's bike and the garage stayed fairly empty. Hayden was the only one who had a car, but he tended to park it in the driveway. Jonathan stepped up the small set of stairs leading to the door that connected the garage with the house.

He crossed the living room and hung his coat in the closet at the foot of the stairs. Jonathan and Paige's rooms were on the second floor, while Hayden and Collin's were off of the living room on the main floor. In the kitchen, he poured a glass of water out of the pitcher they kept in the refrigerator, setting it onto the counter. While he did so, he popped a few precautionary Ibuprofen, painkillers, and water, a ritual he'd developed for whenever his roommates got him out for the evening.

For a moment, he wondered if his mother had done the same when she'd been in college. It was hard to imagine that this was an innovation to college drinking that his generation could claim. He'd have to ask her someday. He smiled to himself as it occurred to him that it would have to wait until after he graduated, or she'd start worrying that he would party himself out of school when she inevitably read too much into the question. Evelyn was like that, always overly worried about college in particular. It amused Jonathan. College was a struggle at times, but he didn't have any doubts he'd graduate. He'd always been more worried about what came after, when real life began and the pressures of the world outside the shield of higher education started making their demands on him.

Thoughts like this should have made him more tranquil, at least those of his mother. They were comfortable, after all; endearing. Instead, he felt uneasy again. It stopped him mid-swallow as he looked over the empty living room. His eyes surveyed the house, looking for something lurking in the shadows. Perhaps it was just too quiet, he thought. The absence of people was unusual here. He couldn't remember the last time he'd been the only one home, and somehow even that thought disturbed him. He stood there for a moment, listening to the silence, annoyed again that the paranoia made no rational sense.

This wasn't even a particularly ominous evening. There was no thunder or lighting; it was Seattle and it wasn't even raining.

Nothing.

"Be brave, Tibbs," he said out loud, finishing off his water.

He frowned as he noticed that apparently he called himself *Tibbs* when he wasn't taking himself seriously. Leaving the pitcher out for Collin and Hayden, he started to climb the stairs to his bedroom. On the second step, he heard a noise and froze. It was so slight he wasn't sure if he'd imagined it, like a dresser drawer being gently pushed shut. It hadn't been a creak of a floor board or some sound that older houses made. Hesitant, he was already wondering if his inebriated mind was playing a trick on him. It wasn't out of the question, given how jumpy he'd been since leaving the bar.

Standing there, it occurred to him that there weren't a lot of realistic options in these moments. It wasn't the first time he thought he'd heard something strange when he was in a house alone. It wasn't as if he could call out and hope that if there was an intruder, a real one and not a figment of his imagination, he would politely reveal himself. He couldn't call the police because he thought he'd heard "something" and felt frightened.

No, Jonathan was going to deal with this the same way most everyone did when these moments came up.

He kept his eyes looking upstairs as he backed down one step. Without needing to look, he reached around the corner and opened the closet door where he'd hung his coat moments ago. Gently feeling around the corner between the door frame and the closet wall, he found the house's low budget security system, the handle of an aluminum baseball bat. He gripped the bat with both hands at chest level, reassured himself that he was being paranoid, and proceeded forth to clear the house.

He crept up each step and reached the landing where it T-ed; on the left was Paige's room, on the right was his own. Straight ahead was a bathroom, but the door hung open and he could see from the staircase that it was empty. He thought the sound had come from his room, so he headed that way, attempting to move slowly, creeping forward.

This is ridiculous, he thought. No one is up here.

His door was open just an inch. Had he left it that way? He could have. He had pretty much just run in and changed his clothes when Paige had asked them to get moving earlier. He usually shut it though. His hand reached for the door knob, then he thought better of it and pulled his hand back.

Tibbs, he thought. Just get this over with.

He narrowed his eyes and used the end of the bat to push the door open slowly.

The room was dark, but nothing stood out as abnormal. His bed and nightstand were against the left wall. His two bookcases stood against the back wall next to his closet. The closet door hung open, and all there was to see inside was shadow. On the right was his desk, sitting under a large corner window, beside his dresser. His laptop sat on the desk. Other than that, the desk was empty except for a small cigar box.

He kept the room spartan, clean, as empty as possible, everything with a function and everything in its place. Even his bed was made, as his mother had drilled the habit into him growing up. The only light coming into the room was the moonlight from the window. At ease, Jonathan stood in his doorway and let the bat come to rest next to his leg.

"Your book collection is somewhat of a mystery for a man your age," said a calm voice from the darkness.

Jonathan jumped, startled. Even coming up here looking for an intruder, he'd never actually expected to discover one, and the voice had spoken the moment he'd dropped his guard. The bat shot back up into its ready position so suddenly he'd almost hit himself with it. The jump back was no less graceful and he nearly lost his footing. Luckily, his free hand had instinctively reached for the wall behind him to keep him from falling.

Leaning against the wall, Jonathan frantically searched the dark shadows of the room for the source of the voice. He saw now why he'd initially missed the figure. He was standing beside one of his bookcases, framed by the blackness of the closet. As the man turned his head to face Jonathan, his movement gave him away, his pale skin and blond hair standing out in contrast to the dark, no longer hidden by the black fedora.

The blond man from the bar stood looking back at him, studying him.

"I did not mean to startle you, Jonathan," he said.

The man's face looked sorry, genuinely apologetic. Jonathan found it unnerving to have such an expression under the circumstances. The man turned with a snake-like smoothness, as though his body were gracefully transitioning to look in the direction that his eyes were already facing.

Jonathan felt rigid and still, failing to think of words to speak and unable to move his mouth to form them. His mind raced to sort out the situation, and with alarm he realized the man had used his name.

The stranger began to come closer, walking toward him with slow, calculated steps. Jonathan fought to retreat, to will himself to move against the adrenaline locking him in place.

"Textbooks, non-fiction, true crime, yet all the novels you own were printed fifty years before you were born. Aren't you odd?" the stranger asked, seeming to look at Jonathan as though he were the question.

As the intruder drew closer, Jonathan finally found control of his legs and began to back away, keeping an unchanging distance between them. When the man stood before him in the doorway, he paused.

"I'm sorry I'm here, waiting in the dark like this, Jonathan. I had to be sure I could slip away if you were not alone. Of course, I doubt a statement like that would put anyone at ease," he said. "I often get curious about people; I find bookcases revealing, usually. Though, yours somehow makes you cloudier."

His eyes darted up and down the man. The stranger stood a foot taller than him, and Jonathan was a solid six feet himself. He seemed to still be waiting for Jonathan to answer, and grew thoughtful when he didn't.

"You aren't a talkative one," the man observed. "Also curious, also different. I'd have expected rage, an instinctual territorialism, yet you hardly seem to want to use that weapon."

Jonathan didn't want to use the club. He wanted the man to be afraid of it and not escalate the situation. His eyes took a quick glance at the staircase. Soon he'd be able to make a break for it, get outside, get to a neighbor's house, call the police, and get this crazy stalker arrested. As though he could read Jonathan's mind, the stranger spoke again.

"Don't, Jonathan," he said. "You would only prolong this."

The man began to move toward him. His face grew heavier with the weight of what he was doing as his hand reached into the front breast pocket of his coat. An urgency surfaced in Jonathan as the stranger reached for that pocket. He knew he had to turn the tables now, psychologically. He had to become the threat giver and not the threatened. If he didn't make a show of strength, the intruder would only be encouraged by his weakness.

Finally, he managed to remove the look of fear on his face, to contort his features into anger as he retreated back. He raised the bat and spoke.

"Don't."

To Jonathan's credit, it actually sounded like he meant to strike should the man keep moving forward.

The intruder took notice of the change in Jonathan's attitude, but didn't stop. The distance between them began to close. Jonathan cranked the bat back like he was cocking a gun, the last warning to the man that he would defend himself, but the stranger only kept the regretful look on his face and moved closer, finally pulling his hand from the coat pocket, holding something small that Jonathan couldn't make out in the dark hallway.

When Jonathan made the decision, every cell in his adrenaline-drenched body committed. Swinging hard, the man discreetly brought his arm up, careful to make sure the bat didn't hit what he had pulled out of his pocket, but would only land on his forearm. It should have shattered the stranger's arm, but when the bat connected, there was a dull thud, and Jonathan retracted in shock. The vibration ran violently through his hand and wrist. It was as though he had swung full force at a bronze statue. The pain, so sharp and unexpected, made him lose his grip on the bat. He yelled out in surprise, dropping down onto his knees, and clutching his hand protectively as the bat clattered to the floor.

The man's free hand reached down and pulled Jonathan up with impossible strength. Moving slowly, he handled Jonathan like he was restraining a toddler, trying not to hurt him though he couldn't allow him to thrash about. He struggled, but kicking and hitting the intruder was useless. The man held Jonathan up with one arm, gripping his shoulder and neck above his collar bone. Jonathan found himself pinned, feet dangling a foot from the floor, with his back pushed against the wall. Realizing that he was hurting himself more than his attacker, he reached for the hand holding him off the ground. He may as well have had him in a vise for how little Jonathan's struggle affected the intruder's grip.

So close to the man, Jonathan saw the stranger's distinct face. Even in the darkness of the hallway, his eyes were wrong, seeming to glow as though they were backlit. They were blue, but an inhuman blue; an unnatural indigo, made all the more eerie by their strange incandescence..

"Jonathan, try to calm yourself. I mean you no harm. Nevertheless, this is going to be unpleasant; I can't help that," the man said. As he spoke, his free hand revealed the small item that he'd pulled from his coat pocket.

Jonathan had known no dread like seeing a syringe brought to his neck, no panic like struggling against a person he couldn't push away, to feel like a rabbit trying to hold open the jaws of a bear. As he watched the needle move closer, the moment seemed to stretch into an eternity. His muscles shook with the futile effort of trying to resist but were unable to even slow the needle as it plunged toward his throat.

At the moment he lost hope, when fear and powerlessness were a storm in Jonathan's thoughts, a single need made itself known. It surfaced in him like a prisoner escaping, tearing off the door to his cage, and brought with it a tranquilizing rage. One question became more important than everything happening around him.

"How do I know you?" asked a steady voice.

Jonathan was surprised to recognize the sound of his own anger in the question. The syringe stopped. The stranger tilted his head to look Jonathan in the eyes. In the light cast from the man's iris, Jonathan saw the slightest curve of a smile break the man's lip. Gone as quickly as it had come, the stranger's face became heavy again.

"You should not," the man replied.

The force behind the syringe began again, and though he never stopped struggling, Jonathan felt the needle pierce his skin, the foreign liquid pump into his vein. The hands that had been taut with the effort of resistance began to feel feeble. His body went slack, his feet going limp as they hung above the floor. His vision blurred, then went black as he lost the strength to keep his lids from shutting.

From within the darkness overtaking him, he heard the stranger speak.

"I'm sorry, Jonathan. This was never how I planned us meeting. You aren't prepared, but you must bear this."

CHAPTER FIVE

SATURDAY | JUNE 18, 2005 | 05:45 AM

THEY SAT SILENTLY in the hospital waiting room. Collin, still wide eyed, stared at the plain white wall across from them. Beside him, Hayden sat with his head bobbing above his knees as he studied the blood on his shoes. He'd been stroking the hair on his lip since they'd sat down twenty minutes ago.

Losing the staring contest with the wall, Collin returned to reality and slapped Hayden's hand to remind him to stop fidgeting with his beard.

"I can't get it out of my head," Hayden said.

They hadn't spoken about it, not since sitting down. Both had felt so useless in the house. They had managed to call 911, but only after a considerably long delay. The police and ambulance had shown up and taken Jonathan immediately to the hospital.

Hayden had wrapped him in a towel. Jonathan had been a distant stammering mess before he'd gone damn near catatonic, and all they'd been able to think to do for him was put him in a towel. Collin still shivered at the look Jonathan had had in his eyes, like his friend had been trapped in some infinite loop as he desperately sought to work something out in his head, but was so traumatized he couldn't make sense of anything. When they had tried to ask him what happened, he could hardly speak.

"I don't—don't know. Hospital. Gotta take me now," Jonathan had mumbled, without really looking at them, his eyes darting around the room like a cornered animal.

Playing it back now, hearing Jonathan's confused and frightened voice in his head, Collin's skin went cold. The image, the way his room-mate clutched at his chest, unable to stop shaking, to get control—Collin wanted the whole disturbing memory wiped from his mind.

They had taken Hayden's car and followed the ambulance to the hospital. The scene at the house had sobered them, though they likely shouldn't have been driving. The ride was short and they had hardly spoken in the car. Their communication had been limited to the exchange of worried glances as Hayden tried to call Paige on his cell phone. She hadn't picked up.

"Should we try her again?" Hayden had asked.

"No, she probably won't see her thirty missed calls 'til her and the Meathead wake up," Collin said.

"Should we call his mom or something?" Hayden said.

Collin had thought about it for a moment and then responded, "I don't have the number, do you?"

Some more time passed before Collin asked the question they were both thinking.

"What the hell could have happened to him?"

"I don't know," Hayden said. "There was so much blood. I didn't think a person could lose that much blood."

"He must have been in shock, right?" Collin asked.

Hayden shrugged.

"Without knowing what happened, he could have been like that for two minutes or twenty before we got home."

The police had questioned both of them for a statement, but they knew so little. When they had returned home, they hadn't entered immediately. Since leaving the bar, they could speak of nothing other than rebooting the New Testament. They'd sat on the porch brainstorming about it for five minutes before even going inside.

The floor had been slick. Collin had nearly slipped in the dark the moment they entered. When Hayden flipped on the light in the kitchen they saw that the pitcher of water from the refrigerator was lying on its side on the linoleum. Then they had noticed that the water was more pink than clear. Finally, they had seen Jonathan's foot from around the corner of the kitchen's center island.

Collin remembered thinking that he must have underestimated how much Jonathan had drunk if he'd dropped a pitcher full of Kool-Aid, neglected to clean it up, and then fell asleep on the kitchen floor. They had both been giggling at the sight until they had turned the corner and found that they had grossly misjudged the situation.

The reality had been like taking a crowbar to the face.

Jonathan laid face-up on the linoleum. His pants and shoes were still on, but his shirt had been torn off the front of him. The remnants of the shirt sleeves were still attached to him. His entire chest was red with blood, his jeans saturated with it. He was in a puddle that had spread so far it had mixed with the water from the pitcher. His face looked like someone had taken a can of red spray paint across it.

For a moment, neither of them had moved. Their feet were like iron weights anchoring them to the floor as they tried to process what they saw in front of them. When Jonathan's body finally took a long, labored breath, they'd snapped back into the moment, stopped trying to understand, and rushed to find some way to help.

They had been forced to kneel in the puddle surrounding their friend, desperately yelling his name. They'd felt the blood, cold from the linoleum, seeping into their clothes and covering their hands as they searched for some way to help him, both frantically looking for the injury where it had all come from.

"Jonathan! Can you hear me? What happened?"

"Jesus! Where is he hurt! Where is the blood coming from?"

Until he'd been put in the machine, Jonathan hadn't been able to close his eyes without seeing the blond man's face, the needle, the blood on linoleum.

The loud noise of the equipment was dampened by the ear plugs. He'd never been in an MRI. On television, the machines had always appeared loud, uncomfortable, and claustrophobic. Jonathan didn't feel any of those things. He found the cocoon of metal safe, the dulled white noise soothing, each a layer of buffer between him and reality.

As a child, he'd often fallen asleep to the sprinkler systems running outside his bedroom window. When the water would stop, the abrupt end of the noise would wake him from sleep and leave him feeling like he'd been abandoned. The repetitive sound was just as comforting now as an adult, but the MRI would only provide this retreat for a short time. It gave him something to focus on, something to hold his panic at bay.

No one knew anything yet. The doctors, the police, not even Hayden and Collin could help piece together the moments between losing consciousness and waking in the puddle.

Jonathan had felt their distrust of his story. All that blood with no wound; it left too many unanswered questions. They hadn't said it, but their eyes gave them away as he tried to explain. Whenever he said he couldn't remember, that he'd been unconscious, the look of skepticism flashing through their thoughts was poorly hidden. At least they kept their opinions to themselves until the facts had been gathered.

He couldn't blame them for it. Overwhelming fear was the worst lens to observe a situation through. It rendered the observer's memory untrustworthy. He heard the words come out of his own mouth and knew his response would have been the same. Jonathan himself questioned what he remembered, doubted it. He found himself leaving out details as they seemed impossible.

Until he'd been made to lie still in the machine, he hadn't really been given enough time alone to try and process it for himself, without an audience, to reconstruct events in a manner that made any sense. He struggled to build a timeline in his head. Alcohol, physical and psychological trauma, drugged sedation, all allied against him to create a fog of uncertainty over everything he thought he remembered.

He had dreamed.

He was a child, sometime near his ninth birthday. He was riding in the passenger seat of a pickup truck, a blue Ford Ranger that belonged to his father. He'd remembered the smell and feel of the plastic canvas car seat, so distinct, not like leather or upholstery. His father drove; he'd tuned the radio to the same oldies station he always had when Jonathan was young.

The truck itself betrayed that he was dreaming. It had been totaled in the wreck that took his father's life. He'd taken this drive with his father as a child.

The dash was too high and he had to push against his seat belt to try and see the road in front of them. He'd forgotten that about childhood. The repeated struggle to see what was happening right in front of him, whether it was because he was being sheltered from it by his parents, or just because he was too damn short to see over the dash.

Perspective, literally and figuratively, was gained with age.

It was early morning, and as they drove he'd asked his father why cats meowed and dogs barked. His father took the question seriously enough, not blowing Jonathan off, not getting impatient at the question of a child that seemed obvious.

"Everything just does what it can," Douglas said.

To Jonathan the statement only begged more questions.

"Why can't cats bark?"

His father smiled, taking his eyes off the road for a moment.

"Why can't you talk out of your ears? Things are all born able to do certain things, and the parts they're born with have limits. Cats aren't born to bark; dogs aren't born to purr."

That had given Jonathan something to think about for a while and some time passed before he'd spoken again.

"Can I have a dog, Dad?" Jonathan asked.

His father had sighed as the real reason for his son's questions was revealed. He looked out the driver's side window quietly for a few moments, thinking of how to respond.

"Son, sometimes wanting something is better than having it," he said, clearly amused with himself.

What Douglas found funny at the time had been lost on Jonathan. His eyes fell to his lap while he pondered, but when he looked back to argue, his attention was drawn away by abrupt changes in his surroundings; changes that didn't belong in the memory.

The daylight seemed to fade away quickly, as though the hours were moving forward at an unnatural speed, pushing them into the onset of night. The weather grew turbulent, rain beginning to pound the windshield as they drove. Douglas squinted through the window, turning on the wipers but no longer able to see the road clearly in front of them. The radio cut out, the music replaced with the static of dead air.

Suddenly his father turned to him, taking his eyes off the road. Douglas' face had become so serious, as though they were having a conversation about life and death, not cats and dogs. It gave Jonathan a chill to see such a sudden change in the way his father looked at him.

"It's got to be close, Jonathan—so close death can't tell you apart."

Unsure what his father was telling him, Jonathan stared back at a loss for what to say. Before he had the chance to ask for an explanation, the speakers blared to life, as though the radio had tuned itself to a new station. No music followed, only a voice that brought a rise of panic inside him.

"I'm sorry, Jonathan. The selection process is not always clear. I don't know that you are right for this," said the voice of his attacker. *"You'll know what to do. I'll be there to help you, when it comes. Follow your—"*

Whatever the blond man had been saying had faded out. Jonathan's mind had shut down completely. Not even a dream could persist.

Waking from those drug-induced depths had been slow, fragmented.

He didn't immediately remember what had happened, and at first it was just unpleasant sensations. The floor he was on felt wrong. Cool and hard against his back, not comfortable like a mattress should be. He was damp. His eyes were shut but the darkness had retreated, and he'd become aware of light hitting the surface of his closed lids. His thoughts had become more lucid.

Did I get sick drinking? Did I sleep on the bathroom floor? He had heard his name over and over again as if it were far away.

"Jonathan! Jonathan!"

He thought he recognized the voices. He could hear their panic, but had still been too distant to share in their fear.

Are Hayden and Collin yelling for me? He'd thought.

Why did they sound so upset, so desperate? He'd felt like he should wake up, see what the problem was, but he couldn't open his eyes. He was caught between states, and couldn't will himself back to consciousness. He'd remembered that he didn't want to wake up, that he didn't want what waited for him in the waking world. He just couldn't remember why.

There had been something wrong with his chest. He'd remembered that the muscles felt like they had fallen asleep. They tingled with the pins and needles that came with lack of blood flow, a sensation he'd had in his limbs, but never his chest.

Hayden and Collin's voices had grown louder. He'd been aware of hands on his exposed skin. There was a stinging jolt to his face. Were they slapping him? The feeling in his chest wasn't fading. It was moving, spreading down his abdomen, up into his shoulders and around his back. As he noticed it, pain surfaced as well. His shoulder hurt; the right side of his neck as well.

My neck. It seemed important. The memories began rushing in, gripping Jonathan in panic.

There was someone in the house. He'd had something in his hand.

He didn't recall bolting up, just that the drowsiness holding him had vanished and been replaced with a tidal wave of adrenaline. Remembering the needle in his neck and the liquid forced into his vein had triggered an onset of fear that overpowered the drugs still keeping him sedated. He'd darted up, gasping for breath, panting as though he'd surfaced from a pool after being held under for too long.

The light stung his eyes and he was forced to shut them. Collin and Hayden were kneeling on either side of him. As he fought to see against the brightness, he saw their expressions. The intensity of the concern in their eyes had driven him deeper into panic.

Time had seemed broken; it moved in fits and starts that he didn't understand. Sounds and sights were dulled and myopic. Within the MRI machine, trying to recall it, the memories didn't seem to belong to him. He thought he must have lost his sanity, and it wasn't clear when he'd regained it—if he'd regained it.

He'd seen the blood, but hadn't at first believed it could be his. His hands were red and wet with it, shaking in front of him. He couldn't make them stop. The trembling wasn't coming from his hands. They were like tree limbs swaying in the wake of an earthquake, a symptom of the tremors in his core. He looked to Collin and Hayden for help. They stared back at him wide eyed, the helplessness clear on their faces. No one knew what to do and it was terrifying.

Suddenly, he'd grown sick and faint. He turned over on his hands and knees, vomiting. His eyes had pinched shut as he wretched. When the contractions in his stomach stopped long enough, he opened his eyes again. The red was everywhere, the linoleum covered with it. He tried to look away but there was nowhere to look. Even Collin and Hayden were tainted with it; their jeans soaked to their calves and their hands turned a shiny crimson.

His mind had seemed to do the math for him. There was too much of it. It couldn't be his—he'd be dead.

"Where are you cut?" Collin's voice, so dull and slow; Jonathan realized then that he'd asked him the question more than once, but it hadn't registered through the madness.

"Hospital."

He didn't remember if he'd actually said the word. It had begun repeating over and over in his head, but he didn't know if it was coming from his lips.

"We called, Jonathan. They're on their way," Hayden had said.

Panic took hold of him again as the image of the man in the hallway resurfaced. His eyes shot around the room nervously; a sudden instinctual need to press himself into a confined space overwhelmed the faculties he had left. Collin and Hayden had jumped back startled as he'd suddenly scrambled on his hands and knees through the blood and wedged himself into the corner between two cabinets. He remembered feeling trapped there, lost, for what felt like an eternity of frantically searching the room for signs that the man was still in the house, still coming for him.

He didn't remember being pulled out of the corner and he hardly remembered the ambulance or getting to the hospital. He recalled speaking, or trying to, grasping for a nurse and begging.

"My chest—he did something," he'd cried. "Please, it doesn't feel right."

They had given him something to calm him down.

Now, within the MRI, his mind rebelled, fleeing from his attempts to reason it out. He succumbed to it, instead just listening to the dull whirring of the machine. He wished he'd stayed asleep.

CHAPTER SIX

SUNDAY | JUNE 19, 2005 | 09:30 AM

PAIGE HAD DIFFICULTY resolving what she'd seen in the kitchen with the person lying in the hospital bed. The room they had placed him in for observation was nothing special. There was a typical tile floor, white walls, handrails, machines used to monitor body activity. There was a curtain that would normally be used to divide the room, but the bed next to him was empty. Paige was glad he didn't have to share the room with a stranger, yet it looked so lonely to her. It was cold, isolated.

She hadn't spoken yet. Jonathan didn't know she was there or that Grant was standing behind her. Lying there, his expression looked like he had a bad taste in his mouth but was too lost in thought to bother doing anything about it.

Collin had warned her, told her not to go home at all. She'd underestimated his concern, but nothing he could have said would have prepared her for the disturbing reality. She'd been able to see every hand print in the blood, every place the roommates had touched after they'd sunk into the puddle to help him. She'd smelled the iron in the air, the vomit. She'd almost been sick herself.

Collin had also warned her that the kitchen made Jonathan's condition appear far worse than he was, but she couldn't accept it until she saw him now.

That so much could happen while they had been separated by a handful of hours seemed surreal. She'd had an unremarkable evening with Grant. Meanwhile, Jonathan had had the most traumatic experience of his life. She had no idea what to expect, no idea what he was feeling. He might not even want to see her yet.

Collin and Hayden had summarized their version of what Jonathan had told the police for her. It had taken a long time for him to pull himself together enough to speak coherently. Hayden had said it reminded him of someone trying to explain a nightmare; like the details had seemed to make some sense to Jonathan, but when he tried to explain it out loud they had lost continuity. He'd paused a lot as he tried to sort it out.

The police hadn't been able to do much with the story. His memory was obviously sketchy, which was to be expected given the nature of the trauma he'd experienced. Though they were skeptical of the details, there was consistency with other information. They had no witness to confirm the assailant had been in the house, but the roommates and the bartender were able to confirm that a man fitting the description of the attacker had been at the bar. Specifically, they'd all noted the height of the man in the fedora. Unfortunately, the suspect had paid his tab in cash and wasn't traceable through any type of credit card. The bartender had been unsuccessful in recalling the man's name from his ID. The police had no similar cases reported in the area.

Jonathan had told the officers that the man overpowered him. He'd mentioned that the man's eyes were unnaturally blue, but he had trouble defining what he meant by "unnatural." He said he had hit the man dead on the forearm with a baseball bat, but the doctors and police all seemed reluctant to accept that he'd successfully connected with the man. It was unlikely a person could take such an attack, as Jonathan described, without injury. They assumed he had missed, probably hitting a wall or door frame, and mistook what happened due to the state of panic he'd been in, although the police had failed to find any apparent damage in the hallway. There were no holes in the drywall or gouges in a door frame. However, the bat was found precisely where Jonathan had said it would be.

The police had asked the standard questions, but Jonathan was largely useless. He didn't have any enemies; he didn't owe anyone money. He didn't have any questionable prior romantic relationships nor did anyone have anything to gain by assaulting him. On top of that, nothing in the house had been stolen.

The bloodwork from the kitchen confirmed it belonged to Jonathan. This had been a relief to the police, but only in that it confirmed the blood didn't belong to another victim. The doctors reported that Jonathan's body didn't show much trauma outside of his psychological state on arrival. Ketamine and various other sleep and paralyzing agents had been found in Jonathan's bloodstream. With no witness to the administration, the doctors assumed that the initial syringe forced on Jonathan had been predominately anesthesia and that the assailant may have followed up with additional shots once he'd been unconscious.

A sonogram, chest X-rays, and the MRI had turned up nothing out of place within Jonathan's torso. Both Hayden and Collin had said that Jonathan had been hysterical about the sensation he was experiencing in his chest, but he'd admitted a few hours after waking that he no longer felt it. The doctors suggested that a numbing agent may have been applied to his chest and that this may have accounted for what he described; if not that, then possibly something to do with the mixture of drugs that he'd had in his system.

The best possible motive that the police could come up with was that the assailant had been there to harvest organs. They guessed that the man had been spooked by the timely return home of Hayden and Collin and fled. Paige understood why the police came to the conclusion; Jonathan had reported the assailant used his name during the assault.

The attacker must have observed the roommates long enough to find an opportune moment to strike when Jonathan was alone. This detail of the story had given Paige a disturbing chill. If true, how long had some stranger been standing in the shadows around them, watching them through their windows, following them? She realized it might not be safe to be near Jonathan if it were the case. The moment she'd had the thought, she'd felt terrible.

You don't abandon family, Paige, she'd reprimanded herself. I can't believe you're even thinking so selfishly with a friend in danger.

She didn't know much about the organ black market and had to assume that the police knew their business, yet it seemed they were ignoring what couldn't be easily explained. All of that blood had to come from somewhere. Why hadn't the attacker moved Jonathan to a different location once he'd had him incapacitated? The cop's theory, riddled with holes, was still the only one.

She knew the police hadn't trusted Jonathan's story. They hadn't implied he was lying, only that they believed that *Jonathan believed* he was telling it how it happened. She was all too familiar with cops saying something like that and knew how humiliating it was, how hurtful to be dismissed as such after being victimized. She knew Jonathan, and he wasn't the type to go looking for attention. She couldn't imagine any reason he would lie. She wasn't going to let him think, even for a moment, that she doubted him. He didn't need that.

She felt a draft and noticed a fan was on in the corner. Grant nudged her from behind, and she stopped stalling in the doorway. When she entered the room, she turned off the fan. Jonathan seemed annoyed at first, his eyes leaving the window when the sound ceased. The look faded when he saw her.

Grant's cell phone vibrated as they entered. When he looked at the caller ID, he excused himself from the room.

There was awkwardness at first, the uncomfortable knowing that there was nothing in particular to say, just the desire to be present, to visit, to be a friend. While she sat with him, she fumbled in her purse, and remembered she'd been carrying around an essay she'd reviewed for him.

"I forgot to give you this," Paige said, pulling the folded paper from her purse. "I proof read it a bit—I thought, I don't know, that you might want to work on it."

She held in her hand the essay Jonathan had been meaning to finish this weekend. They often worked together on such things, their majors being so similar. He'd asked her to take a look a few days earlier. She felt silly offering it now, but maybe later he'd appreciate the distraction.

The paper looked like it was bleeding to death, covered in red marks everywhere she had found a mistake or made a note. He looked at the paper now like he didn't recognize it, like school was something so far from his thoughts that he must have written the essay in some other life. She recognized that look. She'd had it before herself, and she didn't take it personally. She placed the paper on the table. It was pretty marked up; he might not be able to salvage it without a complete rewrite.

Grant returned, looking like he was in a hurry. He said that he'd been called to base and had to leave immediately. At first, Paige thought he might be lying, making up an excuse to leave because he didn't want to be here, but she noticed that he himself appeared uncertain about being summoned so abruptly. Either way, she couldn't blame him for leaving. Jonathan certainly wasn't going to gain anything from his presence. She smiled at him, thanked him for bringing her, and told him to call.

Grant nodded and left.

Jonathan seemed more at ease once he was gone again.

"How are you really feeling?" she asked.

"I'm okay," he said. "I don't even think I need to be here."

"I didn't necessarily mean physically," she said.

Jonathan looked at her for a moment, like he was trying to decide what to say—be honest or put up a facade of normalcy? Had it been Collin or Hayden, he might have chosen the facade.

"I'm worried," he said, quite simply.

"Worried, eh? That seems like the understatement of the year," she said sympathetically.

"I think the doctors and police must be right," he said.

"What do you mean?" she asked.

"I think, with the drinking, and whatever I was dosed with, that I can't be remembering things right."

For a moment she almost felt let down. She'd prepared herself to champion anything he claimed, to believe anything he needed her to believe. This was just like him though. She should have known it before she even got there. He'd sooner doubt himself than trust his own memory if the evidence was against him. Given the circumstances, she had to respect that he was willing to accept that he might be remembering things wrong—it was mature. Had it been her, she'd have slapped any cop or doctor who dared give her a doubtful look.

Jonathan didn't have her baggage though, she remembered.

"It's possible, I guess. Given everything that happened, your mind might play tricks," she said, "but I believe you."

"Hayden and Collin tell you what I remembered?" he asked.

She nodded.

"Well, thank you," he said, "but you can probably see it's better to doubt it. Or else I might need to start worrying about my sanity."

Paige was concerned by the last statement. Sanity seemed a strong word, but she didn't say so. Time passed with nothing said, so she decided to change the subject to something that had been bothering her.

"Hayden told me," she paused. "You forbade him from calling your mother?"

She'd masked the statement like a question, but it was really a subtle reprimand.

Paige adored his mother. Whenever Evelyn visited Jonathan, she spent half the visit with Paige. They'd clicked since the day Jonathan had moved into the house as a freshman. Evelyn had taken time off work to help him get situated. Jonathan didn't realize at the time that it was really his mother's way of prolonging his moving out. Paige had understood and the two had ended up at the kitchen table drinking coffee while Jonathan hauled in everything he'd brought with him from home.

Paige thought Jonathan had found their relationship endearing. He didn't seem to think so now. Defiance flashed over his face. He looked like he was trying to gauge if his little sister planned on ratting him out to their parents, suspicious that she might deliberately go against his wishes. She didn't blame him for the look, because she'd been thinking it and wasn't making any pretenses.

"I'll tell her, I just don't want her coming up here and making things worse. I want some time to sort it out before she over-involves herself," he said.

Hard-pressed to ignore such wishes under the circumstances, Paige nodded, but she didn't like it. They talked a while longer before she started to get ready to go.

"Paige, would you turn the fan back on?" he said before she left. "The sound helps."

An hour south of downtown Seattle, Grant sat in the small room he'd been directed to on Joint Base Lewis-McChord. He'd been stationed there for over a year now, waiting out the end of his service, which was due in the next few weeks.

He'd never been in this room before, let alone this building, and it was becoming unnerving as it bore stark resemblance to the interrogation rooms he often saw on procedural cop shows. There was one door, three chairs, a metal table, and no windows except the obvious one-way mirror with people behind it, watching him. He'd been waiting for nearly twenty minutes now, and no one had informed him what this was in regards to or who he was supposed to be meeting with.

Finally, the door opened and Captain Spencer entered.

"Stay seated, Specialist," he said, and Grant followed the order.

Spencer took a seat across from him, his back to the one-way mirror. He had a manila envelope in his hands. He opened it and read while Grant waited.

"I apologize for the way you were pulled in today," Spencer started. "Rest assured; you're not in any trouble."

Grant nodded and relaxed. Spencer seemed to be speaking to him in a highly formal manner. He had to assume they were being watched by someone important behind that mirror.

"I wanted to inform you that your discharge will be going forward sooner than scheduled. I know this is sudden, but you will be honorably released from active duty today," Spencer said.

That caught Grant off guard; he hadn't expected this, hadn't been given time to plan for it either.

"Captain?" he asked.

"Our superiors have requested I present you with a rather unconventional proposition, Grant," Spencer said. "They assured me that should you decline on any ethical grounds that you won't be punished. However, there will be substantial financial reimbursement for your participation should you choose to accept their offer."

After a pause, Grant nodded slowly.

"Still it must be pointed out, should you decline, you will be sworn to secrecy about the request on punishment of treason. I have documents in this folder that you'll be required to sign before you are presented with any additional details. These documents also require full disclosure of any details that may be requested about your private life, should you wish to participate," Spencer said.

He pulled the paperwork out of the folder and pushed it toward Grant. He then removed a pen from his front pocket and laid it down in front of the documents. There were pages upon pages of legal jargon for him to pretend to read as he thought over what was being presented. Luckily, the places where he needed to sign were highlighted.

Grant didn't think for long. His curiosity was stronger than his caution. Whatever this was, it might be a chance at doing something real, something important. Spencer had said he didn't have to accept. Worst case scenario, all he would be forced to do was keep a secret. He figured he could handle that.

After he signed, Spencer offered Grant his handshake, then got up and left the room, instructing Grant to remain seated.

Again he was left for a period that seemed purposely long. Knowing he was being watched through the window only made time stretch. It was an effort to sit still knowing strangers observed him behind the mirror, and he found he didn't know what to do with his hands. He wondered if this was some kind of test and they wanted to see how long his patience would last.

A woman finally stepped into the room. She was dressed professionally, immaculate in business attire. She wore heels, her hair up, thick rimmed glasses, and carried a metal briefcase in her right hand; attractive, in an FBI-meets-librarian sort of way, but Grant thought she couldn't be military. He reined in his eyes, not wanting to be caught letting them roam down her impressively fit body.

He was irritated now, knowing it was this woman who had been making him wait. Some power play to show how important her time was, and conversely, how insignificant his was. She was likely some Army Intelligence Contractor's overpaid bimbo secretary.

Can we please get to business already, Princess, he thought.

She was the type who used her body to cloud men's judgment, conveying some power with her sex. Grant recognized it. She was probably only here to give him some orientation before he was taken to his new commanding officer. Still, he knew better than to let his opinions show on his face; the man in charge could still be watching through the glass.

She didn't offer her name. She didn't make eye contact with him or smile. Instead, she went through an excessive amount of preparation pulling out her chair and organizing herself, retrieving file folders from her briefcase and placing them in front of her with excessive precision.

Grant didn't appreciate being ignored, or her disregard for observing the pleasantries. It was impolite. What did she think? That she was above shaking his hand or giving her name, treating him with the respect he was due?

Finally, pulling a photo from one of the files she'd carefully laid out, she spoke. "My name is Olivia," she said. "You will report to me from here on."

Grant flinched, but then nodded.

"What is this about?" he asked. "Why all the paperwork?"

Ignoring the question, Olivia held the photo out to him.

"As thoroughly as possible, describe your relationship with this individual," she said. "Be candid; leave out no details."

The desire to say something confrontational swelled after his questions were ignored. He looked from her face to the picture and found himself puzzled. It was a photo of him and Paige. It was clearly taken at the hospital this morning, less than a few hours ago.

This woman had put them under surveillance.

CHAPTER SEVEN

MONDAY | JUNE 20, 2005 | NOON

IT'S TOO BAD mind bleach isn't a real thing, Collin thought.

It was awkward business having recently traumatized friends. Knowing how to behave in these situations didn't come easily to him. He wasn't sure what to say, what not to say, when to be helpful, when he became smothering, how long until it was okay to have fun again. He took most things with a laugh but they were all having trouble finding the humor in this.

When Hayden brought Jonathan home from the hospital, his eyes looked over the kitchen and he just seemed at a loss. Collin understood. What is the appropriate way to say "thanks, everyone, for cleaning my blood off the kitchen floor?" Instead, Jonathan had said nothing.

Paige, Hayden, and he had been up late cleaning the mess off the floor and cabinets, bleaching the towels they'd stained, getting rid of the cloudy red mop water. It was a night he wasn't soon to forget. They'd all been so quiet as they cleaned, he'd felt like a mortician.

It wasn't as though they had done it so Jonathan would thank them. Collin figured it was an unspoken law of humanity: if your friend nearly bleeds to death all over the kitchen, everyone chips in and cleans it up before he has to see the mess. In reality it was a lame, although at the same time genuine, attempt to protect Jonathan from his own memory, to try and limit the reminders. The only thing that would get the blood off the linoleum in Jonathan's memory was time.

Regardless, Collin imagined they'd be doing a lot more eating out for a while.

Jonathan had wanted to head straight to his room. He stopped at the bottom of the stairs, seeming to remember something.

"Will... one of you—" Jonathan had stammered. "Let me know if you aren't going to be—"

"We'll be around. We won't leave you alone until you ask us to," Collin had said.

He'd nodded, then turned and headed up the stairs. That Jonathan wasn't the type to ask for help made Collin feel for him. All things being equal, Collin figured he would have reverted to a three-year-old and wanted nothing but his mother had it happened to *him*. Oddly, that was the one thing Jonathan had forbidden. Paige had said that he wanted to get things straight in his head first. Collin didn't really buy that; he figured Jonathan didn't want her to worry about him anymore than the woman already did. Paige wouldn't have gone along with that, though.

"We need to make sure someone is always home with him," Paige said.

Collin and Hayden didn't argue; if they were being honest, none of them wanted to be in the house alone right now.

"It's making me paranoid," Hayden said. "What if that guy comes back? Shouldn't we have police surveillance, something?"

"I don't know," Collin said. "I mean, they do stuff like that on TV, but they didn't even offer it to him at the hospital. I don't think Jonathan makes the cut for bodyguard status. If this guy is still planning to come for Jonathan, he has plenty of patience anyway. Who knows how long he waited to get him alone the first time."

He noticed Paige shiver visibly at what he'd said.

"I hate thinking someone may be watching us right now," she said.

He didn't know how long he'd been in bed sometimes. He lost track as days and nights ran together. He took the sedatives the doctors prescribed.

He knew he was abusing them, but he didn't want to be awake. Being awake meant remembering, feeling. He didn't want to see the syringe again; he didn't want to remember crawling through that puddle. He didn't want to let himself relive his powerlessness in the hallway.

His friends didn't lecture him for it; they had understood.

"You hurt an ankle, you take some pain killers and stay off it, and you don't jump straight into physical rehab. Who am I to say the same might not be true for an injured mind?" Collin had said.

He'd been talking to Paige, whispering in her room down the hall. They didn't know Jonathan had heard. They'd started to take for granted that he was asleep. It didn't matter; he wasn't offended.

An injured mind, he'd thought. It sounded as apt as any way he could have put it.

At times, when he couldn't will himself to stay in bed, he came down and sat on the couch. They'd talk to him, try to make him smile, but he seldom did. Usually he was only half paying attention to the minutia of their conversations as he was too caught up in his own head. The energy needed to listen was too great and quickly wore him out.

Once, he picked up his school books like he was thinking of doing some homework. He lost his drive before he'd even gotten the bag open. The University had given him a special dispensation; he wasn't expected to attend classes. He felt that he wanted to care, wanted it to be more difficult to cast off all the work he'd put in that quarter, yet he couldn't. Wanting to care simply didn't make it real.

They had tried once or twice to see if he'd talk about the attack, but he'd just shake his head. It only drained him. Sifting through what he remembered, trying to find the pieces he felt he could trust to be real. It was like trying to fix current reality with memories that had to be broken.

One morning, sleep evading him, he stood at his bedroom window, locking and unlocking the latch, wondering if this was how the man had entered into his room.

Did I ever lock this window? Had I ever checked? he wondered.

As he stood there, unable to remember, he noticed a moving truck in the driveway next door. Curious, he watched to see if he could get a glimpse of the new neighbors. The house had been vacant almost as long as Jonathan had lived next door.

All he saw were two large men in gray jump suits—hired movers. Whoever had rented the place must have been well off if they could afford to hire professionals. He watched for a while, trying to get an idea of the new occupants from the furniture he saw. The only telling item was a bed frame that looked like a race car. Must be a family with a child, he thought. When the movers ran out of furniture and only had boxes left to haul, he lost interest.

Absent a distraction, the memories he didn't want returned. He took some pills, made sure the window was locked, and pulled the shade down to block out any light that might threaten to wake him.

Something strange was happening in all their down time. If Hayden was being honest with himself, he and Collin might have been home anyway, but a week and a half of feeling trapped at home was suddenly making them productive.

He was holding open a copy of the New Testament he hadn't read since Catholic school, and it had become an unmanageable cluster of rainbow sticky notes. At first it was just a distraction, a way to pass the time as they played bodyguard for Jonathan. They'd picked up their conversation about writing a graphic novel Bible reboot and soon forgotten they weren't supposed to leave. Hours flew by unnoticed while they brainstormed.

Occasionally, Jonathan would walk through the middle of one of these sessions when he was hungry enough to bother eating. In one instance Collin had actually started drafting some of the comic book panels.

"So when Mary gets impregnated, should we draw an angelic sperm flying into her uterus, you know, with a halo and everything, or just a magic embryo?" Hayden asked.

"Well, which one do you find more offensive?" Collin asked.

"Halo Sperm," Hayden replied. "Oh! and give it a cape!"

Apparently since he was the resident Christian, it was his job to gauge what would be considered more controversial in the retelling. They tried to be more boisterous about it when Jonathan was around, hoping they might pull a smile out of him.

"What should be Jesus' Kryptonite?" Hayden asked once while Jonathan sleepwalked through the living room.

Lost in thought, Collin looked up at the ceiling for inspiration.

"Radioactive pieces of Heaven? Heavon-ite?" Hayden asked.

"No, Heaven didn't blow up like Krypton," Collin said. "How about science?"

"Too obvious," Hayden said.

"Doubt-inite?" Collin said, cringing at the sound of his own suggestion.

"No," Hayden said. "Hell no, jeez."

"Wait, okay, the name sucks, but if Superman gets his powers from the Sun, then Jesus must get his from faith."

"Okay," Hayden replied. "I guess it's an angle."

"Well, think about it; a God without faith is just a superhero anyway," Collin said.

Hayden's eyes narrowed. "What are you implying, Ass Hat, that without faith the New Testament is a comic book?"

"If it's any consolation…." Collin smiled. "It would be a seriously boring one."

Hayden mocked a frown. "If it's any consolation, why don't you go punch yourself in the dick."

Jonathan would just walk out of the room, like he hadn't heard a word of it—no reaction at all.

He woke suddenly. In the darkness, he looked for the clock to see it was six at night.

He'd been dreaming, but could only remember fragments. His father had been there again, speaking to him, but it wasn't clear. Jonathan felt so ashamed, but wasn't sure why.

> *If you can trust yourself when all men doubt you,*
> *But make allowance for their doubting too.*

They weren't his father's words; it was a line from a poem Douglas had read to him as a child, the same poem that Jonathan's grandfather had read to Douglas as a child. It was all he could remember of the dream. It was enough.

Just get your feet on the floor, Douglas used to say to him, when he woke Jonathan for school and he was struggling to fight off the urge to go back to sleep.

He rose in his bed, forcing his feet to touch the wood floor. He looked to the cigar box on his desk, and he knew where the shame came from, even if he couldn't remember the details.

His father had been a big man, strong. He wasn't the type to have a vague poem framed in his office, not something left up to interpretation of the reader. His father would never have hidden like this, wouldn't have drugged himself into a coma just to flee his own mind. If his dad were here beside him now, Jonathan would not have let himself do whatever it was he was doing to himself.

With the thought of his father there watching him, he couldn't bring himself to take another pill. He looked at the bottle for a moment, deliberating on it, and then thrust them into the pocket of his robe. He forced himself out of the bed and down the stairs.

They were gathered on the living room couch waiting for him. Collin and Hayden said nothing, but Paige walked across the floor to him, put her hand on his shoulder, and leaned in close to his ear.

"Jonathan, I think it might be time you took a shower," she whispered, "and maybe changed out of the robe and pajamas. At least wash them."

Jonathan hadn't had the honest inclination to bathe for days. He realized she must be right, that he must smell terrible by now. A look over Paige's shoulder to Collin and Hayden was met with nodding.

"Um," he replied, "right, probably a good idea."

He headed back up the stairs to shed the clothes. He started the water and stayed there longer than he'd planned. The shower was a small walk-in. Tiled with a glass door, it was a tiny chamber. It reminded him of the MRI, the cocoon, the safety of the small spaces he kept trying to hide in. He sat on the floor and let the water run over him. He lost track of time listening to the sound of the running faucet, the trickling of the drain below him.

The water washed away the buildup of human grime. It poured over him, waking the nerve endings that had been numb and unfeeling, the hot steam helping to leach away the prescriptions built up in his system.

He remembered what his mother had said when his father had died. Her words seemed as apt now as they had then.

For now, you'll just have to redefine what you consider normal, he thought.

He had to find a new measuring stick, a new normal; hiding in bed while his roommates stood guard on the house had to end.

Tomorrow, he thought. At least leave the house. Try.

When he finally turned off the water, he stood in front of the mirror. He was halfway to having a beard as thick as Hayden's. So he shaved. By the time he was done with that, it was just a little more effort to brush his teeth and comb his hair. He realized he hadn't worn any of his real clothes since the episode. The hospital had given him scrubs and he had tossed those for his pajamas and a bathrobe upon arriving home. Jeans and a T-shirt actually felt pretty good—sturdier somehow.

He went back down and joined his roommates who, obviously planned, gave him a standing ovation. He pretended to smile—at least it was a start—then handed Paige the pills he'd been prescribed.

"I'll try not to ask for them," he said. "Can't guarantee anything."

She nodded. "If you really want them," she said. "I'll understand."

CHAPTER EIGHT

MONDAY | JUNE 27, 2005 | 9:15 AM

JONATHAN PULLED HIMSELF out of bed. He hadn't slept well. His body had lost all sense of rhythm and he couldn't tell the difference between night and day without looking out a window.

The new normal, he remembered.

He decided to go for a jog. It was exercise, it would force him outside, and he knew he needed it. He put on shorts and a ratty T-shirt, pulled his sneakers out of his closet and got them laced on. He looked back at his bed longingly, fighting the urge return to it.

His eyes wandered to the cigar box on his desk, and like a ghost watching him, his father stood between him and the bed. Douglas shook his head, as if to say, *you can't allow yourself to crumble this easily.* Jonathan turned away, making his way downstairs, surprised by how powerful the thought of failing that ghost had been.

It was clear his friends approved. Paige and Collin were both packing their bags, heading out the door to get to class. Hayden said he would be home for the next few hours, finishing some assigned reading he needed to write a paper on. Jonathan hadn't had to ask; Hayden had volunteered the information. He could see they understood. He was trying to ease himself into being alone again, even if at first "alone" only meant out in a populated area during broad daylight with no one he knew personally. It wasn't as though he thought he might be assailed in his driveway.

He was surprised after a few blocks—he was able to run longer than he'd expected. After hardly moving for two weeks, he expected to be easily winded. It didn't seem to be the case; too much pent up energy, he supposed. It was morning and other joggers passed him, people with dogs and baby strollers; the city alive with the comings and goings of everyday humanity. It was surreal to Jonathan, the degree with which his internal world could change so drastically and the external world couldn't know or care. Life went on no matter what happened to any one person.

He headed to one of the parks near his house, a large community field where a neighborhood soccer team was out practicing. He quickly worked up a sweat, circling the field. The exhilaration of movement, the throbbing of his heart and the quickness of his breath felt novel after such a long stretch of stagnation in a dark bedroom. Briefly, he stopped worrying if he was being stalked, watched from afar by some blond man in dark clothing. It was a fleeting distraction gained only from the act of engaging in something that required him to pay attention to what he was doing.

When the thoughts started to leak back in, he let his legs pull him into a sprint and ran as hard as he could, and the effort pushed them away again, but only until the need to breathe overcame the desire to forget.

As he paced to a stop and put his hands on his knees, the rush and energy of the run started to fade with the slowing of his pulse. He started the walk back to the house, in a better mood than he'd started with.

His mood stayed positive until he stood in front of the house again. Immediately, he felt uneasy. Nothing was blatantly wrong. There was no blond man holding a syringe staring out the front window, but Hayden's car was gone.

Dammit, Hayden.

It wasn't like him to be untrustworthy.

Jonathan stared at the house. He wondered, really considered, if he was going to stand outside just to avoid being alone inside. The answer was simply no. Whatever normal was going to be, he wasn't going to set the bar that low. He could spend weeks being afraid on the inside; he'd endure that, but there was no way he was letting his behavior be governed so drastically.

He hesitated a bit longer, but eventually, he opened the front door and walked in.

The scene in the house was surprising, if not of a horrific nature. There was a child, maybe six years old, sitting pretzel style in the middle of the kitchen floor. The boy had a small pile of toy vehicles in front of him. They were pouring out of an overly colorful and hardly functional looking child's backpack on the ground near him. The kid had singled out two cars. He was pushing them in circles around him as though they were having a race. He made sounds of tires peeling out and vehicles ramming each other for effect.

Jonathan was disturbed for a moment—not by the child, but that the kid sat on the linoleum where he'd lost so much blood.

"Hello," said the boy, looking up at him. "I'm Jack."

The kid was smiling at him. The innocence of it brought Jonathan back to reality. Jack had short brown hair and a thin frame. He seemed alert, aware, like Jonathan's presence was an exciting turn of events. It was sad, Jonathan thought, but even the presence of this child in the house gave him comfort; it was better than being alone. Still, who was Jack and why was he sitting in Jonathan's kitchen?

"Hello, Jack," he said politely. "I'm Jonathan."

Jonathan looked around the room again and searched for an explanation for the kid. When he didn't find one, he spoke again.

"Those look like some cool cars you've got there. I used to have ones just like them when I was younger."

"Yeah? I like cars, but I like motorcycles more. I can't wait 'til I can have one. I mean a real one, not one with pedals," Jack said.

"I have a roommate who likes motorcycles. He has one. Maybe you can come see it sometime," Jonathan said.

Jack's eyes grew wide.

"Speaking of roommates," Jonathan said, "have you seen a big man with a beard around here today?"

"Yeah, he left in a big hurry," said Jack.

"Oh," Jonathan said. "Did he say where he was going?"

Jack thought about it for a moment but shook his head no. "He might have told my sister."

Jonathan realized then that he'd heard the sound of water running from the upstairs bathroom. Had Hayden somehow managed to invite two neighborhood children into the house, then leave, in the span of Jonathan's half-hour jog? Was he trying to show him what it was like to babysit someone?

A moment later, Jonathan heard the bathroom door open followed by the sound of footsteps coming down the stairs. An attractive woman was suddenly in his living room. When he looked into her eyes, she appeared to be as confused as he was.

The woman's face said she'd been put in a strange predicament, but was just choosing to take it as it came. Jonathan was not a good judge of age but she had to be in her early twenties. Her hair was a dark auburn and long, down past her shoulders. She had on jeans and a white tank top, and what looked to be an expensive camera hanging from a strap around her neck. As she made her way over to him, he tried not to be so transparently distracted by the way she walked. His mind had gone blank in an effort to focus his eyes in appropriate places.

She was too pretty to just be in his house like this. It made him nervous; not nervous like when he thought about being followed by an inhumanly strong blond man, but the good kind of nervous, the kind that made him worry he was about to say something stupid, the kind that made him worry he might be on the verge of blushing and she would know his thoughts.

"Make a new friend, Jack?" the woman said.

The little boy nodded.

When she reached Jonathan, she put her hand out, close enough now he could see the blue of her eyes.

"I'm Leah. We're neighbors," she said.

Jonathan took her hand—he was about to respond, but before he knew what was happening, she drew in close to him. He tensed excitedly as she was suddenly whispering in his ear, "Hayden promised you wouldn't be creepy."

When she pulled back, she smiled. Thoughts crashed through Jonathan's head as he tried to decipher the meaning of what she had said. Had he been leering at her?

"Um. Hi, Jonathan," he said, stuttering a bit. "I meant, I'm Jonathan, and yes, I mean no, I'm not. Creepy, that is."

She was still smiling at him, and he realized she was playing with him.

He cleared his throat. "Did Hayden say why he left in such a hurry?"

"Not really. He promised that he'd be gone for less than an hour and that he needed someone to stay here with his roommate while he was out."

Jonathan looked at her like it still didn't add up.

"So how do you know Hayden?" Jonathan asked.

"I don't, actually. I just moved in next door a few days ago. Jack and I were out in the front yard. I was taking some pictures of this interesting little nook we share. Your garden is beautiful, by the way. Anyway, when Hayden came out of the house, he said there was an emergency and that he needed someone to watch his roommate until he got back."

Leah looked at Jonathan with a curious tilt of her head.

"I realize now he was playing the vague pronoun game because I thought for sure he meant the girl I've seen coming and going."

Jonathan was embarrassed now, and he felt it showing on his face. This was bad nervous, and if he ever needed a reason to get over his fears, he'd found it. For a moment, he worried he might have to explain why a grown man would be afraid to be alone in his own house. Or worse, he wondered if Hayden had left out the part where she might be acting as a temporary deterrent to Jonathan's would be attacker.

"Well played on his part," Leah said. "But hey, I'm new to the city, so I guess this is one way to meet people."

Jonathan had to wonder what had gotten Hayden so desperate to find him a babysitter that he tricked their neighbor into it. It must have been pretty serious, especially if he had continued with it once he'd noticed how stunningly attractive she was.

He looked up and realized Leah was still looking at him with that curiosity she had before. She looked like she was struggling within herself to ask a question, then finally decided to take the chance that it might be taken as rude.

"So, what's the story, then? Seems a little odd that you need someone to watch you," she said, quickly adding, "I understand if it's none of my business."

Jonathan, still embarrassed, looked down at the floor. Pleading the fifth was tempting. There really wasn't any good way to spin the truth, no way he wouldn't come off looking fragile at the least. He decided to just be vague; it had worked for Hayden, and it was better than telling her that her little brother was sitting where he'd woke up in a puddle of his own blood last week.

"I recently had an episode, got attacked in the house. It rattled me a bit," he said. "My roommates got a little protective. You really don't need to stay if you're busy. I'll be fine."

She gave him a look of sympathy, then leaned in again to whisper. He liked it when she did.

"Um, yeah, Jonathan," she said. "Sounds like it's time to nut up a bit."

When she pulled away, he could see she was playing again and he smiled back.

"Nut up," he repeated.

The first day back to campus, Jonathan felt like he'd arrived late to the movies. He paid attention, but wasn't sure there was enough time left in the quarter to learn all that he'd missed. Still, the distraction was worth the effort. After classes were over, he showed up for his first shift at the hardware store.

James Fletcher, his boss and the owner, was an older man who had lost his hair long ago and wore nothing but blue collars. His wife had passed away some years earlier, and as a result, he didn't have much in life other than his business, his employees, and a smoking habit he was no longer trying to be rid of. He often said he smoked half as much when his wife was alive because she wouldn't let him into bed smelling like an ash tray. He hadn't expected to see Jonathan so soon.

"What got you up off the mat so quick?" he asked. "The way your roommate described things, I thought I might not see you for a few weeks."

"A pretty girl told me to—well, to be brave," Jonathan said.

Mr. Fletcher thought for a moment, looking Jonathan over, then chuckled. He'd have likely laughed out loud if Jonathan had used Leah's exact words.

"Yeah, that'd about do it, wouldn't it?" James said. "Still, kid, you let me know if you need any time off—people need to take their time with these things."

Jonathan nodded.

The shop had missed him. Mr. Fletcher's other part-timers had covered some of Jonathan's shifts but he got the impression that his boss had covered the brunt of his absence. James said he came from a time where men "worked for a living" and didn't much care for what he referred to as Jonathan's generation's "pussy footing around." He never put Jonathan in the *pussy foot* category, because of all his employees, Jonathan got his work done and never complained, always staying until the job was finished.

"So tell me more about this girl you got busting your balls."

Jonathan shrugged. "Guess I'll have to wait until there's actually something to tell," he said.

"Bah," James said disappointedly. "Speaking of women, how's your mom taken all this?" He asked.

Jonathan looked away.

"I haven't told her," he said.

A time passed and James finally nodded sympathetically.

"I get it, Jonathan," he said.

James turned away then, returning to the cash register and leaving Jonathan to work. He felt gratitude as he watched the old man walk away. It was the first time that particular disclosure hadn't been met with, at least, a look of disapproval. It occurred to him that James was the only person he knew who'd lived through a war. Maybe that was why Mr. Fletcher, more than anyone else he knew, could understand.

Grant and Paige sat on the couch. She was giggling, trying to get control of her laughter.

She'd been listening to stories from his first few weeks in the army. More often than not, they'd made her smile. Grant was so attentive. He'd never been clingy or overly talkative, never pressed her for her time or her feelings, but lately he seemed to want to see her whenever she'd had a free moment.

His presence alone was relieving, not just because he was a shoulder to lean on, but because the man was built like a bull. Since the attack, awareness that they might be being watched by some criminal had lingered in the background. When she'd confided in Collin that the soldier's presence made her feel safe, she could see bringing it up had bothered him, so she tried not to talk about it. The paranoia would subside with time. For now, though, she could tell Grant about her fears, and feel safe with him around.

Jonathan walked through the door, returning from his shift at the hardware store. He waved as he put his stuff down and walked over to visit with them for a moment.

Grant's demeanor changed; he quickly went from relaxed to stiff. He hadn't seen Jonathan since the hospital, she realized. Maybe he was apprehensive about how to behave around him. Then he surprised her, but not in a good way.

"Jonathan, I just wanted to let you know," Grant started, "you ever see this guy again, I want you to call me. We'll make him regret ever coming into this house."

It was so forward, so misplaced, and it exposed how much she'd told him when it was really none of his business.

"I'll give that guy a beat down he'll never forget." Grant punched his fist into his open hand for emphasis.

Paige was dumb struck with embarrassment. She'd specifically asked him not to bring up the attack in front of Jonathan.

"Sure. Thanks," Jonathan said. Paige could see Jonathan's gears grinding—he didn't know how to respond to Grant's bravado. "To be honest, I'm just trying to put it behind me," he said.

Paige let it show on her face that she wasn't the instigator behind Grant's offer. She didn't have to try very hard; her cheeks had turned a hot red the moment Grant started speaking. Unfortunately, Grant only got weirder from there.

"Take this," Grant said, reaching into his pocket.

He pulled out a business card. It read *Grant Morgan, Specialist, U.S. Army*. Paige could see Jonathan was having difficulty taking the card seriously as he looked it over.

Please stop talking, she found herself thinking.

"Thanks, Grant," Jonathan said, putting the card into the front pocket of his coat. When Grant looked away for a moment, Jonathan looked to her with a shrug and expression that captured the awkwardness of the transaction. Paige desperately wanted to change the subject.

"Anyhow, Grant was just leaving. I've got a lot of studying to do," she said.

Grant looked surprised. She supposed he'd expected that he'd be spending the night. Now, she could see he was trying to think quickly as he searched for an angle that would end in her bedroom. He seemed to fail and take the hint.

"I'll call you. Maybe do something this weekend?" Grant asked.

Paige nodded and walked him out. Maybe the guy had meant well, but she couldn't get out of this moment fast enough.

What the hell was that? Jonathan thought.

How Paige could bear talking to the arrogant ass for more than a few minutes escaped him. Besides being the product of hundreds of hours of physical training, he didn't see what she valued in the man.

He realized then that he'd answered his own question.

He'd originally thought Collin's instincts of the guy were a product of jealousy; now he thought they might be genuine. Regardless, he couldn't help but think it was lucky for Collin that Grant wasn't staying the night. His bedroom was right below Paige's after all.

Jonathan had thought about what he would do if he saw the stranger again, and it wasn't what Grant imagined. He wanted to know if he was crazy far more than he wanted revenge. Though he spent most of his hours trying not to obsess about it, he didn't believe the man had failed to accomplish whatever his goal had been that night.

You'll know what to do. I'll be there to help you, when it comes. Follow your....

It was part intuition, and again he found it maddening, but there was something in those words. Perhaps the man had had to escape quickly when Hayden and Collin had shown up on the porch, but he'd done whatever he was there to do. That he must have finished in a hurry didn't give Jonathan any comfort.

Dammit.

All that strength, Jonathan a toddler in the man's hands, and he couldn't have said whatever he was trying to say before knocking him out? Follow your what? He realized Grant's intrusive offer had forced the questions to the forefront of his mind again.

There aren't any answers at the end of these thoughts, he reminded himself.

The table beside the kitchen was often used as a communal study area. He tossed his backpack onto it and started unloading books. Paige came back in shortly after and joined him with her own homework.

"He was honorably discharged a few weeks ago," Paige said upon returning. She still looked embarrassed.

"Oh?"

They looked at each other for a moment and Jonathan softened. She was clearly mortified by the man's behavior. He really had nothing to gain making her feel worse about it.

"He wasn't expecting it. I'm a little worried. He doesn't seem that concerned with what he's going to do for work now," she said, clearly trying to ignore the incident, "and he thought I was joking when I said he should go back to school."

Jonathan listened, but didn't have anything insightful to say. He doubted she was really worried, just changing the subject.

"I'm sure he'll figure something out."

Some quiet time passed. They fell into their old ritual, hitting the books together, and after an hour or so she spoke again.

"I'm glad you're studying again. Hayden and Collin almost never hit the books. I missed having someone to sit here with. It helps me focus."

Jonathan smiled.

"I'll be playing catch up for the next few weeks. I got way behind while I was sitting around feeling sorry for myself."

She looked at him sympathetically.

"A few weeks getting it together after an experience like that isn't feeling sorry for yourself," she looked at him knowingly. "It takes time to process things, especially when there is no closure, no explanation."

He understood the statement came from a well-intentioned place, but he'd heard the sentiment a dozen times since leaving the hospital, so he simply nodded. Part of finding *normal* was going to include being comfortable when friends offered their encouragement.

"Too bad we don't have a Psych major in the house," he said, looking down into his book.

They spoke infrequently after that, both focusing on what they were reading until Hayden and Collin arrived together.

Jonathan had been curious to talk to Hayden about what had been so important the previous day that he'd resorted to asking a complete stranger to watch his roommate just so he could leave the house. When Jonathan brought it up, Hayden looked a little apprehensive before Collin interjected, putting one hand on Hayden's shoulder, and the other in the air as if to mockingly restrain Jonathan.

"My client had an understandable reason for his actions, your honor. You see, he has a well-documented addiction," Collin said.

"I have an addiction," Hayden repeated, nodding in agreement.

Jonathan raised an eyebrow, already knowing this explanation was going to be ridiculous.

"David Tennant was putting on a viral marketing campaign for the new season's premiere of *Doctor Who* and was at the comic store giving away free signed Tardises, but for only three hours," Collin said.

"I didn't understand a thing you just said to me. Is 'Tardis' a real word?" Jonathan asked.

Paige, sitting beside him, nodded as though she'd been thinking the same thing.

Collin and Hayden both exchanged a look that said if he doesn't understand, it would take far too much time and energy to explain it.

Paige whispered, "Comic dorks," under her breath and returned to her reading.

As though there weren't two people in the room studying, Collin and Hayden sat on the couch and started watching television. It was Jonathan's and Paige's turn to exchange looks, silently commenting on their roommate's unconscious rudeness. Jonathan smiled as he returned to his textbook. A night at home didn't get more typical than this. It seemed, with less time than he thought, *normal* might look like a life he recognized.

Then he felt something move in his chest.

CHAPTER NINE

THURSDAY | JUNE 30, 2005 | 08:30 PM

HE'D BEEN TRYING to focus, to ignore his roommates watching television on the couch behind him.

"I don't want to wait for September for the new season of *Lost* to start," said Hayden.

It was a flutter of sorts in his chest, a twitch of his muscles. He didn't make much of it right away, but within a few seconds, he was starting to feel warm.

"Does it seem hot in here to you?" he asked Paige

She shrugged, but didn't answer. A few more seconds passed and he was so uncomfortable he couldn't focus. It was beginning to burn.

His mind made the connection quickly; the burning in his chest and the sensation he had waking on the kitchen floor. He fought the urge to jump to conclusions, to panic before he was sure it wasn't something simple. He didn't want to alarm everyone if he just had a case of hives. He stood to make a line for the downstairs bathroom where he could remove his shirt and take a look.

He never made it that far.

His motor functions were suddenly not in his control. His legs quivered and he collapsed to the linoleum.

"Jonathan, you okay?" Paige asked. "Jonathan?"

He heard her, but couldn't form words. The burning in his chest was pulsing, growing hotter with each beat of his heart, spreading rapidly out from his ribs toward his limbs. Panic began to set in, but for all his alarm, he couldn't move. The burning grew stronger and stronger, his nerves lighting up in pain. It seemed to fill him from the outside in, skin to the bone, until his entire body was on fire, lava in his veins, his brain screaming out for him to act while he was immobilized on the floor.

Paige had stood and come around the table while Hayden and Collin had turned to look from the couch. His eyes suddenly stopped darting from one face to the other and became fixed on the ceiling. In horror, he realized he could not look elsewhere; his eyes no longer minded him. He could feel his hands clenching at his chest out of some kind of instinct, but as the fire expanded, his sense of touch was crowded out by pain.

Paige's face jumped into his vision, she'd dropped to her knees beside him.

"Jonathan! What's wrong?" she asked.

He heard her, but her voice was growing distant. He was too consumed with the flames scorching their way to his fingertips to focus on her voice. The searing moved up his neck toward his head; the surface of his face felt as though he was being drowned in flame. The heat began to sink in, toward his skull, toward his mind. His vision went black suddenly, his hearing completely mute.

Jonathan's terrified thoughts crashed into one another as each sense was taken away. He pleaded, not knowing to whom he begged for help in his thoughts.

Please give it back, please make it stop! Dammit, let me see them!

He was alone in the dark, unable to scream out, and pain was all he was aware of, the only thing letting him know he was still alive. It seemed as though acid had been poured into his skull; it seared into his temples, his eyes sockets, the nerves of his teeth and yet still burned further into his mind.

His thoughts devolved into disjointed panic until they seemed to cease entirely. He lost track of time, the very concept of beginning and end. Fire became all he knew.

"It seems like it's passed," Collin said.

"Was it a seizure?" Hayden asked.

His heart thudded in his ears. He didn't know if he'd been gone for a moment or an eternity.

Suddenly, he felt his limbs. His eyes shot open as he realized his lids were responding. Vision flooded back into him. The burning was gone, the pain suddenly sucked into a black hole within him; thought returned slowly, drifting in from somewhere that language had not existed, becoming comprehensible words again.

"Shit! Shit!" Paige yelled.

He felt her hands drawn back from his chest in surprise as she swore. He became aware that he was on the floor again, staring up at her wide eyes. He could hear the television still playing in the background. His roommates were surrounding him, Paige still on her knees at his right, Collin standing above his head, and Hayden to his left. All staring with their mouths hanging open—but they weren't looking at his face. They stared at his chest as though he had an armed hydrogen bomb ticking away on his torso.

"What happened?" Jonathan asked.

No one responded.

"Guys!" he yelled.

They snapped out of their trance and shut their mouths, looking him in the eye.

"Jonathan, your chest," Paige whispered, bringing her fingers to her mouth in worry.

Slowly, he propped himself on to his elbows and looked down. His chest was flickering, and as he watched in panic, it suddenly became alive with light.

It hadn't just kicked on abruptly. Like a halogen bulb, it had worked its way to full illumination. The light seemed organic, glowing red-orange from beneath the skin and submerged in the muscle tissues over his rib cage. He could see it through his shirt like neon lights had been surgically implanted inside his chest.

His hands moved to touch the light, but then he stopped, unsure if it was wise to touch them. Instead, he reached up and slowly lifted the collar of his shirt.

Three lines ran over his front and around his back. Two of the lines, one on each side of his torso, followed parallel to his arms from his shoulder down to his hip. These two lines were intercepted by the third, running perpendicular to his arms across his chest. The third line reached around from his back. It appeared to start at one lat muscle, crossed over his chest, and terminated in the muscle on the opposite side.

The lines looked like liquid energy running through him.

"What the hell is it?" Collin asked.

Only one thought occurred to Jonathan.

This shouldn't be possible.

How could all of those tests they ran at the hospital have missed something like this in his chest cavity? Jonathan didn't know what to do. He laid his head back down on the kitchen floor, trying to think. His roommates, seeming to fear he was about to go catatonic again, tried to think for him.

"Call an ambulance," Hayden said.

"What the hell for?" Collin asked. "Whatever that thing is, the doctors don't have an ointment for it."

"Well, what the hell else are we gonna do?" said Hayden.

"Why don't you try praying?" Collin snapped back.

While they began bickering, Paige came to her senses, finally taking her hand from her mouth.

"Jonathan," she said softly. "Does it hurt?"

His attention shifted to her when the concern in her voice registered. It was hard to gauge exactly what he felt given the circumstance, but he wasn't in pain any longer.

"No. I mean, there was a terrible pain before, worse than anything I've ever felt. Like I was being cremated and I couldn't move. But it stopped right before this came on," he said, pointing at his chest. "I feel normal. I'm—"

He realized then that something wasn't normal.

"Wait—" Jonathan paused.

Collin and Hayden, seeing that something was developing, became silent.

"There's something tugging at my attention," he said, then shook his head. "No, it's not tugging. It's strange. I can't... I can't *not* notice it."

Jonathan looked up at them, but he could tell by their expressions that he wasn't making any sense.

He realized it had been there for a while now on the outskirts of his awareness. He hadn't been paying attention to it. It didn't feel unnatural, so it hadn't stuck out at first, like choosing not to ignore the sound of the television while trying to study. It seemed as though he was feeling a new emotion, but could only describe it by comparing it to emotions that there were already words for. Instead of trying to explain it, he just said what it was telling him.

"There's something southwest of us," he blurted out, pointing in the direction without looking. "A mile, maybe two."

Direction sense, but with proximity, and it felt instinctual. He might as well have been seeing or hearing it. Such a novel sensation should have been more upsetting, but it felt like something he'd always been capable of. An ability that had always been there, only he knew it hadn't been conceivable a moment ago. Some kind of sensory input was being deciphered by his brain, but what was the source of the input? What was he sensing?

"What's *something*?" Collin asked as though reading his thoughts.

"I don't know," Jonathan replied.

"Jonathan, do you think it could be the man who…." Collin paused. "Did this to you?"

That was a thought.

"Guys, I need to tell you something," Jonathan said, looking to each of their faces. "I didn't tell the police everything."

They clearly hadn't expected that. His story had been pretty unbelievable in the first place for him to be leaving out details.

"The man—I didn't think, uh, I don't think he was human," Jonathan said. "His strength was more than just overwhelming. It was impossible for a man to be that strong. His eyes weren't just a strange shade of blue either. They looked like they were lit up from behind, like a computer monitor. I didn't tell the police because I knew how it would sound. I thought I was crazy, but now that this is happening I know I couldn't have imagined it."

All three roommates were looking at the floor now, all trying to process what he was saying into something that made the current situation make sense.

"I still think we should get him to a hospital," said Hayden.

Paige seemed to agree, but Jonathan hardly saw the point. If whatever was in his chest had eluded their detection after they had run every test they could, he didn't see how they would suddenly know what to do with him now. He needed time to think. He wasn't ready to do something that might make the situation worse. Collin spoke up as though he were reading his mind again.

"Guys," Collin said, "am I the only one who saw *E.T.*? We need to think before we involve any authorities."

Suddenly, Jonathan felt the thing to the southwest move. The signal, if he could call it that, had increased the distance between them. It was farther away than when it had started.

"No," Jonathan said, starting to get to his feet and reaching for the table. "I'm not—"

There was a loud pop followed by the sound of wood splintering. Jonathan found his butt still on the floor.

The table had broken down the center as he'd pulled to lift himself. The two halves crashed in on each other, books dropping in a heap onto the linoleum. The room got quiet as they looked at the mess; the only sound was that of a pencil rolling across the floor.

Jonathan didn't understand. His roommates stood looking at the pile with the same confusion. Finally, Hayden and Collin looked at each other like a light bulb had gone off in both their heads simultaneously.

"I don't think we can blame IKEA for that," Collin said.

"Can you do that again?" Hayden asked.

"What?" Jonathan asked, still sitting on the linoleum.

"Er, break something," Hayden said.

Seeing what they were getting at, Jonathan carefully rolled over onto his hands and knees and gently pushed himself to stand. The roommates all backed away from him. Standing over the broken table he reached, slowly and carefully, for the chair he'd been sitting in a moment earlier. He looked to his roommates, as if to ask permission. They all nodded.

He slowly started to put pressure on the wood of the chair. It creaked once before giving way to the force. The back of the chair broke free of the seat.

He'd hardly pushed on it at all.

"No one get close to me," Jonathan said, putting his hands up as if they were weapons he didn't know how to operate.

It took a few moments to set in. First there was awe, then fear, then disbelief, but eventually, there was curiosity, and they all wanted to see to what extent Jonathan's strength had increased. Hayden eventually ran and got the aluminum bat from the closet and handed it to Jonathan.

"What do you want me to do?" he asked.

"See if you can bend it," Hayden said.

Jonathan held the bat with a hand on each end, then tried bringing his hands together. It wasn't difficult; it bent under the pressure from his arms like it was made of rubber.

Jonathan didn't like it. He felt like they were children playing with fire. There was a reason for this strength, and it wasn't amusement. He walked away carefully, giving each of them a wide berth, and made his way to the bathroom.

"Where are you going?" Paige asked.

"I want to get a better look at this thing," he said, pointing to the light in his chest.

When he got to the bathroom, he removed his shirt and examined himself in the mirror. His roommates crowded around the door. The glow was made of fixed straight lines. There seemed to be one main line to each of the three beams, but along the edges he could see that small threads of light were coming off the main lines and embedding themselves into his tissues. It looked as though the lights were interconnected with his muscle fibers, veins, and arteries. A glowing web of connection under his skin, and it was amazingly complex.

He wasn't in awe of it; this just confirmed his worries. Whatever was inside him was so permanently embedded no surgical operation was going to remove it. It was a part of him.

Carefully, he put his shirt back on. He was going to need something thicker than a T-shirt if he didn't want to attract attention. He left the bathroom, his roommates giving him plenty of space as he exited for fear he might accidentally bump them and send them sprawling across the living room.

He began pacing in front of the television set. They watched him, trying to make sure they could warn him if it looked like he might accidentally put a foot through the coffee table. He kept trying to reason it out.

"Why?" Jonathan asked out loud. "Why do this to someone?"

The signal moved again, farther away, toward the waterfront, he thought. Upon noticing it, he remembered the last thing the blond man had said.

You'll know what to do. I'll be there to help you, if you make it. Just follow your—

"Instincts," Jonathan said softly.

That had to be it. He hadn't been able to put it together because the "instinct" the man had been talking about hadn't triggered yet. Maybe it had taken so long because the man hadn't finished whatever he'd intended? Maybe he hadn't been sure if Jonathan would survive; that was why he'd said "if you make it." The signal in his head was pointing the way.

His roommates had become unusually silent.

"I think you were right, Collin. This compass in my head, it must point to the man. It will lead me to him," Jonathan said.

His excitement hit a wall as he thought about it more.

"Wait, no, why piss a person off, then give him superpowers and paint a heat seeking target on your own back?" Jonathan asked disappointedly as his theory unraveled.

He stopped pacing and looked up at his roommates. They didn't appear to be paying attention to him. They were looking past him at the television set.

"Jonathan, I don't think the blond man is what's southwest of here," Collin said.

CHAPTER TEN

THURSDAY | JUNE 30, 2005 | 09:30 PM

HAYDEN HAD SET the television to mute when Jonathan had broken the table in half, but the news had come on behind him as he paced the living room. He turned around as all of his roommates were pointing at the screen.

At first, there was just a newscaster with an alarmed look as she spoke. Hayden ran over to what was left of the kitchen table and fished out the remote to unmute the sound.

"Footage of the creature has been scant. It appears to have come out of nowhere in downtown Seattle. Currently no creditable explanation of its origins has been brought forth, but theories ranging from alien to a biological weapon have been speculated. The video we just showed you was taken from the window of a local resident. The creature has moved on from that location. Local law enforcement has responded and the area has been quarantined until officers can assess the situation.

"Again, for those of you just tuning in, be advised that a dangerous animal of unknown origin has attacked pedestrians in the downtown area. Not much is known at this time, but so far three deaths and an unknown number of injuries have been reported. At first, this was thought to be a costumed man or a wild animal loose in the city, but as the footage we've received

shows, this doesn't appear to be the case. Reporters are not being allowed into the quarantined zone."

Jonathan could tell from the disjointed manner of the reporting that the newscaster was doing the best she could in a live situation.

"Show the footage again, dammit!" Collin yelled at the television, everyone in the room nodding in agreement with their growing impatience.

"Here is the clip again, but understand that this footage is graphic and that some viewers may find it disturbing," said the reporter.

The video was taken from the second story window by someone who had his lights off to avoid getting the unwanted attention of the subject they were filming. The quality was barely watchable as it was a home camera trying to film a poorly-lit street through a closed window. The only light was from the streetlights lining the sidewalks. Nevertheless, the clip was surreal. It wasn't one of the city's main streets. Jonathan recognized that it was taken somewhere under the viaduct, a raised freeway that bordered Seattle's waterfront.

People on the street were fleeing. The creature, that must have been seven or eight feet tall, made its way into the center of the road, where it stood in the light of one of the street lamps. From what could be made out, it looked like an overgrown gargoyle without wings. Its body was incredibly muscular, seeming to mimic a human male in form, as the creature was chest heavy and V-shaped. The video was too rough to make out a lot of detail, but its skin seemed black and leathery. Its face wasn't looking at the camera, but it had ear-like appendages that stretched straight back from its head like two short samurai swords.

The thing was dragging the body of a man in one hand. Its fingers held the skull like a NBA player palming a basketball. The body was horribly broken, dead. The creature swiveled in the street and let out a loud roar.

Challenger.

Jonathan heard the word in his mind in sync with the guttural roar of the creature on the television, almost as though he'd growled it to himself.

It seemed to be yelling out to the whole city. It looked up and about, into windows, and everywhere it thought a person could hear it. It finally tossed the body of the man through a car windshield with such force that it made the three roommates gasp. The monster stamped the ground, beating its chest once like a gorilla showing its strength. The street lamps shook with it, parked cars rattled, alarms went off.

Challenger!

Again, Jonathan heard the words in his head like a thought, but a thought he hadn't given rise to, an intruder in his mind using his own internal voice to speak to him. It was disturbing. He wanted to believe it was his imagination, that he was somehow unintentionally giving rise to that word.

The person taking the video must have lost his or her nerve and ducked completely under the window sill as the footage came to an end.

The reporter came back on.

"We've received reports that police have engaged with the creature, but that it hasn't been subdued with gunfire. This is purely speculation at this point, but a SWAT team will likely be called in to engage. If this proves ineffective, a military response may be approved. If you're already in Seattle, please don't panic, and stay in your homes. Local radio stations have been advised to air emergency announcements to instruct citizens driving into downtown Seattle not to enter the city until the creature has been subdued to help reduce fatalities. Please, if you know anyone who might be headed to Seattle and unaware of what is taking place, call them and let them know not to enter the city."

"It's looking for a challenger," Jonathan said.

The group looked at him, unsure how he had come to this conclusion. "It was just grunting and growling from what I heard. Seems more like a scared animal trying to establish a territory," said Paige.

"No, it clearly said, 'Challenger,' twice in that video clip. I mean, it was like a bear growling it in another language, but I could hear it," Jonathan said.

From the look on their faces, it was clear they had only seen a creature roaring. He let out a long breath.

"What in the hell could this have done to me to make me understand what that thing was saying?" Jonathan said, pointing at the glowing lights beneath his chest.

Hayden was looking at him. He looked more worried for him than he'd been a moment earlier, more worried than Jonathan had ever seen him. Collin and Paige, a few moments behind him, took on the same expression, as though their own personal puzzle pieces had fallen into place. Whatever they now saw, they didn't like it.

"Jonathan," Hayden said, "I think... I think you know what is happening here."

Jonathan was shaking his head.

"That man, whatever he did to you, he was fitting you to fight that thing."

Jonathan paused for a moment, hesitated, then shook his head. It was too absurd. "That doesn't make any sense. That's comic book nonsense."

Paige looked at first like she wanted to agree with him, but couldn't. "Jonathan, I think Hayden is...." She trailed off, feeling the gravity of what she'd been about to say.

"What do we know?" Hayden asked. "A man, whom you don't believe was human, broke into our house and embedded something into you. A few weeks go by and nothing seems to happen, then twenty minutes ago, you lit up. Suddenly you're impossibly strong. Suddenly you sense there's something southwest of here. Roughly at the same time, a creature of unknown origin appears in the middle of downtown Seattle, southwest of here, and starts yelling for a challenger, but only you are able to understand what its saying."

He finished, looking at Jonathan like the conclusion was obvious. It made perfect sense to the comic-book-blockbuster-movie-obsessed mind. It made none to Jonathan.

"Why? Why would anyone go to so much trouble just to see a man fight that thing? And why now? Why hasn't it ever happened before? Why would there suddenly be a species on Earth that man had never seen? How would it just show up?" Jonathan said, watching the replay of the creature on the news. His roommates didn't appear convinced by his outpouring of questions.

The newscaster came back on. Her alarmed expression had changed; she now looked like she might be ill.

"We're now receiving new footage from a live helicopter camera circling the situation downtown. If you choose to watch the footage, please be aware that it's far more graphic than the original video. The police seem unable to bring this creature under control with their available arsenal. Its exterior skin appears to be unnaturally resilient. SWAT is now engaging the creature."

When the video came on, Jonathan dropped to his knees in front of the television. He understood now why the reporter looked sick.

It still stood underneath the viaduct, but had progressed a few blocks north. Bodies seemed littered in a path to where it stood—some viciously dismembered, others broken, lying dead in unnatural positions. Police and SWAT had formed a circle of vehicles around the monster and had opened fire with automatic weapons. It wasn't being slowed by the attack—if anything, the creature seemed to be getting worked up into frenzy.

It moved suddenly, pouncing onto a police car and yanking up an officer who had been crouched behind the vehicle. Lifting the man up as though he were a kitten, the fingers of one hand closed around the man's legs, the other massive hand on his skull. The video cut out. Jonathan didn't have to see it to know how it ended. He was grateful it hadn't been shown.

The newscaster returned to the screen, at a loss for words. She stuttered that the National Guard had been called to respond to the threat as soon as possible. Jonathan staggered back from the television. He slumped down on the couch. The room was silent.

All he could think was that he didn't want this. He was a twenty-two-year-old kid. He wasn't a killer. He wasn't trained to deal with this. He didn't want to be within ten miles of that thing, let alone pick a fight with it. If he went down there, he wouldn't know the first thing to do. He'd end up part of the mutilated dead lining the street, and for what? So some blond asshole could get a thrill from pitting them against each other.

That didn't seem right to Jonathan, though.

"The stranger, before he put me under—I thought I was crazy, but he said, '*You aren't prepared, but you must bear this.*'"Jonathan looked up at the three of them. "He was right. I'm not prepared. If I go out there, I'll die."

Paige and Collin both appeared deep in thought. Hayden didn't; he looked impatient, and Jonathan knew what the man was about to say.

He started to speak, "Jonathan—"

"No," Jonathan said.

"Jonathan, everything happens for a—" Hayden started to say.

"Shut up!"

Hayden looked at him. "Jonathan—"

"Don't! Don't get self-righteous; don't tell me I have to go down there. I didn't ask for this! You want to trade places, Hayden? You think you'd just march out there to die? I can hardly move I'm so scared."

Jonathan was visibly shaking. He held his hands clasped in front of him, trying to get them to hold still and failing.

"This is reality—if I go out there, it isn't going to matter if it was the right thing to do," he whispered. "This isn't a comic book."

"Yes!" Hayden said. "That is exactly what it is. It's exactly what those stories are about. You have to get down there."

"I didn't volunteer for this!" Jonathan yelled, his fear spilling over into anger at Hayden for taking some moral stance when the situation required nothing of him.

"No you didn't!" Hayden said, getting up off the couch. "And it isn't fair! But what's it going to be, Jonathan? You want Paige to go get your pills? You want to go take a nap in your room while that thing kills a few hundred people waiting for you to show up?"

"Hayden!" Paige exclaimed. "That isn't fair!"

Hayden ignored her attempt to defend Jonathan.

"You think you'll just live with that?" Hayden said. "You think you can just say to yourself, 'It's not fair,' and all those people getting killed out there aren't your problem anymore?"

Hayden's words were becoming heavy, the guilt seeping in. He wanted to ignore it, but couldn't avoid seeing it for the unfair, honest truth that it was. Knowing it still didn't change the fact that it was a death sentence.

"Just give me a minute," Jonathan said.

Panic welled up in him. He rocked back and forth on the couch. He didn't know how to get up. He was stalling. All he wanted was for the seconds to stretch on into hours. He needed time.

"Jona—"

"Give him a damn minute, Hayden!" Paige yelled.

"People don't have a minute. Jona—"

The balance between Jonathan's fear and anger shifted toward the latter. Before he knew what he was doing, he stood, crushing the coffee table in front of them and nearly put his foot through the floor boards. It was just too much to bear being called a coward once more.

Hayden stood his ground, but Paige and Collin were visibly worried that he was pushing their unstable roommate into a rage while he was capable of doing some serious damage.

"What? You holier-than-thou asshole! What?" Jonathan yelled.

Hayden yelled back, "I'll go with you!"

Jonathan swallowed. He felt like he'd just been gut checked. His anger and fear dropped off a cliff. Hayden wasn't posturing, Jonathan could see it. He was volunteering. The man's bravery—it moved him, but it shamed him more than he'd expected.

He turned to look at Paige and Collin. They seemed to struggle with the decision but then nodded. They, too, would go with him. They were all volunteering to help him face this. He hadn't done anything to deserve this kind of loyalty.

He took a deep breath, the word "dammit" escaping as he exhaled. He thought of his father, imagined what Douglas would say if he could be there to say it.

You won't be able to live with having done nothing.

Who was he kidding anyway? Hayden was right. He wasn't going to hide in his house with all those bodies piling up on the street, knowing he was supposed to be the one stopping it.

Yet, of all the things, it was her voice in his head, a flash of the girl next door, that really seemed to make his mind up.

Nut up, Jonathan, he thought.

CHAPTER ELEVEN

THURSDAY | JUNE 30, 2005 | 10:20 PM

"NO," JONATHAN SAID. "You aren't going. None of you are going."

Their volunteering had been enough. They'd been willing to put themselves in danger to help him act. He didn't want to think of seeing one of them get killed just so he wouldn't have to go out there alone.

When Jonathan was a teenager, his friends had taken him out to the cliffs to go diving. He wasn't a thrill seeker, but he'd come along. Some of it had been pride, for sure; all his friends had jumped, but it had really been a test. What would it feel like to step off a precipice like that? His mind understood the safety of the water below but his body resisted, as if it were any other forty-foot drop. He didn't know how long he had stood at that cliff, trying to overcome fear with reason, trying to will himself to jump.

He'd grasped the truth eventually. He couldn't talk himself into jumping, he could only decide. He had to commit to the point of no return. He had charged the cliff, sprinting as fast as he could, so that even if his instincts tried to stop him, he'd still have plummeted over the edge. Instead, he'd jumped. There'd been no thought in his head until he hit the water. That was when the reality of getting back up the cliff became the problem.

He had to commit now, and deal with the reality once he got there.

"Collin, I need the keys to the bike," he said.

Collin nodded, hesitating only briefly, and then shot off toward his room. Hayden and Paige stood uncomfortably. Hayden was still agitated by his own outburst. He looked like he was worried that his anger might be the last words Jonathan ever heard. It had been the right thing, though. Paige looked like she might cry. Jonathan tried not to look at her; it was unnerving. She was a ball-buster and it didn't fit right when she turned so vulnerable. It made him feel vulnerable. He didn't need to see in her eyes that she didn't think he'd be coming back.

"Do you have a plan?" she asked.

Jonathan shook his head. He had no idea what he was going to do once he got there. It hadn't even occurred to him to think that far ahead yet.

"It'll take a few minutes to get there," he said. "I'll try and think of something."

Collin came back from his room. He had his motorcycle jacket, gloves, and helmet in his hands.

"I'd keep the coat and gloves on. They're designed to help reduce injury if you fly off a bike. Can't imagine it would hurt now. The keys are in the pocket." Once he'd handed over the gear he added, "Jonathan, it probably goes without saying, but be careful."

Jonathan thought about the words. *Be careful.* Given the context, what in the hell did that even mean? Don't jump directly into its teeth? Make it work for it? The whole idea of staring down an eight-foot-tall creature from a nightmare reeked of reckless abandon. Regardless, Jonathan nodded and headed for the garage door.

Paige hugged him. She'd come up behind him, her arms suddenly tight around his chest.

"This is happening too fast," she said.

Jonathan tensed, afraid to return the affection when he was unsure of his own strength. When she let go of him, he forgot himself a bit, tearing the door to the garage off its hinges. He grimaced at his forgetfulness and laid the door against the wall next to the now-empty door frame. He was going to have to be careful riding the bike or he might damage the clutch or throttle just from lack of attention to this new strength.

"Watch the TV," he said. "I have my phone. If anything changes before I get there, I might need you to warn me."

They returned to the couch to do as they had been asked but watched him descend into the garage. When the motorcycle's engine came to life, they would know he'd gone.

Jonathan opened the garage door by gently pushing the button that ran the lift mechanism. He put the coat on. Collin was right; the kevlar in the shoulders and the pads on the arms and back were reassuring. Any reassurance was welcome. Then he gently pushed Jenny out onto the driveway. It was amazing how easily the bike moved for him. Three hundred and sixty pounds of metal machinery, and it responded under his push like he was maneuvering a toddler's tricycle. He felt like, if he wanted to, he could lift the thing over his head.

"Didn't think you were the rider," said Leah.

Jonathan was surprised. He hadn't seen anyone when he pushed the bike out. He looked around the yard, but still didn't see her.

"Up here," she said.

He followed the sound of her voice, and saw that she was on her balcony.

"Jack has been asking if he could come by and see 'the neighbor's moto-bike' since you mentioned it to him."

He was alarmed for a moment, scared that she would notice his chest was glowing, but the thick leather of the jacket hid the light.

"It's Collin's, my roommates. I'm just borrowing it. I'm sorry, I need to go, I'm in a hurry," he said.

"Really?" she said raising a curious eyebrow. "Hot date tonight, then?"

"Nothing so pleasant," he said.

"Oh well, I just like to wish my guy friends good luck," she said, "at least when it looks like they need it."

Jonathan smiled. It was funny that levity could be found, given the situation. The way she talked disarmed him, even now. Of course, part of what was funny was how far off her guess was.

"Glad we're friends. Wasn't sure if you hung out with cowa—"

He cut off the word; he didn't like the sound of it. "Well, guys who need babysitting."

She shrugged. "I'm giving you the benefit of the doubt."

They were silent for a moment. The instant of empty awkwardness reminded him he didn't have time for any of this.

"You haven't seen the news tonight?" he asked.

"Nope, not as a rule," she said.

"Well, don't let the kid watch, but you should. I've got to go. Whatever you do, don't go downtown."

He put the helmet on, started the bike, and headed out of the driveway. It was abrupt, considering a moment earlier they had shared a smile, but there wasn't time to explain.

Jonathan slowed for nothing. He swerved against traffic, fighting the flow of cars fleeing out of downtown. He split lanes and drove up on sidewalks when he had to.

He didn't have to pay attention to where he was going, as the signal in his head told him he was getting closer. Collin had never told him what it was like to drive the motorcycle on the streets. Jonathan found it calming as it took most of his focus, and he thought of little else than the task of balancing, turning, not being hit by the panicked drivers, and not letting his strength damage the bike while still maneuvering closer to his target.

With what mental capacity he had left to spare, he was trying to think of what he was actually going to do when he got there. It was one thing to assess the situation once he had a real look at it, but he would like to go in with a strategy at least.

Staying alive is a good strategy, he thought.

There were smarter ways to deal with this than just showing up. He had to go into this thinking he was going to survive. To do that, he needed to start thinking like a survivor. He wouldn't be out here if this thing wasn't killing people, so task one was getting it away from bystanders and housing. If he was going to move it, then it had to be somewhere that gave him an upper hand. That just begged the question, what could possibly give him the advantage?

All he could think of was that he knew the city better than the creature, or at least he assumed he did. For that matter, he could assume he knew the entire Earth better, but how did that help him? He didn't know a thing about the beast, let alone what would kill it.

That wasn't necessarily true, though. If what was true on Earth was true wherever this thing had come from, he might know more than he'd thought. He'd taken anatomy and physiology classes. It had characteristics he recognized. Large incisors and excessive sharp teeth, all predatory features. Long ears indicated a developed sense of hearing. This was just becoming a list of his disadvantages though, none of which helped him.

It walked on two legs—yet, thinking about it now, it had elongated arms, which might mean it was like a gorilla, moving on knuckles and feet when the situation called for it. This meant Jonathan would likely lose in a sprint, as four legs tended to move faster than two unless the terrain gave his smaller body better ability to maneuver. Again, this didn't help him kill it.

Then a thought occurred to him. It seemed like a thin chance if any, but he doubted he'd have an opportunity to think of anything else in the time he had. He'd have to get the creature to—

The headlights of a truck cutting into his lane flashed across his vision and he was forced swerve, narrowly sweeping into the thin space between the car parked on the sidewalk and the little room the truck had left in the lane.

"Pay attention, dammit," he said to himself inside the helmet.

He wondered then if he'd even live long enough to maneuver the creature anywhere. Quickly, he silenced the part of his mind that wanted to go down that line of thinking.

Stop getting in your own way, he thought.

He was nearly out of time. He didn't need the sensation in his head to tell him he was close. He could hear the gunfire over the roar of the motorcycle. When he turned a corner, he finally saw the conflict firsthand a few blocks ahead. SWAT and police cars blocked his view of the creature but the gunfire was deafening. Men opened fire from behind their cars. They looked panicked, some on the verge of fleeing. From where he was, he could see one of the SWAT vans topple over from the force of some impact he hadn't been able to see.

False Challenger! Imposter! said the voice in his head, syncing with the harsh guttural growling in the chaos.

Only Jonathan understood what was happening. The creature thought the men firing at him were challenging it. It was expecting someone more physically capable. It was expecting him.

He pulled into an alley and killed the engine. Leaning against the wall of the building that blocked his view, he pulled the helmet off and dropped it to the ground. He closed his eyes. He hated that his plan was so flimsy. He hated knowing where he wanted it and not knowing how he'd manage to get it there. If that damn blond stranger had just told him what was going to happen, he might have had a real plan. He took in some deep breaths to hold onto his courage. Once he turned that corner, there was no going back.

He reached into his pocket for his cell phone, to see if his roommates tried to reach him. There were no missed calls, only one text message from Paige.

SWAT failed. Army not mobilizing fast enough. Do whatever it takes, Jonathan.

It was that last sentence that disturbed him. He didn't want to imagine what she must have seen, but knew he wouldn't have to. He'd see it for himself soon.

Get a grip, Tibbs, he thought. Need to get the thing's attention off the police. Find its weaknesses. Need to get the advantage. Now move before anyone else dies.

He turned the corner and made his way into the madness. As he neared the scene, he started passing bodies, most in pieces. Half a man's torso laid under a riot shield that had been snapped in half. Empty shells from all the wasted rounds littered the streets. Cars were tossed about, some lying on their sides, others completely turned over. Weapons were abandoned in the streets or forcibly removed from their owners. Jonathan wondered if he would die as easily as these men had. What did it matter that he was strong if he could be torn in half as easily as anyone here?

He dropped down next to an officer firing into the circle. The man ducked back behind his vehicle and took notice of him there. He immediately started screaming at Jonathan for being an idiot; it was a testament to the officer's bravery that he hadn't run. Jonathan got the gist of what he was yelling, although he could hardly make it out this close to so much gunfire. "Damn fool," "no place for a civilian," and "police matter," were in there. Jonathan agreed with the officer. This was no place for him. Why hadn't the blond stranger been smart enough to see that? Now hundreds were going to die, while he was busy being a damn fool.

Imposter! Imposter! The beast roared again.

The translated words, spoken by his own internal voice, were like having his own thoughts turn on him, reaffirming the doubt he already felt.

Then it struck him; a surge of hope was born as he realized it. If it was surprised and angered every time it killed someone so easily, it must not be able to tell who the challenger was; it could not sense him like he could it. He did have an advantage.

Get its attention, Jonathan thought.

He left behind the policeman still yelling at him. Running a few yards, he approached the closest SWAT van still upright. He gauged the jump; no small task when he didn't know his own strength. Aiming to land aboard the top of the vehicle, he reached out with one hand and put his palm on the van roof. The immense core strength he now possessed made the maneuver simple. He landed smoothly with the simple use of his forearm. The strength coursing through him defied gravity without the strain it would put on mere human muscles. Grace was a symptom of the balance and stability that this strength brought.

From above the barrier, he could see what had unhinged these men fighting around him. This thing—it couldn't seem to tell the difference between the people running from it or the people fighting it, or it just didn't care. It was piling the dead, stacking its kills one on top of the other in the street like trophies.

Jonathan wasn't ready to see it; he couldn't take it all in. With terrible understanding, he realized he'd smelled the blood. It pooled in the street beneath them. The odor was a visceral thing, flooding his lungs and threatening to empty his stomach. His eyes darted from one lifeless form to the next; he didn't know what to do with the images and he couldn't understand why he hadn't looked away.

His eyes came to rest on a single color standing out in the pile. It was small and thrown so carelessly into the mass of bodies; pink, impossible to miss against the predominantly blues and blacks of police and SWAT uniforms. A jacket, a child's jacket, a girl; she couldn't have been more than six or seven. She was still, her body so fractured, her limbs and fingers contorted in unnatural angles, her jaw dislodged, turning her childhood innocence into the very essence of wrongness. The little girl—the thing had picked her up and broken her, until nothing about her was right.

Her eyes stared back at him, lifeless, demanding an explanation from within the fallen. His vision a tunnel; the girl was all he could see, her dead gaze questioning him.

Why did you take so long? Where have you been? What did you wait for?

The guilt was so overpowering that there seemed nothing to hold on to inside as the image of the girl's broken body branded itself into his mind. It threatened to break his very sanity, his very ability to be in this moment. Plummeting, he searched for stability within himself, something to halt the unhinging of his mind, to let him move his body again, if nothing else than to let him shut his eyes. He didn't find what he was looking for.

Instead, something terrible seemed to find him.

It surfaced without thought, a thing that had hidden in plain sight for so long that it startled him when it moved within. He didn't recognize this part of himself as it made its presence known, but his intuition screamed out in warning that he wasn't supposed to let it out, that it had been chained down inside for a reason, that it was never meant to do the world any good. It had been forced to wait for his permission, for Jonathan to surrender control.

There was no choice; it had the strength to move that he couldn't find. When he let the thing take hold of him, its fury wrenched his eyes from the broken body of the girl and back to the monster in the street. Part of Jonathan curled down into a ball as the thing grew stronger. It fed on the responsibility, the disgust, the frustration, the unfairness, the very adrenaline pumping through his veins and silenced the part of him that wouldn't act.

There was no desire to flee. There was no more fear of pain or death. He lost himself in rage, became something rabid and focused. He felt a surge of violent strength as it finally took the wheel.

The creature stood next to its pile of trophies, its back to him. There was a break in the gunfire. Jonathan saw now that the remaining police had stopped shooting momentarily as the creature had gotten a hold of a fellow officer and they feared hitting their comrade.

He'd never moved so fast, the strength in his legs propelling him. The SWAT van rattled, the roof caving in as he charged forward. When he hit the ground, the pavement shook beneath him. He didn't hesitate, only forced his legs to push harder, to accelerate. He took one last powerful step before lunging straight for the monster's back. His arms covered his head like a shield, his eyes and teeth clenched shut, waiting for the impact.

There was a heavy thud like slabs of meat clapping together. He felt the connection reverberate down his spine.

He heard a crash somewhere out in front of him. When he opened his eyes, he was on the pavement. The sound of helicopter blades surfaced, muffling the noises around him. His rage made the world feel as if it were moving in slow motion, dulled to his senses.

He saw the police officer next to him scrambling to the safety of the vehicle barricade. The creature had dropped the man when they'd connected. Jonathan looked up to where it had stood. There was nothing there now.

Ahead of him, there had been a bullet riddled semi-truck. It had now collapsed onto its side. The creature had torn through the hull of the trailer and overturned the entire vehicle. Jonathan rose to his feet, his fury focused on what now lay in the truck's hull.

The raging thing inside of him—it seemed pleased with itself.

He took his eyes away from the container briefly, assessing his surroundings. The police were still. They wore astonished faces; their mouths hung open. They tried to blink the gun smoke out of their eyes and believe what had happened. He knew what they saw. A nothing of a boy, barely a man, had knocked the beast from its own battleground.

The moment passed, its ending marked by a loud creaking from the inside of semi's trailer as the thing began to move. He'd jumped off the precipice; now it was time to deal with the climb back to safety. Jonathan could imagine the monster inside the hull, not yet knowing what had hit it so hard, and it stoked the flames of his anger to know he'd rattled it.

The large, clawed hand of the beast reached through the hole its body had torn in the side of the semi. The men surrounding Jonathan snapped out of their momentary lapse, taking cover again behind their vehicles. Jonathan's gaze focused on the claws.

With a quick and powerful motion, the beast pulled itself on top of the capsized semi and crouched beside the tear in the hull. Its white eyes quickly swept the scene, finding where it had stood a moment earlier and coming to rest on Jonathan. It began to growl, speaking in its monstrous dialect.

Challeng—

"I'm right here!" Jonathan roared over it, cutting off the voice as it translated in his mind.

CHAPTER TWELVE

THURSDAY | JUNE 30, 2005 | 11:20 PM

JONATHAN CRASHED INTO one of the cement pillars supporting the freeway. The cylindrical support cracked around him as he hit. He fell onto the street, dust from the fractured pillar raining down on him.

A little over a minute had passed since he'd been staring down the monster. Since then, he'd been kicked so hard he'd knocked over a SWAT car, been backhanded into the asphalt, and now grabbed by his jacket and thrown out of the street entirely. If it weren't for the pillar, he'd still be airborne. He was losing this fight. Worse, the creature didn't even seem to be taking him seriously any longer. He had its attention, there was that, but it was just toying with him. Its interest now only seemed to be gauging how much punishment Jonathan could take. It was all he could do not to accidentally kill bystanders by crashing into them as the creature kicked his ass all over the street.

Since taking that first kick to the chest, he'd learned a lot. On the up side, he was no longer a fragile man. He was hurting, but not the pile of broken bones that he should have been. Whatever the implant in his chest had done to him hadn't been limited to sheer strength. It had made his body denser and far more resilient. On the negative, he didn't know the first thing about fighting, and it was embarrassingly apparent.

It was as though the creature lived and breathed violence; methodical and quick; it was four steps ahead of him with every attack. He had to change tactics. He couldn't stand toe-to-toe with it. Eventually it would grow bored and begin to focus on killing him. Jonathan knew whatever the beast was doing in the fight right now, it was psychological in nature, meant only to show him that he was hopelessly out of his depth. It wasn't as though he hadn't expected this before showing up, but his frustration was rising. He was losing his grip on the fury that was holding back his fear. Even now, looking up at the beast from his knees on the sidewalk, it showed no hurry to maintain the upper hand. It wanted him to attack, it wanted him to fail. It wanted him to do so in front of his entire species.

Reaching his feet, Jonathan noticed the metal pole of a street sign next to him and pulled it out of the cement. It wasn't easy, but the pavement broke away when he put the strength of his back into it. Maybe he could keep the thing from getting too close to him.

He looked up and the creature hadn't changed pace or even given a sign that it registered he'd picked up a weapon. When his panic began to build, he forced himself to remember he had a plan. Turning away, he retreated into the darkened streets beneath the viaduct. It was one step closer to where he wanted it and it lured the damn monster away from the police barricade.

There were no streetlights underneath; plenty of shadows to hide in. He hoped that if he could lose the thing in the dark for a moment he might gain the upper hand. He could sense its location through the signal in his mind, but in the dark it would need to search for him. He ducked out of the creature's line of sight and made for the shadows, pressing his back to one of the pillars. Both his hands clasped the metal bar tight to his chest as he waited for the creature to make its way in.

He sensed it nearing rapidly. The beast must have jumped from the police barricade to where Jonathan had smashed against the pillar when it realized he'd retreated. He could feel the pavement rattle as it landed and rolled into a fighting stance.

The thing moved with an animal-like grace. During the fight, it had dropped kicked him while both hands had been planted on the ground. It changed between a human-like walk and a knuckle crawl when it wanted to move quickly. That it mimicked a gorilla at times was encouraging. That his prediction had been correct meant his plan had a chance.

He focused on the compass in his mind. The beast stood on the other side of the pillar. He could hear its heavy feet and hands on the pavement. Suddenly, the movement stopped, and Jonathan thought he heard the sound of it sniffing the air over the hum of the city's noise.

Dammit, he thought with sudden alarm.

He'd miscalculated his advantage. There were good reasons not to lure a monster into the dark. Even if the thing couldn't target him directly, it could likely hear, smell, and see better than a man. He became aware of how loud his own breathing was and quickly held his breath. He had to hope that their location would mask his sounds, and that the densely populated city would inundate its senses with the smell of other humans. He waited, desperate for the signal to start moving away from him. He needed it to turn its back on him.

He let out each breath as slowly as he could. The creature didn't move for a moment, and the wait made the moment stretch out. Finally, he sensed the gap between them grow larger. It was moving away, checking behind one of the other pillars.

As quietly as he could, Jonathan moved the metal pipe to one hand and edged quickly to where he could see the creature's back stalking away, deeper into the shadows. Whatever he was going to do, it had to be fast. It was too agile, too quick. He couldn't delay; he had to get a few solid strides in before the sound of his boots on the pavement gave him away. When the moment seemed best, he let out the breath he was holding, and took two powerful strides before launching himself at his enemy's back. As he drew close, he brought the bar over his head, aiming to bring it down onto the monster's skull.

At the last moment, it sidestepped and spun. Jonathan, fully committed to his attack, brought the bar down with all his strength, punching a hole in the pavement as he landed. The creature's foot quickly came down on top of the bar as its alternate hand grabbed him by the throat. He realized then it had known exactly where he was the entire time. He felt himself lifted off the ground and spun. The beast's foot on the bar pried it loose from his grip. He found himself slammed against the pillar again, his feet dangling above the ground. A split second passed and the beast's fist connected hard with his face, punching his skull into the pillar, then again and again.

Suddenly, Jonathan's mind was white with pain. It felt as though both of his eardrums had ripped in half. He couldn't focus, he felt his grip on consciousness slipping, and he had trouble discerning what was up or down.

Not weak, said the intrusive voice in his head. He hardly registered the creature's repulsive growling that accompanied the mental invasion. *You embarrass your kind. No fight in you, No Fight.*

He couldn't argue with the words intruding into his mind. He couldn't ignore them either as they seemed the only tangible thing. The rest of his senses floated about in a manner that left them useless. He fought to regain his wits, but panic was setting in with the realization that he was defenseless.

One of the beast's knuckles came to rest lightly between Jonathan's eyes. The pressure was frightening at first, as though it forecasted another barrage of blows that he'd never recover from. Instead, the pressure remained light but steady, and seemed to help his eyes orient. His vision stopped spinning so drastically. The white eyes of the monster waited for Jonathan's to meet them.

Sickens the Fever waits for you to see death, No Fight, said the beast.

Whatever the hell that means, Jonathan thought. His eyes finally let him look back into the monster's patient stare, but he couldn't hold the gaze of those white slits. Staring it down was terrifying.

The beast pulled his knuckle away and shook him.

No Fight degrades Sickens the Fever with his cowardice.

Jonathan hoped that his mind would clear enough for him to defend himself. If the creature was talking, maybe he could buy the precious seconds he needed.

"I've—I haven't—I've never fought, I don't know—don't know how," he said.

The creature's face started to shift into better focus. It looked confused. He thought it was confusion at least, as he couldn't read its facial expressions despite being able to understand its guttural growls. Perhaps what the beast understood of Jonathan's speech was just as poorly translated. It seemed to be hesitant, like what Jonathan said was unexpected.

No Fight, not fragile? it asked. Must bring combat to Sickens the Fever.

The way the beast was talking, it seemed to refer to itself as Sickens the Fever and identified Jonathan as No Fight. As Jonathan grasped this, he felt a small hope. His mind must be clearing. Every second counted; he just needed to keep it from attacking a bit longer.

"Sorry, Sickens the Fever," Jonathan said. "No Fight doesn't have what it takes."

The creature grew furious. It roared into his face as it held him pinned to the pillar wall. The heat of its breath blew past him, the lingering smell of blood on its breath, humid and sickening against his face. The sight of those metallic teeth brought images of flesh being torn from his body. Sickens the Fever's eyes ran down Jonathan's neck, stopping at his chest. The zipper of his jacket had come loose at the top, and the orange glow was exposed. At the sight of that light, its anger changed, and it seemed pleased. Whatever it had realized Jonathan couldn't fathom, but it placed its free hand onto his throat.

His head finally cleared enough that he could struggle. As his senses became reliable, he saw that the creature's neck was swelling, like all the muscles holding up its head were flexing. It craned its head around as the process occurred, like a man trying to pop the vertebrae of his neck.

Jonathan felt its grip start to tighten. He brought his hands up to try and pry the creature's fingers from him. He could feel the claws against his neck. They hadn't yet broken through his skin, but it was slowly increasing the pressure.

Why? Why is it drawing this out?

The monster's neck started to change colors, the black and red skin becoming darker. The darkness grew in pulses, as though some organ inside the creature was pumping a tar-like fluid into its neck, like a heart pumped blood through a man. Once the color filled the contours of its neck, it refocused its gaze on him. The white orbs had changed. The veins throughout the eyes stood out, webbed, black, and fierce.

His gaze locked with those eyes, and the blackness filled them, replacing the monster's once white gaze with a shiny black. He might not have been able to read its facial tics, but in that moment, those eyes hid nothing from Jonathan, and he knew what it meant.

It moved quickly. Jonathan released his grip on the creature's hands and brought his hands up to protect himself from its jaws. He was a second faster than it, having realized what was coming before it sprang its teeth on him. It wanted his throat. His left hand caught the creature's lower jaw, the right landed over the creature's right eye. Its head struggled against him, moving in for the kill. It was stronger. He was losing the struggle an inch at a time, powerless to do more than watch as its jaw slowly pushed toward his neck. Its hands were tightening so much that he was losing the ability to breathe. His mind flashed back to the hallway with the blond stranger, the horror of the syringe moving towards him, the lights going out. Not knowing if he would wake again.

"No." Jonathan strained the word out, his own voice sounding so desperate, half grunting, half wheezing.

He couldn't stand dying like this. Struggling with all his might and yet still losing to an enemy's indomitable strength. The hand over the creature's eye was losing its precarious grip. He felt it slipping, if he lost hold this would be over before he even realized he'd let go.

Where there is a will, there is not necessarily a way, not when deadlines are involved, he thought.

It was something his grandfather had said on his death bed. He hadn't thought of it in years; he'd been so young when he'd heard him say it. Perhaps Jonathan should just give up now. After all, only seconds remained, and he had shown up unprepared. It was clear now that he wasn't catching any breaks.

His thoughts, reduced to desperation and panic, seemed to clear. He felt the thing rising up inside of him again, that fury that had crashed into the monster in the first place. It seemed all for naught; he couldn't change this, no matter how much rage he found inside. He felt himself submitting, but the anger inside refused, only growing stronger at Jonathan's acceptance of his fate.

There isn't a way, Jonathan thought, closing his eyes as his hand slipped.

The creature's face lurched forward a few inches then stopped abruptly, like a dog that had reached the end of its leash. Jonathan, sensing the change, opened his eyes and met its glare. In the quiet of his focused rage, he realized it looked alarmed, in pain even.

Why?

Jonathan looked away from the creature's stare and understood. His hand had slipped off the creature eye, thus surrendering those costly inches, but was now holding tight to the thing's right ear. The beast's grip started to tighten quickly now. He could feel its claw breaking his skin. It was panicking. Jonathan returned to the monster's gaze and locked in its eyes once again.

Can you read my mind, Sickens the Fever?

With the strength he had left, he pulled to the right. The creature wavered, its forward thrust lost out to the agony, moving its head away to reduce the pressure Jonathan was putting on the fragile appendage. As it snarled out in frustrated pain, Jonathan felt the skin stretching, the leathery tissue of the ear separating from the monster's skull. With a final violent jerk, he ripped the flesh from its head.

He fell to the pavement as the monster released him. It reeled back, reaching to cover the hole where its ear had been severed. Jonathan inhaled deeply, finally getting a full breath of air without having to fight for it. He coughed and gasped, trying to recover. The beast stumbled back. It thundered into an uncontrolled rage, one hand holding the right side of its skull, the other beating its fist into the pavement in the throes of a pain-induced tantrum.

Jonathan looked at the leathery flap in his right hand covered with the tar-like blood now pouring out of the creature's body. The black fluid was flung about as the monster lost control of itself. He tossed the severed skin away in disgust, bringing his attention to the monster.

Keep bleeding, he thought.

His rage erupted in its success, growing eager to capitalize on the moment, to inflict more pain. Rolling to where he had held the steel bar, he quickly got the weapon back in hand and charged the beast. Swinging like a baseball bat, he caught the monster viciously in the blackened skin of its throat and sent it rolling between two pillars of the freeway underpass.

He could see immediately the blow had staggered it. It was in immense pain, spitting up the black fluid that now poured out of its severed ear canal. Jonathan rushed in wildly.

Desperate to recover, but seeing the danger coming, the creature's wits surfaced. It ignored its agony and swung out with the free hand. Jonathan's unskilled attack was deflected and before he knew it the creature had its hands around the front of his coat again. It pulled him off his feet and roared into his face, the black blood splattering against his skin unnervingly. Wavering from the pain Jonathan had managed to inflict, it spun quickly, throwing him as hard as it could to the west of them before falling back to its knees.

Jonathan was helpless in his flight out from underneath the freeway. Dizzyingly, he spun through the air, not knowing where he would land. He finally hit the pavement at an angle that kept him from belly flopping onto the street. Instead, there was a hard thud followed by an agonizing journey across the asphalt. Like a stone skipping across water, he absorbed painful blows every time he connected with the ground, powerless to stop his momentum.

Finally, a stack of wooden shipping pallets stored near the dock blocked his path. When he hit, the wood imploded around him. He was covered in the collapsing rubble.

He didn't move for a moment; he wasn't sure how long. Everything hurt. He felt old, tired. Nothing was broken from what he could tell, but his bones and joints begged him to stop moving. He didn't know where the part of him with the strength to stand had gone. Death had come so close tonight.

"Just get your feet on the floor," he said.

Painfully, he got to his hands and knees, slowly pushing out of the pallets. He was still dizzy from the tumble. He stood, then leaned against a crate for support. For a moment, he didn't realize where he was; he was just breathing and becoming aware of new pains he'd never before conceived of.

This whole month has just been shit, he thought, almost wanting to smile at his flippancy.

The night almost seemed pleasant here. It was quiet, calm even. Everything was far away; no monster, no gunfire. All he heard was the distant sound of the helicopter, the waves lapping against the seawall feet from where he stood. He looked down at his right hand and realized the glove was still covered in the beast's black blood. He took it off, throwing it to the ground in disgust much like he had the ear. The stuff smelled terrible, toxic.

Just for a moment, he closed his eyes.

Alarm kicked in as he felt Sickens the Fever move in his mind. It was a subtle change in location, but it reminded him immediately there wouldn't be, couldn't be, rest yet. He didn't have long before it would come for him. It had thrown him away to buy itself this time. He sensed it was about 300 feet from him, a small distance to cover for the beast.

He realized then that he was exactly where he'd been trying to lure the beast all night, and he pushed himself off the crates.

There were a series of docks on the edge of Puget Sound. Two of the docks were close together, but with a good difference in height. The first dock was for small crafts and row boats. The other was taller and meant for much heavier vessels. He forced himself forward. His muscles had already tightened on him, rebelling against being required to move, but he was too close. He had to try and stop this thing once more. He had to do whatever it took. One thought of the little girl in the pink jacket was enough to remember why.

He had the *where*, now he just needed to quickly come up with a plan for *how*. A hurried scan of the area didn't immediately deliver what he was looking for. There were some large crates and more pallets.

He knew that swinging a flimsy piece of wood at the thing would be an exercise in futility. He needed something stronger, something steel and heavy, something entangling. Fighting his body's resistance and sprinting across the dock, he finally found a thick steel chain wrapped around a pillar. It was red-brown from rust and exposure to the salty ocean waters, yet he could feel its resilience; it was still strong.

He had to twist it hard, focusing his strength on a single link of the chain to break a length of it free. He doubted the creature would be able to break it unless it had the opportunity to single out a link like Jonathan had. He ran the loose end through his bare hand, wrapping the steel around his palm and then pulling it behind his elbow and then back through his hand again, closing his fist tight around it.

The creature might have the strength to pull Jonathan's arm off; he intended to make sure no less would sever him from this chain. Now, he just needed a dangerous place to wait, to draw it in close.

So close death can't tell us apart, he thought.

His father's words this time, rising to the surface, clearing all the noise in his mind, bringing with them the resolve to finish this.

He felt it coming.

A circle of illumination exposed him like a beacon as he knelt at the edge of the smaller dock. He feigned injury, holding his side under the opened jacket, laboring his breathing, making a show of not paying attention to his surroundings. His eyes were facing Puget Sound, his reflection glowing back at him from the water. A man more concerned with attack than pain would worry about being assaulted from behind.

His mind was vigilant, waiting.

He wished there was time to have practiced this. He feared he wouldn't be able pull it off with only this one shot. There would be no second chance. He felt Sickens the Fever approaching from the east.

It has to think I'm finished, it has to get in close, he thought. Trust your instinct, do not jump the gun.

He felt the creature moving towards his left flank; it was on the higher dock while he knelt on the lower, a few feet from the edge.

It's got to be perfect, one shot. He closed his eyes, focusing completely on the instinct to guide him, wavering as though he were on the brink of collapse.

Jonathan knew when it took the bait. He felt the sudden movement.

Sickens the Fever must have become reckless and impatient in its pain. It had jumped and was rocketing toward him in an arc from the higher pier, intending to land directly on him, to crush him beneath it. In that moment, where time raced forward yet slowed down, he had to be patient.

Eyes still shut, he felt it breach the threshold he'd set in his mind as his trigger. He could only hope he'd judged it correctly.

He somersaulted backward. The creature was unprepared for the sudden movement, not suspecting Jonathan had detected its presence. It landed on the dock with its back exposed to him, and he exploited its surprise.

From his kneeling position he jumped, bringing the chain up and over the creature's head while ramming his knee hard into its spine. He lurched backward with all he had against the monster's throat while simultaneously pressing both knees into its back.

The thing roared in pain when the shackles sunk into its injured neck. Desperately, it tried to pry its hands under the chain and loosen the hold. Jonathan tightened the noose, wrenching left and right to increase the monster's agony and keep it from getting leverage. It swung itself wildly, trying to throw him off. With a final frantic tug, he forced it to swing to the edge. It lost its footing and pitched the two of them into Puget Sound, locked together in struggle.

Sickens the Fever's panic became chaos as it realized it was no longer on solid earth. Its hands left the chain, wildly searching to pull them up, to find the air. Gravity favored Jonathan; the monster's weight acted like bricks dragging them down into the cold darkness of the water.

Its desperation told him everything—his plan was working.

Gorillas can't swim for crap, Jonathan remembered thinking, and apparently, neither can Sickens the Fever.

It was just a matter of time now, just a matter of who could hold his breath longer. All there was left was to hold on. Sickens the Fever was beginning to choke, to take in water. Jonathan clung to the chain as though it were a part of him.

In that moment, he wasn't afraid to drown; being the solution to this terrible problem was more important to him than breathing. They sank further down into the thick darkness, the glow from Jonathan's chest the only thing allowing him to see as they fell further and further from the light of the pier. It was okay if he never surfaced, but he couldn't let go first. He tried not to swallow in the cold.

Tethered to the monster, Jonathan felt its strength leaving, felt its struggle dying down. He would dig it a grave in the ocean floor, if that's what it took.

CHAPTER THIRTEEN

THURSDAY | JUNE 30, 2005 | 11:45 PM

THERE WAS A familiar thudding in the distance. It seemed to reach him through muffled ears. Rhythmic and constant, it was pleasant, and at first it was all he was aware of. As it drew closer, its meaning started to take shape. He had that feeling again, like he'd never intended to wake up, but wouldn't be given the choice.

"Jonathan," said a voice over the thrum of the helicopter.

There was an urge to cough, then he choked up sea water. It felt like he'd been hacking up for quite some time. His eyes were watering with the effort. When he gained enough control over his breathing, he opened his eyes. He was lying on his back and recognized the dock light above him. He was at the end of the pier.

How had he gotten here? He couldn't remember climbing out of the water. The last thing he recalled was when the monster had stopped moving. Alone, with only the glow emanating from him, he'd been unable to see the light of the dock through the depths of the water. He'd been drowning. He remembered taking in water instead of air.

The sound of the chopper was getting closer. He took another breath and his lungs burned with the effort.

"Jonathan, I know you've been through a lot tonight, but I need you to sit up." The voice seemed more familiar now.

He didn't want to comply. He wanted to lay on the dock forever. He felt hands reaching under him, gently propping him up against a crate. With reluctance and audible annoyance, he let himself be moved. What was one more thing after a night like tonight? Water ran down his face from his hair. He was cold and becoming more aware of it by the second. Sitting was uncomfortable, the movement reminding him of every injury he'd endured.

He could still feel Sickens the Fever on the seafloor below him. How dead would the monster have to be for him to stop sensing its whereabouts? He looked up and searched for the source of the voice.

There he was, the blond man, standing outside the light, his eyes iridescent as he recalled them.

Jonathan couldn't muster the energy to be afraid. He'd never been this tired. No more than a couple hours ago, he'd had a hundred questions for the man. Now he couldn't think of one.

"Just—just kill me," Jonathan muttered. "I'm too tired for whatever this is."

The stranger looked up to the sky, gauging how long before the light of the helicopter might reach them, then he returned to Jonathan, crouching by his side.

"If I had any desire to kill you, I wouldn't have pulled you out of that miserable water," he said.

Jonathan doubted the man, but saw that his clothes were as soaked through as his own. Beside them, the man had removed his ridiculous fedora and coat, having placed them on one of the wooden crates along the pier. It explained why Jonathan didn't remember pulling himself onto the dock. The man looked to be smiling, like he found this situation funny somehow. If the man was grinning because he felt Jonathan should be grateful, he had another thing coming. He was still the reason Jonathan had been drowning in the first place.

"What then?" Jonathan asked. "What could you possibly want?"

"I need you to stay here, Jonathan," he said, pointing to the dock. "Don't go anywhere for a moment. I'll be right back."

If he'd had enough energy to laugh, he would have. As it was, he hardly had the strength to continue sitting up. He dropped his head and let it rest on his shoulder. As he did so, he saw the metal chain still clinging to him. He'd somehow managed to keep it locked around his forearm even after being brought to the surface. He thought about shaking free of it, but even that seemed like too much effort to bother.

The man stood. He paused over Jonathan for a moment, then walked to the edge of the pier. There was the sound of a splash, and a few seconds later, Jonathan felt Sickens the Fever move in his head. His alarm was quickly suppressed as he realized that the man must have swum down to the creature's body. Eventually, the stranger's hand surfaced out of the water and clutched the edge of the dock. As he pulled himself up, Jonathan saw that the beast was thrown over the man's shoulder. He tossed it onto the dock with the respect one would give a dead fish.

He doesn't plan to give it mouth to mouth? Jonathan thought. He wanted to look away; just seeing the thing's dead, black eyes made him uncomfortable. Even now, he didn't trust it to stay dead.

The man placed his hand over the torso of the beast and closed his eyes. His hand seemed to be searching for something. It hovered over the body about an inch above the surface of its skin. Finally, he stopped his hand over a portion of the creature's lower abdomen and turned his gaze back to Jonathan.

The man nodded to him as if to say, *good, pay attention.* The man returned to his jacket and pulled out two crude looking tools—a small but heavy hammer and a thick metal wedge.

The sound of the helicopter seemed closer now.

Up close, the skin of the creature was dark red with a chaotic webbing of black tar surrounding it. The red skin glistened faintly beneath the long black strands of tar, like the smooth exterior of an amphibian. Only on the creature's chest was the red completely absent; there, the black tar looked molded into armor plates suited to the creature's musculature. It was as though that black tar had reached out in ropes to surround the red skin of the monster's limbs and back. Jonathan knew the skin of the creature was made of something unearthly. Its durability alone was evidence to that.

Jonathan watched as the man searched the area he'd focused on before. When he found an imperfection in the skin, he drove the wedge in and began to hammer. Eventually, a stream of black fluid drained out of the crack that the man had made and pooled onto the dock. Jonathan smelled the familiar odor.

The man made a face that Jonathan thought was distaste. He didn't take any pleasure from what he was doing and appeared to dislike the smell as much as Jonathan.

"Metal skeleton," the man said.

Jonathan lifted his gaze, unsure what to make of the statement.

"The creature's bones are iron based, malleable. They can be bent, but seldom break. That and their armor, their musculature, all makes them very difficult to subdue."

The man nodded at Jonathan as his hand slipped into the cavity in the creature's abdomen. It was sickening to watch.

"Why are you doing that?" Jonathan asked.

The man's hand pulled back out of the body, and Jonathan saw vein-like appendages tearing away from whatever he'd grasped within. Jonathan turned away from the sight. The sound of the veins as they snapped free was disturbing. When the man freed the object from the beast's body, he stood and walked toward the water. As he did so, Jonathan, eyes still on the creature's corpse, realized that the signal in his head had moved with him.

He looked back to the man now, who was standing over the water, washing off whatever he'd taken from the body. As it came clean, Jonathan saw a faint red glow in the man's hands. Whatever he held, it was somehow tied to Jonathan's new sense. It, and not the monster, had been what Jonathan had felt since his chest lit up back home.

The helicopter was close now. It must have spotted them on the dock and started moving directly for them. The man returned and knelt next to him.

He opened his palm and showed Jonathan what he'd pulled from the beast. The red glow illuminated Jonathan's face as he gazed down at an opaque stone, no larger than a chicken's egg. The glow came from within, as though at its center was a bright light surrounded by red fluid. It was pretty to look at, remarkable really, but Jonathan couldn't imagine its purpose, or why his mind was linked to it.

"Jonathan, take the chain off your hand. I need you to destroy this," the stranger said.

Jonathan's tired eyes flashed with defiance.

"No," Jonathan said.

The man appraised the look and shifted his eyes down at the stone, then back at Jonathan.

"I know you don't trust me Jonathan. I can't blame you for that," he said, "but please try and understand, it was circumstance that forced my hand."

Jonathan's face didn't change. Nothing this man said could make him obey. The helicopter's light would be on them soon. They would be surrounded by people and this man would have to explain himself to everyone. Jonathan had no doubt the man would flee, but he didn't need the stranger's confession to prove anything. Everyone had seen just how crazy the world had become. At least Jonathan would not be alone in that any longer.

"Jonathan," the stranger said as he looked up at the helicopter. "Destroy this in your palm. Everyone who died tonight does not have to die. You can make it all right again. But you must do this."

A moment earlier, Jonathan himself couldn't have fathomed a thing this man could say to sway him to do anything. Yet now, despite his anger, his hostility, his mistrust, he felt that certainty falter. It was the one thing that Jonathan would risk making his situation worse for—to bring those lives back, to bring that child back.

"How?" Jonathan asked, his voice betraying his desire for the man's words to be the truth.

"This reality is tied to you and this stone. The link can only be severed by you, or it," the man said, pointing to the monster's corpse. "If you do not destroy the stone, this reality will be fixed. All of those who died tonight will remain dead."

"I don't understand," Jonathan said. He was shaking again, not wanting the weight of another terrible decision tonight.

"I promise I'll explain it to you, Jonathan. But now—" He looked again at the helicopter that was making him raise his voice. "But now is not the time. It's your choice. Do nothing, and hundreds remain dead, and you'll never know. Trust me or not, I am offering you the only chance to save those lives."

"Why! Why should I trust you?" Jonathan said, glaring into the man's eyes.

"I can't give you a reason to trust me. We don't have enough time. I can only tell you the rules. If tonight you wish to put the rules to the test, it is your decision to live with."

Jonathan felt his defiance crumbling. The words reminded him of his father. He wanted to grab hold of those words and believe they were meant to steer him wisely now. How could he dare risk doing nothing if that man might be telling the truth?

There was no real choice at all.

"Do you promise? Do you promise they'll all be alive?" Jonathan asked.

"Yes, Jonathan, I promise," the man said.

Jonathan paused.

"Give it to me," he said.

The man nodded and went to place the stone into Jonathan outstretched hand. He stopped a moment before putting it in his palm.

"Jonathan, soon you will be home again. It will be disorientating. You will be confused. Do not discuss this with anyone until we've spoken again. Return to the park where you jog. I will be waiting there; it's very important that you call me by name when you see me."

The idea that this man had a name caught Jonathan by surprise. He had referred to him as "the blond stranger" for so long that he hadn't thought of him in terms of a person.

"Right," Jonathan said with obvious sarcasm, raising his voice over the sound of the helicopter. "Then what's your name?"

"Heyer," the man replied, placing the stone into Jonathan's palm.

Heyer pointed at Jonathan's eyes with his middle and index finger, then pointed at his own eyes with the same two fingers as if to instruct him to focus on what he said next.

"It will be confusing, Jonathan," he said, raising his voice now as well over the helicopter blades.

The wind from the propeller flung their hair about and made

Jonathan chill with cold as he was still soaked through from the water. Heyer seemed unperturbed by the wind.

"Talk to no one. Meet me at the park. Say my name when you see me." Heyer nodded once, then pointed his finger at Jonathan's hand. "Now destroy it."

Jonathan looked at Heyer as though he were mad. He didn't pause long. He didn't take his eyes from Heyer's when he crushed the stone in his hand, like holding the man's gaze would force everything he'd told him to be true. He felt the stone break, like a delicate piece of glass with fluid inside. Heyer stood and backed away from him. As soon as he did so, Jonathan's heart sank. It seemed an omen of betrayal.

The fluid from the stone was all over his hand. It burned as it had when his chest had turned on, searing its way from his hand down his arm. Jonathan no longer felt cold in the draft from the helicopter; he was molten lava again.

Fear gripped him. What had he done? The fire was moving toward the glowing lines on his torso, not away this time. He curled into the fetal position with the pain of it, finally breaking his eye contact with Heyer, pulling his knees up to his chest and gripping tightly as he endured the pain migrating down his arm and into his chest. The world became red all around him.

"Why are you doing this?" was the last thing Jonathan was able to cry out before everything went white.

CHAPTER FOURTEEN

THURSDAY | JUNE 30, 2005 | 8:30 PM

JONATHAN STARED AT his text book. His head was in one hand, hovering over the kitchen table—the table that should have been split in half. Paige sat next to him, reading. She reached down and took a sip of her tea. The TV was on. Collin and Hayden were watching something.

"I don't want to wait for September for the new season of *Lost* to start," said Hayden.

That's familiar, Jonathan thought.

He felt disoriented. He should be sitting on a dock, dead tired, freezing, talking to the blond man. Heyer? Why wasn't he tired? How was he so calm? Had he been dreaming? There had been so much pain a moment ago and now, nothing. He felt like he should be bored, or like he had been until a second ago.

He hit the table with his fist lightly. It didn't collapse. He hit it again harder; nothing, no impossible strength. Disbelievingly, he brought his palm down with enough force to let out a loud smack and cause the table to shake. Everyone in the room turned to the sound.

"What the hell?" Paige said, looking at him as though he was a monkey throwing his poo.

Jonathan stared back at her for a moment, confused by her confusion. He looked about the room, trying to orient himself, make sense of what should already make sense. His eyes fell on the clock and he realized the time was wrong. It should have been closer to eleven, yet it read 8:30. He must have fallen asleep. It must have been a dream.

No.

How was that possible? The monster, all those people and police, the news footage, the helicopters, sirens, gunfire, all so vivid in his head only seconds ago. The rage, the guilt, the fear; it was more real than any dream he'd ever had.

No, dammit.

That was no dream; they were memories. He opened his mouth to speak but then stopped. He didn't know what to say. His last memory was of Heyer specifically telling him he would be disoriented, that he should speak to no one.

Understatement, he thought. He realized Paige was still staring at him.

"Um, sorry, I'm just—it's just a struggle to catch up," Jonathan said.

She raised her eyebrow and went back to her book. Jonathan, still at a loss, pulled the neck of his shirt out so he could look down at his chest. There was no eerie orange glow, nothing.

Talk to no one. I'll be waiting for you at the park. Say my name when you see me.

It had literally been seconds ago that Heyer had said those words to him. Hadn't it? Jonathan rose from the table.

"I need some fresh air," he said, pulling his coat off the back of his chair, a chair that shouldn't have been in one piece. Then he headed for the garage door, which shouldn't have been on its hinges.

"You'll never catch up if you procrastinate," Paige said.

He nodded, but didn't stop. Was he really doing this? Was he really going to go meet this man, this "Heyer" after what he had been through? Of course he was. How the hell else would he ever prove to himself it was real?

Why was he so damn calm? On the dock, his body had been exhausted from adrenaline overdose, and now it was as though he was just beginning to grow anxious. He should have felt like he'd drowned; instead he was as nervous as someone who was late for an appointment.

It just wasn't on the right level; the state of mind and memories contradicted each other. It was making his brain itch somehow. It was irritating.

He shut the garage door and headed down the stairs.

Leah looked up from her laptop when she heard the neighbor's side door open. She'd been sitting on the balcony above their driveway for a little over twenty minutes now.

This had proven, by far, the best part of her new home. On the East Coast, she and Jack had never had a balcony. It made her feel like she was giving in to some storybook cliché for girls just by being so drawn to it. Was this some terrible innate desire to be pursued by Romeo? Had Shakespeare ruined balconies for her? Maybe next she would have an irrational need to own a pony. She pushed the thought away. She liked the little sanctuary too much to let herself over-think it.

Jonathan came through the door and walked up the driveway. He looked deep in thought and a little pale, like he'd just seen something that was threatening to make him sick. She hoped he wasn't always in such a state. He'd be attractive if he didn't constantly appear to be restraining an avalanche of worry.

"Good evening, neighbor," she said, making sure she sounded pleased to see him.

His eyes found her immediately, but the worry didn't dissipate when they made eye contact. Leah thought it got worse for a moment, before he forced his facial expression to look more relaxed and smiled at her. It wasn't the reaction she'd hoped for. He looked as though he'd forgotten how to interact with another human being and was attempting to hide it.

"Hello," he finally managed.

"You know, Jack hasn't stopped asking about the motorcycle since you mentioned it to him," she said. "I think you might be on the hook for showing it to him sometime."

"I'll have to ask my roommate about it," he said. "I apologize, I'd love to talk more, but I need to be somewhere."

"Yeah?" Leah said, a mischievous smile on her face. "Hot date?" She was trying to seem playful, but really hoping he would tell her that it wasn't why he had to go, that he wasn't seeing some girl.

He seemed to hesitate.

"Did you want to wish me luck?" he asked.

"Maybe," she said, in a mocking tone, surprise he'd guessed where she was going with the question. "But only if I thought you needed it."

At first she thought he'd been flirting back, trying to see if she'd be jealous if he was off to see a girl, but he just looked inexplicably puzzled. It was like he was somewhere else entirely, having a hundred thoughts that had nothing to do with their conversation. He was harder to read than he'd been the other day. She wondered if this was what he'd been like before the attack he'd mentioned. Then she realized that he'd answered her question with a question. He hadn't actually said where he was going at all.

He'd taken his eyes off her and was looking up the driveway into the dark streets beyond the light of their homes. Finally, he spoke. "It couldn't hurt," he said.

She found it odd, the way he said it. More like he was afraid of something out in that darkness than excited to see a girl. She frowned as she watched him. He was frustratingly difficult to read.

"Well, goodnight," he said after a final moment of indecision.

Her smile slumped with her shoulders; he really did seem to be in a hurry. She couldn't persuade him to stay longer and keep her company.

"Goodnight," she said. "Good luck, just in case it turns out you need it."

He walked toward the driveway, but turned a moment before he left her sight and called back to her. "Oh, by the way, thanks for that advice the other day. I think—well, I'm pretty sure it helped me."

"No problem," she called back.

In all honesty, she wasn't certain what advice she'd ever given him. He turned the corner and was gone. She found herself lingering on where he'd walked out of the light.

"Why, Leah?" she asked herself when she was sure he could no longer hear. "Why do they always have to be damaged?"

As Jonathan came closer, there was something anti-climactic about seeing Heyer sitting there on the park bench in the dark. He was unmistakable from behind, the blond hair hanging down from that ridiculous fedora.

Jonathan stopped there, a few feet back, hesitantly staring at the back of the man's head and wondering if he was making the right decision in coming. He had no doubt the man knew he was behind him somehow.

I can't trust him, Jonathan thought.

It did appear that the man had told him the truth, or at least a version of the truth. If the time was correct, and it seemed to be, Jonathan could only think of a few possible explanations, all of which were science fiction in nature. Either the events he remembered had all taken place in his head, which was a disturbing thought, or hadn't taken place at all. Yet, Heyer was here, just as he'd specified he would be. When no one else seemed to be aware that anything out of the ordinary had taken place, Heyer still knew somehow.

Jonathan took another step forward. He needed it to make sense— then he paused again. Heyer had told the truth, but he had certainly left out the part about the blinding pain Jonathan would experience. He reminded himself to keep this omission in mind no matter what the man had to say.

"It's a nice park," Heyer said. "I see why you'd exercise here. It's a good place to think."

Heyer's head turned as he spoke. He didn't look at Jonathan; he seemed to be waiting for him to finish hesitating. Jonathan approached slowly, coming around the bench, keeping his eyes on the man, watchful for sudden movement. This wasn't a narrow hallway. If he was threatened, he had the choice to bolt.

When he could see Heyer's face, the man didn't look up immediately, but smiled to himself knowingly.

Finally, those soulful, luminescent eyes turned to face Jonathan. Heyer looked relieved. How did the man appear so villainous, yet at the same time so protective? They looked at each other for a moment. It was unnerving to Jonathan to hold his gaze, waiting for him to speak, to see what the man intended to have happen here tonight in this park.

Heyer broke the silence.

"It is a relief to see you, Jonathan," Heyer said. "I calculated your survival chances to be rather low. In fact, it borders on a miracle that you are standing here now. A good indicator; it would be highly unfortunate to have lost you."

He paused as if to see if Jonathan accepted what he'd said so far, then continued, "I instructed you to call me by name, did I not?"

Jonathan tried his voice, unsure of it.

"You said it was Heyer," Jonathan replied, slightly louder than a whisper.

Heyer nodded.

"We do not have much time, and we have a great amount to discuss," Heyer said. "Jonathan, you must have a considerable number of questions, and since I do not know where to begin, I'd advise you to ask what you will. I will answer as best I can, but I must leave soon; so, I will try to keep us focused on pertinent matters. If I feel you are asking something likely to do you harm, or that I cannot yet trust you with, I will not answer. I apologize for this; some things I cannot tell you for your own good, others for my own."

Jonathan had no choice but to take that statement for what it was. He doubted he'd be able to tell if the man lied to him, although the way he'd phrased it made Jonathan feel like a child being told that he wasn't ready to know how dangerous the world was yet, which was ridiculous coming from the man who had put him through the most dangerous experience of his life.

"What did you do to me?" Jonathan asked, still struggling to put volume behind his voice. "After you put me to sleep?"

"Yes, a horrible act, that was. I apologize for the circumstances by which that played out. If I had any other alternative at the time, I would have allowed you to volunteer. Unfortunately, that was not an option. I would not have left you with such a disturbing waking experience, but complications led the implantation process to take longer than I'd planned; then your roommates came home, and I was forced to leave you," Heyer said.

"What did you 'implant'?" Jonathan asked, already afraid of the answer. "What do you mean there were complications?"

"The device in your chest is biochemical in nature, so to speak. It serves to cause a number of physical changes to your body and mind when the time is right. Upon insertion into a host, it mimics the cellular structure of the individual it finds itself in, taking on the form of the cells of the body that it is replacing, and then lies dormant. It is complicated, but the simple version is this: I cut out a great deal of tissue from your body and replaced that tissue with an implant that can cause remarkable changes to you once it is activated."

"Why didn't it show up on any test they ran at the hospital?" Jonathan asked.

"As I said, while dormant, the device mimics the cells of your body. Upon waking, you likely experienced an inexplicable discomfort in your chest. This was part of the process still occurring," Heyer said. "In a manner of speaking, your nervous system was becoming acquainted with its new cells."

"But… mankind doesn't have that kind of technology," Jonathan said.

"You are correct, mankind does not," Heyer replied, pausing to let his meaning sink in.

"Then you're not human?" Jonathan asked, slowly taking a seat on the bench next to Heyer, his reluctance to continue staring down into his eerie eyes finally winning out.

"No, Jonathan, but I'd advise that my background will not assist you in your current endeavors," Heyer replied.

Jonathan wasn't sure what to make of such an answer. His endeavors? What did that mean? This evening was terrible, but at least it was over. He wasn't endeavoring to do anything but understand it. He felt like he should have been surprised to find out he was talking to an alien, but after spending an evening the way he had, it hardly seemed like a revelation.

"When does it come out?" Jonathan asked.

Heyer's face looked surprised for a moment, but it quickly returned to a placid calm.

"It is not removable, Jonathan, it is a part of you now," he said. "Well, to be more accurate, I could not recover it without killing you. You should not be distressed, though. The implant will function exactly as your normal cells, except when triggered."

Jonathan didn't like the sound of that. A part of him had been torn out, replaced by something alien, something that he didn't understand and couldn't control. He didn't want to hear that it was permanent. Seconds passed in silence. Heyer seemed to be allowing him time to absorb this fact.

"What were the *complications*?" Jonathan asked. For a few moments, his voice hadn't seemed meek, but now he was struggling to get words out again.

Heyer sighed at this question.

"You bled out too much during the procedure and your heart stopped. I was forced to resuscitate you as I waited for the device to adhere. The implant repairs the damage done to the body during the installation process, but only if the subject remains alive."

My heart stopped? I died? Jonathan thought.

Again, this required time to sink in. It was upsetting the way Heyer spoke of this procedure, as if he were upgrading computer hardware. He could ponder his mortality later; Heyer had said they were limited on time.

"Why?" Jonathan asked. "Why me? Why not someone else?"

Heyer smiled; he almost looked proud. "You were selected by an artificial intelligence, a computer, predominately based on a number of genetic factors that make your body highly compatible with the implant. From a genetic level, choosing you was obvious as there were no other potential recipients nearly as well-matched for the device. However, there were also psychological considerations that were weighed...."

Heyer seemed to ponder his next words carefully.

"Psychology is not easily computed. I made that call. I knew I had made the right choice when I saw you entering the park tonight; I knew you must have found a way to survive," he said.

"I don't understand. You knew I survived back on the dock. After I'd drowned that thing." Jonathan looked at Heyer incredulously. "You pulled me out of the water—what did coming here prove?"

"Is that how you succeeded?" Heyer said. "Yes, that would have worked, I suppose, if the creature had not realized it was close to a deep body of water. Water is not present in large supply on their planet." Heyer nodded at Jonathan as if to congratulate him. "Clever."

Jonathan didn't have any interest in the compliment; the alien still wasn't making any sense.

"What do you mean, is that how I succeeded? You pulled that thing out of the water yourself. You ripped the stone out of it, you made me destroy it, you made me agree to come here!" Jonathan said, surprised his voice was becoming louder than a whisper again.

"Jonathan, know this now. Only one person will ever remember what happened tonight," Heyer said. "The time between the moment you became activated and the moment you destroyed that *stone*. I instructed you to come to meet me at the park because I had planned for the contingency. I was sitting here tonight because I knew that, should you succeed, I would instruct you to meet me here."

"How is that possible?" Jonathan asked. "I mean, are you telling me I time traveled?"

"Jonathan, this will be difficult to grasp, but I will try to explain. The device in your chest is activated and powered by the presence of the portal stone that was within the creature's body. Once that beast became present on this plane of existence, with that stone inside of it, you became activated. When this occurred, the device began recording physical changes in your body, as well as endowed you with certain talents necessary to engage the beast on a physical level." Heyer paused and raised an eyebrow as if to ask if Jonathan followed him so far.

"A monster came here with that *portal stone* inside of it. From a 'different plane of existence,' as you put it, and it being here while I have this device installed in me," he asked, pointing to his chest, "activated me?"

"Yes," Heyer said. "When you destroyed the stone, all the events that transpired while it was present on this plane were wiped away."

"But how do I remember then?" Jonathan asked.

Heyer took a deep breath. "The memories that form in your mind result from physical changes to your brain while you experience your life, Jonathan. When you make a new memory, your mind is physically changed; webs of neurons in your brain reach out and touch each other in a manner different than before you created that memory. When you destroyed the portal stone, you didn't time travel, so to speak, but for you, time was returned to the moment the stone first became present in your world. The only thing that is doing any time traveling is your memories. The device sends this information back to you before that timeline is closed off. The information about the state of your brain is applied. The result is, you retain the memory, but you are returned to a version of time where the portal stone never existed."

Jonathan was having trouble. This was a lot to take on trust, even if what the alien was saying did seem to align with what he had experienced.

"So," Jonathan began, trying to make sure he understood what he was being told, "I have memories of something that never happened. Well, didn't happen to anyone else but me."

His mind reeled with the implications of this. What would have happened if he hadn't succeeded, if he'd died? What if he hadn't shown up at all? More important than all of that though, *why bother at all, with any of it, if all that resulted was Jonathan inherited a pile of terrible false memories?*

"Yes, you probably noticed, for instance, that you were quite emotionally disoriented at the time of transition. Your memory told you that you had just survived a horrible life-threatening episode, yet it only inherited the memories from that experience. The information that is downloaded into your mind at the point of return modifies the structure of your brain, but it does not bring with it the physical state you were in when that stone was destroyed. Hence, you had the memories of a man who had just endured a gruesome fight, likely sustaining a number of injuries, but your body was in whatever state it had been in before being activated. The experience is jarring on the mind," Heyer said. "Frankly, I'm surprised the human body can allow it, but I am by no means a neurological expert."

"I couldn't understand my own calm," Jonathan said out loud.

More and more of what the alien was saying was matching up with what he'd experienced. The irritation he'd felt in his mind made sense now. The memories telling him to be on high alert had been contradictory to his body's state upon returning, which was that of sitting at a table, calmly doing homework.

Jonathan nodded, and then looked at Heyer with needy, questioning eyes.

"I don't understand why this needed to happen. If I'm the only one who remembers it, what was the point?"

Heyer sighed again. Jonathan couldn't tell if his questions seemed boring or childish to the alien, or if it was the answers that seemed to make him tired.

"You acted as a shield that repelled that monster. It came here through gates targeted to Earth. These gates exist in that creature's reality. The portal stone, in essence, allowed the beast access through those gates and permitted the creature to exist here. However, it was tied to you upon entering this reality. That monster is dead; there is one less of them to come here. Its corpse now lies in front of the very gate it used to trespass here. Its body was returned to its reality in the state it was in when you destroyed the stone…."

Heyer stopped explaining then.

"Jonathan, I don't want to get too deeply into this now. This information will not serve you well yet. Just know this…." Heyer paused to make sure Jonathan could see his grave face. "It matters. If you were not here to do what you did, a very different scenario would eventually be playing out, and it wouldn't make you happy. It wouldn't make anyone on this planet happy. For now, the status quo has been maintained. The human race remains ignorant of the breach."

Jonathan didn't like the sound of anything the alien was telling him, but his mind came to rest on another question.

"That thing," Jonathan asked, "what was it?"

Heyer drew in another of his long breaths.

"They don't have a proper human name. They are not categorized in your evolutionary trees as they evolved elsewhere. However, I have given them a name based on the human method of categorization," Heyer said. "I refer to them as the *Ferox intrusus,* but generally just Ferox for short."

"Why did this… Ferox—" Jonathan tested out the word. "—why did it come here?"

"Why does any sentient being start a war, Jonathan?" Heyer asked.

"It wants something it can't get peacefully?" Jonathan guessed.

Heyer nodded.

"You didn't answer my question. What did it want?" Jonathan asked.

"It is a rather long story. For now, just know it was here to kill people. You stopped it. Knowing 'why' only makes you a risk to me and will not improve your survival chances."

Jonathan locked up with fear. It hadn't occurred to him before, but Heyer kept referring to his survival as though it was still in peril; but this was over, he'd survived. What was there to endanger him now except Heyer himself?

"What do you mean? It's dead; you just said I repelled it," Jonathan said.

The light in Heyer's eyes seemed to dim. It was as though he'd expected Jonathan to have grasped something already and he hadn't.

"Yes, Jonathan, that one is dead," Heyer said. "Unfortunately, it is the first of an onslaught. This is, in fact, the calm before the storm. I am tracking a number of others inbound. The next one should arrive approximately three months from now, early September. Following that, they will come as often as weekly for a short period. After that, I will not be able to give you much warning at all, if any. Their assault on this plane will be increasing. You are facing down an army, one at a time."

Jonathan felt heavy. His shoulders slumped and something seemed to drain out of him. Call it optimism or hope, the very energy inside him that made him want to live questioned itself. It wasn't shock, he realized. The way Heyer had been speaking, he'd known but not wanted it confirmed. Three and a half months and another of those things would be killing in the streets. It would lure him out again, and he would go, he knew he would, and he could never hope to get so lucky again. It was a staring contest with death.

He began to feel sick again.

"Perhaps it would be best if you took a few breaths, Jonathan," Heyer said sympathetically.

He nodded, not fully hearing what the alien had said to him. He felt as though he were plummeting. He wanted more than ever to wake up from this nightmare.

"I know this news is unpleasant, Jonathan. I hate to tell you this and leave, but I am scheduled for a destination quite far away in a matter of minutes—which is why we need to focus on the things that can help you," Heyer said.

He heard the words but he wasn't listening. He was thinking about how Sickens the Fever had threatened him, pounding him into walls and pavement, staring him down with those eyes that sought to do him such violence. He'd be forced to endure not being strong enough yet again, the panic of defeat, powerless to the whims of the monster and unable to save himself. He'd be waiting to have his throat torn out. And for what exactly? He didn't even get to know.

"Please," he whimpered finally, "I don't want to do this again. I'll die. You know I'm going to die. You have to stop this, please." Jonathan knew as the words left his mouth that his requests could not be granted. He slumped over as he spoke and his head fell into his hands.

"I can't stop this, Jonathan; I didn't put it into motion," Heyer said. A moment passed and the alien spoke again. "All I could do is give the responsibility to someone else. Activate another device and another candidate. He, like you, would be forced to bear this responsibility, though. You would have to live with that knowledge."

"You could create another, a partner?" Jonathan asked.

"No, Jonathan, that isn't what I meant. One portal stone activates one device. I can give the responsibility to someone else, but I can't divide it," Heyer said.

The thoughts in Jonathan's head seemed to collide with the alien's admission, the desire to tell the alien to make it so, but right along with it came the fierce guilt of what it would mean. It would be so easy—he wouldn't know the victim, wouldn't have to see the life he'd be helping destroy.

He couldn't do that; he could never do that. Not even to some stranger. It was the same guilt that had driven him to face the monster in the first place. Something deeper down inside, deeper than his own self-preservation, couldn't bear the thought of having been given the choice, and sacrificing someone else in his place, even if he was the only one to remember it; he'd learned that lesson tonight. He knew the weight of it.

"Why don't you fight them then?" Jonathan said. "You're strong enough, and you certainly didn't let guilt stop you from letting a stranger take the responsibility?"

He didn't look Heyer in the eye when he said it. He hadn't thought of it as an accusation until it escaped his lips. It seemed silly to bother filtering his words for the one person in the universe who knew this was the moment his life had collapsed around him, been stolen from him. Jonathan just stared off into the park, waiting to hear what the alien had to say for himself.

Heyer picked up his ridiculous fedora and held it in his hands before he spoke. "I would, Jonathan, believe me in that. I would not burden any human with this responsibility, as this is no man's fault. The simple truth is, if I were to perish, there would be no one to replace me; there would be no one else to activate another individual such as yourself," Heyer said. "Sometimes, we are not expendable, and with that comes the horrible burden of making choices like the one I had to make for you."

Jonathan closed his eyes. After a moment, he nodded that he understood. Why had he asked this? The answer only seemed to make things worse. To tighten the chains that seemed to be forming around him.

"If I fail, someone else will be forced into this?" he asked.

There was a long pause and neither said anything. Heyer just seemed to watch him thoughtfully.

"Hmm," Heyer said.

"What?" Jonathan said.

"I just find you interesting, Jonathan," he said. "I tell you that you could give the burden to some individual you don't even know, and your first thought is to wonder how *I* could have ever given this burden to anyone. You find out someone else will gain this burden if you perish, and your first thought is that you must not perish. You make sacrifices for people who will never know to thank you. What does that tell you?"

Jonathan couldn't be pondering this now and he knew it, so he ignored the question. Every fiber of his being wanted to sit on that bench and feel sorry for himself, draw in deep and hide from the world. Yet, time wasn't going to give him what he wanted; there was no breather for self-pity. He was wasting time looking for who or what was to blame. It no longer mattered. He had to focus on staying alive, and the only person who could help him might leave any second. He had to start asking the questions that mattered.

"Help me," Jonathan said.

Heyer noticed the change in Jonathan's voice, and his tone adjusted with it. "Yes, Jonathan, I can help you. Start with what happened during the incident tonight. What were your weaknesses?"

"This thing you put in me," Jonathan said, pointing to his chest. "It isn't enough! I don't know how to fight. That Ferox seemed like it lived to fight, and it was stronger, so much stronger and faster than me. I was afraid, but it didn't fear combat with me; it reveled in it. It found me so nonthreatening that it let its guard down and I got lucky, so damn *lucky*. I almost had my throat torn out. I'm not some badass. I have no idea how to deal with a thing like that."

Heyer thought for a moment.

"Jonathan, that hardware inside of you, though an antiquated relic from my species' history, is still powerful. The only limit to its ability to increase your strength is you. Well, more specifically, your body. When you become activated, the cells that make up the device become powered by the presence of the portal stone. The device then releases molecules, unlike anything your planet has ever known, into your body. These molecules change and adhere to all the tissues that they find. Your muscle, your skin, your bones are all altered, replaced, or coated with the materials released by the device, but it can only enhance what it has to work with." Heyer paused to see if Jonathan understood what he was getting at.

"I understand, I think, but I don't see how this helps," Jonathan said.

"The more muscle mass you have before you are activated, the more the device has to work with. The stronger you are naturally, the exponentially stronger you are when triggered," Heyer said.

"So there needs to be more of me?" Jonathan said. "You want me to go to the gym?"

"In a manner of speaking, yes, but it's not just strength. Endurance, flexibility, balance—all of these play a role in how effective you are once activated."

"I'm not an athlete, Heyer. I don't know anything about muscle building," Jonathan said gloomily.

"Well, I'd recommend you look into the matter. Which brings me to your other concerns, Jonathan—one of my main fears in selecting you." Heyer paused as if unsure how to proceed. "Most men of your time in history have a somewhat universal draw to parts of human culture, Jonathan. Yet you seem utterly lacking in that pull. Your bookcase did not hold a single story of a heroic male role model. No action heroes, no spy novels, no comic books. Maybe you described it best; you don't seem to idolize any *badasses*."

"I'm well aware of my bookshelf contents, Heyer. I need instructions. Not observations about myself," Jonathan said.

"Your world's culture is designed to tell men a story about who they should be. That story is of heroics, the making of champions, the defeating of monsters, saving the innocent, stopping the villains. The entire fantasy that most men don't even realize they are engaging in becomes their expectation of their roles. From my outside perspective, most of what men in your world are told seems remarkably useless. I sometimes wonder why these stories of heroism are propagated so much; you would think that if something was irrelevant it would die off. Yet with humans, relevance often has no bearing on what is retained or thrown on the scrap heaps of your history."

"The stories you are describing irritate me, so I don't tend to care for them," Jonathan said. He was growing impatient at not being able to see the alien's point.

"Curious," Heyer said. "Why irritating?"

Jonathan found it difficult to answer. He was finding it incredulous that Heyer was wasting their time with a pedantic rant about human society. "I don't know. They always have," he replied. "But I don't understand. So, man is obsessed with outrageous hero fantasies. Why the hell are you telling me this?"

"What I'm getting at, Jonathan, is that you are one of the few examples that would give those stories a point. You need to know what it takes to slay monsters, defeat a villain more powerful than yourself. Your culture has been researching it for you since the dawn of human storytelling. You just happen to be one of the few who haven't indulged in it. I think if you really go looking for what it takes to slay monsters, you'll find your world is full of information that can help you. After all, interdimensional dissemination of human culture is part of what has led to the Ferox targeting Earth in the first place," Heyer said.

"What do you mean we were targeted?" Jonathan asked.

Heyer paused. He looked annoyed with himself.

"I apologize, Jonathan. It was a poor choice of words. That, unfortunately, isn't information I can trust you with yet. Still, I'm sure you can imagine; tales of heroics will draw those who wish to measure it."

Heyer checked his watch. "It's near time I leave you," Heyer said.

He stood from the bench and started to walk toward the center of the open field in the park. Alarmed, Jonathan rose to follow him.

"Wait! That's it? That isn't a plan! It's not even a start!" he said, his fear and anger beginning to swell up as his one life line was leaving him.

"I'm sorry, Jonathan. I'll see you again before September. We can talk more then."

"Wait!" Jonathan said. "Please, one more thing."

Heyer looked back at him, waiting.

"Why didn't you tell me what was happening a week ago? Why did you wait?" Jonathan asked. "I could have planned something; I didn't have to go down there blind."

Heyer nodded. He seemed to have expected this question earlier.

"It was not my design. Please have no doubts of that. I had worked diligently to arrange events to our advantage, only to have time and circumstances align against me in the weeks leading to tonight. I was unable to return until now—even this was difficult to manage," Heyer said. "For what it is worth, I think you have seen the consequences of inaction tonight. If you are to become what we need you to be, it's good that you understand what is at stake."

Jonathan didn't know what to say to that.

He wanted to argue that it was reckless bullshit, but he grew quiet when the little girl's pink coat, her dead eyes, screamed through his memories. He could never allow himself to sit, scared, on a couch.

"I am sorry, Jonathan." Heyer said. "You may not have chosen this, but, like me, it has chosen you. Just try to remember, fearing it will not save you from it."

Anger, panic, and guilt; Jonathan was a storm of emotions that made it hard to speak. He knew he didn't want the man to leave but didn't know how to stop him from going.

"I'm going to stop this! You can't just trap me!" he yelled in defiance.

Heyer's eyes looked sympathetic. "I hope so, Jonathan, but there is no stopping this, not without casualties. If, somehow, you find a way to freedom," Heyer said, "please show me the way out."

Heyer smiled thoughtfully then.

"You know, Jonathan, it's funny, but you do have me wondering. What was it you said? '*I'm not some badass.*' Begs the question, doesn't it? What if you were? Why would that make the difference?"

He was gone then, suddenly missing from existence, just an empty patch of grass where his feet had been. No flash of light, no portal, no noise, no beam from the sky. He'd simply checked his watch one more time and disappeared. It was as though Jonathan had blinked and upon opening his eyelids, the tall blond bastard was just gone.

CHAPTER FIFTEEN

DATE | TIME | LOCATION: UNKNOWN

WHEN HEYER BLINKED into existence, the environment seemed to press in on him from all around. The sky was always red on the Ferox's surrogate home world. Not the pleasant red of an earthly sunset, but a dense red that made his eyes feel as though he were swimming through a punch bowl. The only contrast against the blood sky was the black smoke rising off the planet's floor.

He supposed he was late at this point. Malkier, his older brother, would understand. It didn't make sense to get impatient about these things; they weren't easy to calculate after all, and at least Heyer was making the journey to him instead of the other way around.

He was surrounded by the perplexing maze of rock-like structures typical of the planet's crust. The formations would've confounded an earthly geologist. Every monolith that rose into the sky resembled obsidian, and Heyer could see his reflection now in the smooth, glassy walls of the black corridor around him.

He stepped forward, leaving boot prints in the black sand that had collected on the ground, making his way toward the incline where his brother awaited him. As he turned a corner, Malkier came into view on the rise above him, and he saw his brother take note of his approach.

Malkier unfolded his massive Ferox arms from his chest. Such posture was body language for showing defensiveness on the human planet, and Malkier was aware of that. The two brothers spent so much time amongst their adopted species that they had embraced the mannerisms of their alien hosts. It was a politeness to observe these little details to make one another comfortable when they met.

In truth, Heyer's body and earthly clothing were truly alien against the backdrop where he now walked. The Ferox wore no clothing, and as such, Malkier almost seemed naked to him. His brother's muscled frame towered over his human form. The deadly black skin of Malkier's exterior was complete; no color, just the glistening dark grey skin and overlaying webs of black tar. The only exception was a ragged white scar that ran down the side of his brother's cheek and neck. Heyer hated that scar.

The Ferox knew instinctively what Malkier's skin meant. It was the sign of an aged warrior who had sired many children, a leader of their tribes. His brother had taken the body of one of the few Ferox alphas, so that his ability to lead the Ferox would not be questioned.

"Hello, Brother," Heyer said as he reached the cliff top.

Malkier nodded. "You've been missed," Malkier said.

Heyer returned his nod.

"I trust you've reviewed my reports," Malkier said, straight to business.

"Yes," Heyer replied, "they indicate that we should continue on our original path."

Malkier nodded. "So you've had no new challenges maintaining our arrangement on your end?" he asked. "Operations as usual?"

"Yes, the inactive districts have been reinforced. I trust you delayed access to the gates I specified?" Heyer asked.

"The delay you requested was initiated; the Ferox did not respond well to this, but now that the districts are reinforced, it seems like this is no longer necessary," Malkier stated.

Heyer nodded. He had to be careful in his diplomacy. He'd hoped to delay attacks on Jonathan's behalf, and had vaguely explained to his brother that he was having trouble reinforcing Jonathan's gate. It was a failed ruse, as a Ferox had still made its entry ahead of schedule. It was a miracle the kid had survived. Still, the delay had bought Jonathan the time he now had to prepare.

"Have you reconsidered any of the other measures?" Malkier asked.

Heyer sighed heavily. "My answer has not changed. Earth has already involuntarily been forced to deal with problems it is not responsible for; they should make no additional sacrifices," Heyer said.

Heyer could see his brother didn't respect his answer. He worried that he'd made a misstep.

"Heyer, do not forget your position; if you were not family, if Earth was not your home, I would sacrifice the entire planet. I have no love for the humans you prize so dearly. They'll exterminate themselves eventually—might as well do something useful with their existence," Malkier said.

Heyer cautioned himself. After all, when Malkier had come to him with his intentions to exploit Earth, it was only after months of arguments and arrangements that their precarious balance had been found. Heyer had, of course, slipped in some clauses to their agreement that provided Earth some fail safes, but he didn't doubt that his brother had done the same on behalf of the Ferox. Regardless, it could all be for nothing if Malkier lost his temper and decided to betray their arrangement entirely. Heyer feared the day that his brother's love of the Ferox surpassed his love of family.

"Please accept my apology. What I meant to say is, I still believe it is important that the beings making this sacrifice for their species be allowed to keep their memories. More importantly, we may face participation complications if we handicap either side involved in the engagements. My ability to keep the humans involved is a thin smoke screen after all. I prefer not to lie to them; I am sure that you, too, know the repercussions should you be exposed in a lie by the Ferox."

"Yes, well, what the Ferox don't know is genuinely for their own good," Malkier replied. "The value of what you choose to tell the humans is subjective at best."

"I can't deprive them of their defeats, Brother, as such; I feel it is only fair that they at least be allowed to remember their victories. It would weigh too heavily on my already-burdened conscience to deny them this," Heyer said.

They both stood looking at each other, Malkier a foot taller than his brother in his Ferox body. They would've appeared odd to either of the species they hid amongst. Heyer was too graceful, too statuesque for a human; while Malkier was too calm, too thoughtful for a Ferox. When it became clear they were at a stalemate, Heyer spoke.

"So we agree to continue per the original arrangement," Heyer said. "Access to the gates will resume."

"For now," said Malkier. "As we may have eventual use for those memories, I'll not demand you ignore your burdened conscience."

Heyer nodded, and turned to leave. Halfway down the slope, he looked back to wave at his brother as a sign of farewell, regardless of their argument, but Malkier was gone. He had already returned to his tribe; likely eager to reinstate full access to the gates, for which he would be praised.

It was a good sign, at least, that Malkier trusted him enough not to make sure he'd departed. He wasn't suspicious that Heyer might be off to anywhere other than his adopted home planet, diligently on his way to making the necessary arrangements that would keep their schemes up and running. Sure enough, Heyer would return to Earth soon. First, though, there were things he needed to see here with his own eyes, suspicions that needed resolution.

It was better that Malkier didn't know, as Heyer's intentions weren't betrayal. They were a wariness of his brother's objectivity. Heyer had to see for himself if Malkier's reports of his adopted Ferox were what they seemed. His brother loved the Ferox too much, and that love could easily alter the information he sent to Heyer under the guise of unbiased observations.

He had no specific reason not to believe his brother, just a rising suspicion. Heyer knew that if it meant saving human lives, he would rationalize every omission he might decide to leave from his own reports. In fact, he'd already made such omissions. With this in mind, he made his way toward one of the Ferox population zones.

He could not delay. Travel between the realms left earth to its own devices longer than Heyer preferred. The split second he experienced traveling here could mean a week had passed back home. A week or a month could be disastrous if the universe turned against him.

CHAPTER SIXTEEN

JONATHAN STARED UP at his ceiling from his bed. Sleep had been impossible and it was early in the morning now.

Sometime during the night, he'd fought through panic over his approaching future. It wasn't gone now, but carefully maneuvered to the side of his mind and held there by sheer force of will.

He'd wondered, now that he found he was unable to sleep, about those two moments when he seemed to be forced back into the waking world. How he'd had such a strong sense that he wasn't meant to wake. He'd wondered if that feeling was because he'd briefly been dead, brought back from the brink twice now by the damn alien who'd caused him to die in the first place.

You may not have chosen this, but it has chosen you. Fearing it will not save you from it.

Heyer's words repeated over and over in his head. At first, he hated the bastard for saying it. Where did the alien get off talking to him about fear? He wasn't the "expendable" part of this relationship after all, was he? No, he'd made that clear, yet somewhere around three in the morning, Jonathan had thought about his options more. He had to accept the truth of it. There was no denying the words. Sitting in his room scared for three months, being angry at an alien, was only going to get him killed. Going about life as if nothing had changed would do the same.

Worse, it wasn't a decision, but a duty. Jonathan didn't want to bestow this nightmare on anyone. It was complete BS that his life had been commandeered from him. He would be damned if it would happen to someone else. It was the only small victory he could see, the one thing he might be able to control.

There is no stopping this, not without casualties. If, somehow, you find a way to freedom, please show me the way out.

Heyer had given him exactly enough information to be nothing more than a tool, and he'd done it on purpose, yet still, the alien's final words kept draining the anger out of him. How could an alien that seemed to be able to move space and time be as shackled to this situation as Jonathan was? He hated not being able to see the bigger picture. How could he tell if he was getting the truth at all?

He needed more information, and that meant living.

Living meant time. Time meant learning and planning. If he could just get time on his side, he could take the bread crumbs of information that slipped through, piece it together, and maybe figure this out. He had to believe he could escape this without victimizing someone else. He could find a way. He just had to make sure there wasn't a deadline in the equation. It meant survival at all costs.

Resolved to this much, he was giving himself one day to think, one day to come up with a plan and move forward. The more he examined every word the alien had said, the more he realized that Heyer had given him more than he'd initially thought.

Clearly, he needed to improve his physical prowess. Also clear was that he needed to see what the world could tell him about this sort of situation. People who could teach him what he needed to learn were out there. Two of them happened to live downstairs. Others, he would have to seek out.

"Grant!" Jonathan said out loud.

Well, he said to call him if I saw the guy. I saw him, after all.

Where was that business card? He'd left it in his jacket pocket, in the closet downstairs. He had an idea, a direction—he would take it! He got up and headed down after the card; as he entered the living room, he overheard Collin and Hayden talking.

"I think Jesus should have serious staff skills," Hayden said.

"Right, cause that way he can resort to violence when the power of faith isn't enough to defeat the demon he is fighting," Collin said, "or if he is felled by doubt-inyte."

"Seriously, we aren't calling it doubt-inyte. It's lame. It goes past lame to just uninspired," Hayden said.

They looked up from their panels when Jonathan entered. They acknowledged him with a halfhearted wave and went back to work. Paige was on the couch watching morning television programs but seemed more entertained by the conversation about Jesus' martial art skills. When Jonathan came down, she stopped watching the television entirely.

"Hey, Jonathan, long walk last night. I never heard you come home," she said.

Jonathan was reaching for his jacket in the closet. "I lost track of time," he said.

"Want to grab a ride to class with Hayden and me?" she asked.

He'd forgotten about school.

His academic career hadn't been on his mind since his chest lit up the night before; which, given what had passed since that moment, seemed like longer than twelve hours ago—fourteen if he counted the time he'd lived twice. He couldn't imagine getting anything out of class today. How could he sit in a lecture hall when every minute counted?

He put his hand into the front pocket and found the business card where he had left it.

"No, not today," he said. "I need to take care of some other things."

She did not seem to like that answer, but didn't comment on it, just gave him a look that said, I thought you were getting it together, but who am I to judge? I wasn't in a pool of my own blood a few weeks ago.

She did, however, eyeball Grant's card in his hand. "One of those chores involve Grant?" she asked.

"Maybe," he replied, "not sure."

"Did I miss something with you two?" she asked. "I thought you hadn't exchanged more than ten words."

"We've never spoken when you weren't around," he said.

She frowned and then took a longer look at him. "You look tired. Have trouble sleeping last night?" she asked.

He shrugged and nodded.

"Guess these things take time," she said politely.

Jonathan, card in hand, went to head back up the stairs, then stopped. He remembered he had to ask the two super geeks in the living room something. He wasn't sure how to phrase it.

"Guys, if you were going to watch a movie," he paused, "something with a guy who needs to learn certain things, like fighting, or killing monsters…."

Collin's eyes were growing large. He seemed to be waiting for Jonathan to give him a complete thought.

"Do you know any movies about people who are badasses?" Jonathan asked, wincing at how ridiculous the question sounded even to him.

Hayden smiled. "You're going to have to narrow that down. I think you just asked me about 75% of all modern mainstream cinema."

Jonathan had an idea. "If you were writing an essay on the modern hero story, and you wanted to start doing research, what would you watch?"

Hayden's eyes seemed to twinkle. He smiled, then looked to Collin, then back to Jonathan. They knew he wasn't writing such a paper—none of Jonathan's classes would assign such a topic, so they had to wonder where his interest was coming from.

"Jonathan, I think most nerds dream about being asked that question. So, if you would like me to sit on that couch and give you my doctoral thesis on every action movie that has been released in the last thirty years, my answer is yes. A million times, yes."

"Count me in for that." Collin put in, grinning.

"Count me out," said Paige, with a look that said, *You can't make it to school, but you have time for this crap?* Paige had mastered the art of speaking with facial expressions this morning.

Jonathan walked down one of the steep sloped streets that passed over the freeway connecting Capitol Hill to downtown Seattle on his way to meet Grant. When he'd called, the man had answered his phone excitedly but soon seemed confused by Jonathan's peculiar request.

"Jonathan!" Grant said. "You find that bastard?"

Jonathan had fudged the truth. "Um no, nothing like that," he'd said. *Technically Heyer found me.* "Grant... actually I was hoping—and I'm not sure how to ask this—but I was wondering if you might teach me a thing or two about putting on some muscle?"

There had been a pause on the phone as Jonathan waited for Grant's answer.

When he finally responded, it was as though he felt a responsibility to say yes but didn't want to.

"Sure, I could help you bulk up," he'd said. "When did you want to start?"

"As soon as you can," Jonathan said. "Today, if possible.

Grant seemed hesitant. Jonathan almost asked him to forget it. The offering of the business card was just an unspoken politeness. Grant was just trying to impress Paige, and now he was putting him out by calling him on it.

Still, Grant had agreed to meet him at his gym downtown.

"You'll need to get a membership, so I'd get there early," he'd said.

It occurred to Jonathan then that he didn't have a great deal of extra money to fund whatever plans he might make. He was going to need to pick up more shifts.

Damn alien tells me to get ready for a fight, he might have thought about what I had to work with.

He was missing school, he was changing his schedule; the reality of what it might take to survive was starting to take shape, and he didn't like what he was seeing. How was he going to maintain a semblance of his life? College students scraping by on student loans and part-time jobs don't have disposable income, and he was already so far behind. What would he tell people?

He'd put three years of his life into college; he'd invested too much of himself, he couldn't just drop it. His mind rebelled at the notion. His freedom taken away, aliens and alternate worlds now a reality, it was hard to believe that the question of school could weigh so heavily on him. As if, should he find the means to escape it all tomorrow, he would go back to the life he knew? Yet he felt he had to get back to that life. It wasn't just his freedom that would be taken if he didn't, but who he was.

Until he freed himself of this mess, he had to find a way to put his real life on hold. The college had already given him the option of a grace quarter. He would have to take it, postpone attendance.

I might be dead at the end of the quarter. Jonathan winced at the thought and got angry with himself. Stop! There's just no damn point thinking that way.

When he turned the next corner, he saw the gym. As he passed the front windows, he walked by a man leaning against the wall talking on his cell phone. His sheer size was intimidating. Jonathan figured the guy must have weighed 250 pounds and it was all muscle. He wondered if that was what he had come here to be and tried to imagine adding that much weight to his body. He couldn't picture it. How long had it taken that man to become what he was?

He couldn't help but question Heyer's judgment as he thought this. If there was a guy like this working out at a gym a few blocks away, how the hell did Jonathan get picked to fight the Ferox? This guy looked like he'd been preparing to fight monsters his entire life, like he was perpetually built to be a warrior. What was the alien thinking, throwing someone like Jonathan into this situation?

Genetic and psychological compatibility, he remembered.

"Really, Carla!" the big man said, yelling into his cell phone. "You want to get your BMI back down to nineteen but you want to reschedule training?"

What's a BMI? Jonathan thought as he couldn't avoid eavesdropping.

"Well, I'm already here waiting."

It was the last part of the conversation he overheard as he entered the double doors into the facility.

The gym was alive with activity. The front desk was checking people in, handing out towels, answering phones. Everywhere he looked, there was someone doing cardio on a treadmill or a StairMaster. High energy hip hop music was blaring over the sound of machines, even though everyone in the place seemed to be plugged into head phones. The floors were carpeted wall to wall with some type of rubber foam, the walls made up entirely of mirrors.

He could smell sweat. It wasn't as bad as a locker room, but it was still hard to miss.

He talked to the girl at the counter briefly. She asked him to wait while she got a membership salesperson to come speak to him. This was nothing like what he remembered from the local gym in high school, even if he'd seldom actually gone in there. The walls near the front desk were lined with shelves and displays. The shelves were stocked with tubs and bags, the kind Jonathan had only seen in vitamin stores at the mall. He had no idea what any of the stuff was supposed to do.

Crap, will I need to know?

He looked at the labels. He recognized some of the words from his classes, but had no idea what function they served as a supplement. What was nitric oxide and creatine? What was a BCAA? Every vial or tub looked expensive to his college student-sized wallet.

As he waited, the big guy from outside came in. He still looked pissed off. He stopped by the front desk to talk to the girl handing out the towels.

"I'm sick of training these wanna-be models," he said. "They all want perfect bodies, then they ignore it when I tell them it's 80% diet and they can't blow off training. You know they're gonna blame the trainer when they don't get the results they want."

The front counter girl nodded at him in agreement. She seemed only half interested though, like she heard the complaint frequently. The big man walked away from the counter, into the gym. Jonathan watched him go. He was so large people moved aside like they would for a semi-truck merging into their lane on the freeway.

He was growing more and more intimidated with just how much there might be to this whole working out plan when the account representative finally showed up. He took one look at Jonathan and something about him seemed to waver, but he quickly put on his sales face. After thirty minutes of Jonathan explaining to the guy that all he could afford was the simplest of memberships, the guy stopped trying to sell him every service the gym offered and finally let him buy a membership.

Standing there alone, Jonathan felt like some kind of tourist as he waited for Grant. His crappy T-shirt and cargo shorts made him stand out. Everyone he could see seemed to be in some dress code he hadn't been told about. Synthetic fibers, tank tops, and various off shoots of spandex were all around him. He was unforgivably aware that he was the only person here who wasn't already in shape. He'd at least expected to see some overweight people on the cardio equipment, but it wasn't the case.

At first he thought it might be a Friday morning phenomenon and the out of shape people didn't show up until after working hours; then he thought about who sent him here. Grant had probably chosen this place because it catered to people who were already athletes.

He grew anxious quickly, unsure what to do with himself. Grant was going on forty minutes late.

He had to remind himself that Grant wasn't aware of the urgency to get started. How could he be? It wasn't as if he had explained to the guy that he had a bout with a seven-foot-tall monster scheduled three months out and needed to make sure he was ready. Jonathan didn't even know if three months would be enough time to matter. How much "mass" could he gain in that amount of time anyway? Eventually, feeling silly, Jonathan tried to start without him.

Almost immediately he realized he had no idea even how to begin. The gym was so full of options and he didn't know if there was, in fact, a right or wrong place to start. There were muscle machines. Should he start with those? Most of the big guys in the gym didn't seem to be using them. They all seemed lined up with the spare benches and dumbbells, but even that was daunting.

Do I just pick up a weight and start pumping? Just go until I can't lift it anymore?

Looking around, he couldn't tell. Some guys seemed to do a certain number of repetitions, others had people around them to help as they pushed until they couldn't lift the weights anymore. This wasn't nearly as straight forward as he had hoped. Finally, frustrated with the thought of such a monumentally small thing getting in his way, he decided he would try the machines.

It was hard to push the atmosphere away. He felt like amateur hour in the presence of hardened professionals. As he walked over to the machine area, he stopped politely to let two girls pass in front of him. They looked to be about 18, a blonde and a brunette decked out in expensive gym attire and makeup. Once they passed, he overheard the brunette talking to her friend.

"Ugh, as if I'm getting a membership here. Place claims it's exclusive. That guy looks like a homeless person buying a membership so he can use the showers."

Jonathan felt his face redden as he turned around to watch them walk away. The blonde was nodding her agreement. He was stunned; he thought this kind of rudeness only existed in movies. Making it worse, he noticed the muscled trainer watching him just then. The guy was scowling at him from behind his cubicle desk. Jonathan couldn't tell if it was that he agreed with the girls or because he thought they were out of line.

He snapped out of it, turning back to the machines and leaving the man's line of sight.

Being embarrassed is hardly relevant. Screw them all and go do something.

He was pumping the leg press machine an arbitrary number of times, trying to get an idea of what to set the weight at when he overheard the trainer answering the phone from behind a set of cubicle walls.

"This is Lincoln," the voice said. "Yeah, like the car or the president."

Jonathan eavesdropped again, he hadn't thought to bring headphones as he'd assumed he'd be taking instruction from Grant, but seeing as how the guy was now an hour late, he only had his troubled thoughts to keep him company. He'd been unprepared for the culture shift in the gym, so he figured that understanding how the place worked might be wise. Lincoln was clearly an indoctrinated member of the place, so he might be worth paying attention to.

"No ma'am, the parking garage is not open on the weekends, but there is plenty of street parking," Lincoln said, followed shortly by a, "You're welcome."

Jonathan heard the sound of the phone hanging up.

Then again, maybe it won't be that insightful.

He continued to pump the leg press until his legs felt like they were going numb. He had to assume that meant he'd exercised them and moved to the next machine. It was some type of shoulder exercise where he flapped his arms like a chicken. The doubt in his mind kept building. He couldn't tell if he was wasting his time on the wrong things; the possibility was a perpetual discouragement. He didn't have time to be wasting, he didn't have time to figure this out; he needed to know what to do so he could stop focusing on if it was the right thing and focus on damn well getting it done.

"Hey, Lincoln," a voice Jonathan recognized as his account representative whispered into the cubicle, "come check this out."

Jonathan stopped flapping his arms and watched as the account representative pointed to the two teenage girls from earlier, setting up a bench press a little ways off.

"Those two over there," said the account rep, "they came in on free day-passes, wouldn't even listen when I tried to sell them a membership."

"Okay," Lincoln said, waiting for the story to get interesting. Jonathan was waiting as well, but more he wondered how the girls had gotten free day-passes while he had to buy a membership.

"So get this, they wanted to make sure this wasn't the type of gym where they would be 'getting hit on' all the time," said the rep incredulously, using his fingers to make air quotes when indicating he was reciting the girls' exact words. "Apparently, they've had 'a lot of problems' with that in the past."

Jonathan took another look at the girls. He didn't see it. They were in decent shape but hardly distracting. Perhaps being snubbed by them earlier was coloring his opinion of them.

Nope, he decided.

This "*problem*" definitely existed in their absurdly inflated self-images. Jonathan frowned as Lincoln stepped to the front of his cubicle. He could see the trainer was frowning as well as he watched the girls setting up the bench press.

"Watch this," said Lincoln, walking toward the girls.

The membership rep looked around nervously, as if he'd just set into motion something his managers might get upset about. When he saw no one was paying attention, he became more interested in what was about to play out in front of him.

Lincoln approached the girls fairly inconspicuously at first, just getting close enough that he might make them uncomfortable. He seemed to be going about his business, a gym employee re-shelving weights and resetting equipment; then, suddenly, his facial expression changed as he picked up a forty-five-pound plate.

The scowl he'd had on since Jonathan had first seen him became an overacting impression of a sleaze ball. He turned to the girls, wearing this face, and performed a slow motion bicep curl with one arm, making a great effort to maintain eye contact with the blonde who was spotting her friend under the bar. When she couldn't pretend he wasn't staring at her, he looked from his bicep, back to the girl, then back to his bicep and let out a long slow breath.

"Ahh, yeah," said the trainer, without breaking character.

Jonathan and the account rep watched wide eyed. It was difficult not to laugh and blow the act from afar. Jonathan couldn't believe the trainer was keeping a straight face. Once the girl purposely stopped making eye contact, he re-racked the weight and walked up beside the spotter.

"Hi," Lincoln said, doing what Jonathan thought was an impression of a surfer.

The blonde smiled awkwardly.

"So, like, mind if I assist your friend here?" he said.

Placing his hands in a spotting position under the bar, he nudged the blonde out of the way with his hip.

"Oh, excuse me," he said. "I forget how built I am sometimes."

The brunette girl on the bench was now in the awkward position of having to look up at him from between his legs.

"Holy crap," the account rep whispered, turning away to keep from laughing.

To finish off this masterpiece, Lincoln took the weight off the brunette entirely, picking up the bar and gesturing towards his biceps again with his eyes.

"Check it out," he said while he flexed. "Pretty sweet right?"

The girls stopped smiling, clearly getting uncomfortable. They walked away hurriedly the moment the brunette was out from under the weights. Lincoln's eyes followed them as they left, still pumping the weight up and down.

"Hey, where ya going?" he said.

The second the girls were out of sight, Lincoln dropped the act and looked back at the account rep. Jonathan could see now that the trainer had almost lost it. The account rep's face was red with embarrassment for the girls, but couldn't hide that it had been worth it.

"Dude, like, was it something I said?" he joked to the account rep in his surfer impression.

When Jonathan realized he was laughing, it jolted him. He hadn't laughed, not a genuine laugh like that, since he'd woken up on the kitchen floor. It was so over the top that he'd actually forgotten to focus on his problems for a few minutes.

Unfortunately, he'd ruined the moment by noticing it.

When Grant finally made an appearance, Jonathan was, at first, grateful he'd shown up.

This didn't last long, as he soon realized that he wasn't going to be of any help. There was a stink of competitiveness that Jonathan didn't understand undermining everything the man told him to do. He seemed far more interested in showing off his own muscle than teaching Jonathan anything.

He had Jonathan begin on a workout that he referred to as his *maintenance routine*, but he repeatedly started Jonathan at a weight level that would result in almost immediate failure. Grant seemed to revel in the failures, like it proved something. He hardly made an effort to hide it.

Jonathan didn't know where it came from. He had never once slighted Grant to his knowledge. They'd hardly spoken at all. The guy was more confused about what Jonathan was trying to accomplish than Jonathan himself. The idea that Jonathan was honestly there just to learn how to body build was somehow an insult to the man's intelligence. Out of necessity, Jonathan tried to ignore it, yet he couldn't help but feel uncomfortable around him. He kept sensing that Grant felt like he was playing at something. Jonathan realized, of course, that he was sort of pretending, but not in a way that should make Grant question him.

Maybe he thinks Paige put me up to this.

He hoped the man's attitude would change. He tried to find some common ground, but it became apparent the common ground was non-existent. The more time they spent together, the more he didn't like the guy, the more he thought of him as an overly competitive idiot.

After an hour, Jonathan called it a failed endeavor. He'd wasted a day and a considerable amount of money on the whole idea and now had little to show for it other than an abused ego and a severe dislike for Paige's boyfriend. If "boyfriend" was even the right word; after today, he hoped "acquaintance" was a better description.

He resolved to come more prepared next time. He'd seen men's magazines at the grocery store. He could go online or find a book at the library, study up on modern muscle building techniques. He winced at the idea that he was losing time to research, even if it was necessary. He needed to do something, anything, to make some kind of progress. Whatever he did, he had to keep moving forward; a setback like Grant being a jackass wasn't going to get in the way.

As he left the gym he "thanked" Grant for his time. The guy was standing on the sidewalk outside of the gym, talking on his cell phone.

"No problem, Tibbs," Grant said, taking his ear from the phone. "Let me know if you want to do it again sometime."

"Yeah," Jonathan said, starting to walk away. "I'll call."

"Remember," Grant said. "You see that blond guy again, you let me know."

Jonathan nodded and started to turn away again, waving without looking back.

As he walked away he was initially perplexed. There was something about the way Grant had said "you let me know" that was intentionally, yet subtly, irksome. What was that guy's problem? Admittedly, Paige was probably still uncomfortable knowing that the "blond guy" hadn't been apprehended, so he understood the bravado in front of her, but what was his interest in bringing it up when she wasn't even there to hear him boast?

He understood suddenly.

He'd been thinking about it all wrong. It wasn't bravado. It was simpler than that. It was a facade. Grant didn't believe the story at all. He thought he was lying and was merely humoring him by pretending.

When it occurred to him, he could hardly pretend to care what Grant thought. Still, it started to make sense. Paige had seemed to make such a point of believing in him. She'd made a show of her support at the hospital. If Grant didn't want Paige being concerned for a guy whom he thought was lying, it would certainly cast the man in a better light.

It wasn't a blip on the radar of his current concerns, not when competing with his more imminent problems. It slipped from his cluttered mind the moment he turned the corner.

Hayden and Collin sat at the kitchen table, Collin's sketch book and a pile of notes scattered before them.

"Come on, Sunday School," Collin said to Hayden, trying out a new nickname, "dig deep here."

"I'm thinking!" Hayden said. "My brain is fried; we've been at this for hours, and I never went to Sunday School."

Paige walked in through the front door, her backpack heavy with books. "How is superhero Jesus coming?" she asked.

"It's back to the drawing board on the story arc. We need to alter certain biblical events to make them more convincing when they lead to action sequences. Young Jesus needs to be more incomplete, kinda like Superboy versus Superman. Then there's the issue of villains...."

Hayden trailed off as Paige looked like she was beginning to regret having asked.

"I mean," Hayden said, "it's good."

"Good," she replied. "Has Tibbs been around?"

"Nope, haven't seen him all day," Collin said.

She nodded, and her phone started to vibrate. Smiling, she answered it and walked toward her bedroom. Hayden could tell from her face that it was Grant on the other end.

He turned his head back to the project in front of him but noticed Collin's eyes still lingered on Paige as she disappeared up the stairs, then they lingered even after she was gone. Hayden sighed. He honestly felt bad for his friend on this one, especially since he knew Collin's bedroom was right under Paige's. That must be brutal.

"Collin," Hayden said, snapping his fingers.

Collin seemed to come back to reality from the daydream his mind had wandered off to.

"Bro, I'm just saying this for your own good." Hayden paused. "Never gonna happen."

He could see Collin get defensive, see his expression change as he was about to pretend he had no idea what he was talking about, then Collin's features relaxed and looked defeated instead.

"Sunday School," Collin replied, his eyes flicking briefly back to the stairs again where Paige had disappeared. "I don't know what you're talking about, but what exactly makes you say that, just out of curiosity?"

"You mean other than that I've never seen her date anyone who couldn't bench press his own weight?" Hayden asked.

Hayden immediately regretted phrasing it as such. He could see it hadn't done Collin's self-esteem any good. He hadn't meant to push a button.

"Yeah," Collin said, "other than that."

"She doesn't think of you, me, or Jonathan like that," Hayden said, "and I get it. She's pretty and kind of awesome in a lot of ways, but…."

Hayden trailed off, trying to figure out how to express this in a way that Collin would see it for what it was without getting his feelings hurt. He leaned in and whispered, not wanting to risk Paige somehow overhearing.

"She's kinda playing house," Hayden said.

Collin frowned, but picking up on Hayden's whispering, he lowered his voice. "What's that supposed to mean?"

"Paige thinks of us like brothers," Hayden said, "and not like she kinda thinks of us that way; she likes thinking of us that way."

"Whatever," Collin said, disbelieving.

"Bro," Hayden said, "have you ever heard her talk about family. Like ever?"

Hayden watched the gears going in Collin's head as he thought it over. After a moment, he shook his head.

"Well," Hayden said, "I only heard her mention growing up once, and it wasn't a pretty picture."

Collin leaned in closer, understanding now why Hayden had been getting quieter and quieter. "Like how?"

"It's not my place to go into it," Hayden said, "but I got the impression that the only family she's ever had was her dad, that they moved around a lot, and he wasn't exactly parent of the year."

They sat in silence for a bit. Collin didn't look like he was going to push for more details. Hayden wouldn't have felt right sharing anymore anyway. He'd already overstepped his bounds.

"That sucks," Collin said, looking down at the table.

"Well, anyway," Hayden said, "us, this place, Jonathan. It's the only place that ever really felt like home to her. And the way she's reacted to what happened to Jonathan… she acts more like, well—"

"Like a sister would," Collin said, "not just a roommate."

"Yeah," Hayden said with a slow nod. "Sorry, Bro."

After the gym, Jonathan headed to his shift at the hardware store. He had to talk to Mr. Fletcher about picking up more shifts. He didn't have a plan B yet if his boss declined. As it turned out, Mr. Fletcher was more than happy to oblige the request.

"You're worth three of these other retards that I have working for me," Mr. Fletcher said.

For a moment, he'd been flattered; then he realized he'd just been given the value of three retards.

"I gotta tell ya kid, I worry that you'll have time to keep up with your studies taking on that much time at the store," he said. "You sure about this? You don't need to feel like you owe me anything for missing shifts last week. It was completely understandable."

"No, sir, nothing like that," Jonathan said. "I may, well—I might have to take the rest of this quarter off, for personal reasons. I need the extra money, though. I don't know yet how the financial aid office will...."

Jonathan trailed off, realizing that he might be over-sharing. His mind was becoming weighed down with the implications again, how he didn't know what things were going to look like for him tomorrow. He couldn't get used to it, not after having such a structured routine.

Mr. Fletcher nodded in understanding.

At least temporarily, it appeared Jonathan didn't have to explain much to anyone. They all still *thought* they knew what was causing the change in his behavior. If Mr. Fletcher was okay assuming that Jonathan had been rattled so badly by his attack that he wasn't able to be functional at school for a quarter, then that served his current needs just fine. The lie of omission really didn't hurt anyone.

They talked more about increasing his schedule, at least until the next school quarter. The gym hadn't gone so well, but at least this had. As it was, by the end of the week he really had no idea what kind of funds he might need access to.

"Any news about the girl you mentioned, the new neighbor?" Mr. Fletcher asked at a slow moment during his shift.

"No, not really," Jonathan said. "She's a photographer—don't think I mentioned that."

His boss seemed disappointed at the lack of new development. It was just so out of character, or at least it seemed so to Jonathan. Mr. Fletcher was such an old fashioned man's man that his sudden change to gossiping about Jonathan's nonexistent love life was disarming.

"Artist type, huh?" he said. "She any good?"

"I don't know. I've never seen her work," Jonathan said. "Camera looked expensive, though."

"I dated an artist once. It was before I was married. Fiery girl; too much passion and spontaneity. It was a thrill at times; got me involved in a lot of stupid antics, but I remember she was incredibly difficult," he said. Jonathan saw a small smile cracking the man's lips as his memories passed through his mind. "Not saying this girl is difficult, just an old man's two cents."

Jonathan shrugged.

"You say she was a red head?"

"I didn't say," Jonathan said, raising an eyebrow. "But yeah, she is."

"Fiery," Mr. Fletcher warned.

Hours later, when Jonathan returned home from his shift, the sun was just beginning to go down. As he turned off the street and down the slope of his driveway, he noticed Hayden's car parked in front of the garage. He frowned as he approached the car's bumper. He'd seen the sticker a hundred times before; he remembered the first time Collin had pointed it out to him.

"It's like he gave the damn thing a tramp stamp," Collin had said, pointing at the car's rear.

"*What would Jesus do?*" Jonathan read out loud.

The question was supposed to show him the answer to his moral dilemmas. Jonathan didn't see an answer to any of his problems there now; perhaps if morality had been his chief concern, it would have been otherwise. If he were Jesus, being the omnificent son of God and all, he could have snapped his fingers and closed whatever gates the Ferox were using to get to Earth. Problem solved. He didn't have any idea how to accomplish this in reality, and apparently the alien who pulled him into this didn't either.

What would a badass do? He remembered.

There was a lot of what Heyer had said the night before that Jonathan had run over and over through his mind. Until now, the ridiculous "badass" comment hadn't been one of them. He remembered the alien's humorous fascination with the question, and he thought he understood it now. It set the bar within reach of a twenty-two-year-old college student and an alien. That, and the answer seemed clear.

Whatever it takes.

He heard a whistle then, and it startled him out of his thoughts. He looked up and saw Leah and Paige smiling at him from each side of the fence that divided their property. Paige was in her gardening clothes; Leah had her camera hanging around her neck again.

"You look like you're over-thinking something," Leah said.

Both smiled at him; he must have been closed to the world to have not noticed them there. Leah held a pink flower in her hand, and Paige leaned over the fence, letting Leah push her hair aside and tuck the flower behind her ear.

"Probably was," Jonathan admitted.

"Paige said she'd model for me," Leah explained.

"Who says no when a photographer wants to take their picture?" Paige asked, not really hiding that she liked the camera's attention.

He saw immediately why Leah wanted the photo. There was something about the scene; it struck him enough to briefly distract him from his own concerns. Paige, clean except for the dirty garden gloves she'd rested on the picket fence, smiling while the sun went down behind her. It all captured her so well. The pink flower Leah had put into the picture was the final detail, the thing that completed it.

Leah hardly knew Paige—still, she'd been able to see what the scene needed. He found himself impressed by the eye of the photographer, her quick insight, as he watched her taking the shots.

"I think she's got you pegged," Jonathan said.

"Maybe you'll let me take some shots of you sometime?" Leah asked.

When Jonathan came down the stairs, his hair was still wet from a shower. After he'd returned home, he'd gone for a run. At least it was exercise he was familiar with. His legs had felt heavy from the gym earlier. Now, he felt the night of missed sleep creeping up on him. It was probably for the best; he'd need to be exhausted to get to sleep.

Collin and Hayden were waiting for him expectantly in the living room. For a second, he didn't know what to make of it.

"It was difficult. We couldn't think of a single time where you even mentioned a movie, but we know the best place to start," Collin said, like he imagined he was about to teach a blind person how to see.

"Thanks!" Jonathan said, doubtful that they'd actually thought about it as much as they were letting on. "So then what are we watching?"

Hayden and Collin were both visibly excited.

You'd think they were about to tell me I'd won the lottery.

"Rocky!" Collin finally said.

Right! Jonathan thought. Sylvester Stallone. It wasn't as though he'd never heard of the film. It was a national phenomenon after all, though he admitted he'd never seen it, just clips and scenes here and there. Mostly things like Rocky at the top of stairs with his fists in the air. He knew it was about boxing. Then, Hayden added something unexpected.

"All of them!" Hayden said.

Jonathan frowned. "How many of them are there?" he asked.

"Let's see, there's *Rocky* 1, 2, 3, 4, then 6 is due out sometime next year," Hayden said.

"What about part five?" Jonathan asked suspiciously, predicting he was being set up.

There was a pause. Hayden looked at Collin as though Jonathan had just acknowledged the existence of big foot.

"What?" Jonathan asked, playing along.

"Tibbs, you'll come to find that there isn't a consensus around whether or not certain films actually exist," Collin said diplomatically.

"Part five," Hayden said, shaking his head at Jonathan in disapproval.

"For instance," Collin said, "Hayden, have you ever seen *Highlander 2?*"

"No such film," Hayden replied, straight faced.

"*Batman and Robin, Halloween 3, Jaws* 4?" Collin asked.

"Collin, are you having a stroke? It's like you aren't even speaking English right now," Hayden said in mocked concern.

Collin pointed to Hayden. "You see my point."

Jonathan was confused. Paige snickered from the kitchen table; she apparently had at least some idea what the two geeks were talking about. Jonathan shrugged at her. "Some movies are so bad, and screw up the stories so much, that nerds decide to ignore their existence so that it doesn't taint the other films in the series," she said.

"That's correct, Tibbs," Collin said.

"Okay, so we're watching *Rocky I,* then?" he asked, fairly sure he was naming a real movie.

When the exhaustion came, it overwhelmed him quickly, and Jonathan only made it through a quarter of the film before he gave in. It hadn't been immediately clear what he was supposed to see in the story and he struggled to keep his eyes open more than he'd given the film his attention. Had it been otherwise, he would've let Collin and Hayden, who were still wide awake, begin explaining the film for him.

The promise of the blankness that unconsciousness would bring became too much to resist. It was all he could do to drag himself up the stairs before he fell asleep in the living room. When his body hit the bed, he was out fast, the comfort of the mattress and sheets embracing him. It was relieving, to be so tired that thoughts outside of sleep ceased to carry any weight.

There would be those few sweet moments in the morning before he remembered what his life had become, where he'd just be Jonathan again, waking up in his bed like any other morning, not this frightened boy desperately trying to find his way to yet another new normal. It would be brief, but it would be there.

He had to sleep.

He didn't have to rationalize it. He had to be able to get up and try again tomorrow. He had another shift to cover at the shop, and there was so much more, so much he didn't yet have a clue where to begin. When he woke, he hoped his mind would do him the courtesy of forgetting reality as long as it could.

CHAPTER SEVENTEEN

SATURDAY | JULY 02, 2005 | 05:45 AM

HE WAS DREAMING. He knew on some level, because his father was standing beside him, a logical impossibility that no amount of wishful thinking could change.

They were walking along an abandoned railroad track deep in the woods. Jonathan didn't remember what had come before, but this was where they were now. It was summer, not many clouds in the sky, warm, but the shade of the trees made it comfortable.

If it weren't for the tracks, he wouldn't have known if anyone had ever been here. He wondered when the last person to come this way might have been. It seemed important, but there was no way to know. The rails were in disrepair, overgrown and rusted. Entire lengths of tracks and ties were missing in places. Maybe a few people, like Jonathan and his father, still used it as a trail, but it had been decades since anyone had used this track for its intended purpose.

His father wore his work uniform. He'd become a mechanic after leaving the army, and the blue pants and shirt were how Jonathan always saw him in his memory. The name tag on the front was a white circle with blue letters that read *Tibbs*. Douglas' hands still had the black grime from car parts; the dirty rag hung out of his back pocket. The only thing that stuck out now was that Douglas was wearing hiking boots, light brown and in sharp contrast with the blue uniform. His father had left work and thrown them on just to take Jonathan on this hike.

He must have been about twelve; he still had to look up to meet his father's eyes. They hadn't spoken; both were enjoying the quiet walk along the track.

Breaking the peace, Jonathan saw a large shadow move quickly through the woods. It had been brief, soundless, at the edge of his vision. He quickly lost sight of it, but his skin prickled in warning. It had been the shadow of a beast, and it somehow seemed familiar, but it didn't feel right. It shouldn't have been there, hiding in these woods. It shouldn't be there at all.

Jonathan looked back to his father, to see if he, too, was afraid. Douglas was looking down at his hand. In it he held a gold pocket watch, a gift from Jonathan's grandfather, a family heirloom that would one day be passed onto Jonathan. He was simply checking the time.

"Jonathan," Douglas said, "don't worry about that just yet."

"I'm afraid of it," Jonathan replied.

"Can't blame you for that, son," Douglas smiled reassuringly. "But it shouldn't bother us for a while. Try and put it out of your mind for now. The time will come for dealing with that."

Jonathan moved closer to his father. Despite his words, it felt safer near him and after a time, the shadow left his thoughts.

As they continued along the track, they came to a tunnel in the side of a stone cliff. It was man-made and as abandoned as the railroad. It had taken hundreds of men years to forge this path through the cliffside, work crews with dynamite, pick axes, and hammers; all that effort and still the passage had been forgotten.

His father took out a flashlight from his back pocket and nodded to Jonathan to proceed. It was dark on the inside, cold. Douglas kept the light on the rails lining the ground in front of them so they could both see where they were going. As they moved farther from the entrance, the light from outside the tunnel grew less and less. They had to walk slowly, to be careful where they placed their feet.

Without warning, the ground started to tremble. All around him, Jonathan could hear pebbles shaking loose from the sides of the tunnel and running down the stone walls. He turned quickly, thinking they would run back toward the entrance. When he looked, all he saw was the outline of a man standing in the mouth of the tunnel. The man was hard to see with the light behind him. Jonathan couldn't make out his features, but he didn't have to. He knew by that ridiculous fedora who was behind them.

The shaking of the walls was becoming more violent. With jarring visibility, he saw Heyer taking some steps into the cave. There was one last powerful swell of the ground and Jonathan stumbled to the rocky floor of the tunnel. He skinned his hands on gravel as he'd put them out to break his fall. The sting of raw flesh shot through them.

With a loud crash, thousands of pounds of stone closed in the entrance, and took the light with it. Jonathan couldn't see if Heyer had made it inside safely. He didn't know if the alien was now buried under stone, or if he could survive such a weight falling on him. For a moment, the earth's rumbling persisted through the tunnel. When it finally stopped, the sound of the large boulders coming to rest ceased. Eventually the sound of the falling pebbles that had come with the onset of the quake dissipated and the passage became silent.

It was hard to breathe with all the dust that the cave-in had put in the air. Jonathan's hands ached. It brought a tear to his eyes. He felt his father's hand on his back.

"Are you all right, Jonathan?"

He rolled over and turned his palms up. His father pointed the flashlight down on his hands and saw the nicks and cuts from the fall.

"It hurts," Jonathan said, grimacing. He didn't sob, but his eyes watered with more tears.

Douglas took Jonathan's hands and looked them over closely to make sure the injuries were only skin deep. His hand looked like it belonged to a giant when it was next to Jonathan's.

"Sorry, son. It looks like it hurts," he said, "but there's nothing to be done for it, not in here. Right now, you'll just have to take the pain."

Jonathan looked back down at his hands and nodded.

His father turned the flashlight back to the entrance of the tunnel, surveying the wreckage. It didn't take an engineer to know they weren't digging their way out. "Well," he said, turning his flashlight in the other direction, into the dark, "sometimes, the only way out is further in."

Jonathan looked up at him, his expression unsure.

"We'd always planned to come out the other side anyway. The only difference is, now we can't turn back."

"Maybe we should wait for help?" Jonathan asked.

"Help isn't coming, son. We're going to have to help ourselves. Just got to keep moving forward; hope there is a way out on the other side," he said. As he did so, he handed the flashlight over to Jonathan. "Here, why don't you take this? You lead the way."

Jonathan took the flashlight in his raw hands. He was scared in the dark, and glad that he wasn't alone. When Jonathan was young, he'd been afraid to be alone at night. He would always ask his mother to leave a light on in the hallway when he went to bed. The thing was, he was fine in the dark as long as his mother or father were there. It was only in their absence that the dark became filled with monsters. Still, giving Jonathan the flashlight made him feel safer. Now he could control what was illuminated in the darkness.

They started to walk away from the cave in. Jonathan kept the light aimed along the guiding lines of the railroad track, trying as best he could to ignore the urge to flash it around, but to keep the light where it needed to be, showing the way forward.

They walked for what seemed a long time. It was hard to tell in the dark just how much time had passed. Sometimes he would take the light off the path and flash it back behind him, looking for the blue uniform of his father following him, and each time he was relieved that the sounds of the footsteps behind him were still his father.

Eventually, the small pinhole of light that was the other side of the tunnel came into view. Both were relieved. As they moved closer and closer, the flashlight became unnecessary. Standing in the sunlight at the exit of the tunnel, Jonathan clicked the light off and turned to hand it back to his father.

With some sorrow, he now realized that the man following him was no longer Douglas; it was just Heyer, wearing his father's uniform, taking the flashlight back. Jonathan nodded, his face taking on a sad smirk.

"Yes, of course, it's you," he heard his adult voice say. "I knew it would be, but the lie felt better."

He turned away from Heyer to finish the journey, but upon turning, he found he was no longer in the tunnel in the woods. He was in the inner city of Seattle, on a street he would never forget.

He was under the viaduct.

It was dark, the only light provided by the streetlamps. The cars speeding by above him sounded more like a river than a freeway. He turned back around quickly. Heyer was gone now, abandoning him. He'd blinked away like he had the other night in the park, no doubt off to run some more important errand.

He looked at his hands. They were no longer bloody or raw; they were his adult hands.

From the corner of his eye, the shadows among the freeway pillars moved. Always at the edge of his vision, it darted from one pillar to the next, just as it had moved among the trees in the woods. His heart began to accelerate, thudding in his ears. No father, no alien; he was alone with it. He couldn't tell where the beast was, couldn't sense it in his mind. He'd see a flash of movement, but wasn't quick enough to know where it stopped. He turned about frantically, desperate to make sure the Ferox wouldn't get the jump on him.

She was there suddenly. Jonathan caught sight of her as he wheeled around and froze, forgetting the shadow.

She couldn't walk, not on her broken limbs, so she crawled to him. Her pink coat was saturated with the blood, her body covered in it, and he knew that she must have had to crawl through the puddle that had spread into the street, the puddle at the foot of Sickens the Fever's pile of bodies. She'd waded through all that to come to him now, and it trailed behind her, leaving a red smear on the pavement. She struggled to get closer to him. One of her hands stretched out, reaching for him with little, broken fingers.

He crumpled to his knees at the sight of her. He could see the death of a hundred in her white lifeless eyes.

"I'm sorry," Jonathan said in a whimper, looking down at his hands as he couldn't meet the child's white gaze. "I'm so sorry."

It didn't seem to matter that in the end he'd saved her. Guilt didn't work that way, didn't make allowances for science fiction beyond its comprehension. It didn't care that this broken girl was banished to a timeline that no longer existed. All guilt knew was that he'd allowed it to happen.

It was then that the shadow came for him, grabbing him by the shoulder and thrusting him against the pillar. The sound of the cement cracking around him, the pain flooding into him through an unforgiving memory—he recalled what it was to cling to consciousness, to struggle against this thing, this Ferox, yet it wasn't enough to shut off the shame.

You're barely more than a child! Sickens the Fever growled, menacing him with the sound of his own inner voice.

He tried to bring his hands up to protect himself, but they wouldn't move. He looked down to see the rusty chain tightening around him. It wasn't just his hands; it was holding his feet, wrapping his legs and stomach like a snake slithering around him and constricting. The compression was starting to hurt, and he could feel the chains breaking his skin as the links dug in around him, securing him to the pillar.

The panic was maddening, impossible to think through. He tried to scream, but his lungs had filled. He choked out seawater, trying to expel, but it leached into his sinuses and burned. If the chains pressed in any tighter, his ribcage would crush in on his heart.

He looked up through all of this to see Sickens the Fever's neck pulsating like it had that night, filling out and turning black. The Ferox's eyes bulged with bloodlust for the kill, its jaws opening.

Jonathan awoke. He bolted upright, his hands flying up wildly to protect against illusions.

He still felt teeth in his neck, yet his hands found nothing out of place. He realized he was yelling. Panic still welled up in him, making it a struggle to believe the sight of his bedroom in front of him.

In time, he pulled himself out of the sweat-soaked sheets. The phantom injuries dissipated; his mind began to accept the dream.

It was disturbing, his body's unwillingness to mind him, believe him when he told it what was real. Had he been screaming in his sleep? Yes, he must have been, but for how long? Had his roommates heard him? They hadn't come to check on him. Maybe they realized what it was. Maybe they understood and were politely ignoring it as to not embarrass him.

He sat at his desk and put his head in his hands, he forced himself to take deep breaths. He was able to get his breathing under control, but his heartbeat was slower to respond. He couldn't stop the fear from raging through him. He wanted his pills back. He wanted to wake Paige up right then and demand them.

The little girl, Jonathan. No. No, dammit!

He had to learn to cope with things far more dangerous than bad dreams. There couldn't be weakness, not like that; there couldn't be anymore hiding. It wasn't just him on the line.

He remembered how he had hoped that there would be a moment of reprieve from all this awfulness, how he'd sought sleep to escape it, thought fondly of those few moments when he might forget what his life had become. He felt grief for the loss of the peace he wouldn't get. That grief soon gave way to anger.

There would be no easy escape from this—no timeouts, not even in sleep.

CHAPTER EIGHTEEN

SATURDAY | JULY 02, 2005 | 9:45 AM

JONATHAN WAS HEADED down the street to the gym again. He hadn't been able to get back to sleep after the nightmare—or, to be more precise, he'd been afraid to try. So he used the rest of the early morning hours to research weightlifting techniques on the Internet. Unfortunately, the research on his laptop seemed to leave him more confused about how to proceed than the day before. There were a lot of different schools of thought about what worked and almost every source appeared to be selling something along with its advice.

He made a list of common exercises that he'd learned about from his research and took it with him. If he had to, he would watch people who looked like they knew what they were doing until he got a clue. If he got desperate enough, he would ask. He couldn't let himself fail because he didn't want to bother a stranger.

When he arrived, Lincoln, the big trainer from the day before, was sitting in the employee cubicle area. He looked pissed off again. Jonathan thought he might have been one of those types who scowled all the time without realizing it. Maybe it was the guy's demeanor. He sort of always looked angry. It didn't help that he was leaning against the desk, arms folded, surveying the gym patrons like a lifeguard at a pool.

Jonathan didn't go to the machines. This time he went to the free weights. The gym was pretty empty today; must have been a Saturday morning phenomenon. He took out his list and started trying to figure out what he could lift. He could figure this out even if he had to start from nothing. He didn't waver in this; he kept picking up different weights and trying exercises, eventually seeing how many repetitions of each he could lift before he couldn't do anymore. He was starting to feel pretty good about it until he turned around and saw the large trainer standing behind him.

The guy still looked angry.

"I just wanted to let you know that everything you're doing…." He paused to make a circular motion with his hands, indicating the space Jonathan had been working out in. "Is wrong." Lincoln was turning to walk away when Jonathan heard him add, "Frankly, I'm surprised you haven't hurt yourself yet."

Jonathan was speechless for a second. It was so direct and, well, rude. He remembered, then, that he wasn't going to let passivity stop him, that this was a chance.

"Like what?" he asked.

Lincoln stopped and turned back to him, like he was wondering if Jonathan really wanted to know or was just being defensive. He seemed to decide the former.

"Your form is terrible. You've likely never worked out before, and you're trying to lift too much too quickly, and the workout you're doing is all over the place. You aren't focusing on any set of muscle groups. That's just for starters," he said. "Seriously, do you even know what you're training for?"

Jonathan didn't know how to respond to most of that. He was just training to be stronger; he hadn't thought of exactly what kind of "stronger" he was trying to be. He didn't know that he should focus on a specific muscle group. He wasn't even sure he could tell what groups he'd just been working on, just that they were common lifts.

Still, it was the other thing the trainer had said, *"I'm surprised you haven't hurt yourself,"* that gave Jonathan pause. He realized how bad it would be now if he did hurt himself; if he got injured in some way that made it so he couldn't exercise at all. He'd be in real trouble then.

He didn't have any time to waste on something like an injury. It could mean death.

"Um, sorry, sir, but could you help me?" Jonathan said. "It's important that I don't get hurt."

Lincoln looked him over again. Jonathan got the distinct impression that the trainer was seriously on the fence about whether he was worth his time. It felt like he was being interrogated; the man was looking for a clue that Jonathan wasn't just like the thousands who bought a gym membership, only to stop showing up after a week or two. Jonathan, of course, knew that wouldn't be the case. He didn't have the option; he had to get stronger and it had to be as soon as possible. Then Jonathan remembered the phone conversation that he had eavesdropped on the day before. Maybe the trainer was trying to tell if he was just another guy who wanted to break into modeling.

Lincoln finally let out a sigh.

"Come over here," he said.

Lincoln instructed him to put his hands out and try to squat down as far as he could without letting his heel come off the floor. Jonathan tried, but he didn't make it very far.

"Jeez man, did they have PE wherever you went to school?" he said. "Have you ever stretched in your life?"

Jonathan could spot a rhetorical question and didn't answer, only shrugged. He had to wonder how this guy kept clients when he was so blatantly annoyed by them. Then again, maybe that was his angle, point out how badly in need of help someone is and he'll listen more when you try to sell it to him. In another life, it might not have worked on Jonathan, but today his desperation was definitely a sales point.

"Do you even know what you want to accomplish here?" the trainer asked.

Jonathan hesitated. He didn't know how to explain what he needed exactly. "Um, I need to put on muscle, a lot of muscle, as soon as possible. But I also need to have good balance and not lose too much endurance, and be flexible, and I need to be fast." Jonathan was rambling.

Lincoln frowned.

"So you basically want to be the perfect athlete, but you want to put on as much muscle as possible?" Lincoln asked.

"Yes!" Jonathan said. "But I can't get injured. It's important and I need to do this as soon as possible."

"Mind if I ask what the rush is all about?" Lincoln asked.

"Yeah, I kinda do," Jonathan replied, then realized it had been a little forceful, "but if you can help me, I'll do whatever you say."

Lincoln raised an eyebrow.

Jonathan wasn't sure he liked the way the trainer's expression had changed when he said he'd follow orders without question. It made him think of a scientist receiving a fresh lab rat.

"I could help you a lot more if I knew *what* you were training for," he said.

Jonathan shrugged.

Lincoln looked at him for a moment before checking his watch. "Alright man," he said, putting his hand out. "I'm Lincoln, what's your name?"

"Jonathan," he said shaking the trainer's hand.

"Well, Jonathan, tell you what—I'm going to show you a few things because I have an hour and a half before my next client gets here. After that, I'll show you my rates. If you want to get stronger, I'll teach you everything there is to know," Lincoln said. "Just don't tell me you want to be a model, as of yesterday I've raised my rates for wannabe models."

"No worries there," Jonathan said, wishing his problems amounted to just wanting to look good.

Jonathan was pretty sure he'd just made a good decision as he walked away from the gym. At least, it felt like he'd found a fast track to getting where he needed to go. Lincoln had spent an hour and a half running him though all sorts of stuff. There was so much more to each thing than he'd originally realized: stretching, posture, form, diet, cardio vs muscle training—it went on and on. Jonathan could tell it was just the beginning, but he was still three times more knowledgeable now than he'd been at the beginning of the day and that was good.

Unfortunately, Lincoln's assistance didn't come cheap. He'd had to use his emergency credit card just to finance the ten hours of training. That wasn't counting the tub of protein and various vials of supplements that were now crammed in his gym bag. He knew to some degree that Lincoln was being a salesman, but at the same time, he didn't doubt that the guy knew what he was talking about. In the last ten minutes before Jonathan had left, he had mapped out a stringent schedule for how often and how many of each of the pills and powders that he was supposed to be taking each day.

Jonathan had only worried about the debt he was going into for a few moments, then he remembered that, if he failed, he wasn't going to have to pay it off anyway.

He couldn't think of all his purchases this way—only those correlated to his survival. He was getting an image, an inkling of how to save himself. Once he knew what he was doing, he could train by himself, without the assistance of a guide. Guides were clearly expensive, but right now they were indispensable. All of the knowledge he was in desperate need of could not be easily pulled from a book. He wasn't going to learn to fight monsters by simply reading a self-defense manual. He needed teachers, he needed experience. He still had so much more he needed to know.

The nice thing about having roommates like Hayden and Collin was that they seldom had anywhere to be on a Saturday night.

Jonathan came home from a day that started at the gym and then six hours at the hardware store to find the two of them ready to drop their comic book panels and resume the Rocky marathon. He didn't understand how they watched these movies over and over again, at least not with such enthusiasm. Of course, it wasn't lost on him that this was exactly what Heyer had been telling him he needed to discover. He could see it in his roommates as they watched, a focus on the story that seemed to evoke some primal emotions in both of them. At times, Collin looked like his eyes had grown glossy.

Jonathan wasn't experiencing whatever it was at first, but still, it was hard not to be infected by Collin's and Hayden's passion. It all changed rather abruptly, right when it seemed that Collin was about to give up on him.

They were in the middle of *Rocky II*. In the scene Rocky and his trainer, Mick, were sitting in a chapel praying. Rocky's pregnant wife was in a coma at the hospital, but he was supposed to be preparing every day for his rematch with the heavyweight champion of the world. He couldn't get his mind where it needed to be because he was too heart sick over his wife.

"Roc, you're gonna be swapping punches with the most dangerous fighter in the world, and you're nowhere near ready," said Mick, as Rocky sat quietly, listening. "Why don't you stand up and fight this guy hard? Don't lie down in front of him like this! This guy doesn't just want to win; he wants to bury you, humiliate you. He wants to prove to the whole world that you were nothing but a freak the first time out—"

Collin paused the movie and looked to Jonathan.

"Seriously, Tibbs," he said, "if I need to explain to you why this speech is epic, then I have to wonder if you'll ever understand what these films are getting at. I mean, I have goosebumps right now."

Jonathan nodded his head then.

No, he needed no explanation. The words of the film were so over-relatable to his life that he was hardly paying attention to Collin's question. He'd felt something, and he knew now why Collin couldn't explain.

Goosebumps had prickled on his own skin. Inspiration from the words sank deeply into him, past his conscious thought, bypassing the barrier of his mind that over analyzed things, stirring something primitive. It wasn't simply motivating; it was angry and rebelling. It was like a drug coursing through him, bringing out the urge to conquer. It pushed to the forefront an unexpected desire for strength and the willingness to sacrifice whatever it took to obtain it. It ignored his limitations, and he felt an angry refusal to be victimized.

In that moment, deep in his core, he'd felt the thing inside of him stir. He'd forgotten about it, that part of him that had rammed itself into the back of the Ferox and dragged it down to the bottom of the black water; that thing that had risen up just when he was losing himself. It was awake within him, resonating with the words of the film, taking strength from them. It had been starving, and was now getting fed after years of being locked in a box.

He briefly understood how words could drive a man to bleed to death fighting. *Don't lie down in front of him!*

Hayden and Collin were both looking at the intense expression on Jonathan's face.

"Fight this guy hard," Jonathan whispered, his teeth tightening together.

This was what he needed; the competitive edge, the desire to challenge monsters that would come here thinking to destroy him. He couldn't just be hoping to survive; he needed to be thinking of how he was going to beat that leathery bastard's face through the pavement for daring to trespass here. That thing, feeding inside him now, felt like it knew all this somehow.

As soon as he had started to over-think it, the feeling seemed to slip away. He found himself hungry for more words, for another hit of that drug. When Jonathan finally looked back to his roommates, he only had one thing to say.

"We need to watch all of these."

CHAPTER NINETEEN

MONDAY | JULY 16, 2005 | 8:00 AM

LINCOLN HAD TO help him return the bar to the rack. He didn't have the strength left to get the weight off his shoulders. He dropped down to the floor and gave into the fierce need for air. He wasn't being dramatic; he had pushed himself to the point of failure again, always trying to do more than he'd been able to before, always trying to break past the previous barrier. He couldn't let himself be happy with anything that wasn't progress.

"I'm on the floor again," he said between hurried breaths.

Jonathan had spent the last two weeks getting his proverbial ass handed to him. He'd amassed a number of new enemies. They had names like kettle bell, dead lifts, and overhead press. He'd lost many a confrontation with his arch nemesis, squats. After the first day, once Lincoln had really started his training, he'd woken up and found he could hardly move through the soreness that had seemed to spread to every muscle he was unfortunate enough to move. Now, Jonathan couldn't remember the last time that some part of him didn't hurt.

Lincoln stood over him now, shaking his head in mock amazement.

"Always with the extra rep, Tibbs?" Lincoln said. "You know, when you first showed up here, I admit, I didn't think you'd have the spirit for this, but sometimes, well, I wish I had some of whatever is driving you."

You really don't, Jonathan thought from the floor.

He didn't remember when Lincoln had taken up the habit of referring to him as Tibbs. It wasn't like when Collin did so. When Lincoln said it, it was more sportsmanlike, the way football players referred to each other. Jonathan recovered his breath enough to get onto his knees and immediately started looking for his shaker bottle, a sealed beverage holder designed for mixing powdered supplements into water; another thing he didn't know existed until two weeks ago. He drank down the protein mixture, trying not to overdo it; he had learned his lesson early on with fluids—too much meant cramps and vomit.

"Convince yourself that if you don't get stronger, you'll die," Jonathan said between sips of protein and attempts to breathe.

Lincoln rolled his eyes. "Psychology games don't tend to work for me. It's too easy to remember I'm lying to myself."

Jonathan nodded his agreement. Of course, he couldn't explain that he wasn't lying to himself.

He knew it was a puzzle to the trainer. He didn't really fall into any gym clichés. It wasn't so much that he was a skinny guy who seemed to have no sports interest and suddenly needed to become as big as possible. There could be reasons for that. It was the urgency. A lot of people showed up at the gym for training thinking that their willpower would carry them to their goals. In their heads, they imagined some kind of delusional montage from a movie where they grit their teeth and sweat themselves into muscles. The reality generally destroyed their illusions within a few days.

Jonathan didn't have that problem; he hadn't come here with a preconceived notion. He'd come out of necessity. He would either do this and do it well, or he would die. That kind of motivation was as unwavering as it got.

Jonathan had been trying to concoct a story. Something he could say if pressed for why it was so important to be hitting the gym so much, but he had yet to think of anything that was very convincing. He wasn't a talented liar. When Lincoln probed, his usual response was just to shrug and hide behind his own face, as though he himself didn't know the answer. Lincoln didn't seem to buy that, but he usually dropped it.

According to Lincoln, the way he was training reflected what he would expect if Jonathan had woken up one morning with an overwhelming desire to compete in the Mr. Universe competition. Jonathan didn't think he could sell that story.

Eventually, it seemed, he would need some kind of explanation, but that moment had not yet arrived. Lincoln, after all, wasn't going to be the one to pester him for information. Like they had discussed on day one, the trainer trained and Jonathan did as he was told.

Following those instructions, he soon found, didn't end at the gym.

"Want to be a monster," Lincoln said, "you don't just train like a monster; you gotta eat like one."

Eating. Meal preparation and constant food consumption had become a full time job. His roommates hadn't seen the kitchen get so much use in the entirety of their living together. He was constantly cooking meals that were high in protein. Collin and Hayden had openly been sickened by the amount of *healthy crap* they now found in the refrigerator. Lincoln had told him that for optimal muscle growth, he was going to have to have food available at all times.

"Tibbs, if you start feeling hungry, I want you to start getting scared," Lincoln had said. "I want you to be thinking, 'if I don't eat soon my body might burn calories from my hard-earned muscle mass.'"

Jonathan had, at first, found this to be a hassle. Twice a week, he was cooking large quantities of food, then constantly carrying around a backpack full of pre-made meals. Soon, though, he understood the necessity. Constant training was causing him to be perpetually hungry, just like the trainer had advised him. When he started feeling hungry, he started to worry.

This was, of course, in addition to the plethora of new supplements he'd been instructed to take at varying intervals. Protein powders, creatine, nitric oxide supplements, in addition to simple multivitamins, which were the only thing he had recognized prior to hiring the trainer.

Still, that hadn't been the end of it. On the second day of training, Lincoln had asked him how often he was doing things like jogging. When he found out Jonathan ran frequently, he just shook his head.

"You need to knock that off immediately."

He'd forbidden him from doing more than an hour of cardio throughout the whole week. Seeing as Jonathan had been running since high school for all of his exercise, it came as a blow. Apparently cardio and muscle building didn't go together well. It had been the one thing he'd thought he'd be bringing to the table at the beginning; now it was considered a hindrance to his progress. He just had to accept it all as the price of survival. If he wasn't making progress, then all he was doing was dying. Few equations were ever so simple.

"What are we watching tonight?" Collin asked Hayden. "Your turn to choose."

"*Blood Sport*," Hayden replied.

"Ugh." Collin frowned. "Are we really including Van Damme movies?"

Hayden didn't dignify the question with a response. Instead, he riffled through the bookcase full of DVDs looking for the box he wanted.

He'd grown accustomed to the shift in routine. Jonathan came home, always appearing exhausted, and Collin and Hayden used his arrival as an excuse to take a break from their Biblical comic book adaptation to watch action movies from their childhood. Which, if they were being honest, wasn't much of a departure from their ordinary routine, except that it now included Jonathan.

Collin appeared to love the company, especially with the way Jonathan seemed to hang on their every word regarding the films. Although, he'd admittedly seemed less and less enthusiastic about it over the past week.

Hayden's eyes finally found the box he was looking for and pulled it from the shelf. He placed the film in the player and turned on the TV so that the menu options would be showing once Jonathan arrived. He felt like a professor getting a PowerPoint presentation ready before class.

To say Jonathan's change in behavior was noticeable was an understatement. Hayden felt that the only way he could be supportive was to provide the distraction that Jonathan seemed to be looking for. The whole house had commented on Jonathan never being at school anymore, or at least they never saw him there, and he was never studying.

Paige had said she was going to talk to him about it, but then the nightmares had started.

Hayden and Collin had both noticed it. Despite the fact that he appeared completely wiped out, he seemed to struggle to stay awake when he was with them, like he was afraid of going to sleep. They had all heard him, crying out in the night, walking around the house, or typing away on the Internet at early hours of the morning. No one had said anything to him yet. It wasn't a courage issue; it just felt impolite.

Paige said Jonathan was showing symptoms of post-traumatic stress. Collin and Hayden had just nodded when she said it. It wasn't like he was qualified to argue, but he wouldn't have anyway. Given their roommate's circumstances, the assessment seemed to fit. Frankly, Hayden wasn't so sure that *he'd* even recovered from that night. Images of blood all over the kitchen floor still made him cringe from time to time. He couldn't imagine being Jonathan, having woken up in it.

Of course, PTSD still didn't explain Jonathan's strange new obsession with cooking. Hayden was putting that in the distraction category, along with the movies.

A few minutes later, the front door opened and Jonathan came in. He moved sluggishly; his legs walked, but only in protest. He waved to them and they nodded, but he immediately ducked into the kitchen. A moment later, they heard the microwave running.

"Ugh," Collin whispered to Hayden. "Chicken breast and broccoli again."

A few moments later, Jonathan sat on the couch and started putting the meal away. He looked tired and distant. He chewed, but didn't appear to be enjoying the meal, just sustaining himself.

"Tonight, we watch *Blood Sport*," Hayden said, hoping to rouse some excitement out of him.

Jonathan nodded. Both Collin and Hayden noticed a change in his behavior. This wasn't less enthusiasm. It was bordering on no enthusiasm.

"What's up, Tibbs?" Collin asked. "Seem kind of disinterested suddenly."

Jonathan looked up at the two of them and paused. He sighed and put his knife and fork down on his plate. "Sorry guys, it's not you; I'm just starting to think this might be a waste of time."

"Tibbs, we are watching action movies from the 80's. Of course it's a waste of time," Collin said. "What did you think you'd be getting out of it?"

Jonathan seemed to think about the question too long. After he wavered for a moment, he finally said, "Not sure exactly. These movies are occasionally inspiring I guess. It's just, they don't...." He paused again. "They don't seem to offer anything practical."

"Practical?" Collin asked incredulously, exchanging looks with Hayden.

Jonathan put his plate on the coffee table. Again looking thoughtful, it was obvious that he was trying to ask a question without actually giving them context, without asking the "real" question. Hayden wanted to tell him to stop dancing around the issue and just blurt it out already, but he didn't. After all, if Jonathan wanted to talk about it, he wouldn't go to so much trouble angling to avoid it.

"These movies, they're starting to feel so formulaic," Jonathan said. "I don't get why there are so many of them, all telling essentially the same story. Why do—"

"Ah-ha!" Hayden said.

"Crap," Collin said right after he saw the look in Hayden's eyes. "Here we go."

"I'm glad you brought this up, Jonathan," Hayden said.

"Here comes the speech," Collin said.

Jonathan looked surprised, like he'd never expect the comment to push a button.

"It's that very formula," Hayden said, looking to Collin as though he'd just won some argument, "that drives the reuse of these stories over and over."

Collin just shook his head at Jonathan as though he'd been betrayed.

"All hero stories basically follow the same rules, Tibbs," Hayden said. "Joseph Campbell wrote an extensive work on this called *The Hero with a Thousand Faces,* but I'll give you a CliffsNotes rundown of my version."

This wasn't the first time Jonathan had forgotten that Hayden was a literature major and such topics could suddenly turn into passionate tangents, usually of interest to no one but Hayden himself.

"I like to simplify the formula down to four basic components: the quest, the entourage, the weapon, and the wise man."

"Okay," Jonathan said, actually appearing interested.

"The quest is pretty self-explanatory. There's the monster to slay, the revenge to seek, the treasure to find, and the people to save. You know, whatever the call to action is for the hero."

"Sure." Jonathan nodded.

Collin picked up his laptop and plugged into the headphone jack.

"Then there's the entourage, the hero's groupies. They could be his fellow warriors or soldiers, a comedy sidekick, etc. Of course, the entourage doesn't even have to know they are the entourage; take Lois Lane and Jimmy Olson, for example. For most of Superman's history, they don't even know Clark Kent is Superman."

Hayden noticed that something about this comment seemed to resonate with Jonathan. He sat up straighter, more alert.

"Wait a minute," Collin chimed in, giving away that he was in fact still paying attention. "Lois is Clark's romantic interest. Shouldn't she be separate from the entourage?"

Hayden flip flopped his hands as if weighing the observation.

"Ehhh. The love interest almost always becomes wrapped up in the quest somehow. She is either the person the hero is saving, or revenging, or will end up being the bargaining chip for whatever treasure the hero finally recovers when the bad guy wants to take said treasure away," Hayden stated, then paused and added, "or she betrays the hero, which inevitably leads to a plot twist, or their downfall."

"You've given this speech a lot," Jonathan said as he observed Hayden fielding the question.

Hayden ignored the comment and continued.

"Then there's the weapon, that which the hero requires to complete the quest. This is vague. It could be literal or symbolic, depending on the story. For instance, we could literally be talking about a special sword or an ax the hero needs to slay the beast, a Medusa head to turn his enemy into stone like in *Clash of the Titans*, or it could be the magic key that seals or closes a portal. Symbolically, it could also be something like belief or self-reliance. For instance, Neo, in *The Matrix*, is a hero but he is only able to defeat the villain when he 'believes' he's the hero."

Jonathan nodded again.

"Last, there's the sage, the wise old man, the person who knows the terrain and can tell the hero what to prepare for; what he needs to be, who he needs to be. This is your Mick from *Rocky*, Yoda from *Star Wars*, and Mr. Miyogi from *The Karate Kid*. Frankly, these are all of your most beloved characters, usually preferred over the hero themselves."

Jonathan seemed to wait for Hayden to continue. When Hayden didn't, he asked the obvious question. "So, if it's all so formulaic, why do storytellers keep rehashing the formula?"

"I guess some argument could be made that the stories tend to require regenerating to fit the times," Hayden said. "I mean it's easier for me to watch Superman fly around Metropolis since the setting and state of the world are more relatable to my time in history, as opposed to reading about Odysseus," Hayden said, "but I don't think that's all there is to it."

"So what do you think?" Jonathan asked.

"I think the formula isn't about practicality, as you mentioned earlier. Its use isn't useful in the standard sense. You don't learn to fight, for instance, through watching an action movie. But you might learn to fight because of watching an action movie."

"I'm not sure I follow. That seems anti-climactic," Jonathan said.

Hayden sat back down on the couch.

"We watch these formulaic movies over and over again because they affect us emotionally, Tibbs. They show the way to anyone who might heed the call to action. They tell the tale of how a thousand different heroes gritted their teeth to be what the situation needed. It's not physical preparation, it's psychological. And this formula has been inspiring mankind since the beginning of, well, stories."

Jonathan sat back into the couch himself. He seemed to be thinking it over. Finally, he picked his plate back up off the table and started eating again.

Collin removed the headphones from his ear.

"Hayden, that sure was beautiful. Seriously, brought tears to my eyes," Collin said, rubbing a fake tear away. "Now, can we watch this already?"

"Hit play," said Jonathan, though he still seemed lost in thought.

Jonathan wasn't hiding the fact that he was working out. He'd just been avoiding questions about it. Three weeks after Hayden's hero story lecture, Jonathan knew that if his roommates hadn't suspected it, they were about to.

The beautiful thing about living in an inner city neighborhood was that if you were looking for something, it would likely find you with little effort on your part. Jonathan had been keeping his eyes peeled for a weight set he could set up in the garage. After all, no one in the house was using the space other than Collin for his motorcycle.

Jonathan showed up one day in a truck driven by a stranger he had paid twenty bucks to help him cart the stuff home. It was a good deal; a full weight set, bench, curl bar, and the guy had thrown in an eighty pound punching bag just because he was so happy to get the crap out of his garage.

The gear had seen better days. The weights looked like they were from the eighties and the bench padding was being held together with duct tape. Collin and Hayden helped him unpack the truck with a hint of excitement, though they tried to hide it behind sarcasm. Jonathan took it as a good sign, considering he'd never consulted with anyone about turning the garage into a gym. Despite their geek-loving demeanor, they didn't hate the idea of the three of them pumping iron in the garage.

"Wow, Tibbs," Collin said, "did you have to go to more than one dumpster to find this stuff?"

After that, he'd stopped any efforts to hide what he was up to from his roommates. He didn't mention that he'd been working out with a trainer, but he was exceptionally knowledgeable for a guy whom they had never known to do anything but run. He stopped hiding his supplements in his room. He didn't know if anyone noticed or cared, but every time he got a glass of water to take pills or mix his protein shakes, he'd felt like he was hiding a secret. His tubs and containers now had a new home on the refrigerator right next to all the cereal boxes. It didn't all happen in one day, but it happened fast enough to get Paige worried.

Soon, he heard her in his doorway. Jonathan shut the screen of his laptop so she wouldn't see what he was researching, then turned to speak with her.

Paige wasn't always so aware of Jonathan's day to day. She was in her early twenties and had an exciting enough life of her own. This need to act like a protective mother hen had started the day he'd come home from the hospital. He'd noticed it from Collin and Hayden as well, but their mild concerns were easily written off. For Collin and Hayden, if a guy woke up in a puddle of his own blood, they could assume he wasn't going to be himself for a bit. Just ignore it, give him his space. Paige wasn't going to leave it at that.

He appreciated the concern, to a degree. At least, he appreciated the attention, even if there was nothing he could tell her to explain his actions. He wished she would stop asking him why she hadn't seen him at school. Their majors were similar enough that they tended to frequent the same campus areas quite often. He didn't want to lie to anyone, but the appearance of sanity required a great deal of omission.

"So when did you start," she asked, "weightlifting, is it?"

"Couple weeks ago," he casually replied.

"Is that what you've been doing?" she asked. "Instead of school?"

He didn't respond. When she could see he didn't intend to, she shook her head.

"I don't get it. Why?"

He shrugged, didn't say anything, the same face he gave Lincoln whenever he asked. She wasn't as quick to drop the question. She knew him well enough to know he didn't do things on a whim or without a reason.

"Come on, Jonathan," she said. "Why? Just try to explain it to me."

He could see it; he knew her just as well. She had come into his room tonight because she wanted to know that he was okay and she wasn't going to accept some shrug. She had no interest in being told not to worry. She didn't want to be put at ease; she wanted to understand.

When he had been putting himself in a coma to avoid dealing with what had happened, that at least had an obvious correlation. It didn't take a detective to see why a man who'd gone through a traumatic experience might resort to medicating himself to escape the memory of it. Dropping out of school as he headed into his last year of college to become a health nut and watch action movies—that wasn't making sense.

So, he told a piece of the truth.

"I can't feel—" he stammered, deciding on different words. "I can't be that powerless. Never again."

She nodded; this did seem to make sense to her. "I can understand that," she said, making a point of maintaining his eye contact.

There was an uncomfortable pause. He thought perhaps that she wanted him to ask how she could understand, but he didn't want to know. He didn't want her to share some intimate detail of her life, not when he knew he couldn't share anything in return, so he looked away.

"I hear you at night," she said cautiously.

Jonathan turned red with embarrassment. The nightmares were too frequent to have gone unnoticed. He'd suspected that she'd heard him cry out. He'd avoided thinking about it, as there wasn't anything he could do, no simple fix. Still, his pride took a blow then, as he realized he couldn't tell the truth. She would think it was from the attack, the hospitalization—something seemingly insignificant when compared to his reality, to the Ferox that ripped his throat out every night in his dreams, to the little girl who begged to know why he'd let her die.

He closed his eyes and said nothing. At least it had been Paige who told him they knew, not Hayden or Collin. He couldn't have imagined how awkward that conversation would have been.

"Is there anything you want to talk about?" she asked. "I'll listen. You don't have to keep it to yourself."

"I'm sorry if I woke you. I've been having trouble sleeping, bad dreams," Jonathan said, still red in the face. "I don't want to take the pills again. The exercise helps. It helps get me tired enough…."

He trailed off and sighed. It was all he could think to say, and he wished he hadn't said as much as he did.

"Do you want to tell me about them?" she asked, taking a seat on the edge of his bed.

Jonathan shook his head; he had no intention of opening his dreams to her. The awkward conversation ground to a halt again as she seemed conflicted between the desire to pry or to respect his boundaries.

"Have you told your mother yet?" she asked, changing the subject. "About the attack? About the hospital?"

He folded his arms across his chest. When he looked back at her, he shook his head slower this time.

"She's your mother. She'll be hurt that you didn't tell her about this," she said.

"I don't see any reason she ever needs to find out," he said.

"That isn't what you said at the hospital."

"I don't see what good that would do her," he said, growing confrontational but trying not to raise his voice.

"No one will ever know what happened to me unless that man is caught," he said, choosing his words carefully. "Telling my mother the gruesome details about it will just worry her, then her imagination would run away with itself. I'd rather not give her something to keep her awake at night."

Paige didn't look swayed by any reasons he'd given, she just looked defiant. He'd have agreed with her if he had her perspective on things. What was aggravating was that he had serious problems, like fighting off an army, yet still had to deal with things like keeping his mother in the dark.

"Paige, I know you mean well, but please don't make my life any more difficult than it is. I would consider it a betrayal if you went against my wishes on this."

Her defiance melted from her face. She seemed shocked, then saddened. She nodded her understanding, then stood and made her way to the door.

"Paige," he said, and she stopped. "I know how it looks. Just know that what you see me doing, though hard to understand, is the best solution to the problem I can find."

"You're right, I don't understand," she said, and walked back to her room. He heard her door shutting.

He turned back to his laptop and opened the screen. The web page he had been reading, "How to Survive a Bear Attack," was near useless. He closed the lid in frustration; he hated how hiding the truth had made him come off as such a thankless jerk to his friend whose intentions were genuinely kind. He had trouble imagining a future, should he live to see it, where he hadn't ended up breaking ties with the very life he was trying to return to.

CHAPTER TWENTY

"ACTUALLY, IT NEVER goes the way you think it would," Hayden said.

The garage was cleared out. Collin's bike moved near the large car door. With some assistance from the hardware store, the punching bag was now anchored to one of the ceiling beams. The bench was set up, and the weights that weren't on the bar itself rested against the wall behind it. Jonathan had found some foam mats to cover a majority of the oil-stained floor.; it made a place for stretching exercises in the room. The doorway between the garage and the house now had a pull-up bar that hung from the door trim.

Collin and Hayden had started calling it the man cave the day Jonathan brought the weights home. They all agreed that Paige was more man than any of them, but she seldom came in. Jonathan was pretty sure she was purposely giving him space. There was an alienation between them since he'd forbidden her from intervening with his decision to keep his mother in the dark. He couldn't blame her; no one liked to be given an ultimatum.

He didn't mind the company of Collin and Hayden. It meant there was someone around to spot him. He couldn't push things too hard working out alone. It was too dangerous. He could get stuck under some weight that he was trying to lift or have it fall on him, but with the roommates there to help if he got into trouble, he could push the envelope more. He still had to go to the gym for most of his workouts but this ensured he was always able to use his time effectively, especially when dreams woke him up at five in the morning and he couldn't get back to sleep.

Collin and Hayden hadn't done much working out yet themselves. They were timid about it. They mostly stood around Tibbs, talking about whatever came to mind while he lifted. That was fine; for them, this was just a hobby or a conscious health decision, possibly an interest in looking good naked.

Perhaps it was inevitable, but three guys hanging out next to a motorcycle with an open garage door, lifting weights while talking about comic books, attracted Jack almost immediately. Leah seemed to like the free babysitting. Collin let him sit on the motorcycle. The kid loved it.

"More often than not," Hayden said to Jack, "Batman actually wins in a fight against Superman."

Jack, who had asked the question, hadn't realized with whom he was in the room. He was now getting a much longer winded answer than he'd initially imagined possible.

"How?" asked Jack. "It should be over in, like, one punch from Superman."

"Well, you're right—if it was just a sudden fight that broke out on the street, Superman versus Batman, Superman would clearly win," he said, "but most of their fights, when they've actually happened, have taken place when Batman knew he was going to have to fight a super powerful opponent."

Jonathan was doing chest presses on the bench. He put the weight back onto the rack and sat up, suddenly interested in the conversation after a half hour of hardly paying attention. Hayden always noticed when he had people's attention. The man loved to talk.

"You have to remember, Batman is the ultimate strategist. He wins because he always has a plan. You give Batman a week before he has to be in a fight and he'll be ready. He'll set the stage, prepare for every contingency, and get his opponent to fight the fight he knows he can win."

Jonathan straddled the bench; Jack straddled the motorcycle. Both listened intently. If Hayden had been paying better attention, he would have laughed at how they both seemed to look identical, hanging on his words—Jack because anything to do with Superman and Batman was of supreme importance, and Jonathan because Hayden might be making a point that could help him survive.

"Of course, you have to remember Bruce Wayne is a billionaire, so anything he needs to make a plan work, he can essentially go out and buy," Hayden said, then added, "Plus, it's a comic book, so if you need a battle suit equipped with kryptonite missiles in a week an engineer can cook that right up for you, no questions asked."

"I still think Superman would win," Jack said.

Jonathan nodded and smiled at Jack. He agreed, of course. It seemed Batman was at an incredible disadvantage even if he could stage the fight. Still, it was worth considering. He wished that these Ferox had some kind of kryptonite. He had no way of knowing if they had any weaknesses, unless Heyer was going to tell him about them, and he hadn't seen Heyer since his disappearing act in the park.

The truth was he knew almost nothing, and most of what he knew wasn't very helpful. Their ears were soft spots, but then again so were his. If he lost an ear, he wasn't going to be doing much more fighting, whereas it had only slowed the Ferox down. He knew they could be drowned, but he didn't know where the thing was going to show up; he couldn't depend on it being close to water.

Even if he was lucky again, Heyer had indicated that they might not all be so easily tricked—the one he fought was injured and overconfident, not a situation Jonathan could easily recreate. He knew that a very strong individual could crack through their skin with a wedge and a sledge hammer, but there was still the matter of getting the beast incapacitated long enough to pound through its skin.

Even if he was a billionaire, he wasn't sure what he could buy in the real world that would improve the situation; not to say money couldn't help. Paying for things like training and supplements, food, and even secondhand gym equipment was causing Jonathan to spend more time at Mr. Fletcher's hardware store than he thought wise. It was time he could have used preparing. It was another problem for which he still needed a better solution. He tried to push it from his mind for a time, as he didn't want to appear troubled in front of everyone.

He looked over at Jack. The kid was just sitting there on the motorcycle, happy to be listening to these "men" talking about man stuff. Jonathan wondered about his childhood. Had he also mistaken some twenty-year-olds as "men" when he was young? What did that word even mean? Would he have looked at a guy like himself and thought "that man" is talking about Batman fighting Superman? It wasn't what he would've imagined men doing.

He hardly thought of himself or his friends as anything but well-adjusted teenagers who could legally buy booze. His father had been a man; his father's friends, those guys were men. As he tried to remember why, he couldn't say what the exact difference was; some sense of agency, a better self-esteem. His father just hadn't ever seemed to waver. Had it been his dad in this situation, he would know exactly what to do. He wouldn't be crying out at night with nightmares—then again, he'd died before Jonathan was even thirteen.

He turned back to look at Jack just then. The kid was trying to carefully get down from the motorcycle, scared that he might tip it over and lose the privilege of sitting on it. His legs weren't long enough to reach the ground and he was struggling, but he was getting there.

Sometimes you're just too damn short, Jonathan thought.

CHAPTER TWENTY-ONE

THURSDAY | JULY 21, 2005 | 9:00 AM

JONATHAN PRESSED THE end call button. He set the phone down on his desk harder than he'd meant to. Then he stared at the floor.

More and more, he was making choices he would never have had to a month earlier. It didn't feel that way, though. It felt like they were being made for him. They all brought a sense of foreboding. The gut instinct that every decision forced on him was a bad one. Being bad, of course, didn't stop it from being the only thing he could think to do.

It was funny how sickeningly easy it had been. He hadn't even had to ask the bank's representative. Once they had his account pulled up, they had led with informing him that he was eligible for a larger line of credit.

"We'd love for you to be hopelessly in debt to our bank," Jonathan said mockingly.

He reminded himself that the logic hadn't changed. There were things he needed, and he might as well pull out all the stops, because if he didn't live, it wasn't going to matter.

At least if I die, the joke is on them, he thought.

He didn't have a realistic means to get any more money quickly. If he had a car, he would have sold the thing, but all he had that would have been worth anything to anyone was the laptop he'd gotten when he graduated from high school. He couldn't imagine parting with that as it was his only means of research at home. If things got rough, he could pawn the gold pocket watch his father had left to him. The family heirloom sat in the old cigar box on top of Jonathan's desk.

He took out the watch and flipped it open.

He had the inscription memorized. Still, he liked looking at it, running his thumb over the words. His grandfather had had the inscription put in from the same Rudyard Kipling poem that he'd read to Douglas, the same poem Douglas had read to him.

> *If you can force your heart and nerve and sinew*
> *To serve your turn long after they are gone,*
> *And so hold on when there is nothing in you*
> *Except the will which says to them: "Hold On!"*

The inscription hadn't resonated until now. After having drowned the Ferox, it brought a different shape to the words in his head. He felt guilty, then, that the thought had even occurred to him to pawn the watch. He wouldn't even imagine such an action again, not until he'd really exhausted all other avenues. He drew a line in his mind, one that he wouldn't cross. If he had to, he'd flush his credit score down the toilet before he'd part with it.

Something needs to be sacred, he thought.

The problem was time and job skills. He couldn't spend any more time at the hardware shop, because he needed to be spending every second he could getting himself ready. Unfortunately, he didn't possess any particular skills that he could use to get a higher paying job. It was hard enough to find a part-time job, and without a skill to leverage, finding one that would work around his schedule and pay well enough was damn near impossible.

Before Jonathan had decided to call the bank, he'd even considered stealing, but that wasn't in his skill set either. He would more likely have ended up in jail. He couldn't risk a serious time killer, preparation wise, like incarceration.

He looked up to the mirror on the back of his door now, staring into himself.

Is this really what it's coming to?

He couldn't believe he was weighing the pros and cons of theft to fund his survival, that anyone could come to such a place in little over a month.

It wasn't just his increasing debt that had money weighing heavily on Jonathan's mind. The university had called, wanting to confirm that he would be returning to school next quarter. The call was a warning about the drawbacks regarding his student loans should he not complete his education.

He didn't know what to tell the adviser. Was he ever returning to school? Was that a lost dream now? His life could end in a little over two months, and even if he lived through that, there was nothing saying he would make it much longer. The student adviser had been briefed on the incident that had led to Jonathan's initial absence, but when did the grace period end? How long could he cling to any hope that he would ever get to finish what he'd poured the last three years of his life into?

He'd told the adviser he needed more time to do some thinking and would call back next week. Jonathan doubted he would actually be making that call. Idly, he wondered if they would call his mother about it. He didn't think they could. He was an adult, after all. It was infuriating that he faced death and still worried that she would discover his dropping out, that she would be disappointed in him. What was worse was he really did care; it got under his skin. The look she would give him, the tone her voice would take, the never ending interrogation for which he could give her no satisfying answers.

The Jonathan in the mirror still stared back at him.

"I'll hold on to you as long as I can," he and his reflection said in unison, "but reality is getting too small for both of us."

"Still not breaking on this, then, Tibbs?" Lincoln said.

He wasn't referring to the fact that another week had gone by and Jonathan was still at the gym. He was past any suspicions that his client would get lazy on him. It was that they'd spent over twenty hours together getting Jonathan in shape, and he still had not said why. Jonathan didn't mind that the man asked. He seemed to genuinely want to know for professional reasons, to improve on the training plan.

From time to time, Jonathan dropped clues out of necessity. Like that he was looking to improve his balance or his punching strength. It was safe to assume that Lincoln would come to the conclusion that Jonathan was bat shit crazy well before he would believe that he was training for an inter-dimensional show down with a super-powered monster. Suffice to say, even though Lincoln had begun to assume he was using the training for something connected to martial arts or fighting, it didn't explain the secretive nature of it.

Today, Jonathan decided to reverse the third degree.

"How about you?" Jonathan asked. "What makes you need to be in such good shape all the time? I mean, I'm assuming that the working out led to becoming a trainer and not the other way around."

"It's a little embarrassing," Lincoln responded.

"Yeah? Well, now I'm all ears," Jonathan said.

Lincoln seemed caught off guard as Jonathan seldom lost focus during their training sessions. He usually was as serious as a machine, squeezing every dollar he'd paid out of the session. The trainer had actually found that part of their relationship relieving as he wasn't forced to promote himself along with the training. Jonathan wasn't paying for a coach or a buddy to keep him motivated; he was paying for experience.

"Well, believe it or not, I actually have a degree in theater," Lincoln replied cautiously. "Originally, I wanted to be on the WWE."

Jonathan set down the kettle bell he'd been hefting. It was like getting the last piece of a puzzle he hadn't realized he'd been putting together. Lincoln suddenly made sense to him.

"I could see you doing that," Jonathan said.

He was partly being polite. He knew little about wrestling other than the few glimpses he'd caught accidentally over the years. Mostly, he'd just seen giant men taunting each other with a microphone. He could see Lincoln pulling that off, especially after seeing how comfortable he'd been messing with the two teenage twerps the day he had first come to the gym.

"Originally, the plan was to graduate with a theater degree, bulk up, and become a pro wrestler. Along the way, I picked up so much about body building that I fell into personal training," Lincoln explained.

"I can only imagine how difficult it would be to break into the WWE, probably as hard as getting any acting gig?" Jonathan said.

"It's like any idea you have when you're young. You go get a degree, you get the look, and you expect that someone will just show up on your doorstep and discover you. Of course, it doesn't work that way. There are auditions and a thousand other guys with the same dream," Lincoln said. "It's okay, though. It helped me develop the skills that pay the bills. I still audition sometimes."

"Speaking of bills," Jonathan said, "I think I am out of training hours."

"Repeat customer, good man! I'll cut you a deal this time around, pretty clear this isn't a one-week foray into the gym world for you."

"That would be great, man," Jonathan said. "I need to save every dime I can."

"Do me a favor, though?" Lincoln asked

"What's that?" he asked.

"Use the money to buy some decent gym clothes," Lincoln said.

Jonathan smiled. "Actually, I've been meaning to ask—do you know anyone, in your circles, that does instruction on self-defense? Preferably one-on-one instruction."

Lincoln raised an eyebrow. "Yeah, I have a few contacts in that world."

CHAPTER TWENTY-TWO

FRIDAY | JULY 22, 2005 | 9:00 PM

"**I AM CONFIDENT** that events can be controlled to our benefit," said Olivia, "but the situation is similar to previous cases."

"Explain," said the man on the other end of the line.

Olivia was wearing the same style of clothing as when she had interviewed Grant; thick rimmed glasses, fitted suit. She seldom wore anything else to work. It was well after hours and she had stayed in the temporary office provided to her on the military base specifically to give this report. She had let her hair down to relieve the headache she was feeling from the long day. Soon she'd be heading home, or at least to the transitory place where her suitcase was living.

"The phone tap is effective. All communications are being monitored, as well as the house's Internet feed. However, as with all previous attempts, bugging the house itself is useless. Audio surveillance equipment used to observe the subject is meeting the same interference as has been the case previously. All reports are coming from the eyes and ears of our agents tailing the subject and staking out the domicile. Still, they can only report what they see and hear."

The most frustrating challenge of this investigation, since Olivia had been brought on board, was being technologically outclassed. It meant problems to surmount that she and her team had previously taken for granted. As with previous cases involving the blond man, something about the domicile was immune to their equipment. Microphones and bugs were ineffective. Camera and video functioned, but the sound on the video recordings was always distorted past recognition. Cellular and Internet monitoring only worked because the surveillance could take place at a location away from the domicile itself.

"Has the phone tap revealed anything of interest?" asked the voice.

"The subject has requested an increase to his line of credit." She paused, then added, "He also appears to be withdrawing from his educational career."

There was a pause on the line. She waited patiently.

"Do you have any theories as to his motives?"

"Nothing concrete, as you know. This Jonathan is unlike most of our previous investigations. He doesn't fit the standard pattern. He may very well have no idea what he's a part of and is simply reacting in a manner within the normal expected range of human behavior given the trauma he experienced. On the other hand, he may be reacting to variables outside our visibility."

"Off the record then, what is your opinion?" the voice asked.

To this Olivia paused.

This was yet another instance where the difference between Jonathan and previous investigations concerning the blond man had somehow seemed noteworthy. It was not only a change in the blond man's patterns but in her superior's handling of the investigation. The man never asked for her "opinion." Usually he only asked for conjecture that could be supported by evidence in the reports. She couldn't put her finger on what was causing this subtle change in process.

"In my opinion, his actions are not what they seem," Olivia said. "Though we couldn't get close enough to listen in, we know that Jonathan has met with the blond man. This took place approximately two weeks after the initial incident. They had a long conversation before the man disappeared. How the meeting was arranged without our detection remains unknown, as per usual."

"Thank you for your analysis. One last thing," the voice said. "This Private Grant—you believe he will be able and adequate?"

She'd been prepared for this question. She'd formulated a scripted answer to put her personal observations regarding Private Grant aside. Her impression of the man had been bleak from the start. Despite that she'd asked him to be candid about his personal relationship with the female of the house; she'd found his over-eagerness to share details about the relationship disturbing.

He reveled in having an invitation to explain his sexual exploits to her during his reports. She had felt his eyes on her during their initial meeting to a degree that would raise the hackles of most women. The man's behavior as reported to her from the agents assigned to observe him gave her further hesitance. If she had to put it to words, she would say he appeared to be "getting off" on the assignment. She pitied the girl. Given the background she had on Grant, she pitied him even more. However, her pity wasn't going into her reports.

"Private Grant is an ideal soldier. We have led him to assume that we're operating under the Office of Homeland Security. Once he believed that this was a matter of national security, insinuating a potential terrorist threat, he was eager to be involved. He asked no questions."

"I read in your initial report that he is romantically involved with one of the occupants. As he is not officially part of the team, nor trained for this type of operation, do you have complete confidence that he can adequately serve his purpose?" the voice asked.

"The intelligence we've gained from him thus far has been fruitful. His relationship with the girl provided us with eyes and ears inside the house that we would have been hard-pressed to arrange without raising suspicions. If it was not for this intel, we wouldn't have had visibility into Jonathan's decline in mental state. Private Grant has been present in the house during more than one of the subject's night terror episodes. This does support the evaluation that, despite Mr. Tibbs' apparent cooperation with the blond man, he was in fact traumatized by whatever events led to their relationship."

"Do you believe that his decline in mental state could make him a danger to himself or to any bystanders involved?" he asked.

There it was again; her superior's question. He'd never cared about the safety of involved bystanders in the past. She couldn't put her finger on what was subtly different about his approach to this case. It was making it more and more difficult to be prepared for these reports.

"As of yet, there's no evidence we should be concerned for the general public," she replied. "As for Jonathan himself, I wouldn't pretend to predict the behavior of a person under such great stress with no training to cope with it."

"Agreed," replied her superior. "Do you believe Private Grant will be able to maintain his cover until disclosure?"

Of this Olivia had no doubts.

"Yes," she replied. "He will be easily manipulated and removed from the equation."

"The staging of the disclosure," the man asked, "any thoughts on our best opportunity?"

"Yes," she replied.

As her report was complete and her superior satisfied, she pulled the files she intended to bring home into her briefcase. Her habitual attention to detail and cleanliness wouldn't allow her to clear out of the office until her work space was perfectly arranged for the next day. As she set about the arranging of her desk, she reached over to power off her laptop. Before she did so, she noticed an email had arrived in her inbox.

The header read: Grant Morgan | Background Details | Oversight.

This wasn't the type of email she wanted to be receiving minutes after having given her report. It wasn't out of the ordinary for the contracted private investigators to make a big deal out of something irrelevant, given they weren't provided insight into what was of importance. Still, with some concern, she set her briefcase aside and opened the email's attachments.

She waited a moment for the decryption process. Grant's basic profile had been provided to her before she'd made the decision to involve him. More thorough background information had come in, but everything had supported her decision until now.

The man's history wasn't pleasant.

With a few insights from the investigators, it wasn't difficult to piece together the shortcomings in his personality. He was exactly the despicable outcome she would expect from a person with his upbringing. Going into the army, though not in and of itself a bad influence, had unfortunately bolstered those shortcomings. Still, that made him controllable. She doubted there was any background she could learn now that would change her decision.

She reviewed the files. The investigator had highlighted the relevant changes, then her face lost its composure for a moment. She'd never have let it happen had there been anyone else in the office to see. She didn't relish calling back her superior.

Jonathan was getting anxious.

He was making progress at the gym, but all the strength in the world wouldn't help him if he didn't know how to use it. He needed to learn to fight.

He didn't have time to waste taking classes in a group setting. He needed intensive one-on-one instructions and he needed to start today. Hand to hand wasn't the only thing Jonathan was worried about; he needed a weapon. There was no point going into the fight with nothing but his fists and some stupid notion that his knuckles were going to win out against teeth and claws. In reality, hand to hand had to be his last resort.

Lincoln had provided some trustworthy leads, but it was going to be expensive. Once he began, he would need to be a machine. His life would be gym, eat, hardware store, eat, weapons and martial arts training, eat, and finally sleep. The trainer had assured him that as long as his martial arts training was not deeply cardio in nature, it shouldn't interfere with his muscle growth, "as long as you're pounding out punches on a bag, it should be fine," he'd said.

If he was still able to keep his eyes open by the end of these rigorous days, he would spend it doing "research" with his roommates.

One such night, as he was beginning to struggle with his heavy eyelids, Hayden excitedly popped a DVD into the player.

"This one isn't that well known," Hayden pointed out, "but it's one of those B action movies that wormed its way into my heart."

"What's special about it?" Jonathan asked.

"Well, I might read into the film more than the director or the writer ever intended. It's the anthropologist in me," Hayden said. "Let's just watch it; you can tell me what you think after it's over. It's a Kurt Russell movie called *Soldier*."

As the film began, Jonathan tried to see what Hayden read into it. Whatever it was, it wasn't obvious.

In an unspecified future, baby boys were kidnapped out of a hospital maternity ward and raised to be experimental soldiers. Not conventional training, as the military had complete control over the children's lives and complete authority to brainwash them however they saw fit. The children were exposed to all sorts of conditioning as the leaders of the experiment attempted to desensitize them to any emotions, any mercy, any fear, anything that would make them hesitate during combat.

Out of the experimental children, a hero emerged. He was exceptional, the best of the best, the champion amongst the soldiers, the leader. Though, for the scientists and army generals to maintain control, this man was never given any authority to lead his men.

By the time this champion had become a hardened veteran, his commanding officer pitted him against a genetically modified super soldier, to which he's outmatched. Left for dead, the hero was found by a community living in a garbage dump planet where his body was disposed of. Through his interaction with these people, the experimental soldier was able to witness a normal human life.

Inevitably, the super soldier that replaced him returned under orders to exterminate the community the protagonist has become a part of. The hero was forced to kill the entire attacking squadron and the commanding officer, saving his new community, his people, from being massacred.

In one scene, the female lead asked the hero, who hardly ever spoke, "What does a soldier think about? What do you feel? You must feel something?"

The hero, though at first unsure how to answer, finally replied, "Fear. Fear and discipline."

The woman was deeply disturbed by this and asks, "Even now?"

The solider replied, "Always."

It was the one moment in the film that gave Jonathan pause; was it simply fear and discipline driving him now?

After the final scene, he looked over to Hayden, who was anxiously waiting to explain why he found the film so noteworthy.

"This one is all you, fat man," Collin said to Hayden. "I've never seen anything more than a crappy B movie here." He'd been watching halfheartedly but was mostly focused on a comic book panel he was completing.

"You have to look at what the story really is," Hayden said to Jonathan.

"So, what is it then?" Jonathan asked.

"All things have a spectrum, right?" Hayden asked rhetorically. "There are an infinite number of shades of gray between white and black. I think the writer of this movie was trying to find the most extreme version, the blackest of black, the dark side if you will, of the warrior story, or at least the cultural myth of what a 'male' is," Hayden explained, smiling, as though this answer cleared everything up.

Collin shook his head. "Crappy B movie."

Jonathan ignored Collin for the moment. "Okay, Hayden, I'm interested. If this is the *dark side* of the male cultural myth, then that begs the question—"

"—What's the myth? Glad you asked," Hayden replied ecstatically.

Jonathan knew then that he'd walked into another of Hayden's pre-engineered conversations.

"Think about it a little and it's not that hard; men are told, directly or indirectly, their whole lives that they're supposed to be expendable killing machines. Stories tell us that an ideal male will fearlessly confront the enemy, using his body as a human shield against all that would hurt our community's women, children, and resources. That we're supposed to be able to turn off all emotions; be cold calculating reason, be fearless, and when necessary, be primal rage. That men are warriors at all times and can work like machines until we collapse."

"I think you're being a little extreme," Collin interjected. "What drugs were you on when you came up with this theory?"

"That is the point, jackass," Hayden said responding to the interruption. "This is the extreme. This is the peak of the cultural mythology about the path of the warrior. In the end, the hero is the man who confronts his fear with discipline, who defends the community because it is his vocation to do so, who is perpetually ready for war, and despite all this hardening of his humanity, is somehow supposed to remain, well, human."

"I thought Batman was supposed to be the dark side of the hero story," Collin said, starting an argument.

Hayden shook his head.

"Young Collin, the hero story has many incarnations," Hayden replied.

"You know I'm older than you, right?" Collin reminded him.

Ignoring him, Hayden continued, "Batman is a vigilante. His story has a lot of the same elements, in that he is perpetually training and he defends his community. The reason his story is not as dark on the spectrum is because, in the end, Bruce Wayne chooses to be what he is. The hero in this story was never given a choice about what he was going to be, not 'til the end, when he's abandoned by those who created him and chooses to fight for his own reasons."

To Jonathan's surprise, Collin looked slightly convinced by this argument.

"What is this incarnation then?" Jonathan asked. "The soldier in the movie, what do you call his story?"

Hayden's head bobbed back and forth a few times before he admitted, "I never named it. I've always just thought of it as the dark side of the mythology."

"Weak," Collin interjected.

"Point of fact," Hayden raised a finger and pointed it at Collin, "if I hadn't been so inebriated when we discussed it, I might have pointed out that this is a flaw in your argument that Superman and Jesus share the same story."

Hayden raised his eyebrow, daring Collin to challenge him.

"Oh, do go on, Professor," Collin said.

"Superman is a champion, Jesus is a savior," Hayden said. "A messiah, if you will."

This was followed by Hayden taking an arrogant bow. Collin rolled his eyes, waiting for the theatrics to run their course.

Fear and discipline, Jonathan thought.

It was later in the evening, and he sat in the garage, reflecting on what Hayden had said. The man's tendency to preach, to get up on soap boxes with his extreme theories, was always reason to dismiss him. Yet, Hayden, even if he may never know his own courage, had been the brave one, the one who had volunteered to stand by him when the Ferox was killing in the streets.

Jonathan was on the end of his bench doing bicep curls until each arm grew unresponsive. Lincoln called this, "working to failure." He wasn't keeping count; he just waited until the limbs felt numb from use and he couldn't lift the weight again. His biceps shivered from overexertion; his skin felt tight over the muscles bulging with blood in his arms.

He had considered his actions extreme, but saw now that there was an entirely different level. He could follow this dark side, go to the absolute black of the spectrum. He couldn't change his upbringing, of course, but he could become the machine he had imagined he would have to be to survive. He could do whatever it took.

The bar fell to the floor with a slap against the rubber mat. He couldn't lift it again.

Dammit, Heyer.

He needed to see where this fit in the bigger picture. He needed to know what he was to the alien's purpose. He needed to believe that the truth would make these sacrifices stop feeling like sacrifices.

Time was on his mind a lot lately. What the alien had said, about the time lines, it didn't make sense. Paradox. It was a word he'd heard Hayden and Collin use so many times; they'd get angry and scream it at the television whenever they watched science fiction shows involving time travel. He understood the word now; he understood the confusion, how irritating it was to contemplate. His problem was simple. How can you erase everything that happened, start time over, and still have a dead Ferox somewhere out there? It didn't make sense.

Sometimes you're too damn short, he thought, reflecting on how the alien had kept him purposely in dark.

Protecting him, Heyer had said, insulating him from some forbidden knowledge. Like a parent changing the TV station when an R-rated movie came on. At times, more than the Ferox, Jonathan was afraid of what he was being sheltered from. After all, withholding reality from a person always boiled down to the same thing. Manipulation.

His phone vibrated in his pocket, pulling him out of his thoughts. He reached down and saw that one of his co-workers at the hardware store had sent him a text message.

"Your order showed up today."

CHAPTER TWENTY-THREE

SATURDAY | JULY 23, 2005 | 2:00 AM

GRANT COULDN'T SLEEP. He sat propped up against his headboard in the near darkness of his room. Paige was asleep beside him, naked except for the white sheet draped across her hips. His eyes were tracing her curves. She'd wanted to stay at his place more often the last few weeks. Probably so she didn't have to wake up to her roommate yelling.

Olivia.

He couldn't look at Paige's naked skin without his mind wandering to his handler. At first, he'd just found her off-putting. That woman, with her professionalism, her excessive attention to detail, she didn't let her emotions reach her face because she didn't want him seeing through her. He knew what she wasn't showing though; the power she thought she held over him.

She was another wall between him and the truth. The meticulous way she arranged her files on her desk before she'd uttered a word to him, that calm and flawless way she carried herself, made their mandatory debriefings a maddening struggle with his patience.

He'd reported to her every detail of his interactions with Paige on a weekly basis. Every time, she acted like she was being forced to interrogate a special education child. The more she acted like the boss of him, the more he found himself thinking of her when he was with Paige.

Princess thinks she's got me all figured out.

When he realized how addicting it was, he found himself with renewed interest in taking his government-assigned girlfriend to bed, eager to put Olivia's face behind Paige's expressions, finally rattling her composure with Paige's bare body in his bed. The uglier the betrayal, the deeper the level of duplicity, the more he wanted to repeat it. Just deceiving Paige had had its own small charm at first, but picturing the woman he loathed while Paige was at her most vulnerable—that scratched an itch he hadn't realized he had.

"Observe and report all of your interactions with the girl," Olivia had said, "and, of course, any interaction you may observe between her and her personal associates as well."

Princess Olivia paid well, too—so nice to get paid for what Grant now knew he'd happily continue doing for free. He went out of his way to give more detail than the woman had asked for; leaving out, of course, that he liked to imagine it was her he was having his way with night after night.

Olivia never flinched, never batted an eye. She just took notes, not reacting one way or the other. He knew she could feel his gaze, his disrespect for her position over him, but he wanted to see it on her face. He'd wanted to turn that table since the first day she started playing this game with him.

The woman needed to realize his potential; he could be so much more than a paid informant. He wanted in on the real investigation. Homeland Security didn't give a damn about Paige. Even if such a highly unlikely coincidence were possible, there was nothing out of the ordinary about the girl. She was just a college student, a well-intentioned idiot who wanted to save the world from poverty and global warming; a sexy idiot, of course, or else it would've been much more difficult restraining his opinion about her ill-placed passions.

Yeah, she had some classic daddy issues, if Grant had to guess—liked her men muscular and controlling. It was his favorite thing about the girl, but not exactly threatening to national security.

Three weeks into this now, and *Princess* was still telling him the investigation centered on Paige. It had long since become insulting. It made him bitter with resentment, that he couldn't tell her to her face that she wasn't fooling him, that she wasn't pulling his strings with her boundless well of taxpayers' money. Maybe she knew full well that he wasn't buying it, but that just meant she found him more irrelevant than he assumed.

Paige, unknowing as she may be to the games being played around her, wasn't exactly innocent. She, too, just saw him as a means to an end, a pretty package with an empty jar head. Her attitude of superiority was a different brand, but it didn't change what it was at its core. She was in college and he was just a discharged soldier with no job plans. No clue, of course, he didn't need a job.

One day, he thought pleasantly, you're gonna find out you were just a job, little college girl, and you'll cry and you'll cry because Daddy got the best of you again.

He'd yet to meet a woman he trusted, not as far back as he could remember. The opposite sex had something he needed, so interacting with them became a necessity, but if it hadn't been for all the damn sexual tension that came with being human, he wouldn't have bothered. It was perpetually irritating the amount of time he had to spend just satisfying his body's needs.

When he was eleven, he was living with his aunt and uncle. He'd never met his father, and his mother, hardly an adult when she had him, had died in childbirth. It put a great deal of strain on his aunt and uncle to take him in, a fact his aunt constantly reminded him of growing up. She'd been a monster of a woman, so unwilling to let a man forget the sacrifices she made for him.

She dressed just like Olivia, so perfectly put together, until she got home and the disguise came off. She was always yelling at his uncle, the closest thing Grant ever had to a father. The man had been out of work at the time, laid off. Apparently, he'd been laid off for too long. He'd come home once in a while with a little money he made doing odd jobs in the neighborhood. It never pleased the woman though; she'd look down on his contributions, like he was some retard holding money out to her.

Grant still remembered how his aunt would come home, walking up the driveway in her heels, putting on airs to the rest of the neighborhood that everything was fine. She couldn't handle the illusion she wanted everyone to see. She spent all day at work being perfect only to come home and take out her stress on Grant and his uncle. Grant remembered watching his uncle's shoulders draw in, his eyes becoming downcast at the floor when she came home. It reminded him of a dog that had crapped in the house and was about to have its nose rubbed in it.

His uncle was a timid man, too timid for his own good. Grant never understood it, from as early as he could remember. He knew how strong the man was; why not put the terrible woman in her place?

One day, while Grant was lying on the living room floor watching cartoons, he heard her car door shut. He cringed. The sound of her heels walking up the drive still echoed in his mind. He was only ever happy during the day when she was at work. Once she got home, it was just a never-ending lecture on his uselessness. His uncle never stopped her, never intervened, even when Grant was standing in tears in front of the woman, unable to please her.

That day was different though. She came home, hell bent on ripping into them. It could've been anything. A cereal bowl left out of the dishwasher, Grant's shoes on the living room floor. Her reaction would never match the offense.

Something had broken in his uncle that day. He'd been in the kitchen. She was yelling again. She slapped him, a common occurrence.

"I'm sick of you just acting like a damn toddler when I'm angry," she yelled. "You're not a man, just a useless drag on my money."

Grant had tried to slip up the stairs, but she had yelled for him to come back. He hated her. He just wanted to go to his room where he wouldn't have to hear her tantrum.

"You see this, Grant?" she said, pointing to his uncle. "This is your future. Maybe if you're lucky, you can find a woman to pay for you to sit on your worthless ass all day."

Grant hadn't expected it, but his hatred of the woman had shown that day. She saw the flash of defiance on his face before he could stop it. Eager to crush what little rebellion he had found in himself, she turned away from his uncle and headed toward him, her hand already rising to slap the look Grant had given her off his face forever.

That was when it happened.

His uncle had grabbed her arm; his face had become red with rage, redder still on the cheek she had struck him. She should have backed down when she saw that look. Instead, she just saw more defiance in her inferiors, and she slapped him again, as hard as she could, with all the rage she'd intended to take out on Grant. The sound of the slap, hand against cheek, rang out. When his uncle finally lost control, when he pulled back his fist and hit her hard in the eye, he sent her sprawling across the floor.

Grant remembered being relieved. His uncle had saved him. He'd finally fought back. It would be clear to her; she'd see who had the power now.

The man didn't look relieved though. His aunt lay unmoving on the kitchen floor. His uncle had reached over to Grant's shoulder with a quaking hand, his fury replaced with a deeper dread than Grant had ever seen on a grown man, a dread that he didn't understand. He'd drawn Grant to his chest, hugging him.

Before Grant knew what was happening, his uncle had fled through the kitchen door. It was the last time he ever saw the man. Grant had realized years later his uncle must have thought he had killed the woman with that blow. When he eventually realized that wasn't the case, he hadn't come back. He'd left for good.

His aunt had been worse than ever after that. The embarrassment was impossible to hide. The neighborhood saw her black eye and that his uncle had left them. It didn't take a detective to figure it out. She came back home after work for weeks angrier than ever before; the embarrassment of sitting in an office with the swollen bruise over her eye too much for her ego to bear. Grant was the only one there to absorb it. Still, he'd learned the lesson, even if his aunt hadn't; he knew there was an answer to his problem.

He'd built himself up in high school. As soon as his muscles would react to the training, he'd started lifting weights. He let her yell at him, slap him. He learned to hide his anger as he gained his strength. He waited for the day he was going to take any power she had over him away; then she would be the one afraid to come home.

When the tides had turned, when she came at him one day to belittle him and tear him down, he had pushed her across the living room floor and watched her slam into wall. She had been so frightened then; he'd seen it in her eyes and he'd never felt so powerful. It was the last time she dared lay a finger on him. He wasn't going to be like his uncle.

He'd left for the Army when he was seventeen.

It had all led him here, and he considered himself fortunate. Something important was happening right now, and if he'd gone looking for Jonathan a year earlier, he might have thought there was nothing to find. Had he asked Paige for a drink back then, he would've been long through with her by now. Probably a week after getting in her pants, if he had been on his usual schedule.

Paige was just another girl, even if she'd originally been a hastily-planned way to meet Jonathan without raising any suspicions. A year ago, he wouldn't have likely found anything out of the ordinary. He'd have told her he'd call to make plans with no intention to do so, and then when he didn't—he would ignore her calls. Eventually she'd get the message.

When he wanted to see how far he could push it, he'd wait a few weeks, call her up just to see if he could get her back into his bed after having so clearly blown her off; see if she'd still let him have her even though she knew he just wanted to get off again. Now, though, with this deception between them, he couldn't get enough of her; making a fool out of her made him feel intoxicated with power.

He didn't have an end game for *Princess Olivia*; getting the government handler into his bed would have to wait. Taking orders from someone with tits was just something he'd have to endure for the time being. Regardless, he sat here now and put both women aside in his thoughts, a difficult task with Paige's naked body beside him. This was, after all, not about them. This was about Tibbs.

Jonathan Tibbs, another person who thought of him as some arrogant idiot. That, though, was by design. He'd gone out of his way to give that impression, coming off like some musclebound moron so the guy would let his guard down around him; poking at the man, letting him know that he knew this story about a strange man attacking him in his home was a cover up for something else.

It hadn't worked out as he'd planned. He'd been trying to feel out how to get a reaction out of the man. Grant had over-stepped somehow, he knew that now. Jonathan was supposed to be the son of an Army ranger, not some pussy college kid. He hadn't expected Tibbs to play at being some kind of wimp.

He'd been able to learn a lot from Paige, carefully coaxing the information out of her. It grated on his nerves, as he realized just how much time she spent worrying about her roommate. He was the one she was sleeping with after all; she shouldn't be so concerned about some friend. It wasn't right of her to make him feel competitive with Jonathan, not when it came to the woman's affections. He had no interest in worrying if he had control of her loyalty. That she was so worried about some other man made his deceit all the more rewarding.

When he succeeded at getting her to open up, share things she seemed reluctant to say, he felt like he was winning battles against Tibbs. If it appeared that he was prying too much into Jonathan's business, he'd confess he was just concerned about his behavior affecting her safety, then she'd warm to him, just to relieve his fears.

Tibbs was bad news. It hadn't been obvious at first, but the more events had unfolded, the more he'd thought about it, and he had spent a considerable amount of time thinking about it, the clearer it became.

That anyone had believed the man's fabricated story made Grant indignant. The guy had become a recluse upon coming home from the hospital and was having dreams so bad that he was waking his roommates in the middle of the night. Grant had been there to overhear a few of those himself; he'd even snuck across the hall from Paige's room to listened to the man tossing in his sleep.

Please. Help me, Heyer. Dammit, I'm sorry.

He could swear he'd even heard him crying out for his father. What kind of stress must a man be under to have dreams so disturbing he'd lose his shit like that?

More curious, he'd dropped out of school. Paige hadn't even known what he was doing with all his time outside the house. Grant hadn't said anything about it, but Jonathan had gotten a membership at his gym; he'd seen him there frequently, though he'd never let Tibbs realize it.

Apparently, when Jonathan wasn't at work or the gym, he spent all of his time in their garage.

He was up to something down there; people with nothing to hide don't just decide to drop out of college junior year, train like an insurgent, and spend the rest of their hours in a garage doing God knows what.

No, little Tibbs has got a bad secret.

Jonathan was why Homeland Security had pulled Grant into this. Paige was just a convenient cover story to get him involved, manipulate a person into the house without having to pull too many strings. *Princess* just thought he would blow the operation if she told him who they were really after. He'd thought she was on to him the moment he'd seen the surveillance photo of him at the hospital. Turned out that arrogant woman just saw a convenient tool for the job, but didn't have a clue why that tool really happened to be there.

He'd find out what really happened to Jonathan that night. All that blood and no explanation—he'd seen the house before the roommates had cleaned. Someone was killed on that floor. Jonathan had covered it up with the story about the attacker, and he didn't think Tibbs could pull that off on his own.

Obviously, something about it had set off a red flag at Homeland Security. It had to have been something important, something specific, for all this trouble to be put into watching him, something greatly significant to U.S. security.

What Grant couldn't figure out was why the operation was going at this so sideways. Why bother getting intelligence from someone like him? Why not just bug the house? Get a search warrant, break down the door, and turn the place upside down until they found what they were looking for? At first he thought that Jonathan must be some Unabomber type and that they had wanted to see with whom he made contact. Grant hadn't known what to expect when he'd gone looking for Tibbs himself, but that didn't seem to fit. If he was just a small piece of a bigger operation that Olivia was controlling; Jonathan had to be involved with something bigger than a terrorist operation.

That was what really drove Grant now. Everything was coming together. The world was finally making all the pieces fit into place, to give him what he was owed—his chance to really do something, to be a hero for his entire country after a lifetime of being told he was worthless. It had all been leading up to this, and all fate needed him to do was piece it together. Destiny was arranging things so he'd be there at just the right moment, to stop Tibbs while he had his hand right over the doomsday button.

"Can't hide forever," Grant said to himself out loud.

Paige roused next to him at the sound, but he didn't imagine she'd really heard him.

"What's wrong?" she mumbled in her sleep.

"Go back to sleep, babe," Grant said softly.

She wasn't awake enough to know she was speaking. She rolled back to her side, away from him, and seemed to drift right back. When he thought her far away, he heard her speak again.

"More bad dreams, Jon?" she murmured.

Grant glared at her. She'd spent all night with him, in his bed, and still she worried about that lying bastard.

CHAPTER TWENTY-FOUR

THURSDAY | AUGUST 11, 2005 | 8:00 PM

IN THE CORNER of the garage, a fan whirred. Sweat ran down his face and saturated his shirt. His eyes closed; he stood on the rubber mats that now carpeted the cement floor, listening to the fan blades, visualizing motions he would execute in his mind.

Strong forearms, relaxed shoulders, palm down.

As his eyes opened, the sting of sweat from his brow threatened to cloud his vision. He observed his stance in the mirrors that now lined the garage walls. His instructor's words ran through his mind.

Pull the strike to the shoulder, not the tricep. Sweep the leg, regain your stance quickly, and roll the staff over your neck, strike.

The movements began, his bare feet gripping the floor mats as he performed the precise combination of attacks. The mirror reflected his hard won grace, the result of countless repetitions.

To Jonathan, the maneuvers sometimes seemed like someone else entirely, such deadly precision reflecting back at him, a lack of awkwardness he hadn't previously been capable of. The thoughts that floated in his mind after hours of training, much like the grace itself, seemed to belong to someone else entirely. He only half recognized them as a part of himself, a combination of the clarity of focus, a quietness of mind, and a fatigue he held at bay. It wasn't his first time experiencing this; it was becoming the state of mind he embraced.

Words translated into movements without being so much thought but as if they were sensed. Every attack was efficient, no wasted step, no imperfect strike requiring him to overreach. His hands landed on the staff precisely where he meant them to; his feet precisely the distance from his imaginary opponent as would deliver the most powerful blow and give up the least of his defense. The weapon danced around him like an extension of himself.

Three hundred and sixty-degree spin, reverse, maintain momentum, two handed figure eight, step and strike, smooth, strong, powerful.

Three weeks had passed since Jonathan had asked Lincoln to put him in touch with his martial arts contacts. He'd experimented with a few alternate weapons, but the staff had felt right from the first time he'd picked it up.

It wasn't as difficult to learn a weapon on a theoretical level as Jonathan had expected. He'd drilled every night with the staff. His forearms had become dense with the muscle from perpetual use, his hands callused. He practiced until the movements became such an embedded part of his muscle memory that he could facilitate the motion required as quickly as they occurred to him. He was far more critical of himself than his instructor had been. He absorbed his training with the focus of a starving man hunting prey.

Watch the collar bone, don't over extend your elbow, don't lean forward, strong stance, trust the staff.

Sometimes, he imagined it was the voice of his father, the ghost standing behind him, pointing out the flaws in his technique, coaching him to try it again, to be better. Other times, when he wanted to quit, he'd see Douglas sitting on the steps leading into the house, encouraging him to stay.

He'd been a mess of bruises after his first two weeks of training, but the fruits of all the pain and perseverance were becoming apparent. The dexterity he'd initially found so elusive now flowed from his fingertips as though he'd known how to wield the weapon since birth. The nerves of his body, his shins, and forearms were deadening to the pain of constant assault. He was more familiar with his muscles than he'd ever been.

Still, the problem remained.

There was no real way to train for this fight. There weren't any sparring partners who could prepare him to engage a Ferox, and no Ferox was going to fight him like a man.

Jonathan steadied himself, finding the balance in his stance. He closed his eyes again. From within the self-imposed darkness, undistracted by the perception of sight, he set the stage. The beast came at him. He whipped the staff around him, dodging to the right as its phantom claw reached for him. As he spun, the staff spun with him, sweeping the monster's leg out from under it. Without pause, Jonathan spun again and lowered his frame to strike downward as he came around, the staff following him, catching the beast in the skull just as it completed its fall to the floor.

Amply executed in his imagination, the only tool he had to train against. Back in reality, the staff struck the padding on the garage floor with an unsatisfying thwack.

He opened his eyes.

His technique hadn't been flawless. He'd felt the slight imperfections in his movement. The combination of moves was fresh to him, so he drilled, alternating between his left and right side to make sure he was capable of it on an ambidextrous level.

As was happening more frequently, he felt the deadly grace rising through the movements, felt himself being watched by something within, something growing stronger.

When exhaustion surfaced, he dropped the staff and peeled off his shirt. It was heavy with perspiration. He took a deep breath, sat on the edge of the weight bench, and faced himself in the mirror. In the reflection, he noticed something he hadn't before. There were marks under his arms, between his chest and around his biceps. They looked like scars.

Stretch marks. Lincoln had warned him this was likely.

"Anyone who goes from never lifting weights to training like an Olympic athlete stretches his skin as the muscle grows faster than the skin can adapt," he'd said.

Jonathan didn't like it. The skin looked webbed and shiny. It was ugly, the product of hours of cruelty to himself. The longer he looked, the more the differences surfaced. He hadn't cut his hair in a month; he needed to shave. He was surprised Mr. Fletcher hadn't said anything. He was getting worse and worse about it as he'd had less and less time; things like grooming became more irrelevant. What he didn't like more than any of it were his eyes. They looked tired, shadowed, and something else, something he couldn't put his finger on.

The side door to the garage abruptly opened and snapped Jonathan out of his self-examination. Paige and Leah walked in together, surprising him. Paige seldom came in through the garage, and he'd only seen the two together that one day in the garden.

It occurred to him then, that he couldn't remember the last time he'd spoken to Paige for more than a few moments, not since he'd told her how betrayed he would feel if his mother found out about his attack. The last few weeks had been a blur. He'd set aside everything human and focused on the task of survival. He'd been a machine.

"Jonathan? Jeez, you look like hell," Paige said when she took in his face.

Her eyes started to travel down his exposed torso, shining from all the sweat. She blushed, realizing she'd been careless with her eyes. The awkwardness of it affected both of them, and he became uncomfortable, looking around desperately for the T-shirt only to remember he'd thrown it into the hamper soaking.

"Just for the record, I don't agree, but you might think about shaving," said Leah.

She was the only one not blushing; still, she had succeeded in making him feel nervous again, somehow even more aware that he was half dressed.

Paige, recovering from her momentary lapse, walked over to him, taking his face in her hand and looking at the shadows under his eyes.

"When is this foray into macho bullshit going to run its course?" she asked. "From the look of you, you aren't sleeping any better."

Jonathan tensed, sneaking a glance at Leah. He couldn't help Paige knowing, but he didn't want their neighbor aware of his problems.

Paige was only half right anyway. Exhaustion was getting him closer to five or six hours of sleep most nights. He spent so much time training when awake that it seeped into his dreams, his actions in the waking world helping to cloud the terror and guilt he held at bay at night. Still, his mornings were haunted with the face of Sickens the Fever, syringes and chains, blood and drowning, fresh in his mind upon waking, and those were the softer nightmares. He was grateful every night that the girl in the pink coat let him be, nights without jolts of self-loathing so intense his body was forced to wake him just to save him from the tormentor within.

"When did you two start hanging out?" Jonathan asked, changing the subject.

"Couple weeks ago," Leah said. "Paige's boyfriend needed some welding done."

Jonathan may have been tired, but nothing he had just heard made any sense to him. He looked to Paige.

"You have a boyfriend, who needed welding done? Which involves Leah?"

"Grant needed, what was it, a catalytic converter?" Paige said looking to Leah, who nodded. "Replaced on his car."

"I'll take your word for it, I've no clue what that even is. How'd that involve our neighbor though?" he said, raising an eye brow toward Leah.

"Jonathan, lately it's like you've been living in a cave," Paige said with a sigh. "She's a metal artist. She's been out in her garage building metal sculptures for weeks. You should look; they're amazing."

"Oh," Jonathan said. That he was impressed was clear on his face. "So the photography is just a side hobby then? You weld and do mechanic work just to keep things interesting?"

Leah smiled, enjoying that he was impressed.

"Hey, why not get your sweaty roommate here to take a shower and come out with us tonight," Leah said to Paige, without taking her eyes from him.

"He can't," she said. She shook her head then as she realized it had come out more rudely than she'd meant. "Sorry. I meant you won't, right, Tibbs?"

Apparently there had been a meeting, and now everyone he knew had agreed to call him "Tibbs" when they wanted to push his buttons. He saw Leah mouthing the word, silently trying it out, and smiling as she held his gaze.

Unfortunately, Paige was right. Jonathan had a demanding schedule to maintain and going out with his roommates and their admittedly impressive neighbor would not help his longevity.

"No, I can't. Sorry," he said. "I'd have liked to though."

Paige looked down at the floor and noticed the staff lying there. She'd never seen him training with the weapon before. Her eyes lingered on it before she looked at him again. Her worry was mounting, and Jonathan could see it in her expression. She held in the urge to ask about the weapon, or maybe just decided she didn't want to know.

"Next time, okay, Jonathan? Seriously, I can't remember the last time I saw you have any fun." She tried to say it casually; her worry led him to think there was something else there.

Jonathan nodded, just as casually.

"So you promise?" Paige asked.

He hadn't expected a mere nod to put him on the spot and it showed on his surprised expression.

"You said you'd like to, so what is the problem?' she asked.

"I'm trying to stay focused," he said.

"Take a break, Jonathan, stop being a hermit. It will be good for you," she said.

"Please," Jonathan leaned in and whispered into her ear, so Leah couldn't hear. "Remember what happened last time."

It had come to him so quickly. He hadn't stopped to think of the ethics. He'd made the decision to manipulate her; and the only thing stronger than Paige's worry would be her guilt.

She flushed at understanding what he'd meant. It wasn't as though he was connecting a night out with his roommates as a way to end up bloody on the kitchen floor. She'd forced him to tell her he was afraid to be put in a situation where he'd feel vulnerable.

Jonathan cringed inside with the magnitude of his own bullshit. He couldn't believe it had even come from him. He wanted to take the lie back. Paige didn't deserve to feel like a bad friend just because she was trying so hard to be a good one.

After a moment she nodded, looking sorry. She turned to walk towards the steps up into the house and stopped before leaving the garage.

"I'll just grab some clothes and be back in a sec," she said to Leah before she left, leaving her and Jonathan alone.

For a moment, the anxiety he was feeling showed on his face; another lie, another manipulation, another omission. It wasn't hard to see where it ended. How long would he even be able to have friends? He was jerked out of this when he remembered Leah was watching him.

Half naked and alone with her, a nervous excitement pushed out his concerns. He always felt it with her, even in their briefest interactions, yet she never appeared uneasy herself.

At that moment, she just looked curious, obviously wondering what Jonathan could have said to Paige to side step her request so abruptly. She walked up to Jonathan and tilted her head at him, like a puppy that just heard a noise and didn't recognize it.

"So what is it you aren't saying?" she asked.

Jonathan felt the untimely need to swallow, and tried not to do so.

"What do you mean?" he asked.

"Come on, you're a terrible liar, Tibbs." She smiled at already having already found an opportunity to call him by his last name.

He frowned at her.

"Terrible liars don't do it for trivial reasons. You hardly know me. There isn't anyone I'm going to tell. I can keep your secret," she said. The smile gave way to a more compassionate expression, "That, and I can tell you want to tell someone; you don't like lying."

Her perceptiveness was both relieving and concerning; attractive and at the same time dangerous. It didn't matter how right she was, of course; she'd never be able to understand. He indulged the fantasy of dropping his weight onto her willing ears; the thought that at least someone would know, that someone would see the necessity of his lies and all his actions. She could tell him he didn't have a choice, that he was doing what he had to.

That fantasy was just a lie in itself, though, a sad desire to not be alone, and it was for nothing. The relief would be fleeting, if existent at all, and inevitably lead to more problems not solutions: worried looks, fear for his sanity, advice to get help, perhaps a padded room. It wouldn't end with him no longer alone in his nightmare. It would leave him more alone than ever.

Jonathan started to lie, to tell her she was mistaken, yet when he tried, he hesitated and the words didn't come out. He wanted that fantasy so badly. Trying to weigh it in the moment was impossible. Could he trust her? Could she be so damn pretty he'd ignore reality and let himself make such a bad decision?

When he didn't speak, when she could see his concentration turning the tides against opening up to her, she looked disappointed and backed away. He didn't like it, didn't like that she was backing off instead of coming closer.

He reached out to stop her, gently taking her forearm. The action surprised him as much as, if not more than, it did her. He'd never touched her before. Her eyes widened, and she tilted her head again.

"I'm afraid." The words escaped him, and he shook his head as he wished he could take them back. He started to stutter. "I wasn't—I'm not—"

"—Hey, Leah, on second thought, come help me pick something to wear," Paige called down into the garage.

Both startled by the interruption, a moment passed before she called back up to Paige.

"Okay," Leah yelled. "One second."

When she turned back to Jonathan, her hand reached up, touching his arm.

"Tell me," she said softly.

The interruption had snapped him out of whatever hypnosis she'd had him under. Every cell in his body seemed angry that he was changing course. What had he ever planned to say anyway? He let go of her hand, and smiled at her. The smile didn't reach the disappointment in his eyes.

"Damn," she said quietly, her face returning from compassionate back to curious.

Aware that the moment was lost, she turned to head up the stairs. As she left, a thought jumped into Jonathan's head and he blurted it out.

"You know, I might need some welding done myself."

She shrugged at the top of the stairs. "Happy to help," she said. "Just let me know."

CHAPTER TWENTY-FIVE

SATURDAY | AUGUST 13, 2005 | 10:00 AM

COLLIN FAVORED HONESTY. He'd always been drawn to the ugly and often offensive truth. It was a character trait that won him few friends. Still, he held that it was what he wanted from the people around him, and as such, he would have to give it to get it.

"Tibbs, as your friend," Collin said, "I'm going on record and reiterating that I think this is a bad decision."

"Keep an open mind, I guess," Jonathan said. "I don't need your opinion; I just need you to make sure it works."

Collin frowned at Jonathan.

When did Tibbs become such a dick?

Did the guy realize how rude he would have come off had he been talking to someone, anyone, else? Statements like, "I don't need your opinion," were becoming more and more frequent, when the guy even bothered making a statement. It was disturbing how much a person could be changed by one little incident.

Okay, not so little of an incident, Collin reminded himself. Even now, the image of Jonathan crawling through all that blood was something he forced out of his thoughts when it arose.

They were sitting on a bus headed out of downtown Seattle. It was the third transfer they'd needed to take to get to the White Center area of the city—not the friendliest looking neighborhood they were heading into. Collin had never been there on foot; the idea of trekking through the neighborhood evoked fears of being mugged at gunpoint. Tibbs had asked him to meet at an address, but he'd decided to ride the bus with him instead.

"Tibbs, I don't mean to pry," Collin paused. "Well, no, that's BS. I do mean to pry…."

Jonathan looked impatient, closing his eyes as he appeared to know where this was heading. Collin knew he wasn't the first to ask, but he might be the first who wasn't going to sugar coat it.

"What is up with you?" he said.

"I'm fine. Sorry, I didn't mean to be rude," Jonathan said.

"Come on, Tibbs, you're not 'fine.' Paige has been worried about you for weeks now. Hayden told me he's been praying for you. I've been ignoring it. I figured, after what happened, you earned a few months to get it together," Collin said, "but come on, how much should people ignore?"

Jonathan touched his fingers to his eyelids. Clearly, he was sick of feeling like his behavior required explanation. Of course, the guy could put it all to rest by just explaining it. Collin wasn't especially interested in being overly involved in anyone's business, but he couldn't live with a person who was acting nuts and turn a blind eye to it. That's how people woke up one day to find out their roommate took a sniper rifle to a rooftop while they'd been too busy minding their own damn business. Collin hadn't doubted that Jonathan had his reasons, but Paige and Hayden's concerns had cracked his confidence.

As such, Collin knew his place in their household dynamic. If something had to be said, and everyone was too polite, Collin cleared the air. Admittedly, these issues were usually more like "stop leaving your damn nail clippings in the sink," but still, Paige and Hayden were not going to tell Jonathan that they were afraid of him.

"Let's just say it, shall we?" He paused. "When I say 'worried,' I'm being polite. Paige is past worried. She's closer to afraid for you, of you."

There, it was out.

Jonathan didn't like the word *afraid*; it was obvious on his face. Collin thought he looked almost nauseated by it. How could Tibbs really not have realized it? Be so unaware of his own behavior as to not notice when he had crossed the line of *peculiar* to *deeply concerning?*

"Why?" Jonathan blurted out, immediately reigning in the concern in his voice. He let out a long breath. "How could they be afraid?"

Collin did not detect any hint that Tibbs was being disingenuous. That was what made it even more puzzling. How caught up in his own world had Jonathan become to be so surprised? It was hard to believe that he would have to explain to him how he looked to everyone else in the house, yet that was exactly what needed to happen.

"Tibbs, imagine you're this guy, and you live with a bunch of roommates. No, not just roommates—you started out as roommates but now you're all friends. One day, one of these friends, a pretty standard guy, if not a bit of a workaholic, has something just, admittedly, unimaginably terrible happen to him."

Collin paused, he didn't want to bring up the incident but there was no way around it.

"You understand that this friend of yours is a mess. Frankly, you'd be worried if he wasn't a mess. So you and the rest of your friends do your best to be supportive. Then, this friend, he seems like he's started to process things, like he might pull himself together. But, unfortunately, he's more broken than he realized. He tries to go back to school but he just isn't ready, which again, you understand. You don't even judge him for it, because you can't begin to imagine what he's going through."

Collin stopped again, wanting to make sure it was understood that he made no claims at comprehending what Jonathan's trauma might have done to him.

"You start to feel terrible for your friend, because you hear him screaming at night. He's clearly scared shitless. You know you shouldn't say anything. You don't need to add embarrassment to his problems. You don't think your friend has a damn thing to be embarrassed about though. So you say to yourself, hey, if he wants to talk, I'm here for him."

Collin took a long breath. Jonathan was staring at the seat in front of them, but he was listening; he seemed to want to know what it looked like from the outside.

"Your friend never says anything, so you take the hint, and you don't bring it up. Then he seems to take an interest in things he never cared about before. He wants to watch action movies, he wants to talk about superheroes, he even seems to care when your other idiot roommate goes off on ridiculous rants about these things. He is overly interested in *art reflecting life reflecting art,* blah, blah, whatever. You don't care because you assume that your friend is just trying to distract himself. That he might even be afraid to sleep, or even be afraid to be alone. He just needs time, and if he wants a distraction, hell, it's the least you can do.

"Then, stranger things seem to start happening. He's gone most of the day, but he isn't at school. He starts eating like a health nut. He starts exercising like it's the only thing in life that matters. Still, though, there are worse things a guy could do between semesters. So, you even try to work out with him a bit.

"You start seeing less and less of him. You tell yourself, maybe he met a girl. That would be great, just what the guy needs. But that doesn't seem to fit. Your garage transforms slowly into a gym. Your friend, when you see him, is exhausted. You go days at a time without speaking to him. You catch a glimpse of him one night and his shoulders and arms are covered in bruises. When you talk to him, sometimes you seem to be talking to someone else. Then he starts having this look is his eye that you don't recognize and it's intimidating. He never smiles—well, at least, when he does, you think he's faking. You start to worry that maybe he's so afraid of something that he's becoming dangerous."

His friend looked concerned, though Collin actually found that to be relieving. Jonathan must have underestimated what it would be like to live with him the last few months. The wakeup call looked like it was far worse than he'd suspected.

"Paige said that Leah even asked you to come out the other night and you blew her off. Which, Tibbs! When a woman like that wants you to go out, the word 'no' should have been erased from your vocabulary."

Jonathan's eyes were closed again. He was nodding as he took it all in, but his shoulders were slumping and his expression looked like he had something bitter coating the inside of his mouth that he couldn't spit out. He didn't appear to be denying any of it, and again, Collin found that relieving.

"Now there's this excursion, which, don't get me wrong, I'm kind of excited about, even though I don't get the hurry," Collin said. "Tibbs, it's not like you to do something like this, so hastily. The way things are going, I wouldn't be surprised to find out you went nuts and blew up a Walmart or something."

They sat in a silence, the unspoken finally said. Jonathan sat deep in thought as he stared out the window at the passing streets; Collin stared at the bus seat in front of them. Minutes passed while Collin waited for him to get defensive, to explode with some explanation that he was a misunderstood victim, but Tibbs didn't. He didn't even look worried anymore, yet the words had made him heavier somehow.

When he'd started to worry that he'd done some irreparable damage to their friendship, Tibbs finally spoke. "I don't know what to say," he started. "I'm not crazy; I have no plot to take out Walmart." Collin smiled with relief that he'd said something. "No, I know. I was going too far with that one, but still, you must see that you aren't 'fine' at least."

"I've been taking some instruction in self-defense. I'm trying to get stronger," Jonathan trailed off; this didn't seem to be the road he wanted to go down, so he started over.

"When I needed to act, I froze. When I needed to think, I couldn't," he said, looking Collin in the eye now. "You say you can't imagine what this has been like. You're right; you can't imagine it at all. You have some idea about how someone is supposed to react, like there's some right amount, some appropriate response."

Jonathan stammered, restraining some anger, but Collin didn't think it was directed at him.

"Next time you have to look some monster in the eyes as he forces a syringe into your neck, then we can talk about what an appropriate reaction is."

Collin blinked; he felt himself stiffen.

Jonathan hadn't talked about the attacker, not since that first week. The mere story Jonathan had told about that syringe going into his neck made Collin shiver. Tibbs was right; he couldn't imagine being the one who had to own the real memory of it, the one who had to see it again and again in his nightmares. He thought to apologize for making him explain, but Jonathan spoke again before he could.

"I can't be a person who this can happen to again, Collin. Next time something tries to go for my throat, they can't, they won't be dealing with a scared kid pissing his pants and hoping something will save him." He said this as he pointed to his chest. "They have to be dealing with someone else."

Collin nodded. He looked down at the seat in front of them, breaking eye contact. It would be easier for Jonathan to talk without someone trying to stare into his soul as he did so.

"I don't know how long it'll take, okay? What I do know is that school books and drinking with girls isn't the answer. It's not going to help. I'm not afraid of getting a job after college, or of being lonely. I'm just afraid."

A long time passed and the bus rolled on as they sat in silence. When Collin decided to speak again, he tried to make it clear he aimed to steer the conversation away from such seriousness.

"You know what it is, Tibbs? It's that you're actually doing something, that's what is scaring people."

Jonathan frowned. "I don't follow."

"Horrible things happen to people," Collin said. "Crap, not so horrible things happen to people. They get emotionally scarred; most either self-medicate or go to a therapist and get medicated. Almost everyone openly whines about it though."

"I still don't follow," Jonathan said.

"I'm just saying, when 'Jonathan Tibbs' got scared, he went on a yellow brick quest to find courage and didn't think for a second that he needed to explain himself to anyone. It's actually a little inspiring. Or at least it would be, if you lost that creepy look you've been getting."

Jonathan made a face like his eyes were about to cross. "Really?" he said. "The cowardly lion?"

Apparently Tibbs disapproved of Collin's reducing his explanation to a children's book analogy. Collin laughed. "Well, it's true, Tibbs. I don't think a wizard will give you a badge, but how else can this end? You either find you always had it or you don't."

"No," Jonathan said, and Collin detected a note of defiance, "some things you have to build, you have to become."

Jonathan felt an unexpected relief after talking to Collin.

He'd only told a shadow of the truth, but it hadn't been a lie. The outcome was the same as far as Collin need be concerned. Perhaps when Paige and Hayden heard what he'd said, and that Collin had believed him, they'd stop worrying.

Had things been different, Jonathan would have considered himself blessed to have such friends. Few people, himself included of late, could spare the time to step out of their own little existence and express such concern for another. Few could spare the time to pay so much attention.

Rarer was a friend like Collin, who would risk giving an honest opinion about what he saw, even if his delivery left something to be desired. He'd still made it clear that Jonathan needed to rein in the things that were going to make him seem dangerous to his friends. He needed to make a real effort to pay attention to the face he let the world see.

He knew the "creepy look" Collin had spoken of; he'd seen it staring back at him in the mirror so many times now he no longer thought of it as a stranger.

When they got off the bus in White Center, Collin suddenly seemed wary of his surroundings. The area was littered with gas stations, auto shops, nail salons, and convenience stores. They quickly turned off the main drag and started walking a few blocks into the neighborhood. Collin relaxed once they were back into what looked like normal suburbs.

Collin had been pushing to get Jonathan to go out with the rest of them that evening since they had gotten off the bus. What had been strange to Jonathan was that he was trying harder than usual this time. Jonathan couldn't tell who Collin was pushing so hard for, Paige or himself? Finally, Collin had reminded Jonathan that it was Paige's birthday, as he'd clearly forgotten. His resolve had faltered at that.

"Paige bringing Grant?" Jonathan asked.

"Maybe," Collin replied.

"I don't like the guy," Jonathan said.

"Hate him," Collin agreed.

"So, is that why you're pushing this more than usual?"

"No, not the only reason. We told her we'd try to get you to come."

"I thought you said Paige didn't want to ask me?"

"Yes and no."

"What?" Jonathan asked, getting confused.

"Yes, Paige wants you there, but not *just* Paige," Collin said

"So, who else?"

"Your mom," Collin said.

Jonathan's eyes went wide and he spun in his tracks to find Collin giving a sarcastic expression.

"I'm kidding, Tibbs," Collin said, surprised by Jonathan's concern over a bad joke from the nineties. "The neighbor girl, Leah; she wants you to come. I don't think I was supposed to tell you that, though."

"Sorry," Jonathan replied. "I just freaked a little because I haven't told my mom about school yet."

"Hasn't the school notified her that you took a leave of absence for the quarter anyway?" Collin asked casually.

"No," Jonathan said, concerned by Collin's tone. "Why would they?"

"I'm assuming she co-signed on your student loans, right?" Collin asked. "Seems like they'd at least notify her."

That this might be possible hadn't occurred to Jonathan. He made a mental note not to delay following up on it now. Unfortunately, it was a Saturday, and there was no one to call until the work week started.

"I haven't formally dropped out yet; they are giving me a quarter off," Jonathan said. "I still need to call about it. I need to decide."

Collin just looked at Tibbs like he thought it was a mistake. As understanding as Collin had been, missing a quarter was one thing; dropping out entirely was just stupid.

"I've been avoiding it," Jonathan explained.

"Whatever, man. Your life. I'm not judging, dumbass." The last part he said in a fake whisper. "What about tonight?"

"I'll think about it," Jonathan said.

The conversation ended as they reached the address they were looking for. When they knocked on the door, an older lady answered.

"You the one who called about that piece of crap in the garage?" she asked.

Jonathan had five hundred dollars in his pocket. It was all he'd been able to pull together for this purchase. "Pull together" in this instance meant that for the last few weeks any purchases that could go on a credit card had: food, training, supplements, everything but rent. It was the only way he could hold on to enough money from his actual paychecks for things he couldn't finance.

"So he's test-driving it?" the old woman asked.

Jonathan nodded.

"But you're buying it?" she continued.

Jonathan nodded again.

He waited on the sidewalk with Eileen, the old woman who had answered the door a few minutes earlier. It was semi-awkward; his presence there was more to assure her that Collin wasn't stealing the motorcycle they had come to see, Jonathan being the collateral should Collin not come back from his test drive.

"You going to need to test drive it as well?"

"No, ma'am. If he says it runs fine, that's all I need," he said.

"Good," she said. "Don't want to be missing my soaps over this."

They heard him coming long before they saw him. Collin pulled up on a Honda Hero from the mid 90's. It looked like something he'd expect to see in a bad post apocalypse movie. Its original paint job was black. The fuel tank was dented and the paint scratched off. Whoever had owned the thing had dropped it going pretty fast; he could see that it had skidded to a stop over a paved road. The left foot pedal was bent from the fall but still usable. The seat cushion looked as though it had cracked from sun exposure. He killed the engine and pulled the helmet off.

"Well?" Jonathan asked.

Collin shrugged.

"Well, it's safe to ride. It handles for crap, but it's got a bit of speed on it. I can fix the foot pedal in the garage. I heard a rattle but I think I can fix that too," Collin said, looking confident.

"Is it worth five hundred dollars?" Jonathan asked.

"Well, just because it might be worth it doesn't mean I'd buy it. But yeah, it'll run. Most of the damage is cosmetic. Frankly, I'm surprised you found this thing, and she's throwing in the helmet and the cover?"

"Throwing it in?" exclaimed Eileen. "The ad said you have to take it all. I want the damn thing out of my garage."

"It took a lot of patience and Craigslist searches," Jonathan said to Collin, as he handed Eileen the money, then he held his hand out to Collin for the helmet.

"Wait, you expect me to walk home now?" Collin asked.

"Hey, man, I asked you to meet me here, didn't I? Anyway, I need to get Paige a birthday present," Jonathan said.

Collin glared at him.

"I really don't get why you can't just borrow my bike," Collin said.

"I'm thinking of making some alterations," Jonathan replied.

He pulled into the garage and parked his motorcycle. On the ride home, he'd named her Eileen, after the impatient old lady that had sold it to him. He had to agree with Collin; Eileen wasn't as agile as a newer bike. She was decrepit, damaged, and poorly taken care of, but none of it mattered; when the time came, she'd carry him swiftly to his destination.

He pulled off his helmet. It, too, showed the marks of the rider that had taken the fall. Collin said he should replace it, that it wasn't a good idea to wear secondhand gear. Jonathan didn't have the money for that though. He set the helmet down to rest on the bike seat, and then walked across the yard to knock on his neighbor's door.

Jack answered. He was still in pajamas.

"Oh, hi, Tibbs," Jack said with a mischievous smile.

Jonathan frowned at the child. He'd been put up to calling him that name. "Your big sister around?"

"She's working in the garage. I'll show you," the child said.

Jack ran past Jonathan and out to the front driveway, the way all children do when they're excited to be of help to an adult. Jonathan followed. When they stood in front of the garage, Jonathan could hear the sounds of an air compressor being masked by loud classic rock music from behind the door. Jack indicated for Jonathan to pull up on the door handle near the bottom.

"I can't lift the door yet," Jack explained.

"Maybe now isn't a good time?" Jonathan asked. "Sounds like she's busy in there."

"It always sounds like that," said Jack. "She usually leaves it open. It's just a bit cold today."

Jonathan nodded, reaching down to pull up the door.

Immediately, he understood how Paige had been incredulous at his not knowing what had been going on in their neighbor's garage. Leah's back was to him; her hair was braided down her back. She had on welding gear: a mask, thick gloves, and an apron that covered her clothes. When the door opened, she turned to see Jonathan standing beside Jack with his mouth hanging open.

The statue sat on a platform at the back of the garage. It was almost completed from the looks of it. The piece stood tall, only a foot from touching the ceiling of the garage. It was made of steel strips that had been meticulously bent to form the contours of a man. The light from the open door reflected off the surfaces. It didn't shine like stainless steel; it was a dark brushed metal. To Jonathan, it looked like a man holding a blacksmith's hammer. She was still working on its last arm. The finished arm held the hammer. The skeleton of the other arm looked like it was holding a piece of unfinished scrap metal.

"Well, that's the expression I always hope for," Leah said after she'd flipped up the lid of her helmet and killed the torch.

Jonathan closed his mouth, pulling his eyes from the statue to Leah.

"It's amazing," he said.

She was pleased that he liked her art. It showed in her eyes, but her lips scrunched like she had just tasted something tart, and she tilted her head at him as she was prone to doing when she got curious about something.

"Oh, everyone says that," she said. "What I'd like to know is what it makes you think of?"

Jonathan looked at the statue again. The question felt like she was a therapist holding up a Rorschach inkblot and asking him what he saw.

"It looks like a steel blacksmith shaping steel. As if you're saying…." Jonathan paused. "That man shapes himself?"

"Hmmm," she said, looking at it again from Jonathan's perspective. "I was curious what it would evoke. I hadn't been thinking of the symbolism, but I do like your take on it."

"Not sure it's the truth, though," Jonathan said.

She frowned at him. He didn't see the look right away, as he was still gazing at the statue. Finally, he turned back and noticed her staring at him with a perplexed face.

"What?" he asked.

"Just weird that you of all people would say that," she said.

"How so?" he asked.

"I don't know a ton about you, but the one thing I've noticed since I moved in is that you work a great deal to shape yourself." She nodded back to the statue. "Steel shaping itself, flesh shaping itself, same difference."

Jonathan understood her perspective. People around him didn't know that circumstance was shaping him, not any decision he'd made himself. She might have seen all the work he put into his body as some form of creation, some kind of art, something comparable to the work she'd put into the statue to bring the shape to life. She couldn't know he was bending to someone else's design.

He wasn't creating something to be marveled at; he was trying to build a weapon scary enough to frighten monsters.

"You're shaping the statue. You are creating the illusion that he is shaping himself of his own choice," Jonathan said. "The statue just has to hope you have his best interests in mind."

"That's a depressing take," she said. "It takes away any say he has in creating himself."

She mused over the idea.

"Meh," she said, "that's just the kind of bull that comes up when you try to make art that reflects life. The rules applying to art aren't the rules applying to man."

Jonathan grinned and looked down at the ground.

"What?" she asked.

"My roommate, Hayden, would've loved to have been a part of this conversation." He looked back up at the statue then and changed the subject. "It doesn't have eyes. Is it supposed to be a blind blacksmith?"

"I'm working on getting it some eyes," she said. "Though for now, I kind of like the idea of a blind blacksmith shaping itself. Maybe I'll just tie a blindfold over his face."

Jonathan looked up at the metal statue one last time and remembered why he had come over in the first place.

"I wanted to see if you would take a look at something for me," he said.

"This about that favor you needed?" she asked.

"Meet Eileen," he said.

"Wow," said Leah as she set eyes on Jonathan's motorcycle. "Where did you find this piece of junk?"

"Blue light special at the flea market," he joked.

She grinned, but her face betrayed that she wasn't sure if he was kidding. Jack, content just to be sitting on it, didn't seem to care that the bike was a mess.

"I had Collin check it out. He says it'll run. That's all I need it to do," Jonathan said.

She nodded, but still looked skeptical. "So what do you need from me?" she asked.

Jonathan walked over to the cabinet where he stored his training staffs. Beside the practice weapons was a thick steel demolition bar. It was heavy, hexagonal in shape, coated with a rust resistant black oxide. The bar was the same length and height of the practice staffs, but thicker, with ends that looked like giant flat head screw drivers. He held it parallel to the side of the bike.

"I need to weld on clasps for this so that I can easily clip this bar on to the bike when I'm riding. I need to be sure it won't slip loose and that it doesn't hinder any of the operations of the bike. Also, I need to be able to get it free easily," Jonathan said.

She looked up at him questioningly from beside the bike. He could see this wasn't the type of welding she'd imagined him asking for.

"No big deal to do the alteration, especially since I don't think you'll care how it looks. We'll put it on the side where the fuel tank is dented and the paint is scratched off. But...." She paused as she rose from kneeling beside the bike. "Why do you need to carry an oversized crowbar around?"

"It's a demolition bar, a rather expensive one that I had to special order," he said. "I've been looking at getting a side gig on a demolition's crew, but I don't want to leave this at work sites."

The beauty of this lie was that it wasn't a lie at all. Jonathan had been looking into an employment change with a demolitions crew as Mr. Fletcher had offered to help him with his current monetary issues. Running a hardware store gave the man a wide net of acquaintances that were always looking for a hardworking young man whom a trusted colleague like Mr. Fletcher could vouch for. The part about needing a special crowbar was complete crap, but at least if the story ever came up, it would sound legit to someone like Leah.

"That sounds like it's half BS to me," she said.

Or not, he thought. Jonathan was about to defend his story, but she stopped him.

"Tell you what, Tibbs," she said. "You come out with us tonight, I'll do your welding, and I won't ask what it's really for."

Her offer not to require he explain himself was relieving, but much like buying the motorcycle had usurped his schedule, it now looked like this evening was going to be a wash as well. Luckily, he didn't have a shift at the hardware store today, so he still had the rest of the afternoon. September was looming closer. The deadline was charging at him, whether he was ready or not. The only reason he could agree to forfeiting a night of training was if it was at least in an effort to move forward. Of course, it being Paige's birthday also weighed in; he might not be there for the next one.

"Tibbs," Leah said. "It's getting offensive that you need to think about it this long."

"Deal," he said, sticking out his hand for her to shake.

"How formal," she said, shaking his hand.

CHAPTER TWENTY-SIX

SATURDAY | AUGUST 13, 2005 | 3:15 PM

HE STRUGGLED TO keep from growing frustrated as he threw his strikes into the punching bag, the familiar feeling of sweat beading up onto his forehead. With every punch that landed on the canvas, he reprimanded himself for the imperfections in his technique.

His hand-to-hand wasn't progressing as well as his weapons training. The fighting style couldn't be learned as quickly. This realization, with his slow and disjointed rate of improvement, crept into his thoughts, regularly poisoning his confidence.

To be a master of hand-to-hand required a greater degree of fluidity gained through sparring and real life experience, a development of movements that needed to be instinctual, but on a deeper level than the staff. Jonathan was hard-pressed to fit such a transformation into his deadline. If he'd already been acquainted with a fighting style, the standard body movements from an earlier age, it would have helped him immensely on the onset. As it was, Jonathan had never so much as taken a kickboxing class as a child. His mother had never pushed him toward such things and he had never pushed himself.

Through Lincoln's contacts he'd been able to gain private training from a professional, much like his staff instructor. His teacher gave him praise for his degree of focus and commitment. The praise was, of course, lost on Jonathan. He was used to this reaction, much like with Lincoln training him at the gym and his staff instructor; they seemed to covet what they saw as raw determination.

The teachers could not find it in themselves, because they still believed that what they were seeing was "determination"; a desire inspired by an aspiration could not contend with need. Desire might gain strength from praise, but it did nothing for true need.

The instructor he'd chosen taught the Keysi Fight Method. Having no background from which to draw on, Jonathan had picked KFM because it was principled on effectiveness. It wasn't a martial art meant for recreation, but for reality. It was a hard decision to research, as reality would be bent when he fought a monster capable of knocking him through walls with a single strike.

Keep your chin tucked in, shoulders up, he chastised himself.

He caught himself dropping his arms again and turned away hastily.

He fumed for a minute and forced some deep breaths. It was better to let his irritation run its course, he'd found, than to force himself to try and struggle through it. Frustration could sometimes lead to a completely wasted training session or even a back slide if he allowed it to become strong enough.

Take a moment, his father would say.

It was then, while he tried to let his anger seep out, that he noticed he was no longer alone in the garage.

The blond man with his fedora stood against the wall, watching him train.

"Crap!" Jonathan jumped, his irritation replaced with shock.

"I apologize. I didn't mean to startle you, but you looked so focused," Heyer said. "I thought it best to wait."

Jonathan laughed at himself. Here he was training to be some kind of warrior and he'd practically jumped into the rafters.

"It looks as though you have taken my instruction to heart," Heyer said. "I'd wager you are twenty pounds heavier than when I saw you last."

He'd expected he'd be angry when he saw the alien again. Instead, a tension he'd blamed on the stress of his circumstances relaxed. It was one of many burdens, but still, as it happened, he became aware of how much it had weighed on him, how he must have adapted unconsciously to carry it. Only as it lifted did he realize how heavy it had really been.

"Let's hope it's worth it," Jonathan replied. "If I end up dying anyway, I could have spent the last three months in a drug-induced coma instead of wasting the time I had left."

Heyer's expression looked concerned at Jonathan's grim outlook.

"I don't think you ever would have done that, Jonathan," Heyer replied.

Jonathan frowned at him.

"Oh, you were being comical," Heyer said.

"I'm glad to see you," Jonathan said, letting it show on his features that he was as surprised to say it as Heyer likely was to hear it. "Frankly, I question my sanity sometimes."

"I apologize that I have been absent so long," Heyer said. "You know, it's funny—all the technological advancements of my species have colluded to make me busier than any one man should be required. I can't imagine being constrained to a 24-hour sleep pattern as humans are. But I digress; I returned as soon as I could."

Jonathan found it odd that the alien referred to himself as a man.

"Don't suppose I can ask what you were off doing?"

"I was engaged in a matter of diplomacy on the East Coast until a few moments ago," Heyer said. "Off planet before that."

Jonathan nodded. "So you're just going to be purposely cryptic then?" he said. "I guess I shouldn't be asking anyway."

Heyer halfheartedly smiled and began to pace around the garage. Tapping his foot against one of the weights Jonathan had left on the floor, reaching out and pushing the punching bag to see it sway, he seemed more human for a moment as he busied his body with the examination of the room. It reminded Jonathan of the way his grandfather used to look when he'd taken him garage sale shopping as a kid.

"It's not my aim to keep you in the dark, Jonathan. But the less you know, the safer we both remain. In the end, there is nothing I could reveal to you that will serve you in any useful capacity. Still though," Heyer paused, appraising Jonathan before committing to anything. "I understand what it is to want to know what you are a part of. It is not, after all, a desire unique to man."

"What does that mean?" Jonathan asked.

"Perhaps...." Heyer emphasized the word and let it linger. "Once you've repelled the next inbound, we will discuss *some* of your questions," Heyer said, stressing the word *some* as deliberately as the word *perhaps*.

"What?" Jonathan said skeptically, unsure of what the alien seemed to be offering. "Is that your idea of a reward?"

"No, Jonathan, I would not consider knowing anything about our arrangement a reward," Heyer said. "More of a responsibility."

"I don't get it. What difference does it make if you tell me now or later?" Jonathan asked.

"There's still some time to pass before that next Ferox breaches the gates," Heyer said. "Between then and now, you and I may find we need to be able to trust each other."

The word *trust* seemed to cause them both to pause. Jonathan hadn't previously thought of trust as something Heyer would need of him. Reflecting on the notion, Jonathan wasn't sure if he could ever trust the alien.

"I'm not sure how people in a situation like ours go about building trust," he said bluntly.

"Nor I, in fact," Heyer said, with a small grin, "but, despite how difficult things may seem now, information is a heavier burden than you imagine. There may be a time when you think fondly of these days, when your only concern was killing a monster, when you may wish you could go back to being in the dark."

Jonathan began to argue, but Heyer put his hand up to stop him. "It is not a point of debate, Jonathan. It is my responsibility, and I must decide the burden you are prepared to carry. I do not think it wise that you carry any more weight into your confrontation with the Ferox."

They stared at each other as the alien's decree sank in.

"Time is drawing near, Jonathan," he said. "You have had some time to adapt to your situation, to think about the challenges ahead. I came to see if there was anything I could do to help you."

Jonathan teetered back and forth like a rebellious teenager, not wanting to be told that the discussion was simply over, but seeing the necessity of changing topics. Finally, he quashed his rebellion and started asking other questions.

"Do the Ferox have any weaknesses?" Jonathan asked.

"No, at least not outside of what you already know. Drowning or blunt force trauma," Heyer replied.

"Can't you give me some kind of weapon to fight them?" Jonathan asked. "A space gun or something?"

Heyer looked like he was coming close to rolling his eyes at such a juvenile question. "No, Jonathan, if things were that simple, there would be no need for our current arrangement. Outside of the device implanted in your chest, I cannot help you by any means that are not of this Earth." Heyer said.

"That sounds like—" Jonathan paused. "That sounds like a rule."

"In fact, it is," Heyer replied. "But for the record, I do not possess an armory of the kind you are imagining."

"If you can't help outside of the device, can you make the device itself stronger?" Jonathan asked, pointing to his chest.

"No," Heyer replied.

"Why not?" Jonathan asked.

"I did not build the device; I do not know how it works on an engineering level," Heyer said.

"What do you mean you don't know how it works?" Jonathan asked incredulously.

Heyer, looking slightly exasperated, glanced around the room until he noticed Jonathan's cell phone on top of a cabinet. He walked over and picked it up, holding it before Jonathan.

"Jonathan, do you know how to operate this cell phone?" he asked.

"Yes," he said.

"Do you know how to build one, or make this one any better?" Heyer asked.

"No," Jonathan said, dejectedly seeing Heyer's point.

"It's the same with technology from my civilization," he said. "I'm not an engineer. To give you better context, I once had to make a modification to your device. If an engineer of my people had seen that attempt, it would have been like watching a toddler trying to break the encryptions around the Pentagon."

Jonathan found himself disarmed when the alien compared himself to a child. Heyer always seemed so grave in his explanations; it seemed inconsistent that the alien did not in fact take himself just as seriously.

"With the assistance of artificial intelligence, it took me over ten years to make that one adjustment," Heyer explained.

"Well, fine, fair enough," Jonathan said. "Can you get an engineer from your species to help?"

Heyer sighed. Clearly, these weren't the sort of questions he had intended to be fielding.

"No," he said. "It is not an option."

"Why wouldn't someone help you?" Jonathan asked.

Heyer shook his head. Apparently this information was off limits as well.

"Let's try to stick with practical matters, Jonathan. Just accept that if there was some simple technological way for me to make your confrontation any easier, I would have already told you," Heyer said.

Jonathan thought about that for a moment. Like most things Heyer told him, there was little more that he could do than accept them as truth, as skeptical as he might be. There was no way to fact-check the alien.

"Heyer, what would you be doing if you were me?" Jonathan asked.

"I think you have the right idea, Jonathan. I've only seen a Ferox brought down by those who brought a superior offense; no small task, I know, but not impossible, as you've proven. As you've surmised, our inability to plan beyond knowing the window of time it should appear in, and knowing roughly a ten-mile radius of where, makes setting up a trap almost impossible," Heyer said.

It was disappointing to Jonathan; the man who knew all the real details of what was happening and what he was up against had not been able to come up with a better solution than Jonathan had flying nearly blind. Yet, there was one piece of information that Jonathan realized he hadn't known previously.

"Wait, a ten-mile radius of where exactly?" Jonathan asked.

Heyer paused.

Had the alien slipped and told him something he hadn't intended? He looked Jonathan in the eye now, as though he was carefully choosing his words.

"Let's just say, roughly within ten miles of where we stand," Heyer said.

"Why would my garage be the center of a ten-mile bull's-eye for these damn things?" Jonathan said, hearing the anger creep into his voice. He felt this disclosure reeked of some betrayal on the alien's part, but he already knew that Heyer wasn't going to answer him. This detail—it seemed to be screaming something at him but he couldn't put his finger on what it was.

"Jonathan, please. Let's return to matters of utility," Heyer said, and before Jonathan could argue he changed the subject. "What is your strategy? You don't intend to face your enemy with nothing but your hands."

Jonathan's inner struggle was showing on his face again as he did not want to relinquish the pursuit of his previous question. In the end, if the alien wasn't going to explain; there was nothing he could do to make him. So he dropped it for the moment and responded.

"No," Jonathan said as he walked to the cabinet where he stored his practice staffs and opened the door.

"Yes," Heyer said, "the bo staff; an ideal choice."

"I've trained every day with this. The problem is," Jonathan said, "there's no way to practice fighting a monster."

Heyer nodded, understanding the complication. "Yes, I imagine it would be odd to persistently request your sparring partners fight you unarmed," he said. Heyer removed his trench coat and laid it over the weight bench, then checked his watch. "This I can help you with, Jonathan. You will attempt to strike me."

The alien went about removing his shoes as though he'd not said anything out of the ordinary. He placed them neatly under his coat.

It made a sort of sense. Jonathan remembered hitting the alien with the baseball bat. It was unlikely that he could hurt Heyer without the aid of the device in his chest. He paused a moment, mulling over if he could truly attack the alien now, but quickly embraced the opportunity.

It was the best practice he could hope for, unless he could talk Hayden or Collin into running around the garage in hockey pads while he tried to take their heads off. This was considerably less dangerous.

Jonathan nodded slowly and picked up the training staff. They faced one another in the center of the room. He noticed, then, that there was a glow from beneath Heyer's shirt. It was not unlike the glow Jonathan had seen on his own chest when he'd been activated. Heyer's glow was yellow though, and less pronounced. The lines were smaller, not reaching around his entire torso but centered into the place where his chest and stomach met. None of the yellow lines crossed; they ran parallel, one on top of the other.

Heyer, seeing Jonathan distracted by the light, addressed his unspoken question. "Yes, it is not unlike the device in your chest, Jonathan. Its power source is not tied to the presence of a portal stone. Do not let it distract you. Focus on striking me."

Jonathan nodded, and readied himself. He started with a display of skill, whipping the staff around him in a manner that demonstrated his aptitude with the weapon.

Heyer raised an eyebrow. "I'm not sure if a display of pointless maneuvers will intimidate a Ferox," he said. "Strike me. Do not hesitate should you succeed. Follow through with any combinations you initiate. The enemy will not stop to applaud you at each success. Nor will I."

Jonathan stood, unsure of himself after Heyer's instruction. The way the alien spoke indicated to him that he was familiar with the weapon. He would not likely be engaging a clumsy opponent.

He began to circle the alien. Heyer matched his movements. Finally, he let loose with a series of strikes. Most swiped air; some the alien was forced to block with his forearm. Occasionally, it appeared he purposely let a blow land on his back to gain better footing. The maneuvering ceased when Heyer's hand found Jonathan's throat.

Jonathan stopped and made eye contact with the alien, afraid of the strength he knew the hand on his neck was capable of, acutely aware of how the moment reflected their first encounter.

If Heyer made the connection, he didn't let on.

"Do not stop because your defense failed, Jonathan," said Heyer. "React like you would to a Ferox with a claw on your throat."

Jonathan felt his jaw clenching as aggression rose up inside, pulled forth by Heyer's challenge. He sensed the rage there, more and more often, observing him as he trained, growing stronger as it watched him become a weapon. He still felt a distrust of it, a fear of letting it take control, and yet, as he looked into the alien's eyes, its presence dulled his fear, overshadowed it with a resolve, a focus, a predatory gaze.

Fight-This-Guy-Hard.

He brought the staff up into Heyer's wrist, simultaneously kicking the man in the chest, propelling them apart. He landed in a ready stance and refused to let the alien have a moment to think, moving back in with a new combination.

He held back nothing now that the rules seemed clear. They sparred like this for over an hour. Heyer, obviously the better fighter, never let Jonathan land a real strike. That was fine by Jonathan, although frustrating. He wanted to know that when he succeeded, he'd done so because he had outwitted his opponent, not because the man had let him get a shot in to boost his ego. The alien wasn't a paid instructor giving him praise; he understood the necessity of the training.

Heyer never broke a sweat. Meanwhile, Jonathan's clothes clung to him. He never hit back, only tapped Jonathan when he'd left himself open. They both knew they couldn't risk an accidental injury. Jonathan getting hurt before being activated would be too devastating to their efforts. Jonathan wished it could be possible to train like this every night. He already felt deadlier than ever, even if he'd never succeeded in landing a single strike. The sparring revealed countless flaws in his technique, things his imagination couldn't have predicted. It was the best experience he could have to prepare for the Ferox.

When Heyer noticed Jonathan was visibly exhausted, he put his hand up as to indicate that they were done. Jonathan accepted the offer and resisted the urge to drop down on a knee and divulge the true level of his fatigue.

"Jonathan, that you have achieved this level of skill in such a short time shows a true understanding of what you face."

Jonathan shook his head, gasping for air. "Heyer, I didn't land a single strike," he said.

"I am no Ferox," he said. "I've trained in your species' various martial arts longer than you have been alive. I never had any real expectation that you would hit me, but a Ferox does not fight like a man. Their sense of strategy is different. They rely on their formidable strength and speed, their senses and instincts, their armor. They do not train like you. I watched you adapt as we sparred. You learned quickly, corrected your flaws almost immediately. I believe you will outwit them."

Jonathan nodded. At least this compliment came from someone who actually knew what he faced.

"I need to leave," Heyer said, checking his watch again. "I will come by again soon."

"Wait," Jonathan said, his sudden concern obvious. "Is there a way I can reach you? A cell phone number, an address, something?" Jonathan asked.

Heyer put his coat on and slipped back into his shoes. "I will consider this, Jonathan. Right now I do not have a good means for you to contact me. I know how it sounds, but you have to understand that typical human communication methods are easily traced," Heyer said.

Jonathan found the statement as odd as when the alien had compared himself to a child. When did a being who could teleport around the globe start worrying about being traced by someone? It hadn't even occurred to Jonathan that Heyer might have such a concern. He didn't have long to consider it before the alien spoke again.

"Before I go, I am curious. You do not intend to take one of these small sticks into combat with the Ferox?" He pointed to the staff in Jonathan's hand.

Jonathan shook his head and walked back to the cabinet, pulling out the demolition bar. "It's not ideal, as I can't train with it in my current state. It's too heavy, but once the device activates, it should be manageable."

Heyer inspected the bar and looked unsure.

"It's the highest quality steel I could find," Jonathan said defensively. "I had to special order it."

Heyer looked at the bar again and then back to Jonathan. "Is that so?" he said, putting his fedora on and handing the bar back to Jonathan. "Perhaps, then, there is a way I can assist you without going beyond Earthly means."

Then he was gone, just as before in the park, leaving Jonathan alone in his garage, holding a heavy metal bar out to no one.

"Bye," he said.

CHAPTER TWENTY-SEVEN

SATURDAY | AUGUST 13, 2005 | 9:15 PM

PAIGE WALKED ACROSS the hall to Jonathan's bedroom. She did this less and less now. Conversations between them tended to leave her feeling like she'd done something wrong. It hadn't been easy on her. It wasn't that they had ever been overly conversational, even before Jonathan had been attacked. Still, they had spent so much time together, most of it in quiet company as they studied. She missed his presence. She missed their routine. She didn't like that they were becoming strangers.

She knew she was over-thinking things, but it was confusing to miss a friend who wasn't really gone, who lived right down the hall.

I will not make him feel guilty, she promised herself.

She hadn't planned to request Jonathan join them at all. Leah and Collin had convinced her that she should ask. They'd said that Jonathan would make an exception for her birthday. If he'd forgotten, Paige thought it was understandable, given how little they spoke anymore. She was going to ask him to come, but she wasn't going to be hurt when he said no.

When she reached his door, it wasn't shut like it normally was. It was open wide enough that she could see him standing in front of the mirror. He was clean shaven, he'd combed his hair, and he was buttoning a shirt. Her eyes drifted over to the edge of his bed, where a purple envelope sat.

He remembered, she thought as she turned away from the door.

"You got her a card?" Collin asked Jonathan incredulously.

"It's the thought that counts," Jonathan said, pretending to be defensive.

"You made me ride the bus all the way home, after doing you a favor no less, so you could stop at a drug store and pick up a card?" Collin wasn't really mad, but he wasn't going to let it slide by unnoticed either.

Jonathan nodded.

"Jonathan. That card had better be amazing. I swear, if it doesn't bring tears to her eyes with its thoughtfulness...." Collin trailed off as he hadn't thought of a good punishment to follow that sentence with.

The men sat around the table Collin had reserved at Paige's favorite pub. They each had a beer in front of them. All but Jonathan had an empty shot glass as well. In the middle of the table were a few, as yet, unopened birthday presents. There were two empty seats with half empty mojitos on the table. Paige and Leah danced together a ways off. The bar didn't have a dance floor, yet no one was complaining.

"How is it that the two hottest girls in this bar are here with us?" Hayden said to Collin.

"Let's not over-think it," Collin replied without taking his eyes off the girls.

Hayden glanced at the girls. "Why do girls dance at bars when there isn't a dance floor?"

"Let's not over-think it," Collin reiterated.

Grant was quiet. He seemed to be watching Paige, yet more than once Jonathan caught the man's eyes leering over to Leah. He tried not to notice, but it seemed intentional, like Grant was trying to antagonize him without letting him be certain if it was on purpose. He feared he was being paranoid, but he felt a twinge of jealousy each time he saw it. It was disturbing to think Grant timed those looks, that he intended for Jonathan to catch them.

From what Jonathan had gathered, no one understood why Paige still bothered with Grant. She no longer spoke excitedly about him as she had originally. When she had come down the stairs that evening and seen everyone in the living room waiting to take her out for her birthday, she'd been ecstatic, yet it seemed like she was more excited about the going out than the "going out" with Grant.

Collin had said, before Grant arrived, that he thought she was going to blow the guy off. Apparently, Grant had done or said something to change her mind. That, or Collin was just seeing what he wanted to see. It was curious though, what had Grant done to get on her bad side?

"You're in a good mood this evening. Finally seen the wisdom in giving in to peer pressure?" Hayden asked.

"Perhaps you forgot what happened last time I went out with you guys," Jonathan replied.

He tried not to imply it the same way he had with Paige. Still, it caused a moment of uneasiness until they saw he was earnestly joking and relaxed, happy that he'd made a remark so flippant about the incident.

"Fair enough," Hayden replied, smiling. "Still, though, what gives?"

Jonathan thought about it for a moment. "Let's just say I had some wins today."

"I wouldn't call that motorcycle a win," Collin said, "but if it makes you happy, then—"

"You look like you've put on some weight," Grant interjected. He hadn't been participating in the conversation, and now he seemed impatient with it.

The three looked up at him, and Jonathan nodded.

"Happy to be of assistance," Grant said.

He can't be serious.

Jonathan smiled and nodded anyway. When Grant looked back to ogle Paige and Leah again, Collin gave Jonathan a questioning look.

"I'll tell you about it later," Jonathan said, shaking his head.

When Paige and Leah returned, Hayden and Collin teasingly booed that they hadn't continued dancing. Paige blushed; Leah seemed more inclined to give a bow.

"So when are we going to open these?" Collin asked Paige, nodding at the gifts on the table.

She smiled and reached for one of the boxes with brightly colored wrapping paper. Grant's pocket started vibrating as she opened it. He pulled out his phone and checked who was calling.

"Sorry," he said to everyone, excusing himself. "I need to take this. Don't wait for me."

He leaned down and kissed Paige on the forehead as he left. Jonathan thought Paige looked perturbed that he'd chosen the phone over her. His eyes followed the man as he left to take the call outside. He looked back at the table and realized he didn't see anything from Grant in the pile.

He didn't get her a gift.

As the thought occurred to him, he found himself looking out the bar's street window at Grant, infuriated with the meathead, but when Jonathan's eyes found him, he was surprised by what he saw. Whatever call Grant was getting, he was upset about what he was hearing; he appeared to be on the brink of yelling at the caller. He thought he saw spit flying from the man's lips as he growled into the phone.

"He already gave her a present," Leah whispered to Jonathan.

She'd leaned in close to him, so only he could hear. He turned to her, realizing the disdain he felt for Grant must have been showing on his face; either that or Leah had read his mind.

"Oh," Jonathan said, letting his face relax.

She leaned in a little closer, and whispered again. He felt the special brand of nervous excitement she gave him as she drew nearer; he could feel her breath on his skin.

"Her ears," she said, flicking her eyes toward Paige.

Jonathan looked over at Paige and understood. She was wearing what looked like expensive earrings. He hadn't thought Grant would be spending that kind of money, especially since Paige mentioned Grant wasn't currently working.

"Between you and me," Leah whispered conspiratorially, "those bought him a guilt week."

"Not sure what you mean," Jonathan said.

"I mean, she was going to break it off. But then he gave her those," Leah said.

"She tell you that?" he asked.

"Nope," Leah said, "but she wasn't bringing him tonight originally."

So, Collin had been right after all, Jonathan thought.

"Don't worry," Leah said, "she won't keep them. She just lost her nerve when he sprung them on her."

Jonathan nodded. "Any idea how he got on her bad side?" Jonathan asked.

Leah shrugged slightly.

"Doesn't trust him. It's things like this, where he has to leave the room to answer his phone," she said. "But you didn't hear that from me."

"Hey," Collin said toward the two of them. "You aren't whispering loud enough for the rest of us to hear."

They both returned a sarcastic smile to his calling them out.

"This one is from Jonathan," Paige said, picking up the purple envelope.

Jonathan smiled as he waited for her to open the card. When she finished reading, she looked like she might smile herself into tears.

"Thank you, Jonathan," she said, putting the card in to her purse before anyone asked if they could see it.

Grant returned from his phone call. He didn't appear angry, at least not as angry as he had when Jonathan had spied him through the window. He looked like he'd gotten news so bad he couldn't process it. The whole table still picked up on his change in mood. When he sat, he immediately took a long drink from his beer, finishing it.

Paige reached over, putting a hand on his knee. Grant snapped out of his thoughts at her touch.

"Sorry, I just—" Grant paused. "I just got turned down for a job I'd interviewed for. No big deal, just thought it was a good fit."

"Sorry, man," Hayden said, genuinely sympathetic. The rest of the table nodded in agreement.

Grant, wanting attention off of him, tried to smile. "Hey, it's your birthday." He reached for a present on the table and handed it to Paige. "Let's forget about it."

Paige took the present from Grant's hands. It was the last one on the table.

"This one is from Collin," Paige said, starting to peel off the wrapping. Collin shrugged as though it were nothing special. Jonathan could tell he was really brimming with eagerness as Paige removed the paper.

Once she'd opened, he couldn't see what she was holding. For a moment, she looked down into the wrapping paper and appeared uncertain. Then a spark came to her eyes, and the fingers of her free hand came to her mouth.

"Collin! Is this what I think it is?" she said.

"Pretty sure it is," he said.

She finally pulled the item from the box so everyone could see. It was a hardback book, but he could see by the way she held it that she prized it.

"It's a first edition," Paige said.

Jonathan recognized the title. It was a copy of *Ishmael*. He hadn't read it himself, but he'd seen Paige reading it a number of times and knew it had a reputation amongst Environmental Studies majors.

"Open the cover," Collin said.

She reached down with her spare hand and carefully lifted the lid of the book and gasped again. "No way! It's signed!" she said. "How did you even know?"

"I'm not blind," he said. "I've seen three copies of that book in the house since you moved in, not to mention you reading it a dozen times."

Jonathan snuck a look at Grant's face as he took in Paige's reaction to the gift. It was only for a moment; Grant looked at no one. His eyes appeared to be looking through the table, his mouth pinched, his nostrils flared. When he looked up and caught Jonathan watching him, he quickly let the expression go slack and replaced it with an emotionless facade.

Apparently, Paige hadn't been this excited about the earrings.

As the night moved on, conversations ebbed and flowed. Eventually, Jonathan found himself alone at the table. He was on guard duty, watching the group's various coats, purses, and presents.

Outside of watching movies with Collin and Hayden, it was the longest time he'd spent with his friends since he'd killed Sickens the Fever. Collin and Hayden had fallen into their familiar rhythms. From what he had overheard, they were much further along producing their rebooted Bible comic book than he'd realized. They spoke excitedly about story arcs, the presentation of certain panels, the layout of the first title page, Internet publishing.

The more he heard them talk, the more he thought back to how Paige had looked at him in the garage a few nights earlier, how he'd forgotten about her birthday until Collin reminded him, how her relationship with Grant had reached its near end without him knowing, how she and Leah were suddenly friends.

Then there was Leah herself, right next door, building massive metal sculptures with an arc welder. All within a stone's throw of his bedroom and he'd been too closed off to notice. They might as well have all been living in a timeline that couldn't exist for him, much like his fight with the Ferox didn't exist for them.

Hiding in a garage, building muscles, practicing violence in every spare moment, his focus on staying alive brought with it this tunnel vision. The longer it continued, the further removed he would become from his real friends leading their real lives. The Jonathan he recognized would eventually cease to exist entirely. More and more he came to terms with this; the part of himself that was withering away put up less and less resistance, but it was the relationships belonging to that part of him that he mourned. The Jonathan he was building didn't have friends; he only had an alien and some untold number of enemies.

He'd been immersed into superhero movies by his roommates. The heroes with the secret identity always had friends, or what Hayden called their "entourage." They grounded the hero, kept him human, and inspired him to persist. Protecting them was the very reason they divide themselves into two different identities in the first place.

Jonathan always had to see the story through a cracked lens, because the heroes had something Jonathan didn't get to have; their two identities existed on the same plane of reality. Jonathan only fought in a place that no one but he could see or remember. His story could never be like theirs; his alter ego could never be unmasked. He would never be the hero revealed, and therefore, never the hero.

Jeez, that's the booze talking, Jonathan thought, making a mental note to cut himself off.

"You look like you are over-thinking something again."

She'd come back to the table while he'd been lost in his depressing thoughts and he hadn't heard her sit down. When he looked up, he was surprised to find her watching him.

"I'm glad you came," Leah said.

"I think I'm glad I did too," he replied.

She pulled her chair closer to him. "So tell me, Mr. Jonathan, what scares a guy like you?"

He could tell by the way she said "Mister" that she was a bit tipsy. Still, the question was a means to return to their awkward moment in the garage.

"You know, I'd rather talk about you," he said. "What's your story, Ms. Leah?"

"What would'cha like to know?" she asked.

"What brings you to Seattle, for starters?"

She looked a little uncomfortable. "Well, it's a bit of a long story, but the short version is that I had the opportunity to get a change of scenery and I took it."

"Why Seattle then, I guess?" He asked.

"It was far from the East Coast," she said.

"Not a fan of the East Coast?" he asked.

Again she looked uncomfortable. It threw him off; he didn't know as much about her as he would have liked, but the one thing he knew was that she didn't get knocked off her guard easily. Gracelessness under interrogation was his arena.

"I'm just gonna lay some things out for ya," she said. "I know it must be strange that I'm hesitating answering some pretty straight questions. So it's like this. My parents died a few years ago. I was only nineteen, but I got custody of Jack. They had a life insurance plan that got put into a trust. Jack and I live off that."

She looked at him then, like she expected something from him. He wasn't sure what it was. He started to say that he was sorry to hear about her parents, when the rest of the table seemed to return all at once. They brought laughter with them, and Grant.

"Anyway, no one likes explaining their baggage," she said, making her tone more upbeat with the return of their friends. "It's just true what they say, 'everything reminds you,' so I came here to, well, you know."

"To stop being reminded," Jonathan said.

He didn't need any explanation. He'd experienced the same feelings when he'd lost his father.

They shared a smile, but soon it was clear that neither knew where to take the conversation. When they started laughing at their own awkwardness, she put her hand on top of his; he turned his hand over and clasped hers gently.

"Anyhow," she said, changing the subject, "what are you studying in school? Paige said the two of you have crammed for a lot of finals together. Environmental Sciences?"

"No," he replied. "I used to study Biology."

"Used to?" she asked.

Now Jonathan hesitated. He hadn't forfeited his college career. At least, he didn't think he had made that decision, but perhaps his subconscious was more of a realist. *Used to* didn't sound like something you planned on going back to.

"Oops," she said, smiling at him. "My turn to ask the wrong question?"

"I'm on a break is all," he said, trying to keep the levity going.

"What caused the break?" she asked carefully, like she was feeling out if the question was okay.

Jonathan felt himself turn red, not sure how to respond.

"Yeah, Tibbs," Grant interjected, "explain to the girl how you woke up in a puddle of your own blood. We all still want to know how that really happened."

When Jonathan looked to Grant, he could see that the words weren't flippant. They weren't some slip, some drunken bad behavior. They were pointed and arrogant. He'd made no attempt to hide the malice in his voice and now made no attempt to hide his satisfaction with himself.

"I mean, if you plan on taking a girl to bed," Grant added, "don't you think you'll have to explain why you wake up screaming for your daddy every night?"

CHAPTER TWENTY-EIGHT

SUNDAY | AUGUST 14, 2005 | 12:00 AM

AN HOUR LATER, he stood in front of the punching bag, halfheartedly hitting it, not really putting anything into the punches. He was just watching the bag sway back and forth in front of him.

He hadn't known what to say to Grant. He'd excused himself and left. Actually, he didn't remember if he'd excused himself. It was a blur. The last thing he'd heard as he'd walked away was the sound of Paige shouting at the asshole.

Thinking about how he'd walked away was making him boil inside. He kept seeing it from Leah's eyes. How red and stupid his face had looked. How he'd put his head down like a coward. The humiliation of the moment had been too much for him. He kept trying to transform his memory of reality to one in which he'd asked the man to step outside, but the reality refused to change.

Violent images surged through his mind, feeding the storm inside of him. The images kept growing worse, more visceral, until he was seeing Grant's blood on his hands as he pummeled him into the sidewalk. He was growing drunk with it, not wanting to calm down, not wanting to feel better. All he wanted was to have stopped thinking and acted.

He wanted to give the rage what it needed.

He hit the bag, hard this time, grunting with the effort. It felt good, better. He pulled his arm back hard and struck again. It smacked with the sound of fist hitting canvas.

Who did Grant think he was? The arrogant shithead had sat there, eavesdropping, waiting for the perfect moment to make him as angry as possible.

It should have worked.

Grant had miscalculated. Jonathan didn't have a short enough fuse. He'd been too shocked to be angry at first. By the time he'd worked himself up enough to want a fight, the window for violence was lost to him, and now his anger pleaded to go back to that moment and make a different choice.

He heard the garage door open and Collin and Hayden walked in. They took one look at him and knew. Luckily, Collin had no interest in pretense.

"Asshole!" Collin declared; Hayden standing beside him, nodding his agreement.

Jonathan didn't want to, but he choked trying to keep a chuckle from escaping. They were probably the most harmless men he knew. They were as aware of this as he was, but the way they stood before him like they wanted to head out into the night and pummel Grant with him was priceless.

He almost resented them for making him laugh. He was trying so hard to keep his rage fueled.

"Um, what—" Jonathan paused. "What did Leah say?"

"Don't worry," Hayden said, seeing Jonathan diffusing himself. "We made sure she didn't think it was anything like the way Meathead made it sound."

For some reason, that didn't soothe his fears.

"What did you tell her?" he asked.

"Honestly, I don't think she knew what to think. We made sure she knew you'd been attacked. You know," Collin paused. "Not self-inflicted or anything. That was all we said. She seemed to already know about that much; though, maybe without the more disturbing details."

"That's it?" Jonathan said

There was a pause as Hayden and Collin looked at each other.

"Well, I mean, you know, she could tell that it must have been pretty bad. The way you left, she knows you're not…." Hayden trailed off, not wanting to finish his sentence.

"That I'm not okay," Jonathan finished for him, nodding slowly then looking down at the floor.

There was an awkward moment before anyone spoke again.

"Paige is definitely breaking it off with him," Collin said, failing to hide how happy he was about it. "I've never seen her so angry. It was a little scary."

"Where is she?" Jonathan realized he hadn't thought to ask why she wasn't with them.

"Last I saw, she was publicly humiliating him on a street corner. We didn't stick around to watch. Collin and I walked Leah home," Hayden said.

"It's too bad her birthday got so epically messed up," Collin said.

That's when they heard the yelling from the front yard.

"You're being ridiculous, Paige. I drank too much," Grant yelled. "Come on, I'm sorry."

The sound of Grant seeped into Jonathan like gasoline on the cooling embers of his rage. The thing inside of him became aware, climbing to the surface, fixated on the man's voice. Jonathan was headed for the side door, passing Hayden and Collin like he'd forgotten they were there.

"Jonathan," Collin said sheepishly. "You've—you've got that creepy look—"

"Just go home, Grant," Paige yelled.

If they were loud enough that Jonathan could hear them in the garage, then half the neighborhood could hear this domestic disturbance.

"Holy crap," Hayden said excitedly to Collin. "I've always wanted to be on Cops."

All Jonathan was thinking was that maybe he hadn't missed his window after all.

She stood defiantly in front of Grant in the driveway. Jonathan could see she'd been crying, and her makeup looked smeared down her cheeks.

She'd taken the earrings he'd given her out. Seeing her so upset only made it worse, made him think less, made him want to fight more.

"Leave!" she screamed at Grant.

He was about to fire something back, but stopped when he saw Jonathan rounding the corner.

"Oh," Grant said in disgust, "here he comes."

"She doesn't want you here," Jonathan said.

Looking at the man's face, it was as if Grant truly believed he'd somehow put the events of the evening into motion; engineered it so that he'd look like a victim while Grant came out the villain.

"You have them all fooled," Grant said, "but you and I, we both know you're full of shit."

Jonathan couldn't imagine what had driven Grant to indulge in this delusion, and he didn't care.

"What, Tibbs, you want to get in my face, try and make me look like an asshole?"

He stepped between Paige and Grant, knowing he was making the man angrier, wanting him to snap.

"Go inside, Paige," Jonathan said without taking his eyes off Grant. "He won't follow you." *Fuel to the fire.* "And, Grant," he said, "you are an asshole."

Grant smiled.

He'd wanted it; he'd been waiting to bring it out, to see Jonathan pushed far enough that he stopped worrying about control and did something stupid. He turned his head, just for a moment, as though he were building up for some clever retort, some harsh put down.

Instead, his sudden movement caught Jonathan off guard.

Grant's fist connected with his face. It spun Jonathan around and he fell onto his hands and knees. The gravel of the driveway cut into his palms as he stopped his fall. The ground wouldn't hold still, the socket of his eye throbbed, growing warm where the fist had connected.

Take the pain.

"Who's the asshole now?" Grant taunted him.

"Grant! Leave!" Paige screamed, her voice betraying her fear as she moved forward to get between them again.

Jonathan wasn't scared; he felt a smile on his lips.

It was laughable to him that two months ago he wouldn't have known what to do in this situation. No *man*, let alone Grant, was enough to scare him now, not after being accosted by an alien and having half his chest ripped out; not after facing Sickens the Fever, not after drowning.

He had nightmares that Grant wouldn't understand if he lived to be a thousand. Getting punched in the face was just something he needed, to see he wasn't fragile, to bring the fighter all the way to the surface.

He shook off the pain and turned to stand.

"You're still the asshole," he said as he reached his feet.

Paige turned, startled that Jonathan was standing, unnerved by the tone in his voice, the look in his eyes.

Grant knew how to fight, Jonathan had no doubt of that. Still, Grant had drunk five times the amount of alcohol that he'd had this evening, and Jonathan trained at his violence on a daily basis. When Grant came at Jonathan with a haymaker meant to take his head off, Jonathan moved to the outside. The punch sailed past him as he came in close and caught Grant with his elbow. Jonathan's attack was swift and hard. The sound of bone hitting forehead was crisp and rewarding.

Grant staggered back.

The blow would've rocked anyone. Jonathan gave him no time to recover and used his backward momentum against him, quickly stepping into him while tripping him from behind with his leg. Grant hit the ground before he knew what was happening. Not waiting for him to regain his wits, Jonathan thrust his fist down hard into center of Grant's torso. The man gasped as the wind rushed out of him.

It was a blow to the solar plexus, Jonathan knew. His instructor had shown him the place to put the force. Grant wouldn't be getting himself together soon.

He wheezed and coughed, trying to regain the breath that had been knocked out of him.

Jonathan struggled, then, as he hovered over him; he didn't want to reel his anger back in yet. The thing breaking loose inside of him didn't want to be locked away again; it wanted to beat the man's face until he couldn't recognize it. He was right there, vulnerable in front of him, begging for Jonathan to vent his rage.

"Jonathan," Paige said.

He didn't want to hear her. His mind was too balanced on the edge between walking away and giving in.

"Jonathan, don't...." Paige pleaded.

It wasn't the words, but the fear, the desperation in her voice, that made him hear her.

This isn't it, Jonathan. This is not about him.

He knew that if he let himself go now, that there wouldn't be any coming back. Not to Paige; she'd see him beating a helpless man into the pavement and she'd see it again every time she looked at him. It would confirm her fears about him.

This is not the moment.

He looked away from the man on the ground and forced himself to breathe, exhaling his anger. His muscles lost their tension, beginning to relax. His fists unclenched. He became aware of the sound of Grant gasping on the ground, the hot throbbing over his eye, the rawness of his hands. He looked back to Grant, and somehow, barely, he found mercy. He turned away, walking back to Paige, leaving Grant on the ground.

"I'm so sorry, Jonathan," she whispered, genuine, but relieved he hadn't lost control.

Collin and Hayden were ten paces behind her. They'd seen it all. Jonathan could see it on their expressions.

"What is it, Jonathan?" Grant asked, trying to speak between coughing. "What the hell makes you so important?"

Jonathan ignored him. A few more steps and he'd do his best never to think of Grant again.

"Answer me, dammit!" Grant began to raise his finger to point at Paige. "You think I care about her! They made me stay with her!"

Jonathan slowed.

"They made me," Grant said, "so I could tell them about you."

Jonathan stopped.

"Yeah!" The arrogance in Grant's voice was returning. "You see? He knows I know. He knows he's in deep shit."

Jonathan turned, facing the man still wheezing on ground, not knowing what to think. He couldn't tell if Grant was trying to screw with him. It was too much to process. The only thing he knew for sure, no matter what was actually going on, he had to get Grant to stop yelling about it.

"Oh yeah, Tibbs, they know." He was smiling at the look on Jonathan's face. "You aren't fooling shit. They know all about you."

"Paige, please go inside," Jonathan said. "Please, don't fight me on this."

He let her see his face, the wrath no longer in control. He let her see his concern. She was confused. After all the drama, this new level of unexplained crazy talk from Grant was hard to comprehend.

"What's he talking about, Jonathan?" she asked shaking her head.

"I'm not sure," Jonathan said. "I'll find out. Please go inside. I'm not going to hurt him again."

She looked at Grant, bewildered, her eyes still shining from the crying and confusion. Then back to Jonathan, who nodded reassuringly. He couldn't imagine what she was thinking, but she started to walk toward the house, toward Collin and Hayden.

"Take her inside," he asked of them.

They seemed unsure, but nodded at his command. Paige reached for Collin, tugging at him for support. Jonathan nodded back to them as they walked into the house before returning his gaze to Grant.

He knelt next to him slowly, like he was approaching a growling dog he didn't trust not to bite. At least, Grant didn't look like he wanted to fight anymore. He was reveling in the reaction he was getting from Jonathan, staring him down, looking for signs that he'd regained some power that he thought was stolen from him.

"Whatever you think you're on about," Jonathan said in a low voice, "I doubt it's wise for you to yell it so anyone listening can hear."

Grant's eyes seemed to lose their assurance. "Maybe," he said, only loud enough for Jonathan to hear, still wheezing a bit.

Grant started to get to his feet and Jonathan rose off his knee as he stood. When they locked eyes again, Jonathan got the feeling that Grant was trying to read his thoughts.

"What you're involved in," Grant said, spitting the words out. "They know you lied about what put you in that hospital."

Jonathan said nothing.

"They're smarter than you. They're just waiting for you to slip up."

Jonathan felt like the man was baiting him, a desperate bluff to trick him into talking. It was the way the man made accusations without giving specifics.

"They?" Jonathan asked. "Who's they?"

Grant's glare contorted with angry incredulity. "Don't play games with me," he whispered.

Jonathan wasn't playing games, though. Someone may know something, but it wasn't Grant.

"Good night, Grant." Jonathan said, turning to leave him in the dark. "Leave Paige alone."

When he'd gotten about five steps away, Grant spoke again.

"Uncle Sam," he said, his voice beginning to betray desperation.

Jonathan stopped and took a deep breath.

"Make it easier on yourself, Tibbs," Grant said. "Let me take you in; they'll go easier on you if you surrender. Give up whoever you're protecting."

Jonathan hesitated for a moment. Then he left Grant in the driveway.

CHAPTER TWENTY-NINE

SUNDAY | AUGUST 14, 2005 | 12:30 AM

GRANT WATCHED JONATHAN'S back receding up the drive. The lying prick didn't look back, and when the door shut, he felt the finality. It was sobering.

He stood there another moment, unable to make a decision, before he saw there wasn't anything left for him to do, no move left to make. He'd underestimated him; he'd been manipulated somehow.

No! That stupid woman set me up to fail!

Olivia—he should have expected it. Whatever game she had been playing, it had backfired. Jonathan hadn't confessed to anything. All Grant had accomplished was to blow his cover.

She didn't know what the hell she'd done.

As he turned and walked up the driveway, the night was darker than he remembered. There weren't as many street lights illuminating the shadows. He'd followed her orders; well, maybe not exactly, not all of them. Jonathan knew now, but she was going to say he'd disobeyed. They weren't going to trust him. They might kick him out of the investigation.

What if she had him dealt with? He felt a sickening in his stomach as he realized that it might be much worse. The night suddenly had eyes. He had to explain it to someone. He had to make them see that he'd still made the right call.

He shoved his hands in his pockets, turning out of the driveway. He started to shake, the weight of his miscalculation growing, the implications he imagined starting to give rise to paranoia. He was walking faster and faster, desperate to get somewhere populated, a busy street. Somewhere he could be in the safety of civilians.

He made it a block and a half before he knew it wouldn't be allowed. The man stood before him on the sidewalk, blocking his way. He wore a government issue suit: black tie, white shirt, black blazer. Grant stopped in his tracks. The man didn't move, just stared at him like a snake waiting on a mouse.

"It's not my fault," Grant said, his hushed voice betraying his panic.

The man took a step forward, and Grant's instincts took over. When he turned to flee, he only had a moment to realize that he'd done exactly as they had expected. The fist of the other man, the one he hadn't realized was behind him, connected with his face. His legs buckled, his vision blurred, and he fell to the pavement.

Before he knew what was happening, the two men were on each side of him, one arm under each shoulder, picking him up off the ground.

He whimpered, "Please, I can explain!"

Neither man dragging him said a word. They didn't even care what he'd done, probably didn't even know. They were just obediently following orders. Then he heard the sound of her heels approaching on the sidewalk, and cowered inside. When they turned him around, he saw Olivia, standing in the street in front of him.

She was dressed as she always was, her tailored suit and heels, but now with a heavy coat on to keep out the cold. He couldn't read her expression. As per usual, she wasn't wearing one.

"Please listen," Grant said, "I figured it out. I—"

She batted her eyes to one of the men holding him, and a fist hit him in the gut.

"No," she said, waiting for Grant to understand she didn't care in the least what he had to say. "When," Olivia asked, "did I ever order you to figure out anything?"

A moment passed as the meaning of her statement was allowed to seep into the man.

"When," Olivia asked, "did you get the idea that you were to do anything other than what I ordered?"

"What are you going to do?" Grant asked sheepishly, afraid to be hit again.

She took in a slow deep breath and let it out.

"If it were up to me," she said, "you'd disappear."

Grant blinked.

If it wasn't up to her, then who was it up to?

With her eyes, she signaled to the men restraining him and they began to drag him towards a car parked a few feet away. He didn't struggle. There was no point and he didn't want to be roughed up anymore. They opened the door for him. He looked to each man's eyes. He didn't see any mercy in them, just impatience, so he eased himself into the back seat, and they shut the door. The locks triggered a moment later.

It was black leather interior. He was alone in the back seat. Next to him was a thick yellow envelope. There was an opaque black glass divider between the front and back seats.

He was afraid to move. His legs shook; he tried to will them to stop but they refused to obey.

"You've proven yourself to be a gross miscalculation, Mr. Morgan," said a man through the car speakers, the mask of the voice modulator disguising its owner.

Grant swallowed.

"You were given three explicit instructions. One, reveal your role in our investigation to Mr. Tibbs exclusively; two, offer him immunity in exchange for his cooperation; and three, remove yourself from contact with any of the household's occupants," the voice said.

After a moment, Grant thought the voice was waiting for him to speak. When he dared to open his mouth, he was immediately cut off.

"You were not instructed to antagonize him in front of five of his associates, to raise suspicions of our operation to his entire household. You most certainly were not instructed to pick a fight with him in earshot of the entire neighborhood and request his surrender."

"I—I thought—" Grant stuttered.

"My report informs me that you were upset and initially non-receptive when you received these instructions tonight, Mr. Morgan," the voice stated. "Am I to understand that, despite the extreme care with which you were brought into this investigation, that you're such a worthless soldier you'd let yourself endanger our entire operation?"

"I figured it out," Grant whimpered.

"Oh? Please enlighten me, Mr. Morgan, to exactly what insight you believe you've uncovered," the voice requested arrogantly.

"I realized that," Grant started, "we needed Tibbs to slip up. When I was instructed to blow my cover, I knew you must be desperate, that you needed to rattle him. Get him to make a mistake, call one of his contacts."

"And exactly," the voice asked, "who do you assume to be Mr. Tibbs' 'contacts'?"

Grant looked around the car dejectedly.

Jonathan Tibbs was a liar, a dangerous manipulative liar. He had everyone fooled. Grant knew it by the way they all seemed so protective of him. He'd been covering up something big with that bullshit story at the hospital. Why was this man still pretending it wasn't obvious? Grant knew where Jonathan came from; this man behind the voice must know as well, so why were they still playing games like this?

"He's a terrorist," Grant said, his voice betraying that he knew nothing more than what had been alluded to the day he'd been brought into the operation.

This moment from his daydreams, where he showed them they underestimated his value, where Olivia saw that he had always been the real one in control, wasn't going how he'd imagined it.

He felt humiliated by his own words, by being forced to play their game. "I can stop—"

"Mr. Morgan, I've heard quite enough," the voice said. "May I remind you that your orders were to keep tabs on the girl? Yet, you ignored these orders and fixated on Mr. Tibbs. Do you care to explain yourself?"

Grant stopped talking, staring down at his knees. He felt tears on his cheeks. He hadn't been aware of them before. He couldn't tell now—did they know all or nothing? Were they trying to trick him into confession, or manipulate him for information? His eyes and nose were running as the voice on the other side of the glass passed judgment on him, called him worthless. Grant said nothing, just waited.

"The envelope on the seat next to you," said the voice, "is the payment you were promised for your participation. Take these funds and do not come anywhere near this operation again. If you are so much as spotted in this neighborhood, near Jonathan or the girl, your already useless and expendable existence will end."

Grant let out a grateful breath and reached for the envelope. He didn't like it, but at least he was going to live. The doors to the vehicle audibly unlocked, and he wasted no time exiting, fumbling with the door handle as he tried to leave.

"Mr. Morgan, there will be no second chances," said the voice.

Grant stopped, then nodded to make sure the voice could see he understood the implication.

Outside the car, he risked a glance at Olivia. Her thugs stood to each side of her. She took in his red eyes, the snot that had been running from his nose. Her face revealed no disdain, just blank disregard.

Humiliation dug into him. He turned up the street and around the corner. When they could no longer see him, he ran.

They don't know.

He felt it in his gut; they suspected but they didn't know. That was why they played their game; that was why he was really still alive.

Trying to pull himself together, he made promises to himself. One day, he would see that woman so powerless, that she'd cry out for his help. He wouldn't help her though, not until she begged. Jonathan, that conniving bastard, was going to find out that Grant Morgan wasn't so easily cast aside.

Grant was still alive, and it meant the world still wanted him to be the hero. The world wanted him to be the one who stopped the monster.

Olivia sat down in the backseat of the Sedan.

"Orders?" she asked.

"Keep the house on surveillance. Make sure that the secondary protocol is adhered to. No men are to engage Jonathan Tibbs or the other house occupants under any circumstances," the voice said.

"The other civilians in the house weren't meant to gain awareness of our operation, especially the girl," she said.

"Given Mr. Morgan's theatrics leading up to the disclosure, it remains to be seen if plans will need to be adjusted," said the voice.

"And Mr. Morgan himself?" she asked.

"Whatever he imagines is so far from reality that he poses little threat in and of himself. He's certainly done damage to our credibility with the subject, but Mr. Tibbs' cooperation was never a likely scenario. If the man has a sense of self-preservation, he'll follow orders this time. Still, keep him under surveillance, see if he becomes a problem," the voice said.

"Understood," she replied as she reached for the door.

"Olivia," the voice said, halting her exit.

"Yes?" she inquired.

"Mr. Morgan's reaction to his removal and his fixation on Jonathan— it all supports your hypothesis regarding what the private investigators uncovered. The connection between them is no mere coincidence."

"Agreed," she replied. "Do you wish me to pursue this?"

"I've taken the liberty of doing so based on your initial hunch. I bring it to your attention now because of what we've uncovered."

"Please continue, sir," said Olivia.

"Every electronic record and paper hard copy that could be used to follow up has been deleted or misplaced. There is only one being we know capable of breaching our security to such a level."

Olivia swelled with pride, but didn't let it reach her face. None of her predecessors assigned to this investigation had come close to what this news might mean.

"That such care was taken to remove the evidence reveals more than it hides," she replied. "I'll compile a list of all eye witnesses still living who can provide testimony."

"Start with Evelyn Tibbs," said the voice. "Now that Jonathan is aware he is being watched, I advise you approach her with discretion."

Jonathan awoke.

Surprised he'd been able to sleep at all, he tried not to cry out. His morning ritual began. He laid his head back down on the pillow and waited for his heart to slow, trying to think about something else. All that came to mind was Grant.

When he'd come back into the house the night before, they'd given him his space. Collin had handed him an ice pack. Paige had looked to Jonathan, then the floor, like she couldn't decide what to think, and because of it, didn't know what to say. They hadn't asked what Grant said, they had just let him go to sleep. Now, after what Collin had said to him on the bus, Jonathan wasn't sure what he would be to them when he went down stairs.

It had occurred to him before that someone out there had to know something. A being like Heyer couldn't exist and Jonathan be the only one to know about it, but there hadn't been a way to search out such a person. Now it was clear that some operation out there had known to watch him after he ended up in that hospital. The question was, what did they know? What did they want? More importantly, what did it mean for him?

We'll need to trust each other, Jonathan remembered.

Some things made sense now that this was out in the open. This was why Heyer was so reluctant to give him a means to contact him, why he only gave Jonathan the little information he needed to survive. Regardless of what it revealed, it caused far more questions. Why Grant? Why make such a sideways maneuver to keep tabs on him? Why not listen in when he'd been out in the open with Heyer in the park? If he was being watched, the house must be bugged. Why hadn't they done something when the alien was standing in his garage yesterday? Had Grant been planted before he'd even been assaulted by Heyer—was that possible? Had these people somehow known Heyer would come for him? How could that be possible?

He wasn't about to start fooling himself. Espionage, surveillance, and undercover activities were all outside his ability to deal with. He couldn't hide anything from a surveillance team.

Did he want to? He couldn't help but wonder, if someone knew about what was happening, why hadn't they revealed themselves to him sooner? After all, wouldn't they know he was forced in this? Wouldn't they know all he wanted was a way out?

I don't know what the hell I'm doing.

She poured pancake batter onto a griddle in the kitchen. It sizzled as it hit the pan. Cooking had never been Paige's thing. No one had ever tried to teach her. She was fairly sure she was either going to burn the pancakes or that they would still be liquid batter in the middle. She pressed on anyway.

Jonathan would be walking down the steps soon, no doubt with a black eye. She'd be thinking of Grant every time she looked at him until it healed. She didn't ever want to think about Grant again, but it wasn't like she would need a bruise on Jonathan's eye to remind her; the look on Grant's face, the vitriol that had suddenly been bursting out of him. He'd been so hell-bent on tearing Jonathan down, demeaning him, even if it meant humiliating her on her birthday. How could she have gone to bed with that monster and not have known what was writhing under the surface?

It was what Grant reminded her of that made it all so disturbing. The way he'd been; too much like her father, all too familiar. She loathed herself, felt a fool that she could be blindsided by it.

It had been years and she made efforts not to dwell on her childhood growing up with that man, yet how could she so glaringly make the same mistakes as her mother, without seeing the signs, the rage hidden underneath the facade. Had she fooled herself somehow, ignored it when it was right in front of her? Her blindness had now caused even more damage to Jonathan.

Embarrassed by her own choices and angry at herself at the same time, one emotion fed the other in a vicious circle.

Never make this mistake again, she thought. Every time you cringe, every time you remember, just repeat it: "Never make this mistake."

Some time passed; she eventually had a healthy looking stack of pancakes on the counter. She hadn't tried one yet—she just kept going. It helped to keep her mind busy. At least until she ran out of batter.

Hayden and Collin were up before Jonathan. They didn't appear to have lost as much sleep over last night's debacle as she had. For a moment, it reminded her of breakfast commercials where the entire family smelled Mom cooking and slowly made their way to the table in pajamas with uncombed bed heads. They were endearing in a way, like children.

"This is new," Collin said, watching her.

She nodded but stayed focused on what she was doing. Hayden yawned, then gave a look like he'd remembered something important.

"So, did anyone else dream that Jonathan kicked Grant's ass last night?"

Paige struck the pan with her spatula.

Collin gave Hayden a dirty look. "Seriously, bro, read the room."

"No, it's okay," Paige said. "It was the one part of last night I look forward to remembering."

She could hear his footsteps, then—Jonathan coming down the stairs. Paige took in a deep breath in anticipation. All she wanted was to give him the apology she'd been too upset to express the night before, to make sure he knew he wasn't responsible. Was it really all on her somehow? Was Grant her responsibility?

She noticed his footsteps had stopped, like he'd gotten halfway down the stairs and hesitated. Was he so unsure if he wanted to face them? The memory of him humiliated, trying to excuse himself at the bar, flashed through her thoughts again and she cringed. She was relieved when the footsteps resumed and he was there, standing in the living room, looking like he'd been hit in the face with a softball.

"As I was saying," Hayden commented idly, "couldn't have happened to a nicer guy."

Jonathan, taking them all in, looked unsure of himself. Unsure of what, she couldn't be certain. When he looked to her and the scene in the kitchen, his features changed. She thought he looked ashamed somehow;

then he approached her slowly, like he was afraid that if he moved too quickly he would frighten her. She couldn't stand it; his silence, his slow movements. Whatever was going on in his head, she could tell, was weighing heavily on him.

When he stood next to her and still looked like he didn't know what to say, she felt like she was going to start sobbing. She'd been crying off and on all night—it was all too easy to start up again. She reached out to touch his face, below the purple mark that Grant had left. Then she worried it might be tender and pulled her hand back.

"I'm just so sorry, Jonathan," she said, a sob escaping. "I feel like an idiot. He was so terrible to you."

She hugged him then. She didn't care if she was being ridiculous, or if Hayden and Collin were watching. He seemed to stiffen for a moment, caught off guard by the sudden affection, but then he melted and embraced her back.

"You don't need to apologize for anything," he said to her quietly, so Hayden and Collin didn't hear. "I'm just glad you aren't afraid of me."

The way he'd moved so slowly, the way he'd seemed to be relieved that she'd hugged him, it made sense then. He'd thought that she might see him differently somehow. After all, it wasn't like him to fight. If someone had crossed the line with him two months ago, he never would have thought violence an option; then again, two months ago she didn't think he'd had a line to cross. Still, even when he'd been angry in a way she had never seen him, he hadn't let go; he'd pulled himself back. It was losing that grip that would have made him into what he was so afraid she would now fear.

"No, of course not," she said. "I made pancakes and you're eating them."

"All I'm saying is," Collin said, "you can't always spot the crazy ones. Sometimes crazy just strikes and no one sees it coming. Don't beat yourself up about it."

They sat around the table, eating. Jonathan hadn't expected it, but Paige wasn't stoically suppressing her feelings regarding Grant. She'd seemed a bit embarrassed when everyone, even Hayden, admitted to not having liked the guy from the get-go. That had been overshadowed by her relief when all three admitted that they never had any suspicions that he was a nut case, let alone dangerous.

"Seriously, when I was in high school, I worked at a video store," Collin said. "One day, this guy I'd worked with for months just loses it, starts talking about how aliens have been watching him. How they're plotting to take him back to the mothership. I had to call his mother to come take him to a shrink. He'd been perfectly fine the day before, just like any other day."

"Ever see him again?" Paige asked.

"Yeah, three weeks later he came back to work, but he was different," Collin said sadly. "Apparently his brain had just turned on him one day. The three weeks he'd been gone he'd spent with a doctor trying to get his prescriptions strength adjusted so he could function. It scared the hell out of me, still does really, how his mind had just decided not to make a certain amount of some hormone one day, and suddenly he was someone else entirely. That our personalities are so fragile; it's disturbing."

Jonathan had been listening to his friends discuss Grant's strange behavior with a mixture of emotions. He felt such loyalty from them; they hadn't considered a word of what Grant had suggested. The very notion that the government was watching them had immediately led them to the conclusion that Grant was paranoid, crazy, and belonged in a psych ward. At the same time, he felt guilty, because they trusted him so much that they didn't realize the man hadn't been paranoid.

"I keep thinking," Paige said, "it makes sense now that the Army discharged him. I bet he had some kind of an episode or something. I always thought it was weird that he never told me why he'd been let go early. Maybe he was getting disability for it? That would explain how he had enough money not to worry about a job."

Paige's theory fit her knowledge. The pieces were falling into place differently for Jonathan. Grant was discharged two days after he'd been in the hospital. He'd been taken off assignment because he was an available soldier already in a position to get information the government wanted. He hadn't needed to worry about work because he'd still been on the government payroll.

"What do you think, Jonathan?" Paige asked. "Why did he fixate on you?"

Jonathan shrugged. "I'm not sure I want to know."

It wasn't a lie. Until he knew what the people watching him hoped to gain, he had no idea what to expect, and little hope that it would make his life any less complicated.

After breakfast, Jonathan headed to the garage. Now that he had transportation, crappy as it might be, he didn't have to bus everywhere. When he got there, he found the garage door wide open and motorcycle gone, just an empty space next to Collin's Suzuki. For a second, he thought it had been stolen, but it would be ridiculous for a thief to take his wreck when Collin's bike was sitting right next to it. He could hear the familiar sounds of classic rock playing next door.

When he approached Leah's driveway, he saw that she had the bike out and was fitting the demolition bar into the two latches that looked like modified carabineers. She'd managed to fit it so that the bar's hexagonal shape sat perfectly into the holsters. It was amazing that she could have done this in just one morning.

She looked up when he approached. He smiled awkwardly. Her eyes lingered on his bruise for a bit.

"Deal is a deal," she said, "even though I got cheated on time."

Jonathan ran his hand over the bike, gave the demolition bar a tug to see how stable it was in the holster. It was perfect. It would be able to stay in place while he rode but would come free when he reached for it.

"It's great," he said in genuine gratitude.

"Of course it is. You doubted me?" she asked.

"No, I didn't," he said.

He was at a loss as to what else to say. The previous night loomed between them.

"Jack hasn't stopped talking all morning about how you knocked Paige's boyfriend out," Leah said.

Startled at first, Jonathan grew a little embarrassed. Had the kid been up late enough to have witnessed what happened? Hadn't the babysitter put him to bed?

As though reading his mind, Leah explained, "That ass was yelling so loudly when they got back he woke up half the block. Jack is a light sleeper." She pointed to the balcony, where she'd been sitting the night Jonathan had drowned the Ferox. "I had a pretty good view myself."

He followed her finger and nodded. It hadn't occurred to him. He'd been nervous about Grant yelling at the top of his lungs, but only in a general way. He had no idea what Leah would think of what she'd heard and seen.

"I'm sorry Jack saw that," Jonathan said.

She approached him, reaching for his face just as Paige had, tilting it to get a better look at the black eye. He stiffened at first, reminded by her touch just how beautiful a woman she was. He tried to relax, let her survey the damage. If there was ever an upside to the bruise, it was that it gave her a reason to put her hands on him.

"I'm sorry he saw it, too," she said, still holding his face, "but I'd be lying if I said I was sorry I saw it."

She took her hand back; had it lingered a moment longer, her touch might have confessed something other than concern. He hadn't minded; he missed the connection immediately.

"Paige is mad at herself," Jonathan said. "We were all caught off guard last night. I'm sorry I left like I did."

Leah raised an eyebrow. "I didn't take it personally. It was pretty clear that he'd…." She paused. "Known what buttons to push."

"Yeah," Jonathan said, "he did."

"Everyone's got at least one," she said. Then her face changed from a look of sympathy to one of curiosity. He thought he knew what was going on in her head. She was weighing the urge to mind her own business with the stronger urge to ask personal questions. He knew she would end up asking, but still, he liked that she always thought about it before she did.

"Any idea why he would be instructed to infiltrate the Tibbs entourage?" she asked.

"Oh," Jonathan said, "well, I think that's why Paige is so mad at herself."

"I don't follow," she said.

"She thinks Grant was discharged from the Army early because of mental health problems," Jonathan said.

"Oh, she thinks he was a nut case," Leah replied. "Is that what you think?"

Jonathan shrugged. "It's what everyone seemed to think at breakfast," he said.

She looked at him conspiratorially. He wasn't fooling her, and he knew it. She saw right away that he had side stepped the real question. It was not the first time it had occurred to him he should be more careful around her. She was too perceptive. It was just so attractive a trait that it disarmed him before he could remember how dangerous it was. He needed to watch what he betrayed. He needed to commit to his lies, but he struggled, because no part of him really wanted to.

Jonathan looked down at the bike to break away from that look. Testing how it functioned with the alteration in place, he swung his leg over and sat into the suspension. The fit was good; though his left leg had to make room for the demolition bar, it wouldn't bother him while he was riding.

He looked up after a moment and saw she still looked down at him now, her face unchanged, her interest not diverted.

"You know," she said, "my father used to say that the best liars were men who say very little. He obviously never met you."

"Paige made me pancakes," Jonathan said. He smiled at his own blatant attempt to change the subject.

She put her hand on the handle bars and bent down to look at his eyes. "Just promise me you're not a terrorist," Leah said, and let a smile touch one side of her lips.

"I promise," he said.

You need to stop this, he thought.

He didn't need to introspect to know what was really happening. Yes, he was a terrible liar, but was that really an excuse? Was it reason to let suspicion gain any ground in Leah's thoughts? In his head, he had a responsibility to keep his secrets, because he didn't know what danger the things he knew posed to innocent bystanders, especially to his friends. He could only imagine how comforting it would be to have someone he could confide it all in. Leah was right there, so perceptive, so unjudging.

He'd already slipped in front of her, wanting to let go, when he'd betrayed his fear in the garage. He had to rein it in; his emotions weren't going to care for his responsibilities. They weren't being subtle; they were trying to trick him even now. They tried to tell him that if she somehow put the pieces together without him telling her the truth outright, then he hadn't really betrayed himself, or Heyer, or the world.

He almost laughed at himself then, realizing how ridiculous it all really was. Even if he blatantly explained it to her, she might not understand; he wasn't even sure he understood. It's why his roommates had seen nothing in Grant's accusations; the idea that the man was insane was so much more believable than the truth could ever be.

This is why the alien keeps me in the dark, Jonathan thought. This is what he means by trust.

It was one advantage, he realized, that he had over a surveillance team. He never had to fight in front of a world that could remember. No one could ever begin to piece together the reality from what they might observe watching him. The only way to know the truth would be if someone explained it. If Jonathan was interrogated, even tortured, he didn't know enough to compromise the alien.

CHAPTER THIRTY

SUNDAY | AUGUST 14, 2005 | 12:00 PM

"TIBBS, DID YOU get laid or something?" Lincoln asked.

He'd brought his attention back to Jonathan after looking out the window trying to fathom why his client would have purchased the beat up motorcycle parked in front of the gym. His expression said he hadn't come to any conclusions before losing interest.

"What… do you… mean?" Jonathan replied between pull ups.

"Well, you just seem, I don't know, happier today," Lincoln said. "If you were a girl, I'd ask if you were pregnant."

"Nope. Not pregnant," Jonathan said, starting to struggle to finish the reps.

"The black eye?" he said. "That have anything to do with all this training?"

"No," Jonathan said, dropping from the bar, "I stepped on a rake."

Lincoln smirked. "The rake deserve it?" he asked

"That rake got exactly what was coming to it," Jonathan said.

"Ahh, well, there ya go. Nothing quite as nice as being the person to give a rake what it had coming," Lincoln said.

Jonathan—despite feeling the drag from drinking the night before and having an unmistakable mark over his eye that told everyone who saw him that he'd been punched in the face—had been in a good mood all day. It had snuck up on him, after his concerns for his friends had been put to rest.

What was funny was that after a decade's worth of grammar school teachers telling him violence was never the answer, he was less afraid, more confident than he'd been in years. Even the ache over his eyelid gave him a sense of pride. He could see it was sad, considering where the feeling came from, but it didn't change it from being true.

Jonathan hadn't been in a real fist fight since the sixth grade. There hadn't ever been an instance where it sounded like a good idea, where he could have justified the action to himself. More, *the would be Jonathans* of the world putting *the Grants* in their place only happened in the movies Collin and Hayden had him watching.

"You ever watch the Rocky movies?" Jonathan asked Lincoln, changing the subject.

"Sure," Lincoln replied. "I'm a personal trainer after all."

"Well, I think the montage scenes in action hero movies are complete crap," Jonathan said.

"I'm listening."

"Well, they never show the guy pull a muscle, get stuck under the weight he can't lift and need a spotter to pull it off him, or get shin splints," Jonathan said.

Lincoln nodded. "Yeah, they still make me want to work out though."

There was a pause as they looked at one another.

"Yeah," Jonathan agreed.

"Technically, *Rocky* isn't really a hero movie," Lincoln said.

Jonathan looked up at him and frowned.

"It's a sports movie," Lincoln explained, "again, technically."

The trainer was right. Really, a lot of the movies his roommates had had him watching were sports movies if he thought about it. Life and death consequences seemed to be the fine line that divided Rocky from Rambo. That neither Collin nor Hayden had made the distinction yet seemed to hint at something, but Jonathan couldn't put his finger on it.

"You have a favorite?" Jonathan asked. "Sports movie, I mean."

"Yeah, I got the wrestling bug after I watched this crap movie from the 80's called *Vision Quest*," Lincoln said.

"Never heard of it," Jonathan said.

"I have a copy," Lincoln replied. "Let me know if you ever want to borrow it."

A few days later, Jonathan sat at his desk looking over a map of Seattle. He'd cut out a roughly fifteen by fifteen mile square with his home in the center. The alien had said he could expect to see the Ferox show up within a ten-mile radius of the house, so he'd placed markers in roughly half mile intervals throughout the map. He didn't have the time, money, or resources to setup elaborate traps, but he could at least know what locations might give him an advantage, or if not an advantage, at least a plan.

He'd never looked at a map this way before. It was encouraging to find out how much of the terrain was covered by water. Maybe if he was lucky, the damn thing would appear right over Lake Washington and drown. It was a pleasant thought, but if this alien technology could bring a Ferox to Earth from a different dimension of space and time, it would likely be sophisticated enough to land its passenger in a safe location. After all, it would be even better if the monster plummeted to the Earth from ten miles above him in the stratosphere and he could just side step it as it crashed into the pavement—not likely, though.

He hadn't seen Heyer again, not since they had sparred in the garage.

Jonathan stood, reaching for the duffel bag under his desk. Steel toed boots, Kevlar armored motorcycle jacket, gloves, hair clippers, an empty 1-gallon gas can, and some road flares. The gas can and road flares were recent additions. Most of the items were protective gear. He didn't know how resilient his skin would be once the device was activated. It didn't seem like these precautions could hurt.

He spent more time than he would've liked trying to find the jacket. It had fit perfectly, not hindering his mobility with the staff. He'd practiced training with it and the gloves on just to get used to it. The thickness of the materials between his skin and the bar made it so that he needed to learn to trust the movements without necessarily being able to feel the staff, and he didn't want to drop the weapon just because he hadn't been prepared for the increased difficulty. Also, the jacket had to remain snug. If it was loose, it was just an easy way to get ahold of him and would hinder more than it would help.

Jonathan didn't know if the beast could be intimidated by his size given how much bigger the Ferox was, but the coat made him appear larger as well. Jonathan backed down from large dogs even though he might outweigh them, but he didn't know if the same psychology would work on a Ferox. Still, given the choice, he'd rather look like an angry Doberman than a barking Pomeranian.

Like the jacket, his hair couldn't be an easy way to grab him. He needed to cut it short, hence the clippers.

As he looked over the gear, it occurred to him that he hadn't actually bought anything to carry it in; a duffel bag wasn't going to work if he needed to move quickly. In the corner of the room he saw his backpack, the one he'd used to carry his books to school. It had been sitting in that corner since the night Sickens the Fever had attacked—months now.

He reached over and placed it on the bed, dumping out its contents. Most of what poured out was textbooks, but there was also the folder with his half-finished paper. The same marked up draft that Paige had brought him in the hospital.

It still reminded him of a murder scene. There was no reason to keep it, he knew that. The quarter had ended and he hadn't turned it in. He wasn't prone to sentimentality. He should have just put it in the trash bin, but it tugged at him. He remembered thinking in the hospital that the draft had been so unrepairable. The wording was vague; the research did a poor job of supporting his theory. There were a few paragraphs here and there that were solid, but the rest read like he was attempting to trick a teacher's assistant into giving him a passing grade.

Now he wondered why he'd even bothered writing it if it was so poorly thought out. He'd have been better off starting over, picking a different topic. He put the textbooks onto his bookcase; he found himself trying to summon regret as he did so, but it felt disingenuous. He couldn't turn this into a heartfelt Hallmark movie moment for his lost dreams because it simply wasn't.

What came to mind was something his mother had told him once, when he was a teenager, just having had his heart broken for the first time. She'd found him in his room staring up at the ceiling, struggling to come to terms with the rejection, the future he'd imagined with the girl whisked away.

"At first, you'll want the hurt to go away, to find some way to cut the feelings out of yourself. Then, as time passes, you'll find yourself clinging to that pain. Somehow, your heart believes that to stop feeling hurt is a betrayal. That it calls into question your own faith in your commitment to the passion you had.

"Life is clever, Jonathan. One day you wake up and realize it doesn't hurt, yet there was never any betrayal. It's not that your emotions changed, but that you're no longer the person who felt those things in the first place. That person is in the past, and his feelings were real, but you are no longer him.

"That person will have become a story you tell yourself to remember who you thought you were."

She'd been right, of course, and now here he was again, unable to connect to the things he'd placed so much importance in months earlier, barely able to recognize that person who had been a student. He hardly even knew that Jonathan's thoughts or motives any longer, like a stranger who had worn his face in another time.

He folded up the map he'd completed and fitted it into the front pocket of the jacket.

Maybe it wasn't who he planned to be, and maybe no one would ever see anything other than a guy who threw his life away when he was young. That was how he was going to look to the world after all, a man constantly readying himself to be a warrior with no war to fight. Of course, he really was getting ahead of himself—chances were he'd only be this person for another fifteen days, give or take. Even if he survived the Ferox, how could he possibly survive the onslaught? That poorly-written paper was a reflection in the mirror. He, like it, had needed to be replaced.

After putting the gear away, he headed down to the garage to train. He was halfway across the living room when his roommates stopped him. They'd been watching a movie he didn't recognize and had paused it when Jonathan entered.

"Jonathan, wait, check this out!" Collin said excitedly, approaching him with his laptop.

On the screen was a comic book cover that showed a mockup of Jesus basking in light from behind and far more muscular than Jonathan remembered ever seeing him. His garb looked more Jedi-like than the robes of a poor carpenter's son. He held a gnarled staff that appeared to be radiating with some kind of mysterious comic book energy. Jesus' eyes glowed with light that hid his pupils.

"Wow, is this the cover of the first book?" Jonathan asked.

"Yeah, we've got the first three sketched and colored. We're releasing on the Internet as a digital download, so we don't have to deal with comic book publishers. We've been hyping this up on comic book forums since we thought of it. Got about six more follow up books written, but they aren't sketched yet. We just need to name the series.

"Let me know if you like any of these," Hayden said, consulting a list they had on the table. "Jesus-man, God-Man, or Christ-Man?"

Jonathan raised an eyebrow. "Those are terrible."

"Man from Heaven? or The Adventures of the Son of God?"

Jonathan attempted to smile but knew it must look forced.

"We need feedback from someone who isn't heavily into comics," Hayden explained.

"The New Testament Reloaded?"

"The First Coming?"

Jonathan held a hand up to stop them. "I'm sure you'll come up with something that works."

Hayden continued brain storming regardless. "Hey, what if each comic has its own unique subtitle? I mean, we can do whatever we want, right?"

"So what are you thinking?" Collin asked.

"I want to call the first book *The New Testament Reloaded: Christ Begins,*" Hayden said.

"As the story arc progresses, we'll change the subtitle for each issue then?" Collin said.

"Exactly," Hayden replied.

Jonathan had walked away, thinking they must now be lost in their creative world again, then noticed their voices were following him into the garage.

His practice staff was leaning against the weight bench. He must have forgotten to put it away the night before. He picked it up, making a mental effort to tune out his roommates as he fell into the motions, warming up.

His grace with the weapon was breathtaking at times. He was deep in his mind, imagining the various attacks he might encounter from a Ferox and implementing a response to them in the real world. He realized, suddenly, that he no longer heard any of the chatter that had followed him into the room. He looked up and saw Hayden and Collin watching him. They didn't snap out of it until Jonathan had stopped moving and started staring back at them.

"That was amazing, Tibbs." Hayden's voice was filled with awe.

No one other than Heyer and his staff instructor had ever really seen him practice. That it affected his roommates to the point of open-jawed amazement caught him by surprise.

"Yeah, man, you've got a real talent with that," Collin agreed.

Jonathan was flattered briefly, until Collin snapped his fingers and exclaimed, "Let's go back to the scene where we flashback to Jesus staff training with his father. I want to make Joseph divinely inspired by the power of the Holy Spirit!"

"Nice!" Hayden agreed as they both turned and headed up the stairs.

Two hours later, Jonathan found himself drenched in sweat and exhausted, another day behind him. He took off the bag gloves and unwrapped his hands. He remembered the first time he'd attempted to use the bag without the wraps supporting his wrist. His hands had shaken for an hour afterward and he couldn't understand how boxers could hit a bag for so long without damaging their hands and wrists. It

turned out certain safety precautions got left out when you bought a secondhand heavy bag at a garage sale.

He hung the wrist wraps and gloves on the wall where he'd built a
place for them, then found himself staring down at his hands.

They were young looking, callused, but not the massive hands of
a man. His father's hands would make his look like they belonged to
a child. He couldn't help but think they would never be enough. The
Ferox could probably swallow his entire fist without even choking. How
could these hands ever stop the beast? It wasn't a confidence building
thought, and it wasn't the first time he'd looked down at his hands and
worried about how fragile they made him feel.

He needed to look down at his hands and see weapons.

He was about to leave the garage when he saw his staff lying on the
floor. He picked it up to return it to the cabinet and noticed the contents
were not as he had left them.

The cabinet usually housed his two practice staffs and the metal
demolition bar. Today, there was an additional item. It was as long and
tall as the demolition bar but was wrapped in brown recycled paper with
a piece of twine. There was a note attached to it. Jonathan pulled it out
and sat on the bench. It was heavy, but not as heavy as the demolition
bar. The note was typed, not handwritten, and simply said:

This is within Earthly means, but barely.
It will not break. I promise.
Will be around soon.

The note wasn't signed, but it didn't need to be. Heyer had left this for
him. He'd even wrapped it.

Jonathan pulled the staff from the paper and stared into a reflective
surface. It was an exact replica of the demolition bar as far as dimensions
went, but it wasn't the same material.

Beautiful, Jonathan found himself thinking, no other word coming
to mind.

His eyes got lost in its reflective surface like a man mesmerized by a
camp fire. He didn't know anything about metal working, but he'd seen a
lot of different materials in his time at the hardware store. This, he didn't

recognize. It was smooth to the touch and it caught the light strangely, as though it were dark graphite at one angle and then silver at another. He could feel its resilience. Perhaps it was an alloy that was hard to come by or that humans didn't know how to isolate or temper; maybe it was the way the weapon had been forged, but it felt invincible.

He ran his hand down the surface and felt some imperfections in the steel near the center. He flipped it over to see that the alien had put an engraving into one of the surfaces.

"Excali-bar," Jonathan said out loud.

He smiled, rolling his eyes at the alien's sense of humor. It occurred to him that he'd never thought of Heyer as having a sense of humor.

He tested its fit in the motorcycle holster and was pleased to find it clicked into place as well as the original. For a moment, he thought he might show it to Mr. Fletcher, see if he knew what it was, but realized it wouldn't be wise. Better to keep it hidden until he needed it, especially if it might border on being otherworldly.

Confidence seemed to flow through the staff into him. He saw himself before the beast holding this weapon, and briefly, felt something he hadn't before: impatient. He looked forward to standing in front of his enemy with this weapon, to strike the monster down with it. It was iconic, something a knight would slay a dragon with; something a king would pull from a stone. It reminded him of the stories his roommates indulged in over and over again.

He was honored just to hold it. He'd never felt this for the device implanted in his chest. That had been forced on him, and he could never set it down. The implant owned him; it wasn't a weapon so much as it was the chain shackling him to his future. This was different; he'd earned this weapon, and it made him feel like fate was finally trying to level the field.

He didn't believe in such things; it wasn't his nature. Still, it felt good to think that maybe, the universe saw him, and was on his side.

CHAPTER THIRTY-ONE

WEDNESDAY | AUGUST 24, 2005 | 8:15 PM

JONATHAN PUT THE phone down on the bed next to him. He took a deep breath as he finally released his grip.

Telling his mother, with no real explanation, that he hadn't attended college for the last quarter was like his nightmares; not for the fear, but for the shame. Her disapproval had been raw and genuine.

Like all of his conversations, it was overshadowed by his frustrating silence in the face of the question *why?* It was worse with his mother, because he'd kept her in the dark about the night in the hospital. He couldn't just rely on her taking pity on him; she wouldn't assume that something inside him was injured and needed time to heal. It felt like, to her eyes, he was purposely and self-destructively throwing his life away.

He started the conversation by explaining that there was nothing to be done, he'd waited until registration for the coming quarter had come and passed. She hadn't exploded in anger. He'd caught her so off guard that she'd been at a loss on how to deal with the news. At times, there had been a silence on the other side of the phone line that disturbed him to his core.

This was far from the last of it. Evelyn would show up in person soon. She'd be upset with Paige for not having told her that Jonathan was having such an unexpected shift in his behavior. He'd have to explain that he'd forbidden her and again be left unable to explain his actions.

Why? The looming question he faced gave him sympathy for Heyer. There he'd been, demanding answers the alien felt he had good reason not to give. What was truly worse, not knowing the answer, or being forced to carry the truth alone?

When he'd finally succeeded in getting off the phone, he knew he'd be screening his calls for weeks unless he could think of something to say, a lie that would satisfy her, a story that fit the appearance but wasn't the truth. Maybe, when she showed up on his doorstep, he'd have to tell her about the attack. That was a problem for a future Jonathan to deal with. Right now, he had to be concerned with getting to that future.

He took some solace in the thought that at least he'd told her. She hadn't heard it from a student loan adviser; she wouldn't just find out when he ended up dead in the weeks to come. Given the time-traveling parallel dimension-jumping paradoxical complexities of the whole mess, Jonathan didn't know what it would look like to the people he left behind if he died. He would have to ask the alien; of course, that didn't mean he would get a straight answer, or any answer, for that matter.

No. He would demand to know this much.

It was with these thoughts that Jonathan rested his head that night. He'd ceased to be afraid of sleep. Troubling dreams were just a part of what he was now, perhaps a part of his training. He was quite familiar with the sensation of fear. He got a lesson every night.

A few days later, he looked up from his computer screen to see Heyer's reflection in his window.

The alien either came into existence in his bedroom or had entered the house so quietly that he hadn't heard him. Both were possible, but at least Jonathan hadn't jumped this time.

"I was starting to worry you wouldn't be back again," Jonathan said.

"I said I would be here," Heyer said, "so here I am."

"Yeah," Jonathan replied, turning in his chair to face him.

"How are you faring?" Heyer asked. "The gate will be breached soon."

At first, it seemed like a commanding officer asking a soldier for a progress report, but Jonathan wasn't in the military. The question was a kindness, a concern for his state of mind.

As the day drew nearer, Jonathan's self-preservation refused to come to terms with the realities. It was possible that nothing Jonathan did between now and the moment the Ferox arrived could ever make him strong enough to defeat it, and this uncertainty in the face of a slow, tortuous death begged him to search for an escape. Beg as it may, the situation was a cage with no door: no way to flee, no lock to pick. Knowing it and accepting it was not the same thing.

"I'd like some straight answers on a few things," Jonathan said.

If Heyer noticed the blatant side step of his question, he showed no offense to it.

"I'll do my best to accommodate," Heyer replied.

He studied the alien for a moment. "If I die, if the Ferox kills me, what will happen?" Jonathan asked. "What will it look like to my friends and family?"

"Jonathan, I think it best not to entertain the—" Heyer began.

"Please, don't, not on this. Just tell me," Jonathan said.

Heyer paused at being interrupted, seeming to look into Jonathan's eyes and weigh his motives. Jonathan just hoped he would see his need for certainty on this of all things.

Soon, the alien took a breath and let it out slowly.

"Your body will disappear from this plane of existence. If you are in a room with people, it will appear that you blinked away. The time of your disappearance will correspond to the moment of your activation. The moment the gate begins to open on earth."

"Aren't you worried someone will notice?" Jonathan asked.

"No; if this contingency is to occur and someone is looking directly at you, they will most likely not be believed upon reporting. More than likely, over time, they will simply assume that they misremembered what happened, that you got up and left or some such scenario, and disappeared later. Even if the worst case scenario was to occur and multiple witnesses corroborated that you had vanished, what would come of it?" Heyer pointed out.

Jonathan nodded. It was elegant in its own simplicity, really. Even he, after all, had questioned his own memory when what he remembered seemed impossible. As for multiple witnesses, they may not question their memory, but the world would.

"What happens to my body? Where does it go when it disappears?" Jonathan asked.

"Through the gate," Heyer said. "Much like the corpse of the Ferox."

"Why?" Jonathan asked. His eyes were closed, his head shaking as he yet again grew frustrated with the senseless rules of this conflict.

"I'm sorry, Jonathan," Heyer said. "It is best I don't answer that. It's for both of our protection."

Jonathan opened his eyes, anger showing on his face.

"Our protection," he said, his tone questioning the alien's honesty. "You really mean your protection, so stop making it like you are doing me any favors."

Heyer seemed surprised, almost hurt, that Jonathan questioned his statement.

"Don't look at me like that. I know that we're being watched right now," Jonathan said. "I know they've been watching me, at least since the night I went to the hospital."

"Yes, this is true," Heyer said. "I'm curious to know how you came to be aware of it?"

"Oh, are you? Well, I curious to know why you didn't tell me about it! I was completely blindsided. I wasn't sure I should—" Jonathan stopped. "I wasn't even sure I should tell you."

Heyer was hard to read, but again, Jonathan thought he looked pained by his statement. "Why would you think to hide this from me?" Heyer asked.

Jonathan's frustration erupted at the question. Heyer told him so little that he couldn't even have a conversation with the man. If the alien would just trust him, stop deciding for him what he needed to know, then this didn't have to be so difficult. Time was drawing near, and Jonathan couldn't escape. He couldn't see what harm remained in letting the alien know how infuriating it was to be kept in the dark.

"Has it never occurred to you that I didn't want this? Does that really come as some surprise? You've never proven that you can be trusted, and the fact that my country's authorities are investigating you doesn't make you seem any more trustworthy!"

He was like a teenager revolting against his parents after years of being told what to do. Pointing this out to the alien after they both ignored it for so long, it was like forcing him to acknowledge the elephant in the room instead of just letting him discount it with the promise that answers would eventually come.

"How do I know you aren't using me? How do I know I'm not involved in something evil? That these people aren't investigating you because you're the villain?" Jonathan asked. "How else am I supposed to get my life back? I don't see how I ever get my freedom if I blindly follow you. You'd have me forfeit everything because you tell me to! On what? Faith? You're just an alien who broke into my house, ripped me apart, and enslaved me to this thing you put inside my chest! You think all this didn't occur to me when I found out there were people out there who might help me if I turned you over to them!"

He tried to calm himself down. Somewhere in his tirade, the anger had neared sobbing. It wasn't how he'd imagined the outburst going in his head. It made it more difficult to think about what he wanted to say.

"I don't have a clue what your motives are, and you've taken everything from me. Why shouldn't I just lead them straight to you? That's the big secret, right? They're watching me to get their hands on you!"

Somewhere in the middle of Jonathan's outburst, Heyer had taken on a look of patience rather than surprise. He'd folded his arms and stared at the floor, the ridiculous fedora covering his eyes as he waited for Jonathan to finish, for him to regain his composure.

"That you have chosen the course you have," Heyer said, "instead of trying to use this knowledge as a weapon against me… it represents the very trust that I spoke of."

Heyer paused as he seemed to think this statement more weighted than Jonathan immediately understood.

"I will answer some of your questions Jonathan, but first let me ask you something. Why didn't you choose to betray me?"

"I didn't choose anything," Jonathan said.

"But you did, when you didn't seek out the government cell that you've become aware of. Why not go to them? Why not offer your participation in my apprehension? Why not stand on your doorstep and yell that you'll tell them anything they want to know? It's a chance to escape, isn't it? Why didn't you take it?"

Jonathan looked up at Heyer.

"I'm not sure," Jonathan admitted, almost growling the answer and then breaking the stare to look at the floor. "Intuition. Something didn't seem right. I don't like gut feelings, Heyer; a person is stupid to trust them for long without knowing why they're there. My gut told me that helping them apprehend you would hurt the world more than it would help me."

"I understand this," Heyer said, taking a long breath. "I am not good or evil, Jonathan. Such concepts are for the simple-minded, and I think you know that. I admit, it would be easier to think of things as straightforward, easier to ask a man to forfeit his life if he believes he is playing the part of the hero.

"I can only make you two promises about my motives. I am doing my best to follow my own moral compass and I will always try to push you in the direction I think best for your species. I give you my word on this."

Heyer let what he was saying sink in, taking a moment to appraise Jonathan's reaction, before he continued. "The truth is, this was *never* about good or evil."

It was as real an answer as Jonathan would get. Heyer believed he was doing what was best for mankind, but recognized that he could be wrong. Yet, the very admission, that recognition that he knew he might be wrong, made Jonathan's intuition strengthen its belief in the alien.

"Okay, but," Jonathan sighed, "why are the authorities after you then?"

"Your government took interest in my activities a long time ago," he said. "Believe me when I tell you that we've been playing this game for quite a while now. They detected the presence of a technologically advanced being on their planet due to some of my early mistakes. As human technology improves, the task of staying a step ahead grows more difficult. Rest assured, you, Jonathan, are ten times more knowledgeable about my activities than they are," Heyer said, "and that is why they are watching you. The more they believe you know, the more aggressive they will be in obtaining this information."

You're in deep shit. Grant's words echoed in Jonathan's thoughts.

"How is it, Jonathan," Heyer asked, curiosity on his face, "that you became aware of their surveillance?"

"They had a man dating my roommate," Jonathan said. "A few weeks back he lost his composure, told me I was being watched, tried to trick me into telling him what I knew, tried to get me to turn myself in. I think we were lucky that they hired an idiot."

Heyer began to pace the room, bringing his fingers to his lips. His movements, even when he was lost in his thoughts, were a combination of human and precision. They made him appear so familiar, yet different.

Angelic, Jonathan thought.

He remembered that when he'd first seen the man, as an intruder in his home, the grace he failed to hide had been so sinister, snake-like. Now, he wondered, had their initial meeting been under different circumstances, would this grace have been comforting instead of vilifying?

"This is…." Heyer stopped. "I haven't seen a surveillance team be so sloppy since long before the Cold War."

"What does that mean?" Jonathan asked.

"It means that I find it doubtful that this apparent accident was unplanned," Heyer said.

"Why would they screw up on purpose?" Jonathan asked.

"That is the question," Heyer said. "It's either a genuine mistake or a tactic."

"Heyer, aren't they listening to us right now? Isn't this place bugged?" Jonathan asked, pointing his finger in the air and rotating it.

Heyer looked up from his thoughts and stopped pacing. He smiled at Jonathan.

"They can see us. They know I am here right now," Heyer said. "However, they cannot hear anything we are discussing. And yes, the room is bugged."

"How's that?"

"Human technology, or at least devices for interpreting, amplifying, or recording sound waves, is easy to manipulate. I monitor and block certain coordinates throughout the globe. One of those coordinates is your home. I initiated the block weeks before we met. Stationary things, like a location, are easy and require nothing be physically present. In other words, since the house doesn't move, no 'alien' equipment needs to be left here to maintain the block against unwanted recording devices."

When he referred to his equipment as alien he'd pointed to himself to show the irony.

"Unfortunately, I cannot always arrange conversations at a specific location; the device in my chest tracks me, indiscriminately blocking the space around me as I move," Heyer explained. "End result, the only way to eavesdrop on us is to be within earshot physically, with an actual ear. When I'm present, you won't even be able to make a phone call."

"That does explain Grant," Jonathan said. "I'd wondered why they used him at all, but if you can't listen from afar you'd have to find a way to get someone inside."

"Yes," Heyer said, "but it also calls into question his actions; why go to all that trouble inserting an asset arranged to monitor you, only to let you find out about it?"

Jonathan sat back in his chair. It was all a lot to think about. Still, though, Heyer hadn't said anything about the most important question he had asked.

"You still seem troubled, Jonathan," Heyer said.

"Heyer, I appreciate your honesty on these things, but you didn't answer the question that really matters in the end. I'm worried that you can't answer it."

"The question of your freedom," Heyer said. Heyer sighed. He was more human suddenly, perhaps because he seemed to grow tired.

Jonathan didn't answer. He waited.

"Jonathan, I've lived a long time," he said. "If we want to measure a life by rotations around the sun, as is your Earthly custom, I am thousands of years old."

Jonathan didn't know what to make of this admission. He didn't know what he expected Heyer to say, but he hadn't expected him to reveal something like his age.

"I have watched man's society evolve. I've considered more men, more human beings, to be my friends throughout your history, than I have any of my own species." Heyer looked up at Jonathan. "In a lot of ways, I know more about you than you truly know yourself. You were identified before birth as a primary candidate for the implant. Due to the course your life took, I feared that the process that selected you would be voided. I didn't come to the decision to give you this responsibility easily. All that said, and after having seen you survive even when everything said you should have died, I think you are lying to yourself about what you think it is that you want."

"I know I don't want to die this way," Jonathan said.

"No, I don't doubt that you wish to live, Jonathan—what I doubt is this attachment you have to your previous life trajectory," Heyer explained.

"My life trajectory." Jonathan felt a stir of anger at his previous endeavors being reduced to two stupid words. "You sound like a damn guidance counselor. You don't know a—"

"—What was it for, Jonathan?" Heyer interrupted.

"What? What do you mean?" Jonathan asked.

"You went to college; you chose to study the life sciences. What did you want to do with that knowledge Jonathan? Why was it so important that you devoted over three years of your life to it?" Heyer asked.

Jonathan was flustered by the question. The alien asked it like it should have an obvious answer. It didn't, and it couldn't.

But shouldn't it? He wondered.

"Did you want to cure cancer? Did you want to be a doctor? Did you want to save the environment?" the alien asked.

Jonathan searched for an answer; it was difficult, on the spot like this. He felt like he'd known the answer, that at some point he decided it was his path, but the reasons wouldn't come to him.

"I didn't have a five-year plan, Heyer. Knowing what made life work was important to me, gaining that knowledge was supposed to point the way. I figured I'd find what I wanted to do eventually," Jonathan said.

Heyer shook his head at the answer. "You've worried about this freedom you want back. This has weighed on you for nearly three months now. Yet, you do not know the answer to this question. Do you not find that curious? Do you not know what it is you want this freedom for?" Heyer said.

Jonathan felt he was being manipulated, like Heyer was just trying to make him feel stupid for wanting control of his own destiny. He clenched his jaw, but didn't try to hide the anger building as he listened, refusing to look at the alien.

"You are a smart man, Jonathan. You're scientific in nature; wise beyond your age. You don't believe in anything past what you can prove. You don't like gut feelings, and you choose not to delude yourself about the world. All things are admirable in and of themselves," Heyer said, "and yes, you would have finished college, but only because you are dedicated. Yet, you lack the fundamental thing that would've made any of it mean anything to you."

In a low, skeptical voice, still unwilling to look at the alien, Jonathan asked, "What's that?"

"Call it what you want, Jonathan—a vocation, a calling. You've never had a sense of the true meaning of those words because you've never felt them. You'd run the danger of spending your whole life as a powder keg of potential, dying to be ignited, your own brain repeatedly getting in the way. You'd never have been able to find a good reason to do anything because you don't believe in anything. You don't stand for anything. You are missing the very spark that ignites ambitions."

"It doesn't mean I'd never have found it," Jonathan said, starting to feel drained by the words the alien spoke, surprised he hadn't argued.

"Jonathan," Heyer said in a low voice, "I know the future waiting for you. I see you doing a job you've admitted to yourself long ago that you hate. Then, one day, you realize you've lied at interviews, pretended to care about things you don't, all in pursuit of something you never wanted, because you didn't know what else to do. That day, you realize it happened so slowly, one compromise with yourself at a time, that you somehow forgot it wasn't right to have to be what you've become."

For a moment, Jonathan found himself disturbed at the thought that Heyer might mean he knew "the future" literally.

"You keep surviving, but you are unsure why you bother. You are desperate for the world to tell you what to do with yourself, because you never found that spark, the thing that would give it all meaning. Desperate for someone to tell you that you are the one to do something and the world needs you to go do it. Desperate for anyone to tell you what you should give a damn about," Heyer said sympathetically. "But most of all, you would be desperate to find a way to believe that 'someone' if he ever showed up to tell you."

Heyer waited a moment before continuing, not wanting to move ahead and leave Jonathan bewildered. No one liked to be told someone knew them better than they know themselves.

"Jonathan, do you know why human stories are so filled with spirits, angels, gods, mythical creatures, even aliens, that show up and guide men to what it is they should do?" Heyer asked.

He thought about it, but the answer came quickly.

"Because if it was just another man," Jonathan said, "it wouldn't be enough."

"So here I am, the only being on this planet who will ever fit the criteria. I tell you this road has meaning for you, that your previous one did not. It's an opinion, from a being outside your species that you would never have heard without that device 'chained' to your chest. But I'm not a salesman, and I do not want to sell you on this, and I certainly don't want to lecture you. What I think is pretty straight forward.

"This world is not meant for everyone. It doesn't hold that spark for all of you; it can't. People like you, Jonathan, will never find purpose in anything short of the unquestionable. So yes, I ask you to forfeit your life, in the defense of your species. It's the closest I can get you. I ask you to stop focusing on having a choice, and really ask yourself if the choice that was made for you isn't one you wish you could have made for yourself—because all this worry over freedom and choice, it's just a smoke screen for something else if you don't know why you want it."

They didn't speak for a long while.

Jonathan rocked back and forth a bit, staring at the floor. He toiled around in a swamp of changing emotions and thoughts. He didn't want to admit to himself that it felt true, any of it: that he'd never really known what he was doing, that he worried he never would, that he tried to ignore it by sweeping it under a rug of life's realities. After all, in this world, it didn't matter if you had a drive behind what you did; you had to find a way to live, fulfilling or not. Heyer had taken his freedom, but had he given him something more important?

"It's too much to ask someone staring death in the face to accept that they would've preferred it this way twenty years from now. Even if it's an alien doing the asking," Jonathan said.

Heyer nodded his understanding.

"I'll try to think about it."

It meant something to Jonathan that Heyer at least conceded it was a bigger question than he could be expected to answer in the heat of an emotional lecture. Jonathan wasn't one to argue for argument's sake. He felt enough self-doubt to think that Heyer might be more right than he wanted to admit. He wasn't ready to concede it, though—not yet.

"Do you know when the Ferox will arrive? Do you have a better idea now that it's closer?" Jonathan asked in a whisper.

"Late Friday, September fourth, most likely. Possibly the morning of the fifth," Heyer said.

Twelve days, best case. Jonathan took a deep breath and nodded.

It was comforting that Heyer hadn't checked his watch. He hadn't shown any hurry, no rush to be off to other chores.

"Have you ever been in a war, Heyer?" Jonathan asked.

Heyer seemed caught off guard by the question, the shift of focus. It was more personal than anything Jonathan had ever asked him. He'd always been so focused on himself and his own problems in the presence of the alien he'd never thought to ask him something like this, something a friend might ask.

"Yes," Heyer said.

"Were you afraid?" Jonathan asked.

Heyer looked up into Jonathan's eyes.

"I was terrified," Heyer said.

Jonathan nodded. "How did you keep it from stopping you, the fear? How did you do what you needed to?" Jonathan asked.

"There was a saying where I came from," Heyer said. "It doesn't translate perfectly, but the gist is this: *fear is the heart alone.*"

Jonathan nodded, waiting for the alien to continue.

"The first time I was in combat, I was lucky. My brother was in the trenches with me. Had I not known he was there, I don't know that I would've survived," Heyer said.

Jonathan nodded. "It's like kids in the dark," Jonathan said. "Alone, it's terrifying, but if someone is with you, sometimes you can forget to be afraid."

It was Heyer's turn to nod.

"Unfortunately, that doesn't help me much," Jonathan said, defeated.

"Jonathan, if it helps to know, I will be there when you fight. You won't see me. I won't be able to help you, I cannot intercede, but should you fall, someone will have witnessed that you tried."

It should have been little comfort, as from what he understood, his efforts would be banished to a nonexistent timeline in his death. Jonathan tried not to think of that; instead, he tried to be grateful that someone would be there while he was still breathing.

After that, what did it really matter?

CHAPTER THIRTY-TWO

HE DIDN'T REMEMBER when he'd started to think of the garage as his friend. It was really just a cocoon large enough to contain him as he was forced to change. He'd found the same protection, the same isolation, in the MRI machine at the hospital, in his drug-imposed coma, huddled on the shower floor.

Its interior had changed along with him these last few months until it was hardly recognizable.

The poor man's Batcave, Jonathan thought as he lay on the padded floor, looking up at the rafters. He listened to the hum of the fan, the rain hitting the roof, and the sputtering of the gutters outside.

He hadn't focused a great deal on gymnastic moves, but he'd drilled on the "Kip Up" repeatedly. He wanted to know that no matter how bad a blow he took, no matter how dazed his head might be, his body would be able to perform this maneuver. To get him back to his feet. It had taken him a long time to get the hang of it. Now, he hadn't failed the maneuver in over a week, but it was important that he keep the motions fresh.

He planted his hands on each side of his head, his legs went up, and the motion rolled down his body, until he thrust to his feet in one graceful movement.

He stopped practicing when the door to the garage opened.

She hadn't knocked, and she didn't look surprised to find him there alone. The rain outside had gotten to her as she made the short walk between their houses. Her hair was hanging down around her shoulders, curling where the water had touched it. Her camera hung around her neck. She seemed to shiver, but shook it off as she stepped into the garage.

This girl had to know how nervous she made him. Jonathan was frustrated with the paradox of the feeling, the excitement to be near her mixed with the fear that held him away. He didn't know why she had invited herself over. It became clearer when he saw she held a bottle by the neck in one hand and two empty glasses in the other.

People get the luxury of drinking to forget the problems that infect their days, or at least the luxury of trying. It wasn't that it hadn't occurred to him that it might be healthy to forget his life, even if just for a few hours, even if just to get a decent night's sleep. He'd allowed himself on Paige's birthday, knowing it might be the last birthday he ever attended. That hadn't turned out so great. If he wanted to die without any excuses, there could be no time wasted. But, he didn't think of this now; all that occurred to him was that Leah was here, the two of them alone together in his cocoon.

She didn't have to ask him. She didn't even have to speak. He simply looked to the bottle in her hands and up to her eyes and nodded. He walked over to the weight bench and sat with his back to the metal bar. She sat facing him, putting the bottle and the glasses between them, using the bench as a makeshift table. Then she poured.

"Thanks for not making me ask," she said.

"Thanks for thinking of me," he replied. "Should we drink to something?"

"If you want."

Jonathan tried to think of something that didn't sound like a cliché, something personal to them. It didn't take him long.

"To less awkward moments," he said.

She smiled at him, and they both drank. It was a strong liquor, some type of whiskey, dark with amber hues, like the color of her hair. He could feel the burn run down his throat, could feel the garage getting warmer around him. It was right somehow, perfect; it was what he would have imagined a girl like Leah drinking if the thought had occurred to him to imagine such things.

"You go next," Jonathan said.

"To forgetting September 1st," she said.

He'd never been sentimental about dates. If someone had asked him what day his father had died, he couldn't have said. It wasn't because he hadn't been scarred; it was that the date didn't have anything to do with it. It was a lot like the way Heyer had described birthdays, just another trip around the sun. Even if he never got it, he wasn't about to be the jerk who pointed it out. Clearly, today was one of those dates for Leah; clearly, she wanted him to know.

It didn't take many rounds of this until Jonathan had to confess he couldn't drink anymore. She started to pour again and he waved his hand at her in defeat. She put the bottle on the ground, carefully, and then the glasses.

She turned around, sliding across the bench toward him, and then reclining into him like a chair. Her head against his chest, he sat back until the bar holding his weights caught him. He crossed his hands around her and held her.

"I didn't want to be alone," she said. "I knew you were here. I could hear you hitting the mats over and over again. I don't need to talk about it, I just wanted company."

"I'll try to be good company," he said.

Some time passed. No one spoke. He couldn't see her face, just her bare feet crossed at the end of the bench. She didn't seem to be waiting for him to say anything, so he just enjoyed her warmth against him. Finally, she broke the silence.

"Doesn't this place make you lonely?" Her tone was different than it had been a moment ago; inquisitive, as though she'd been distracted from whatever memories she'd been avoiding by examining the furnishings of Jonathan's cocoon. "You're always in here, by yourself."

"I get lonely, but I like it here," he admitted. "When I'm around people, they always want to talk. Somewhere along the line, talking got too exhausting, too complicated."

She tilted her head so he could see her face, smiling at him. "Yes, well, we've seen you struggle on that front."

"Humph," he responded, a laugh that only lasted one breath. "It's hard to find someone who's comfortable for long in silence."

She nodded, and then she pulled away from him. He missed the warmth of her. She turned and looked him in the eye, her head tilting seductively.

"Can I take your picture, Jonathan?" Leah asked.

"Now? Here?" He asked.

"Yes," she said. "This place is you, but without you in it, it's just a garage."

She took the camera from around her neck and turned to face him. She looked at him through the lens, turning the focus to capture him how she wanted. She shook her head. He could see from her concentration, she wasn't finding what she'd hoped. With her hand, she indicated for him to stand.

He was unsure what she was looking for, but he rose from the bench and walked about the garage. She watched him patiently. When he turned back to her for help, she only nodded, as if to say, *I'll tell you when I see it.*

Finally, when he stood in front of one of the large mirrors, she asked him to stop. He waited, looking at his reflection, unsure what to do with himself, unsure what she saw. She snapped a few shots and frowned.

"It's missing something," she said.

He shrugged, not knowing how to help.

"It's your face," she said. "Your expression isn't right."

She gave him that look he liked so much, when he could tell she wanted to ask him something, but didn't want to cross a boundary. He already knew she was going to ask; her restraint always lost to her curiosity.

"That night, with Grant, you had this look," she said. "After he'd hit you, when you stood, when you picked yourself up and turned to face him. It was your real face."

He thought he should be more alarmed at what she was bringing up, more uncomfortable. He wasn't. She was the first person who ever seemed to want to see that face.

"It was—it was just rage," he said.

She shook her head.

"No. It wasn't a snarl; it wasn't mindless anger. I knew when I saw that expression that Grant was in real trouble. It was exciting, in a way," she said. "I thought, *this is the face of someone who won't be stopped.*"

He was quiet for a moment, looking at her reflection behind him in the mirror. "I can't do it on request," he said.

She nodded. Then he could see she was trying to think of a way around the problem.

"What happened? In your head, what changed at that moment, after he'd hit you?" she asked.

He thought about it. Only one word came to mind.

"Permission," he said.

"Permission?" She tested the sound if it, seemed intrigued by it. Her expression changed then, she nodded and she set the camera down, apparently having given up on capturing what she'd hoped for. She stood and walked to him. When she was within his reach, she stopped.

"Permission to what?" she asked.

"I'm not really sure," he said.

She held his gaze awhile longer, but seemed to believe he wasn't being vague on purpose. A moment passed, and she stepped closer.

"You know why I like you?" she asked, changing the subject.

He shook his head slowly.

"You…." She poked him gently in the chest. "Are always so busy. A girl wouldn't have to worry about you getting clingy or overly attached, if…." She paused. "If she were looking for someone who wouldn't get clingy, or overly attached."

"I suppose you're right," he said.

When she kissed him, he knew he'd lied. He could easily get overly attached. If she knew, then for the first time, she hadn't called him out on it.

She was asleep next to him. He could see her bare back rising and falling with her breath in the dim light coming in from the window. The room was pleasant, Jonathan thought, though sparse for a girl with so many hobbies: no mirrors, no art, just dark wood furniture and the bed. He liked that. The bed itself was the only extravagance, a queen with a white down comforter. It was like a bed sized cotton ball in an otherwise elegant room. The digital clock on her night stand said two o'clock in the morning in large, blue light.

He didn't remember falling asleep or when she had rolled away from him in the night, the liquor fogging his memory. He no longer felt its effects, but he was thirsty.

He slowly got out of the bed so as not to wake her. It was tomorrow after all, the anniversary was over; if she slept deeply and woke without a hangover maybe she would just remember the good parts of yesterday. He found his jeans and T-shirt on the floor and silently slipped them on. Jack had been asleep for hours, but he didn't like the idea of the kid finding him walking around their home in his boxers.

When he got to the kitchen, he poured himself a glass of water, then he turned and noticed that the light was on under the door to the garage. There had been no light a moment ago, he was almost sure. Maybe Jack was awake after all. Why was he in the garage at 2 a.m. though? Jonathan walked over and slowly opened the door. Peeking in, he didn't see anyone, just the metal statue. It looked more complete than he remembered, so he stepped inside to take a better look.

It occurred to him, then; he was dreaming.

The light was coming from a workbench off to the side of the statue. Sitting on a stool in front of the bench was a man, his back to Jonathan, wearing a blue collar shirt and hiking boots. Between them was a hoist, suspending a truck engine from chains. Jonathan remembered the engine from his father's garage, the one he'd thought to fix himself the day of the funeral. The one he'd quit on before even starting.

He hadn't dreamed of his father again, not since the night after he'd drowned the Ferox. The dreams betrayed themselves, never lulling him into a false illusion of reality for long. Their inconsistencies with the world he recognized were always glaring in the details; a man who should be dead, an engine in the wrong garage.

Things out of their place in time.

As the day drew closer, Jonathan had expected more of the same dreams he was used to: moving shadows, chains, choking, the face of monsters, the little girl in the pink coat, but not his father.

Douglas had been a mechanic after leaving the military, yet Jonathan hardly knew a thing about cars. Meanwhile, the woman sleeping next to him could weld a "catalytic converter," to a vehicle like it was just something everyone knew how to do. He wasn't being sexist; something just seemed to have gone wrong. It still troubled Jonathan, since his father's death, that he hadn't spent more time in their family garage with the man. He'd known so much—he could have taught him so much. Why couldn't he have been wise enough to know there wasn't a bottomless well of time to learn it?

I don't even know what I need to know, he thought.

"You'll figure it out," said Douglas from behind the engine.

Jonathan walked barefoot across the cement floor, taking care not to step on metal shavings and leftovers from the construction of the statue. He stood next to his father and watched him work on the engine.

"I have a confession," Douglas said as he wiped grease off the wrench in his hand with an old rag from his back pocket.

"What's that?" Jonathan asked.

Douglas' hands now clean, he pulled off his glasses.

"I didn't know what was wrong with this thing either," he said. "I never had enough time to figure it out. If you had been old enough, I'd have had you help me."

Jonathan smiled. "When did you know you wanted to be a mechanic, Dad?"

"Didn't happen all of a sudden. I had the knowledge; I was sick of working for someone else. Eventually I had the capital, so it happened," he said.

"I guess I meant why did you want to run an auto shop then?" he said.

"I was good at it, son," he said, "and it made me happy to do something I was good at."

"Did you ever think I was good at anything?" Jonathan asked. "What did you think I would be?"

His father put his glasses back on and looked at him.

"Jonathan, when you were a kid, no one knew what the world was going to look like when you were grown. As a father, I tried to see your character more than I looked for talents. You weren't quick to emotion; you worked hard when it mattered." Douglas laughed, then. "And nothing pissed you off more than making decisions when you didn't have all the facts. I can see that hasn't changed."

Douglas tilted his head and looked at him over the rim of his glasses.

"I knew you were clever, Jonathan. You weren't going to let the world outsmart you. When you didn't know what you should do…." Douglas paused. "You never stopped trying to figure it out."

"Clever isn't enough to win," Jonathan said.

"No," Douglas said understandingly. "But if you can't win with your head, you'll just have to want it more than the other guy."

"I don't know how to do that," Jonathan said. "I don't even know what these damn Ferox want. How can I want it more?"

"What made you go out and face the Ferox last time, Jonathan?"

He thought about it, but didn't like the answers that were coming to him.

"Death. Dead children," Jonathan said, looking away from his father in shame. "Guilt, revulsion, anger. I was so afraid, that somehow people would know I'd had the power to do something and I hadn't shown up to do it, that I'd be blamed for their deaths."

Jonathan cringed as he faced the memory. How Hayden had been willing to follow him to face the Ferox even though he knew the danger, to drag Jonathan through his own cowardice.

"But that was before it all got so complicated. Before I knew that the only deaths that matter were the Ferox or my own," Jonathan said.

"Son, we both know in our guts that damn alien isn't lying about the implications. I don't think anyone goes to the trouble to make a man face a monster in an arena outside of time and space if there isn't a damn good reason," Douglas said.

Jonathan nodded. "I'm afraid," Jonathan said. "I'm afraid that whatever these monsters want, they want it so badly I won't be able to stop them. That winning is more important to them than their very lives."

"Don't bullshit a bullshitter, son," Douglas said.

Jonathan smiled. Douglas had often made him laugh as a child by using that old phrase. He'd always done it when his mother wasn't around to hear him swearing in front of Jonathan.

"I'm in here with you, Jonathan," Douglas said. "It's not as though you're alone in a box describing the insides while I am on the outside, taking your word for it. I know the contents of this box as well as you do."

"I'm not lying, Dad," Jonathan said defensively.

"No, you're deluding yourself. It's subtly different," Douglas said.

Jonathan looked at Douglas with a frown, but his father had grown quite serious now.

"Don't let that damn alien make you see what he sees. He means well, but he isn't all-knowing." Douglas paused. "You know there is a part of you that wants this more than anything you've ever wanted. You felt it in that hallway when Heyer had you by the throat. It pulled you into the fight when Sickens the Fever had you crippled with guilt and fear. You almost gave it the wheel when that arrogant asshole picked a fight with you in your driveway. You feel it when you train; you sense it watching from behind your eyes, learning. You've seen it looking back at you in the mirror."

"You think that's the answer?" Jonathan asked. "My inner psychopath?"

"Don't call it that, Jonathan. Don't try to give it a silly name so you can cast it aside. Don't try and make it separate from you. It isn't. Stop trying to bury it and try to understand it," Douglas said.

"What's to understand?" Jonathan said. "You say it's part of me, but it feels more like something that wants control of me."

Douglas nodded and let out a heavy breath.

"You've been angry for a long time, Jonathan. Maybe since the day I left you and your mother," Douglas said.

He put his hand on Jonathan's shoulder. "Your anger comes from an intense desire to change something, Jonathan. You see, you couldn't give that anger what it needed, you couldn't put a face to a villain. You've been holding in all this rage because you couldn't give it anything to destroy. Even as a child you started tucking it away. You chained it down inside because you couldn't find a compromise with it, hoped that if you starved it to death, it would die. I think you were wise in that; it's been for the best that you did so. Until now, that fury you've kept locked up wouldn't have done you a damn bit of good."

"Dad, that doesn't make sense. I never hated anyone. I never wanted to hurt anyone," Jonathan said.

"No, but that is part of your problem," Douglas said. "Violence from anger is one of the crudest tools. It can't solve complicated problems. You don't remember what drove you to study biology, but you forget how angry you were when I died. You wanted so desperately to find a way to get your hands around death's throat. The things you've spent your life angry about are the things you couldn't find a solution to, couldn't imagine any way to change. It wasn't just my death; that was just the start. It was the lifetime of unfair realities you didn't know how to rebel against."

Jonathan listened. He didn't want his father to stop. He felt like there was finally a voice within him telling him the truths he couldn't see on his own.

"Most people eventually make their peace with things they can't change. Instead, you pushed them down until they became a violent thing hibernating inside of you. An anger that's been waiting for a fight for so long it won't take no for an answer now that that fight has come. I admit, Jonathan, you're outmatched, and you're right to be afraid. But that rage inside you won't tremble. It isn't ashamed; it doesn't hesitate. It wants you to take off its chains. It wants its freedom."

Freedom, Jonathan thought, remembering how he hadn't been able to tell Heyer what he needed it for. Did this part of him know the answer?

Jonathan looked at the floor, silent for a while as he considered. "It's neither here nor there, Dad. I can't turn it on or off."

Douglas nodded, his eyes showing his sympathy. "I don't think you'll need to, Jonathan," he said. "Somewhere past the pain and fear, it won't need to be given permission. It's waiting for its moment."

Silence fell over them for a time. Douglas put some of the tools back on the workbench, turned on the stool, and looked back up at the metal sculpture that had loomed in the background. He smiled as he folded his arms over his chest.

"I think she likes you more than she lets on," Douglas said with a lighter tone.

"Why is that?" Jonathan asked.

"This; it's done," Douglas said, pointing to the metal statue. "She used your idea."

Jonathan looked the statue over and saw what his father meant. She had taken a cloth and wrapped it around the statue's head where its eyes should be. The exposed skeleton of the arm was now completed. The missing piece of metal had been welded on. Instead, the statue now appeared to be finishing work on a set of eyes.

The blacksmith was still blind. It couldn't change what it had been shaped into, but it was fashioning its eyes. Soon it would be able to see itself. Once it knew what it was, it could take control over what it was going to be.

"Dad," Jonathan said, "Heyer said I was chosen by a computer, for genetic and psychological reasons. Do you think it was this thing? Do you think he somehow knew about it before I did?"

His father didn't look away from the sculpture. "No, son," he said. "That's not the reason."

When he awoke, he was relieved. There was no panic.

He lay on his side, his eyes facing the clock, its blue display reading four in the morning now. Still coming out of sleep, he became aware of her hands on him, pulling on him. She'd woken him, interrupted his dreams before they turned to nightmares.

She'd rolled back to him, pressing herself to his back. When he turned to face her, she pressed her lips against his, pulling her body on top of him, her long hair hanging down around them.

"Couldn't sleep," she said, looking down at him, "put me back to bed?"

His hands found their way up her curves. When his thoughts were on the brink of being engulfed by his lust, he had that feeling again, like he could choose to believe that the universe was pulling strings on his behalf. That it had sent Leah, and somehow she was there to level the field. How dare he die, if he might be the one who could put her back to bed?

CHAPTER THIRTY-THREE

STOP PUTTING THIS OFF, he thought as he stood in a towel in the upstairs bathroom.

He walked over to the bag and grabbed the hair clippers. The time to remove the unkempt handicap on his head was here. He started shaving before giving himself too much time to think about it. He didn't want to look like a skinhead so he cut the hair just short enough that it couldn't be used against him and called it good.

More than ever, he didn't recognize the Jonathan Tibbs looking back at him. His face and jaw were more chiseled than they had seemed before. His black eye from Grant had healed. His shoulders seemed broader, his muscles more prominent. He seemed older. He must be 25 pounds heavier than he had been three months before, and he carried it all in his chest, back, and legs.

He felt like a Marine, as he examined himself now without the long hair.

He showered and let the cuttings run off of him and down the drain. He'd left Leah's bed to get ready for his shift before she had woken again. He left a note that said he had to get to work and wanted to be gone before Jack woke up. He'd wanted to say something romantic, but remembered her warning of getting attached. It was for the best; he might cease to exist in the next three days. If she hadn't meant what she said, what good would it do to give her another reason to hate September?

When he arrived for his shift, Mr. Fletcher clapped at seeing him.

"Thank God! You finally cut that mop you called hair," he said. "I was beginning to think you were becoming some kind of hippie."   .

Jonathan nodded and smiled, "It was time."

"Good thing, I'd say. Mr. Donaldson is coming by to give you an impromptu interview today. Make sure you'll fit in on his demo-team. Don't worry. You don't need to know a damn thing about it before you start. They'll have you doing all sorts of labor before you need to do anything technical," Mr. Fletcher said.

"I can't thank you enough for your help, Mr. Fletcher," Jonathan said. "I really need the money these days."

"I could tell. All those shifts you'd been wanting," Mr. Fletcher said. "Any thoughts to when you're getting back to school?"

Jonathan hesitated at the question. He didn't want to tell the man he wasn't likely to be going back. He didn't want a lecture on his future. Obviously, he couldn't explain that his future was precarious at best.

"To be honest, I'm taking an extended break, sir. This year has been a bit of a wakeup call. Biology is fascinating, but I'm not sure it's the right road for me," he said.

Jonathan didn't think that would get him off the hook but Mr. Fletcher surprised him.

"Nothing wrong with that, Jonathan, especially these days; I can't go a week without hearing on the radio about how all you college kids are drowning in student loan debt with degrees you aren't even using."

"Thanks, just wish my mother felt the same way," Jonathan said.

Mr. Fletcher shrugged. "You're a grown man. At some point parents have to understand that you have to make your own decisions and mistakes, if it is a mistake."

"You haven't met my mother," Jonathan smiled.

"Speaking of women, anything ever come of that redhead next door?" Mr. Fletcher asked.

Collin sat at the kitchen table, his school books laid out around him. He was behind in some classes, as all the work on the comic book had taken up his spare time, but that wasn't his chief reason for being there now. He tried to give the appearance that he was deep in the throes of a long study session when Paige came home.

She walked through the door and looked surprised to see him at the table. He sat back when she entered and waved. He sat where Jonathan used to, when Paige and he would study together. She walked across the kitchen and sat in her spot.

"Hitting the books?" she asked.

"Yep, got some catching up to do," he said.

She nodded and pulled some of her own books out of her backpack.

"Never seen you study out here," she said. "Don't you usually hide in your room when you're cramming?"

Collin shrugged. "I figured I might absorb some of your study will-power if I sat out here with you," he said.

It was hard not to look up at her. He kept his face in the book, feeling sure she would see through him; a boy with a crush, trying to find a good excuse to be close to her.

He'd never have said it to Jonathan, but he'd been jealous of the time the two had spent together studying. Tibbs had no interest in Paige and Collin knew that; he just wished that he'd had a good reason to spend as much time in a room with her, even if it was mostly spent in silence. It was obvious she missed the company. Collin thought now that Jonathan wasn't attending school for another quarter, maybe he could sit with her.

Couldn't hurt his grades, he'd figured.

Her gaze shifted off of him and onto the book she had open in front of her. Collin tried not to smile.

Some time passed. She seemed to reach the end of a page and she spoke.

"I wanted to tell you again. My birthday present—it was really thoughtful," she said.

Collin glanced up at her. "The idea came to me one day, and I knew you'd go nuts over it," he said.

"It's one of my favorite things," she said. "I'll hold onto it forever."

"I'm glad you like it," Collin said.

They sat there for a few hours. They spoke infrequently, just as she had with Tibbs. Collin found it hard to study as he was just happy to be where he was. Eventually there was a knock at the door. They both looked up at one another.

"Expecting anyone?" she asked.

"Nope," Collin said, "and it's too late to be a Jehovah's Witness."

Paige got up from her seat to answer the door. He couldn't see who was there. He could only see the door and her beside it.

"Hello?" she said.

Collin noticed her body language change subtly. Her weight shifted onto a hip, and her voice seemed lighter. He knew her well enough to know she was flirting.

"Hi, I'm looking for Jonathan," said a man's voice.

"Oh," Paige said. "Jonathan isn't home yet. Do you want to come in and wait?"

"Yeah, that'd be great," said the voice. "I'm Lincoln."

Collin felt his joy receding at this interruption. Maybe he misread it. Maybe she was just being friendly; then the guy walked through the door. He was bigger than Grant.

"I thought I knew all Jonathan's friends," said Paige as she stepped aside to let him through the doorway.

"I'm his trainer," Lincoln said.

Paige looked at Collin then. "Did you know Jonathan had a personal trainer?" she asked.

"Nope," Collin said. "Explains a lot though."

"Jonathan said he'd be home around now," Lincoln said. "I was just going to drop off this movie we'd talked about."

"You can leave it with us," Collin said. "We'll make sure to give it to him when he gets here."

"What's the movie?" Paige asked.

Lincoln smirked at her. "Just a bad movie from the eighties."

Paige looked at the DVD box. "What's it about?" she asked.

Collin sighed. He had no doubt that Paige could care less about the movie.

When he arrived home, Jonathan was approached by Paige before he ever made it down the stairs to the garage.

"Friend of yours stopped by," she said.

"Oh?" Jonathan said. "Right. Crap, I'm later than I expected."

"He brought this for you," she said, holding out a DVD case.

Jonathan reached out to take the box, but she pulled it away and tucked it behind her back.

"How long have you been keeping your personal trainer a secret?" she asked.

At first, he thought it was another interrogation. Then she bit the side of her lip and raised an eyebrow at him and he recognized it as the face she gave right before asking a favor.

"Awhile now, I guess," he said.

"How come you've never invited him over?"

"Uh...."

He turned off the light in the garage around nine o'clock and walked up into the living room. Collin had come down to visit a little while before he'd finished training.

"You lifting weights tonight?" he'd asked.

"Not tonight," Jonathan had replied. "Why?"

"I want to start," he said. "Not as much as you do, I just want to try and put on some muscle. Let me know next time you're lifting?"

Jonathan had nodded, unsure what brought on the renewed interest.

Hayden and Collin were at the table when he came through the door. As he walked towards the stairs, he stopped. He'd noticed a DVD that Hayden had left out, one the roommates had already made him watch.

"Mind if I borrow this?" he asked Hayden, holding up the *Karate Kid III* case.

"Go for it," Hayden said.

After he'd showered, he played the DVD on the laptop in his room, fast forwarding to the climactic end scene. The story's protagonist, Daniel, had been beaten and humiliated. He laid on the arena floor, panicking, needing to stand up and fight but frozen on the ground, failing to find the courage. All the while, his more experienced opponent ruthlessly taunted him, eager to inflict as much pain as possible should Daniel stand again.

Daniel, with nowhere to turn, cried to his teacher: "Mr. Miyagi, it's over! I can't fight him! I want to go home! I'm afraid!"

Miyagi laid a hand on Daniel's shoulder, to help calm him.

"It's okay to lose to opponent," said the teacher, "but must not lose to fear."

A few months ago, the teacher's words would have rolled off Jonathan as the cliché antics of the early nineties. Now, he didn't have to project himself into this scene; he understood it from having lived a nightmarish reflection of it. Daniel's moment wasn't life or death, but the chaos he felt around him was the same brand.

The music fell into sync with the teacher's words for dramatic effect, tinkering with viewer's emotions. Jonathan felt the inspiration that these films were designed to bring out. It was too easy to remember his own fear as Sickens the Fever had beaten his face into that pillar under the viaduct. How he had struggled and struggled but found himself unable to match his opponent's violence, how his panic had overwhelmed his thinking.

As he watched, he felt an unexpected anger rising up, the thing inside him again struggling to be freed of its chains, enraged by the very idea of what was happening on the screen. He thought he understood, then. His father, in his dream, he had been right; he'd known. It was the things that weren't fair. The things he couldn't fight with his fists.

Things like abandonment.

These wise men weren't there in the real world; they didn't show up when the protagonist needed them. There would be no heroic music, no referee, no family or friends on the sidelines. Most of all, though, there would be no one to tell him exactly what he needed to hear.

When Jonathan's time came, there would be an alien standing in the shadows, powerless to intervene. There would be a city in chaos around him, watching something they couldn't understand, but there would be nothing and no one to help him.

Nothing but what he brought with him.

CHAPTER THIRTY-FOUR

MONDAY | SEPTEMBER 5, 2005 | 3:45 AM

WHEN HAYDEN WOKE, it was early morning. The clock on his bedside table read three forty-five. He rolled around a bit trying to get back to sleep, but failed. He heard movement in the house and knew Jonathan was likely awake. How his roommate slept as little as he did and still had the energy to train in that garage for hours on end was beyond him.

When he reached the kitchen, he filled a glass from the tap. He hadn't seen him when he walked in, but Jonathan was leaning against a table, staring out their front window. It wasn't a comforting scene.

"Jonathan, FYI, it's creepy to wake in the middle of the night and find your roommate with his new militant haircut staring out the window at four in the morning," Hayden said, taking a sip from his water.

"Can't sleep," Jonathan said.

"What are you looking at, anyway?" Hayden said, joining him by the front window.

"Absolutely nothing," Jonathan said. "I'm just daydreaming."

Hayden shrugged, and turned to head back to his bedroom.

"Hayden," Jonathan said, "would you stay up with me for a bit? I wanted to ask you something anyway."

Jonathan looked lonely, and Hayden detected a note of anxiety in his tone, even if he hadn't meant it to be there.

"What's up?" Hayden said, taking a seat at the table.

"Well, you're the only person of faith in the house. I don't know what Paige believes, but Collin isn't religious. I don't want to offend you," Jonathan said, "but is it the fear of death? Is it the idea of ceasing to exist? Is that why you believe in God?"

Hayden didn't like this question, and it wasn't because it was offensive. It just made him reappraise what he might have walked in on. He felt a tinge of nervousness. What might be the real reason for Jonathan's creepy hundred-yard stare out the window at nothing?

"Well, it's part of it—maybe the root of it, but not all of it. The idea of ceasing to exist has always been unpleasant," Hayden said. "What's got you thinking about the afterlife?"

Jonathan returned to looking out the window before responding.

"I just think the fear might be misplaced." Jonathan seemed to be looking for a better way to put it. "I guess—life is a lot of work. It's exhausting, really. It seems like it might be nice, at the end, to just 'not be' anymore."

Hayden grew more anxious. It occurred to him that he might start looking around to make sure his roommate hadn't taken a bottle full of pills. He'd never heard Jonathan talk like this before, not even in the weeks after the hospital.

"Jonathan, I know you've had a rough few months." Hayden hesitated. "You aren't thinking of doing anything stupid, are you?"

Jonathan looked confused by Hayden's question before realizing how this might look from Hayden's perspective. "No, nothing like that. It's just one of those things you start thinking about at four in the morning when you can't sleep," Jonathan said. "Seriously."

He seemed to be holding in a laugh. The levity did make Hayden relax.

"Suicidal, really?" Jonathan asked. "Is that how this looks?"

"Little bit, bro," Hayden replied, smiling now.

"I just wanted to ask. My family wasn't ever religious," Jonathan said.

"Well," Hayden replied, "it's not that I don't see what you're saying, but the idea of ceasing to exist makes my soul quake."

Jonathan looked like he was thinking about it. A moment or two passed before he spoke again.

"I'm afraid of pain, broken bones, drowning, being mauled by a bear. I'm afraid of feeling helpless, like when that man attacked me in the house. I don't think I'm afraid of what comes after," Jonathan said.

Hayden shrugged. "Call me a coward if you want, but it disturbs me."

Jonathan frowned, suddenly growing too serious in Hayden's estimation. "Hayden, I'll never call you a coward. You're probably the bravest person in this house. You might be afraid of the end, but I know you would put that fear behind you if your friends needed you."

Hayden raised an eyebrow. What the hell had gotten into Jonathan this morning? Maybe he should be looking for an empty bottle of booze somewhere instead of worrying about finding a suicide note.

"Thanks, Jonathan," he said slowly. "So, what have we been drinking then?"

Jonathan just smiled. "Speaking of religion, how are things going with the gospel reboot?" Jonathan asked.

Hayden smiled. "We had a pretty awesome breakthrough for the next story arc," he said excitedly. "I mean, assuming the first run does well enough to bother with a second."

"Do I get to hear about it or is it a secret?" Jonathan asked.

"Come on, Tibbs, you're in the circle of trust—of course," Hayden said. "Jesus is going to find out that the Son of the Devil is also on earth at the same time as him."

"That seems kind of obvious, plot wise. Why is it so exciting?" Jonathan asked.

Hayden, so pumped to talk to someone other than Collin about the new ideas, didn't know where to start.

"Tibbs, you have to understand, in comic books superheroes and super villains are essentially the same character," Hayden explained. "The hero or villain has something bad happen to him, and then they either become good or bad. Bruce Wayne's parents die, he becomes Batman. Harvey Dent gets his face blown off, he becomes Two-Face. Uncle Ben gets killed and Peter Parker becomes Spiderman. Erik Lehnsherr loses his family in the Holocaust and becomes Magneto," Hayden said.

"Okay, so how does this play into Christ and the anti-Christ?" Jonathan asked.

"That's the beauty of the plot! You see, as our story unfolds, Jesus will find that there's nothing intrinsically good about him, and the anti-Christ, whom we are calling Damian for now, will find out that, likewise, there's nothing intrinsically evil about *him*."

"Okay?" Jonathan said, still seeming confused.

Hayden finally just blurted it out. "There are only a couple of times in the real Bible where Jesus' humanity is played up. He flips over tables in the cathedral, getting angry at the merchants, the agony in the garden, and the cry of being forsaken on the cross. It always bothered me as a Christian that Jesus was somehow inherently good because he was the Son of God. His faith isn't faith because he *knows* God exists. What's impressive about being perfect when you're made that way? What is impressive about having faith when it isn't really faith at all? Nothing, right?" Hayden asked.

"I guess I never really thought about it," Jonathan said shrugging. "Sorry."

"Tibbs! Come on, everyone has thought about it!" Hayden replied. "Well! Anyway, in our new version, we see Jesus making choices. The reader gets to see the consequences of those choices weigh in on him, affecting his decisions," Hayden said excitedly. "Jesus and Damian could go either way; it's all a matter of how they respond to what happens to them. There's no sure bet that one will become the savior."

Jonathan frowned. "Isn't that like trying to change the ending of Titanic?" Jonathan said. "It's not like everyone doesn't know where it ends."

"It's the journey that gets you there that makes a story relevant," Hayden said, "not the ending."

Jonathan nodded, and they stood quietly for a moment.

"Do you ever think," Jonathan asked carefully, "that, for a savior, God seems to ask for a lot of, I don't know, recognition."

"Not sure I follow you," Hayden said.

"Don't you think that a god who doesn't get any credit for being the

world's savior, but does it anyway—that that god would be the more…
heroic one?"

"I suppose," Hayden said, "but it's really neither here nor there,
because no one would ever know to thank him."

Jonathan's face had gone pale all of a sudden, his hand reaching for
his chest.

"Are you alright, Tibbs?" Hayden asked.

"Step away from me, Hayden."

CHAPTER THIRTY-FIVE

MONDAY | SEPTEMBER 5, 2005 | 4:20 AM

HEYER. THE ALIEN'S face had been the last thing that had gone through Jonathan's mind before the change replaced all thinking with fire.

He knew, now, why he trusted the alien. No one had asked him to step in on man's behalf, yet he had. He'd never looked to Earth to give him any credit. He'd gone out of his way to conceal his actions on their behalf; watched over mankind for no reason other than that he had the power to do so.

"Jonathan!" Hayden cried out. "How are you not—how are you being so calm!"

"Don't worry, Hayden. The pain is past," Jonathan said, "step back a bit."

Once Hayden moved, he got up carefully as to not to accidentally put a hole in the floor with the strength of his legs.

Collin burst out of his bedroom, his eyes frantic, as though he was expecting the house to be on fire. The last thing Jonathan remembered hearing before the change muted his external senses was Hayden screaming for help.

"What? What's going—" Collin fell short as he noticed that Jonathan was glowing from beneath his T-shirt. "Holy crap!"

"Stay calm, guys, I'm okay," he said this as he was on the move heading for his room.

When he reached the foot of the stairs, Paige popped her head out of the hallway at the top. She, too, was still in her sleep attire. She looked as startled as Collin. Her speech failed her just as quickly when she saw him, chest ablaze, carefully walking up the stairs toward her.

She quickly stepped aside. "What's going on?" she asked, as he turned towards his bedroom.

In his room, he pulled the jacket on over his torso. The roommates all stood in his doorway, staring at him, waiting for him to explain why his chest had turned into a neon light. They seemed unable to form complete thoughts until Jonathan hid the glow under the leather of the jacket.

"Jonathan," Paige asked, "what's happening? Why do you…."

He grabbed his motorcycle keys, helmet, and his backpack, and headed past them again, straight for the garage. They parted as they saw him heading toward the doorway. He couldn't tell if they were afraid of him or if they could see he didn't mean to be slowed down.

He realized as they trailed behind him that if he survived tonight, he would have to experience something like this every time he was activated. They would always stare at him like he was suddenly an alien in Jonathan's body. They were trying to process something so unfamiliar, while he didn't have time to stand still and explain it to them.

"Jonathan, stop! Stop moving! And tell us what's happening!" Paige said, starting to sound more angry than upset. "What's wrong with your chest?"

Her voice was quivering. He could see she was afraid for him.

"I have to go. There is no good explanation. A monster just got let loose somewhere to the west of here and I need to—" Jonathan hesitated. "I have to kill it."

It was relieving. They'd never remember all this, but at least he could tell them all his secrets for a moment and not have to hide anything. It wasn't like he'd have to prove it, especially if he made the news again. Hayden and Collin seemed to be trying to process what Jonathan had said. Paige didn't look satisfied in the least.

"That isn't an explanation! What monster? Why do you have to kill it? Jonathan!" Her voice followed him into the garage. He was careful not to pull the door off the hinges this time.

He pushed the garage opener and the mechanical door started to rise. He walked over to the cabinet, removing the practice staffs and the facade he'd installed to hide the bar Heyer had made for him. They watched him as though they didn't know him at all, yet at the same time as though any theory they'd had about what he was up to the last few months was flying out the window. It must have been like watching Batman run down to the Batcave and jump into the Batmobile, if Batman had the salary of a part-time hardware store employee.

"I don't have all the answers, Paige," Jonathan said.

He placed the staff into the latches Leah had welded on. It lodged in with a satisfying click, then he started the bike's engine. He pulled on the harness he'd fashioned to tie the staff across his back and quickly got it into place over his jacket; the knapsack he put under the cargo net on the back of the bike. He was efficient; he'd practiced all these steps before, except without super strength threatening to snap the leather garments and three roommates staring at him wide-eyed.

He mounted the bike. He was about to put his helmet on and blaze out of the garage when he remembered it might be the last time he saw them.

"Guys, no matter what you might see on the news tonight, stay out of downtown. You won't remember any of this. I know you don't understand, but in case this is the last time I see you, thank you for everything," Jonathan said to all of them, then he turned to Paige. "You're like family to me."

He wasn't a poet. It was all he could think to say.

"Jonathan, I don't understand. Why is this happening? What are you going to do?" Hayden asked.

He paused before he put his helmet on. "Batman," he said, "is going to try and take down Superman."

Hayden looked like he remembered the conversation, but he couldn't decipher Jonathan's meaning in the moment. He pulled the helmet over his head and carefully hit the throttle.

There was no point, not when every second counted. Live or die, these words were for him; they would never exist for his friends.

There wasn't any traffic to watch for this early in the morning and the roads were cold. The compass in Jonathan's head still pointed west, the same spot he'd initially sensed the Ferox's presence; it hadn't moved.

With great effort, Jonathan kept his mind where he needed it, focused on the implementation of the plan; cold and machine-like, disciplined, every piece of him centered on what he was doing, not why he was doing it.

Must not lose to fear.

He drove as fast as he dared, the target in his head drawing closer as he poured on the throttle. He concentrated on predicting where this would begin and plotting that point in his mind against the map he had in his front pocket. He didn't need to look at it. He'd memorized it from hours of study. He'd only kept it in his pocket as a precaution, in case his mental state became too panicked to access the memories he needed.

The instinct directing his route was still novel, but easily understood. It was taking him into downtown Seattle. This was good. Jonathan wanted the beast surrounded by walls and concrete; square blocks of order. Sky scrapers, city streets lined with automobiles and infrastructure he understood and could use to his advantage. He wanted it somewhere completely human in design, and foreign to what he had to imagine its natural habitat would look like.

Though he had alternate strategies, he didn't want to fight the Ferox in a suburban area with nothing but wood houses and fences, structures it could easily move through. Worse, he didn't want to be out in a forest somewhere, trying to engage this thing in the dark.

Downtown gave him the best chance, and plenty of water.

It was not long before he sensed himself close. The three-dimensional aspect of the instinct became more useful now as he realized the Ferox was not at street level. He looked up and saw that he was targeting a six-story parking garage a little ways up the block. He pulled off the street and killed the engine in an alley.

Jonathan pulled Excali-bar free from its road mounts and slipped it into the harness on his back. He swung the knapsack over his shoulder. As it looked like he'd be going up the side of the building, he was going to need his hands free. Fortunately, the parking garage was a cement structure, only partially enclosed on the upper levels. He wanted to remain as stealthy as possible. He had no qualms about sneaking up on the beast if he got the opportunity; kicking in a metal security door or ripping a garage door off its rails was bound to be noisy. A parking lot security guard might see him on a camera, but that wasn't going to matter as soon as he saw the Ferox.

It was exhilarating to be able to move this way again. Heyer hadn't over exaggerated the potential in increasing his muscle mass. His strength was plain now. It felt like he could bench a pickup truck, run through walls if he had to. It was not just raw power though. He felt stable, balanced, like he would have to be hit by a tank to lose his footing, the frailness of the physical human condition no longer present. He knew not to let it go to his head. After all, nothing had changed about the fragility of the human mind. It might be deadly if he misjudged his limits.

He almost effortlessly jumped to the third story and slipped into the garage. Limits were becoming a real question. If he'd wanted to jump to the roof, could he have? How far could he fall before his legs would break under the impact? It was impossible to know the boundaries anymore.

Tonight, he was going to find out.

With that thought, he freed Excali-bar from its harness. The Ferox felt as if it were on the next level up. He made a line for the ramp leading to the next level of the garage.

When he reached the ramp, a warning entered his mind. Something wasn't right about this. At first, he couldn't pin down what was troubling him, but then he realized it was that the compass still hadn't moved. When he was miles away, it made sense, as he couldn't detect a movement of a few paces from that distance. Now, with a matter of yards between him and the enemy, the target in his head hadn't moved at all.

Sickens the Fever had attacked the city by this point, hadn't he?

The first moments from that night weren't so clear. They were obscured by panic, clouded by his lack of understanding of what was happening to him, even more by the traumas he'd experienced. Had the Ferox stayed still this long before finally venturing out? Could one behave so vastly different from another? More important than all of these questions, could this be a trap?

Jonathan stopped, cutting the thoughts off in his mind. Letting his worry run rampant like this couldn't be allowed. He'd made every effort to think of all contingencies to avoid the road to doubt.

Whatever the case, Jonathan's move was stealth. If anyone was going to get the drop, it would be him. As he came up the cement ramp connecting the third floor of the garage to the fourth, he hugged the corner, trying to get sight of the creature before engaging with it. He heard nothing; no heavy feet on cement, no guttural grunting or monstrous breathing. The quiet was unsettling. Was the damn Ferox standing perfectly still?

He took a deep breath and poked his head quickly around the corner, and it all became clear.

It wasn't as Jonathan had imagined it, though he'd momentarily experienced it himself. A red light emanating out of him and surrounding him, thickening and insulating him until a flash of white had returned him to his kitchen table. The pain had been so great that night on the dock. It had stopped him from having awe for the phenomenon now in front of him.

As he approached it, the gate was all fluid and energy. It was nearly as wide as the parking space it hovered over; the outer shell a turbulent liquid, a thick red and black cloud of fluid held in the shape of an orb by forces outside Jonathan's comprehension. It was a beautiful thing, but only in the manner of beauty that unnatural things can have. Nature, after all, had never expected its laws could be bent to create this thing. Science and technology had manifested it, the power of thought seeming to break the rules of reality.

Why was it here like this though? Why hadn't it just been as short-lived as the one Jonathan had experienced? He stood hypnotized by the light it was giving off and wondered. Perhaps the experience of time inside and outside of the orb was simply different.

The fluid on the surface of the gate was becoming more agitated.

Currents of electricity were cracking within and accelerating in their frequency. Jonathan could smell static in the air around him as he neared it. He pulled the knapsack off his back and put the contents at his feet, tucking one of the flares into his back pocket. The sensation in his head was becoming sharper. His grip on Excali-bar tightened on instinct, his body reacting before his conscious mind formed the thought.

Within the sphere, a figure had begun to form, a dark shadow within the red. The shape he'd seen so frequently in his nightmares. He eased into a fighting stance.

Wait for the flash.

The moment built, arcing electricity coming to a crescendo within the gate. The shape solidified. The white light flashed, threatening to blind him. He clenched his eyes shut as the gateway delivered its trespasser, and swung. Excali-bar moved through air and connected with something solid.

The Ferox crashed into the garage wall and fell down onto a knee, stopping itself from falling face first on the cement floor with one hand. Before it had a chance to know what dimension it was in, a red rubber gas can exploded against the wall behind it, covering the beast with the fluid.

The Ferox's eyes looked up, aware of the cold liquid running over it, searching for the source.

The sound of a flare igniting would be foreign to the beast, as was the smell of the gas it found coating its body, but the noise helped it to focus on the direction of its attacker.

Challenger?

Jonathan heard his own voice translate, asking the question in his mind over the abhorrent dialect of the Ferox.

He stood ready, the staff held behind him with one hand, the other holding the lit flare.

"Technically," Jonathan said, tossing the flare into the gasoline, "I'm the defending champion."

CHAPTER THIRTY-SIX

MONDAY | SEPTEMBER 5, 2005 | 4:55 AM

IT SEEMED TO take the blaze without concern, bringing its arm up to examine the fire now burning away on its skin.

This beast wasn't what he'd expected. It had the same body, the same black tar chaotically wrapping its exterior, but it didn't have the face or coloring of Sickens the Fever. This creature's undertones were a dark green, frog-like beneath the black tar. Its ears were attached to its skull, short ridges running along the sides of its head and down its neck, as though the appendages hadn't yet freed themselves, hadn't fully formed. Its face was angrier, its white eyes spaced further apart, darting around its surroundings rapidly, more birdlike than the predatory gaze of the first Ferox. The most noticeable difference was that this one had a tail.

Jonathan didn't like the sight of the tail. He hadn't been training to fight something with a fifth limb.

Flames, Challenger? the beast asked. My world flows molten.

Its jaws moved, rapidly clicking together as the beast studied him, as though its mouth was only half under its conscious control, like its teeth had a will of their own. Its entire body seemed to be held at bay, as though its instinct to kill was impatient with its mind's warning for caution. This Ferox was not the controlled, discerning, and comparatively calm nightmare that Jonathan had fought before. This wasn't what he had prepared for; this thing looked rabid. The fire engulfing the beast only added to its presence, enhancing its demon-like qualities and the chaos he saw within its eyes.

The blazing beast took a step away from the cracked garage wall, easing itself into an aggressive stance. He let it pull away from the wall and mimed its movements, drawing it into the open garage. Circling one another, both watching how the other moved, measuring their enemy. Jonathan had wondered if an animal staring down a hunter with a spear knew the spear was deadly or simply focused on the hunter. The Ferox had studied the staff in Jonathan's hands and its eyes had lingered on the pointed ends. He studied its tail. Like the creature's jaws, it seemed to move outside of its conscious awareness.

Eyes locked, the distance between them shrinking, both waiting for who dared make the first move.

A sharp ringing filled the air. The alarm, followed almost immediately by the downpour of water from the buildings sprinkler system, surprised the Ferox. It pounced at Jonathan on instinct.

He'd waited for the trigger—he spun, sidestepping the beast as it lunged for where he'd been standing. He came around, swinging hard, using his momentum to put more power behind the attack. Excalibar connected hard with the creature's back, sending it airborne over the garage floor and then rolling over the cement. Its claws dug into the ground, trying to halt its motion, but it couldn't get the traction it needed on the wet floors. Its nails raked the ground, sparks trailing them, as it reoriented itself, turning to face him even as its momentum pulled it away. It came to a halt against a pillar.

From where it stood, its tail seemed agitated. The smoke from the now-extinguished blaze wafted off its skin. The water flowing around it caught its attention, and it seemed to falter, hesitate. He'd hoped for this, the downpour of water foreign, possibly something that could evoke fear in a species that couldn't swim and came from a planet without rain.

"My world is covered in oceans," Jonathan said.

His enemy seemed to inspect him anew, its head bobbing as it looked at him with one eye, then angled its head to take him in with the other.

Its impatience won out; it dropped to all fours and charged him.

Jonathan moved out of its attack as it neared, dropping into a shoulder roll and coming up ready with point of the staff between them. The Ferox whirled, coming to a halt in front of the point.

It was the calm before the storm.

He swung and the beast reacted, leaning back to let the blow sail past. The claws reached for him as he moved but found only air. He retreated, parrying the attacks with his staff as the beast reached for him. Neither stood still; movement was life, each maneuvering for a damaging blow. At times the Ferox seemed to move more like a lizard, and he felt he was fighting a wingless dragon. Blows were landed, but not solid enough to do real damage.

Overzealous, Jonathan brought Excali-bar around and down hard. Missing the creature and striking the cement with a loud ringing clang, the bar puncturing a jagged hole in the cement. It had been a mistake; he'd left himself open.

He had to roll backward, retreating through the pooling water on the garage floor, keeping his grip on Excali-bar, to avoid the beast's claws, but it was still on him. He brought the staff up to help defend as the Ferox rammed him with its forward momentum, disrupting his guard and leaving him open for a backhand punch that caught him hard across the chest. The fist jerked him off his feet and sent him into the wall of the garage facing the street.

He landed on his feet and ignored the sharp pain. It had been close, but not fatal. He had to be more careful. Still, it wasn't lost on him that he'd taken the hit without getting the urge to wet his pants.

You have a plan, follow it—move the fight now.

Sure that the beast would pursue him, Jonathan gripped Excali-bar and turned, throwing himself through the opening in the garage wall and free-falling four stories down to the street. The air was cold as it swept up past him in his soaked clothes. He landed hard, the sidewalk cracking beneath him, but his legs could take it. He didn't need to look; he could sense it following him as he leaped forward.

He adapted quickly to being able to leap great distances. The strength in his core allowed him to adjust for his lack of gymnastics skill. The months of martial arts training and gym work combined with the power surging through his body and gave him grace. The ability to absorb so much force on his legs and push off allowed him to keep moving despite obstacles. He could pounce off the side of a building mid-leap if need be.

He knew where he was headed, the closest spot he'd scouted. He didn't bother looking back; he could feel the thing chasing him, could hear vehicles flipped out of the creature's path when it was impeded, but he needed to make sure it stayed close, that it didn't start thinking it was being led into a trap.

Keep it pissed off.

He allowed the Ferox to close the distance between them. When he could see his destination through the city skyline, he made his move, coming to a stop after he felt the Ferox was already in mid-leap and headed straight for his back. When the instinct in his mind screamed that the Ferox was about to crash into him, he turned, swinging Excalibar like a baseball bat.

It caught the beast full-force in the abdomen. He felt the blow vibrate down the shaft of the bar into his hands, heard the concussion of the hit in his eardrums. Its body shot away from him like a missile, crashing through the wall of a brick apartment building across the street from him.

His eyes widened at the hole in the building, bricks still falling loose. He knew it had felt that one.

Still, the sheer destruction they were capable of was frightening. If things got out of hand, they could level buildings. He strapped the staff back into the harness and waited for his adversary to show his face at the mouth of the hole.

It reminded him of waiting for Sickens the Fever to come out of the overturned semi, the fear he'd felt that night threatening to seep into this moment; he fought it down in his mind. He couldn't allow what had happened to him before force its way in on this.

The boy who got his ass kicked three months ago is not here right now, Jonathan.

Finally, that ugly face emerged from within darkness. Jonathan gave it a moment to take a good, long look at him. The Ferox was angry, but it wasn't about to make another mistake. He could see its eager, bloodthirsty impulse struggling with the caution that warned that its opponent was cunning.

Jonathan raised one hand and pointed into the sky. The creature's eyes followed to where his finger indicated. "We fight there," Jonathan said, letting his eyes linger. He refused to show the beast any of the fear he held at bay.

He could see it understood. It wasn't going to take a time out and stroll down the street with him, but it knew that Jonathan was choosing their arena.

"How bad do you want my life, trespasser?" Jonathan asked.

If it had wanted him dead before, he could see the beast wanted it twofold now. Jonathan turned, leaping in the direction he had indicated. With his hands completely free his balance and maneuverability was all the more efficient; in no time, he was a block away, the Ferox in pursuit.

The construction site came into view. Jonathan had never been inside, only observed it through the fences. It was deserted for the night, and he leaped the barbed wire without pause. The construction of the sky-scraper's skeleton was nearly complete, forty floors—500 feet of steel and rebar-reinforced concrete floors.

It has to be enough.

He'd chosen the site because the arrangement of the adjacent build-ings made it possible to leapfrog to the top. He didn't want to have to scale the walls with the Ferox on his heels but he would if it came to it. He was trusting in his imagination; there hadn't been any way to test how well getting up this building was going to go in his mere human state.

He ran, and launched himself as high as he could. Safety lights were on in the structure, illuminating each floor, but he had no idea what level he was going to be able reach as the wind rushed passed him.

He realized he was going to touch down between floors and used his hands to thrust his trajectory upward, pulling his feet up with the momentum and rolling onto the cement.

He sensed the Ferox clearing the construction yard fence behind him.

He turned back to the edge to see the Ferox's reaction. It stood where he'd jumped from and seemed to be assessing its pursuit. It roared at him from below, enraged at being forced into chasing its prize, impatient to have its war. It charged and leaped as Jonathan turned away, breaking into a sprint across the cement, dodging building supplies like an Olympic hurdler as he made his way through the interior of the skeleton toward the other side.

He couldn't leap between floors. The ceiling above him was reinforced cement. He didn't stop when he reached the other side—the Ferox was catching up, but it wasn't going to get hold of him here. He jumped again, as hard as he could, watching again as he rushed airborne toward the adjacent building, desperate to reach the top.

He didn't clear it. He crashed into the outer rim of the building's roof as his hand reached for the top, grabbing on for life.

The force of his body hitting the wall wasn't pleasant but he took the pain and kept moving, pulling himself up quickly and running to the center of the roof. The beast raced toward him in his mind.

The sound of the Ferox slamming into the rim of the roof chased him; when he turned he saw its one outstretched hand keeping it tethered over the precipice. He sprinted back, straight towards the construction site, one more jump back to the rooftop of the unfinished skyscraper.

He could feel the creature reach for him as he once more took to the air, its claw coming within inches of grabbing him.

He halted himself against one of the skeleton's exposed I-beams when he landed. The top wasn't as completed as other levels, building material sat in stacks all over the floor.

Immediately, Jonathan pulled his weapon free. He turned to the roof he'd stood on seconds ago, looking down on the Ferox. When they connected eyes, Jonathan took the staff in one fist and beat his chest twice over his heart. The creature didn't have to translate. It beat its chest back at him and let out a roar of intimidation, backing away from the roof's edge to gain the running space it needed to make the jump to Jonathan.

The language for *come get a piece* was universal.

CHAPTER THIRTY-SEVEN

TUESDAY | SEPTEMBER 5, 2005 | 5:15 AM

SHORTLY AFTER THE Ferox joined Jonathan on the roof, it had begun to rain. It made the cement slick on the exposed surface, easier to lose his footing. Red and blue flashing lights had begun to surround the construction site. The fire alarm, the chase through the city, the hole they'd put in the building below—the sightings of the Ferox and all the activity must have led to enough 911 calls to pull the police out in force.

Jonathan heard the low, familiar thudding of a helicopter in the distance. Soon, the entire city would be watching.

He crashed into a pile of building supplies. Though his head was still spinning, he jumped into an offensive stance as he had practiced and let his instincts guide him. He caught the Ferox with a hard upward strike to its chin as it attempted to pounce on top of him. He whipped the other end of the staff around and struck the Ferox again, hitting hard against its right flank and rolling it off its feet back into the center of the cement floor. This maneuvering had gone on for a while now, largely at a stalemate. Blows hurt, but not enough to turn the tides.

Mere minutes had passed, yet Jonathan and the Ferox had experienced their own private war. The beast understood the stakes. It knew Jonathan intended to drop it off this roof and maneuvered accordingly, but it didn't seem to want to win this way itself. It made no effort to corner him on a ledge, no attempt to catch him with a blow that would send him over the side. It didn't want to play king of the mountain.

His head cleared.

They fell into circling each other's footing yet again. Every time the Ferox landed a blow, the pain and threat caused him to teeter on the brink, forcing him to push down his doubt. He couldn't let the monster into his head. He couldn't panic or this was over.

The Ferox's expression, the vicious combination of lizard and alien features, suddenly changed. Its jaw drew shut, no longer clicking like it had a mind of its own. Its tail grew still, rigid. Alarm screamed out in him at the change, but he forced it down, not allowing the panicked thoughts to rip him from his concentration.

He maneuvered to strike and found that the Ferox had left itself open. He reacted on impulse, realizing a second too late what the Ferox was doing. It took a painful blow to the ribs, but caught the staff under its arm, quickly bringing its forearm under and over, gripping the staff with its claw.

Its arm now a vise entangling his weapon, Jonathan hesitated and the beast capitalized, pulling the staff and him with it. Unprepared and being thrust toward the beast, he was forced to let go as the Ferox spun, its tail whipping toward him too fast to be dodged. It took him off his feet when it connected. Sideways, he crashed into one of the exposed I-beams, pain shooting down his spine as he dropped to the ground.

The beast waited for him to raise his head.

It dropped Excali-bar to the ground before him, using one of its feet to kick the staff behind it, far out of reach in a pile of building supplies. He didn't understand why it hadn't thrown the weapon from the roof. Did it want Jonathan to focus on retrieving the weapon? Did it just want inside of his head? Lifting himself off the ground, leaning against the I-beam, he looked down at his fists. They still seemed so inconsequential, useless.

How was he going to win this? He felt panic seeping in through the cracks in his mental shield. The Ferox seemed to become invincible and terrifying.

Dams the Gate. Jonathan's stolen inner voice spoke the words as the

Ferox pointed to itself with claws, growling at him in its alien dialect, naming itself. *Wants the Challenger's life more....*

It roared at him from the center of the floor, but his own voice intimidated him from within. It beat its chest again, daring him to try to reclaim the staff, or, even better, to fight unarmed.

Jonathan didn't have a plan for this. All he could think about was the beating he'd taken at the hands of Sickens the Fever. Now here he was, with no escape and nowhere to hide. He'd lead himself into a death trap.

Your blood will run in puddles, Challenger.

Unable to escape Dams the Gate's voice within him, he lost what little grip he had on the adrenaline surging through him, heard the desperate sound of his heart racing in his ears.

The Ferox stepped toward him, beginning to close the gap. Jonathan's body shook as he stepped away from the I-beam. The Ferox seemed aware of the change in him. The bloodlust in its eyes gained fervor, the predator's impatience at the closeness of its victim more evident.

You wear your fear, Defending Champion, Bringer of Rain.

As they approached one another, the Ferox drew down lower to the ground, its head bobbing like a snake coiled for attack as it watched Jonathan with one eye and then the other. It seemed pleased with itself at seeing his hesitance, its teeth clicking again in anticipation. It moved toward him suddenly, and he overreacted, committing to a dodge. He knew immediately that it had feigned the strike, used his fear against him so he would leave his guard open. It rushed toward him then, capitalizing on his mistake, catching his face hard with its solid fist. Jonathan could hear metallic knuckles clinking together against his eye socket as he was spun violently around.

Defenseless, his back exposed, he whipped back with his fist, trying to force the Ferox to dodge. The strike sailed futilely through the air and was returned by a jaw-cracking fist that forced his eyes to the sky and loosened the teeth in his mouth. Dizzied, unsure where his enemy now stood, he lashed out again, desperately hoping to connect.

There was a loud clap and he was brought to jarring halt. The Ferox's claw seized his arm mid-swing, gripping him by the wrist, and before he could react he was pulled off balance by the monster. He felt it release his arm as he was flung forward. Helpless to stop his momentum, an anvil came down on him. The monster's clasped hands hammered into the back of his head, sending him straight at the floor.

Jonathan felt his feet leave the ground and his skull thrash against cement, heard the surface cracking around him as his head broke through the concrete. Dazed, he rolled, barely quick enough to keep the foot coming down for his head from crushing him back into the ground. Dams the Gate's stomp shook the roof as he rolled further away, hurrying to put distance between them. It charged him, kicking into his abdomen so hard he was ripped from ground and sent shooting across the roof.

Jonathan crashed through a stack of building supplies that exploded around him, only slowing him enough to drop him into a roll. Disoriented from the barrage, he reached out to stop himself and felt his finger gripping the rim of the roof edge as the surface ran out below him.

Jonathan scrambled to pull himself back onto the roof.

The fight became a blur of pain.

He was hesitating, taking blows he should have dodged, not capitalizing when the beast made a mistake. He tried to defend but the creature was getting in too many hits. Every blow was a failure resonating in his mind; he felt himself coming to know the battle was lost.

The viaduct all over again; the creature toyed with him. He was rolled over the pavement, smashed into the steel beams, slowing down, and stiffening as the blows added up. Finally, the creature lifted him, grabbing him by the front of his jacket. He felt his body spun, thrown across the roof.

He thought it was the end, that he'd soon feel himself falling as he plunged from the building. Instead, he slammed into the metal doors that housed the temporary elevator shaft that the construction workers used to get to the roof.

He'd have broken straight through and fallen to his death at the bottom, but the lattice metal doors were held shut by a padlock and heavy chain. The doors bent around him until they absorbed the full force of his impact and spit him back onto the cement.

His ears were ringing, the wind and rain pounding him there. He coughed and blood spat onto the concrete in front of him. He knew what it meant; internal bleeding. The red puddled in front of him, bringing him back to the kitchen floor, whispering to him what seemed so obvious now. He was always going to die. He had been dead from the moment he'd woken up that night, been headed right back to that puddle since the moment he dared to crawl out of it.

He wondered, then, if Heyer was seeing this now. Would he really not intervene—would he watch him fail? Would the alien close his eyes when the Ferox tore the life out of him, only to have the whole ordeal cease to have ever been a moment later?

Despair gripped him.

A beam of light hit the Ferox. It was the helicopter finding them, now, when his hope was lost. Perhaps his friends would all see him die up here before this timeline ceased to be. The light on the monster made it all the more menacing, casting its shadow onto Jonathan. Dams the Gate hesitated in the light for a moment, pulling focus from its prey until it decided the helicopter wasn't a threat.

Jonathan heard the thudding now, the sound of the helicopter's blades tuning out the rest of the world's noise. It was calming, having the chaos of so many sounds reduced to one. He turned his head and saw the chain dangling from the elevator doors.

He knew he had to get up, but he didn't want to; he wanted to let it be over.

Don't lie down in front of him.

It was the voice of some wise old man, the words someone was supposed to be there to say to him, now, there in his thoughts. A hot spark of anger awoke in Jonathan as the isolation he felt pressed in on him, reminding him that no one was coming, that he was alone. The thing inside of him, stirred by the injustice of it, came alive and growled.

Dams the Gate should have been on top of him by now. What was it waiting for?

He looked again and found the monster taking its time walking over to finish him. This savoring of their victory seemed to be a species trait.

Even this one, so impatient for the kill, wanted him to keep fighting, wanted his death to be drawn out.

His eyes fell back to the ground, to the blood before him. The rain had begun diluting it, washing away the red. The anger screamed out from within him, desperate to be heard.

This is the moment.

It surged up in him, showing him the things he couldn't bear; the stacks of dead, the murdered trophies of Sickens the Fever. The shame he'd endured for allowing it to happen.

I do not feel guilt. I will not lose to fear.

The voice was his, and yet it belonged to the part struggling to be freed inside of him. It showed him the face of the little girl. Her broken body, her innocence contaminated.

I can be whatever it takes.

Like a fuse being ignited, the rage took hold of his perception, changed the way he saw things. His abandonment ceased to be his weakness. His isolation wasn't a curse. No one was watching; no one would ever remember.

The rage didn't see despair. It saw permission. It saw freedom.

CHAPTER THIRTY-EIGHT

TUESDAY | SEPTEMBER 5, 2005 | 5:20 AM

JONATHAN KNEW, THEN, why he was lying near-defeated on this roof top. He'd come down here with his shiny new weapon, like some damn knight riding a horse. He'd been trying to protect himself from the truth of it all, save what was left of him from the last real horror.

As he pushed himself to his feet, it all became so simple. Dams the Gate wanted to be here, and Jonathan was still looking for a way out. The Ferox desired every moment of this, wanted him to get up and keep fighting, wanted to feel pain and give it in return. It wasn't conflicted, it had no doubts about its goals; it was primal rage and taking his life was its only purpose in this existence. It came here eagerly, through a gate to another world, to find him, and he'd still been running away.

He wasn't supposed to recognize himself when this was over. He wasn't walking away unscathed. He couldn't be normal or ever hope to find normal again. He'd been naïve to hold onto the hope that he could.

The dark side of the story, Jonathan—you know its name.

All of this, every last atrocity, was happening in a place where only he and Dams the Gate mattered. The world didn't need to like what he'd have to become to save it. Today, mankind didn't need him to be a champion, it didn't need him to be a savior.

It just needs a killer.

Jonathan felt himself let go, felt himself give permission to the part of him struggling for its freedom. The panic muted around him, pushed out by the fury rising to the forefront, and as the change touched his eyes, the light, the spark in them that could be a victim, went out.

Reaching his feet, the eyes of a killer found the Ferox stepping toward him. Jonathan reached up, finding the zipper of his coat, and pulled it open. The light from his chest spilled out of its confines, and Dams the Gate grew insane with bloodlust at the sight of it.

Its neck began to bulge, darkening as the thick tar surged into its jugular, blackening its eyes. Jonathan's hands dropped to his side as he waited, letting it all happen, letting the beast come to him.

Death won't be able to tell us apart.

He didn't move, not until the Ferox, sure of its impending victory, drunk with the anticipation of violence, lunged for him.

He reached up to intercept it, his hands grabbing hold of its chest and neck, the beast's momentum sliding him back over the wet cement toward the shaft of the elevator. Its jaws snapped at his face like a raptor trying to sink its beak into prey. He could feel the force of the monster pressing in on him, trying to shorten the distance between them, trying to make his arms bend to its strength. Jonathan's feet skidded across the ground, unable to find traction on the wet cement.

They stopped abruptly when his boot found leverage against the elevator shaft. He held it off there, pushing back against the metal doors. He remembered the syringe in the hallway, the pillar below the viaduct. His nightmares, now powerless over him, only fueled his rage, feeding the violence he'd let free within.

As he pushed back, growling with the effort, everything he had was brought to bear against it, and he felt the Ferox begin to lose ground.

Its inability to force its will on him was a revelation. He gazed back into the monster's eyes as the truth revealed itself, a smile cracking his lips as he returned the monster's stare. The beast, becoming agitated, shook with effort as it realized what was happening. He saw, behind those white eyes turned black, it recognized it could be the one to die.

In its moment of fear, he brought his hand down from the beast's chest, gripping it into a fist. No longer fragile or small, the hand was steel. He let out a roar as the fist smashed into the monster's throat. Its legs buckled as its hands instinctively came up to protect its neck. Its guard down, the Ferox dropped to its knees in pain. In an instant, he kicked hard into its chest, rolling it back across the roof.

Jonathan, eager for more, began to step forward, but stopped as a thought occurred to him. He turned to the chain dangling behind him, gripping the padlock with his hands and crushing the mechanism in on itself. Quickly, he pulled it free and returned his attention to the injured Ferox.

The helicopter had circled and the light now shown down on Jonathan's back, making the monster flinch to keep its eyes on him. It was hunched over, one hand on its neck, hacking up its black blood, its eyes watching Jonathan step toward it with uncertainty.

As he closed the distance between them, he wrapped the chain around his right glove tightly until it felt like a part of him, making his hand into a hammer.

"You know, Dams the Gate, I wish I could send you back alive. So you could tell every last one of your kind what waits for them here."

As the Ferox tried to stand, Jonathan charged. The creature's legs were unsure; it hesitated, not knowing if it should attack or protect its injury. It made the wrong decision. It covered up defensively and was knocked hard across the roof, ramming into one of the I-beams protruding from building's skeleton.

He was on it again in a second, giving no mercy, feeling no pity. It would not be allowed to collect itself.

Halfway risen to its knees, he caught it hard with the chained fist, its jaw wrenched to the side as it took the blow. Black fluid slapped the pavement. His free hand darted in, grabbing holding of it, keeping it in place. His fist rained down blows. Beating the beast into the building, the steel beam bent inward from the rage he'd set lose on the monster.

He looked down at his enemy, and saw that it had no strength left to stand, saw that links of the chain had broken in the barrage and embedded themselves in its face and throat. It struggled to breathe, to hold onto consciousness.

Jonathan heard the guttural growling of a man losing his sanity, and realized the sound came from him. Blood dripping from his lips, he roared down at its defeated body. Unclenching his fist, he wrapped what was left of the chain around the half conscious creature's neck and pulled it to its feet against the beam.

From between gritted teeth, the thing inside of him spoke. After lying dormant so long, waiting to have Death by the throat, waiting to have the power to change something, it knew exactly what it wanted, knew exactly what war it was meant to fight.

"I will be the end of your species."

The Ferox's eyes tried to focus, but Jonathan had no interest in savoring the moment. It could think about his words on its way to the ground. He swung Dams the Gate toward the edge and let go of the chain, watching his enemy fall out of sight as it plummeted from the roof.

He scaled down the side of the building, the light of the helicopter and the wind from its blades making it all the more difficult to do so. At least it had stopped raining.

Excali-bar returned to the harness on his back, he dropped a few stories at a time, reaching out to halt his momentum every few levels. He dropped again and again and it hurt every time. Even with the device activated, he could feel his injuries draining him. It didn't matter. He'd be done bleeding soon.

Pain was just a warning that something was damaged, a little alarm saying *you might want to stop what you're doing before you break something permanently*. As long as he destroyed that stone, the pain in his body could complain all it wanted. He only had to bear it a little longer. When there were only six stories left, he dropped to the ground.

The helicopter light followed him. The police had the construction site gates open. He was grateful for that. The idea of having to jump over anything else tonight hurt just to think about. He worried that the police would try to stop him, tell him to freeze or to put his hands up, that he would have to push through them to get to the beast's body. He didn't want tonight to be the night he found out if he was bulletproof. Luckily, that didn't happen. They didn't seem to know what to make of any of this, let alone Jonathan, walking toward them with his chest ablaze.

As he approached, he saw open mouths; he might have heard murmurs of confusion, but he couldn't hear them over the helicopter blades, the perpetual thudding noise drowning out what otherwise would have been a noisy city street.

The police parted for him again as he approached the body. They let him walk into a ring where officers surrounded the Ferox. It had put a hole in the city street—large cracks emanated from the point of impact.

He realized then it wasn't dead. It was bleeding out, gargling on its own insides. It struggled to move, desperately reaching out for something, like it was hallucinating. What a Ferox might reach for in the throes of death, Jonathan couldn't imagine. He wished it had died; he wished it would realize that all there was left to do was die.

As he looked down at it, he remembered that the Ferox was as alone as he was here, beaten to near death and surrounded by people who were about to forget it existed. This arena that pitted them against each other outside of place and time was isolating to the both of them.

He didn't know how it was possible that his pity had returned, that such a pure rage could crawl back inside of him and make room for other emotions. Jonathan unsheathed the staff once again. He wouldn't make it wait for release, it felt too cruel. He couldn't help but feel it could be him struggling in the street, reaching out for some last vision of life.

It was the last time this Jonathan would feel these things; he knew that sympathy for his enemy could only get him killed. He looked for the largest chink in its armor and hammered down blows until there was a crack large enough to impale it.

He was glad he couldn't hear the people watching. He didn't want to know what their reactions were as he reached into the body, dumping that black sludge, still warm, all over the street. Why were they watching him anyway? Why did they have to watch this savagery? He supposed he was like any soldier. The world didn't need to know he was out there. They certainly shouldn't want to watch him do whatever he needed to do, become whatever he had to become. They'd reap the benefits of his existence regardless.

Once Jonathan had his hands on the stone, he ripped it free, just as he'd seen Heyer do on the docks before. He walked away a few feet and sat in the middle of the street. The people watching him may as well have already ceased to exist. He removed the gloves he'd been wearing. Sitting there, he wiped off the stone, until all the black blood was gone and all that remained was the glowing red orb. He took one last deep breath, his ribs reminding him they were cracked.

Jonathan shut his eyes and clenched his fist.

"It's all a matter of how they respond to what happens to them. There is no sure bet that one will become the savior," Hayden finished.

Jonathan's face looked more serious than Hayden had expected. A moment ago, he'd been interested, now he looked out of sorts. The change had been so sudden, and Jonathan didn't speak for a moment.

"I think it's a good story," Jonathan said. After a brief silence, he excused himself, saying his drowsiness was finally catching up with him.

Hayden, of course, found that completely reasonable. After all, it was four in the morning.

CHAPTER THIRTY-NINE

IT WAS LATE afternoon when Leah pulled into the parking lot. There was one other vehicle there, as she'd been advised would be the case. She parked and stepped out of her car. As she approached the black sedan, the rear passenger door opened and Olivia stepped out of the vehicle, holding the door open for her.

"So good to see you," Olivia said, her words polite and business-like.

Leah reached into her pocket, retrieving a small memory card and holding it out to Olivia. "Here is a compilation of all the most recent photos I've been able to take of the subjects," Leah said.

"Excellent," Olivia said taking the card. "I look forward to your report."

Leah stopped before taking the seat being offered to her.

She didn't want to make an enemy out of this woman, but she reported to one superior, and Olivia wasn't that superior. Leah never made any pretense of undervaluing Olivia's role or responsibilities, but in this she knew she must always be clear.

"I mean no disrespect," Leah said as discreetly as possible, "but I'm only reporting to our commanding officer. He'll make the call as to what details you're to be briefed on."

If her statement had come as a surprise, Leah couldn't read it on the woman's face.

"Of course," Olivia said. "I didn't mean to create any confusion."

Leah smiled and nodded while Olivia's features remained cemented in place. She climbed into the car, and Olivia shut the door behind her.

"Hello, Leah," said the voice.

She was still staring through the window at Olivia's back. She waited a moment before responding.

"I don't think your lead likes me much," Leah replied.

"Admittedly, I wouldn't trust her if she did," replied the voice. "She has the highest security clearance her department has a designation for. I don't know her real name myself. She is charged with observing, containing, and controlling this operation. As such a task is highly volatile and any failure inexcusable, she is under a great burden to execute the protocols flawlessly."

"I've given her no reason to doubt me," Leah replied, still staring out the window.

"It's not the point. You're the one member of this team who she did not hand-select and who isn't under her orders. She has no visibility to your background outside a vague report indicating your involvement in the development of the secondary protocol. To her, you're another variable that she has to control."

"Well," Leah replied, "perhaps you could divulge to her that I wrote the protocol she is implementing."

"It wouldn't change the fact that your involvement in the field is highly unorthodox," the voice replied. "Your recent choices, I have to admit, have given me my own doubts as to whether or not I should have allowed your involvement."

Leah closed her eyes. She knew that he received reports on her every action. It was part of the arrangement. It didn't make the conversation she was about to have any less awkward.

"General Delacy," Leah said, then rolled her eyes. "Dad, there's no need for the voice modulator."

There was a delay. Finally, the window dividing the back and front seat began to roll down.

She mentally prepared herself for the conversation about to take place. There was no level of professional etiquette that was going to make this situation less disturbing. He'd allowed her to work with him on this operation, but it wasn't going to change the reality of their relationship, even if that relationship was only apparent when they were in a sound-proof vehicle together.

As her father came into view, she saw he wasn't in his uniform. He was wearing a suit and tie, dressed much like the male version of Olivia.

"You sit on this side of the car long enough you forget it's there," he said, his voice uncloaked.

He turned to look at her.

"I never wanted you to feel you needed to prostitute yourself," he said.

The uncomfortable nature of this conversation was heavy, despite the practical reality of the situation. It was the only scenario she could imagine where she'd be required to discuss, in detail, her decision to invite a man into her bed with her father. She had, after all, demanded this opportunity, spent over a year getting him to make it happen.

"I'd hardly call it that," she replied.

"Jonathan Tibbs is aligned with the mark," he replied, "the very being responsible for Peter's disappearance. You must realize the kind of person you may be dealing with."

Leah knew that she and her father had a different idea of the nature of Jonathan's involvement with the alien. She'd been keeping it to herself, but now was the time. She was the person on the inside, and though she knew her observations might be clouded, he needed to be aware of them.

"I don't believe Jonathan volunteered to be in the position he's in. For that matter, we both know Peter was a good man, and from what we know, Jonathan's experience is playing out almost exactly as Peter's scenario did," Leah replied.

"We need to remember that whatever Peter was wrapped up in with the alien may have been of his own volition, Leah," her father said. "Do not let your desire to believe in your brother's honor cause you to ignore that he was involved with the enemy for weeks leading to his disappearance. He made no attempt to notify the authorities. It appears this Jonathan has also elected to take the same course."

"Peter's actions weren't voluntary!" Leah said. "He wasn't some villain! The alien had something over him, something that forced him to hide, even from us. You can think whatever you want, lecture me on the importance of being a passive observer, but you don't believe any more than I do that Peter chose the alien over mankind."

The father sighed.

"Just explain to me what you're doing," he said.

Leah took a moment to gather her thoughts, her eyes again returning to Olivia's back.

"We are still flying blind," Leah said. "Jonathan has been under observation longer than any other subject, yet we've hardly learned anything. The alien is too elusive. If Peter is still alive, the only way to get to him is through the alien, and only way to get to the alien is through Jonathan."

The father listened but said nothing.

"Jonathan is like Peter in so many ways. It's plain that he's scared shitless, even if he is doing his best to hide it, yet, he's been forging himself into a warrior for months now despite this fear. I've observed this change. It's evident from watching him that he isn't doing this for himself. He is...." Leah paused. "He believes it is of dire importance; it's been to the detriment of every other facet of his life. He's given up everything to become a weapon."

"How does this push him into your bedroom?" the father asked.

She looked out the window for a moment, gathering her explanation despite the terrible awkwardness. Her father was a pillar of professionalism. She was his only blind spot and she knew it. It was the only reason this situation had ever come to be. If Olivia ever got an inkling of their familial relationship, she'd likely lose her cement-like composure.

"We have no idea how long before he could suddenly disappear on us. He might be standing in his garage one day and be gone the next. He knows he's being watched, but he hasn't made any attempt to reach out to authorities, and you can't blame him after the oversight with Grant Morgan."

"It wasn't ideal; we had to work with what we had. At least Mr.

Morgan took the attention off you, and got us the intel we needed within the house until you could integrate yourself. No one will be suspecting a young woman renting the house next door with her little brother. I don't think the alien will even see you coming," her father said.

He didn't have to explain; it had been Leah's design in the first place.

"I understand—still, Jonathan either doesn't trust this operation now, or doesn't believe it can protect him from the alien. With our limited visibility, it might be something else entirely, but it doesn't convict him as a willing participant."

Leah gave her thoughts time to sink in before continuing.

"Jonathan is dedicated. I could hardly distract him from his undertaking despite openly throwing myself at him. I don't mean to be immodest, but it's no small deed for a twenty-two-year-old to be so unwavering. I believe he is trapped in this situation that he sees it as more dire than his own life," Leah said. "The last few weeks, I've seen that something is drawing close. It's in his eyes, building up. He is so afraid and unequipped to deal with that fear."

"What are you saying?" her father asked. "Have you taken him to bed out of some sense of pity? Mercy?"

Leah felt a rush of anger at the judgment in his tone. She wasn't a child. He was still seeing his daughter and not a member of the team, not a capable woman who knew what she was about.

"He needs to open up to me. I need to gain his trust, but I can't push him. I can't make him the least bit suspicious. He has to see me as a woman he shares a common history with. He has to see a woman who'll understand him. That kind of trust can take months, even years to build. We don't likely have the luxury of that much time," Leah said, then paused for a moment. "Maybe there was a small element of mercy. Before Peter disappeared, he was at his wits' end. He had no one, just as Jonathan is now so alone, becoming more and more isolated. Even his roommates think he's just damaged from his initial assault. My gut told me…."

She stopped before finishing that sentence. Her father still seemed dissatisfied, although perhaps not as much as he had been initially. Leah stopped explaining like she was giving a report. She knew, now, what her father wanted to hear.

"For what it's worth, General Delacy," Leah said, "if I had met Jonathan under different circumstances, the result may have been the same. Albeit less rushed." She flushed red at having said it, yet the look of disapproval seemed to waver in her father's eyes.

"If you develop feelings for him," her father said, "you may jeopardize us."

Leah shook her head. "I've got it under control," she said.

In her thoughts, she wasn't as sure. She felt that if she wasn't as real as she could be, vulnerable, that Jonathan was never going to trust her like they needed him to.

"Try to remember, Leah," her father said. "We probably can't save him."

CHAPTER FORTY

AT DUSK, JONATHAN lifted the garage door. It was time to train again. Heyer had said, so long ago, it would be a matter of days or weeks before he'd be activated again, that the Ferox would only increase in frequency moving forward. The dread was there, but less now. Any one engagement with the beasts wasn't a death sentence; it was the unending horde that would eventually kill him.

Though he would have been hard-pressed to put it into words, things were different now. This role was his. The skin he wore seemed more his own, the habits more familiar. His desire to go back to the way things had been fading away.

The emotions might have been left in the dust of a nonexistent timeline, but the memories resided in his head like any other. Jonathan supposed killing a sentient being was the same no matter what the species. With the first Ferox, Sickens the Fever, there had been no philosophical burden, because Jonathan had felt more like a victim then. Dams the Gate, in its last moment, had left a mark on him. The way it reached through the pain at the end, before he had beaten the life out it, its eyes no longer filled with rage, just desperation, haunted him. It was too human, even if it had been a monster.

Jonathan figured it would have to be this way for a while. People drew lines in the sand. Then something happened and they stepped over them. After it happened once, it got easier and easier to cross the line again. Eventually, he'd forget there ever was a line in the first place.

When he pulled the garage door shut, the alien was there, fedora and all.

"I'm glad to see you, Jonathan," Heyer said.

Jonathan nodded, shutting the door behind him.

They talked awhile. The alien asked what had occurred the night before, how it had played out with the Ferox. Jonathan gave him the highlights. How the Ferox had been of some different variety than the first, how he'd lured it to the roof. He stuck with the facts, not how he felt about them.

Heyer listened. He took most of the story without interruption until Jonathan brought up the creature's physical form. Jonathan saw the alien's concern then, as he described the thing's body structure, its color, its behavior.

"I can see you're thinking about something, Heyer. I know we agreed that if I was still here today you'd give me some answers," Jonathan said. "To be honest, though, if you think it's best for me not to know, I'll trust you."

The alien looked into Jonathan's eyes then; he seemed to be looking for a sign of sincerity in them. Jonathan expected he would find it. He didn't put faith in things. He hoped Heyer saw now that this was what he was offering, his faith.

"Curious, Jonathan," Heyer said. "I've seen your need to know, the quest for the truth, plaguing you. What could change that you would relinquish that virtue?"

Jonathan thought about how to answer the question. "You were right," he said, "about almost everything. I clung to claims for my freedom, not because you forced me into this, but because I was afraid. If I had had the choice, I'd like to think I'd have made it. I was holding onto a story I told myself, about who I thought I was. I didn't want to see it was a facade.

"Still, it was when I thought about your actions that I made my peace with it. You found a planet; you came to love its people. When that planet was threatened, you came to its aid. We aren't even your species and you asked nothing. I felt that, should I turn out to be wrong about you, I could live with the choice I'd made with what I knew."

Heyer nodded. He seemed moved. Perhaps it was one thing not to ask for thanks—it was another to have it given anyway.

"It would seem we have found a way to trust each other," Heyer said.

Jonathan nodded. "Guess it doesn't matter much, really. I don't want to fight blindly, but I will if you believe it's for the best," Jonathan said.

"Jonathan," Heyer started, "I will never fall under the illusion that your enslavement wasn't morally reprehensible. The only comfort I have is that the alternatives were far worse, but I have spared you of other enslavements. I have not demanded that you believe in what you must do, only that you do it. I've not demanded you choose to participate. I have taken the burden and freedom of that decision from you. I've not demanded you trust me, as I have given you little foundation to support that trust. If you wish to know the truth of things, I will give you this truth. Please consider that there is no way to ever un-know what I might tell you. Consider whether or not you really want to carry this weight into your next confrontation."

"Given the option, I'd prefer to know what my actions mean," Jonathan said. "I've been considering the weight of it for months."

Heyer nodded. "It's undoubtedly the same decision I would make," Heyer said.

They fell into silence. Having this wall between them for so many months, neither was sure how to start breaking it down.

"Where do we begin, Jonathan?"

"The Ferox…." Jonathan said. "Why? Why show up on earth, start killing innocent civilians? Why kill children? It seems so blatantly evil, senseless. What do they want?"

Heyer looked at Jonathan for a minute, thinking deeply. He looked like he was about to speak, but then changed his mind and asked a question instead.

"Jonathan, can I ask you something?" Heyer asked.

"Sure," he said.

"What do you want the answer to be? If there was an ideal reason for the Ferox, one that would make you resolved to continue fighting them, what would it be?" he asked.

Jonathan shook his head. It was hard to think of a reason one would hope for.

"I guess…." Jonathan hesitated. "This will sound strange, as I don't believe in demons, but if you told me they came from Hell and that all they wanted was to torture and murder the innocent, that I was fighting the Devil's minions… that would be the easiest answer."

Heyer looked at the floor and nodded. "Wouldn't that be so uncomplicated?" he replied.

"It's not so much that it's uncomplicated, just that it's fair. Be evil, be killed," Jonathan said. "Justice."

"I don't need to tell you that 'fair' does not have much to do with real life," Heyer replied.

Given his circumstances, Jonathan found the statement amusing.

"Go ahead, Heyer," he said, "complicate things."

The alien nodded.

"They aren't killing indiscriminately, Jonathan. They can't see the difference between a child and an adult any more than you can discriminate between the ages of the Ferox. If you doubt this, understand that the green creature you killed the other night, formidable as it may have seemed, was a child. The coloring, the unformed body type, the tail, the uncontrolled rage it was struggling with," Heyer said. "For better context, you killed the equivalent of a teenage boy."

Jonathan let that sink in for a bit. He didn't doubt the explanation. Frogs lost their tail as they made the transition to their adult form, and the Ferox's ears had seemed prepubescent.

"The first Ferox, he called himself Sickens the Fever," Jonathan said. "That name, it seems to embrace suffering."

Heyer's face changed into a grim half-smile.

"Names do not translate well. They bring with them a cultural baggage that the simple explanation of their root meaning cannot contain. Take your own name. 'Jonathan' means 'Jehovah's gift' in Hebrew. How do you think that would sound to an alien unfamiliar with your planet's beliefs? What if that species came from a culture that didn't have religion as your world knows it? The machinery that allows the translation fails to capture such subtleties. Further complicating the issue, the translator only has access to the vocabulary in your head. What does the name Jonathan really say about you? I'd imagine nothing. Names have just become a noise that you associate with yourself."

"Fair enough," Jonathan said, "the teenager, the green Ferox, he called me *Brings the Rain*. Why did he give me one of their names?"

"I'd be guessing," Heyer said, "but likely it was an expression of respect. Perhaps it found you quite formidable. Perhaps it wanted you to see that it valued you."

"Valued?" Jonathan asked.

Heyer waved it off. "We'll get to that," he said, "the point is, they choose what their name means as much as you do."

Jonathan sighed. Even if it was interesting, this wasn't important.

"Why pile the bodies?" Jonathan asked. "Sickens the Fever seemed to relish killing us."

"It's more instinctual than it is evil. But, that isn't the real reason it did so the night you fought. The easiest answer to that question is because that was what the Ferox was instructed to do."

"Instructed?" Jonathan asked.

"It is only looking for one human. It will continue to kill whatever it sees until that human is drawn out by the atrocity," Heyer replied and stared at Jonathan until he made the connection.

"They come here for me," Jonathan said.

"In a manner of speaking," Heyer said, "yes."

Heyer hadn't lied; this was getting more complicated with every explanation. Jonathan couldn't see how this made sense. Why would the Ferox come for him? What did the alien mean "in a manner of speaking?"

"Jonathan, I'll try to give you some context, something a human can relate to."

"Okay," Jonathan said.

"Imagine that tomorrow the governments of your world locked away every female on the planet. All men on earth are told that mating is no longer allowed. All mating privileges, all access to sex at all, is only on government permission. What do you think the response of the men of Earth would be?"

Jonathan thought to reply with a shrug, but as he considered the implications they became ugly in his head rapidly. There was no good ending to that story. "I'd imagine the most violent rebellion in human history," Jonathan replied.

Heyer nodded. "Well, in this analogy, you, Jonathan, would be the government requirement. Well, to be more accurate, killing you is the key to unlocking their females," Heyer said.

"How is that possible?" Jonathan asked desperately.

"You, of course, aren't guilty of literally keeping the male Ferox from their females. Still, to the Ferox, you are what stands between them and their species extinction, their ability to bear children," Heyer explained.

Jonathan still didn't understand, but was starting to make connections in his head. The way the Ferox had desperately tried to keep fighting even after it was doomed—he knew now what it reached for. Jonathan wasn't only taking its life; he was taking their future. They saw him as the key to unlocking the salvation of their species. He sat down on the weight bench and rested his forehead into the palms of his hands. Somehow, he was the ultimate evil to them. His threat to the Ferox, "I am the end of your species;" could it have been exactly what they already believed?

"Go on, please explain."

"The Ferox have always been a highly formidable species Jonathan. The planet they reside on now is not their origin planet—it is not unlike the Hell you wished they came from. That said, it is an immensely larger planet than Earth. They've evolved there, becoming intelligent and dangerous predators.

"Originally, the Ferox shared their surrogate planet with two other species of similar intellect and lethality. They had reached a balance with these other species and co-existed in a natural equilibrium.

"Unfortunately, the Ferox have evolved to require combat as part of their reproductive cycles. For the male of the species to become capable of impregnating the female of their species, they must engage in combat with an enemy species of paralleled combat ability. Likewise, for the female to achieve fertility, she must be presented with evidence of this combat from the male," Heyer said. "It's more complicated than this simple explanation, but it is enough for now."

Jonathan, listening intently, interrupted. He'd taken enough evolutionary theory to know that what he was being told sounded highly unlikely. "That doesn't sound possible, Heyer. I can't imagine what type of evolutionary pressures would have had to be in place to create such a temperamental reproductive system," he said.

Heyer nodded, seeming pleased that Jonathan was keeping up.

"Unfortunately, that is correct, Jonathan," he replied. "Their evolution wasn't strictly natural. Their current reproductive problems are due to the intervention of another species. Artificial selection, not unlike what humans have done to the wolves of this planet."

Jonathan knew what Heyer was referencing. Though difficult to imagine, all breeds of dog came from the original genetic stock of wolves. Human intervention had formed the breeds to its wishes.

"Now, imagine similar manipulation in the evolutionary process of the Ferox, this time on a rapid scale with intervention coming from a technologically advanced civilization bent on creating a weapon. Genetic modification of the Ferox is performed. The resultant breed grows stronger with every generation because the only members of the species that are able to reproduce are those that are capable of seeking out, engaging, and inevitably killing a creature of similar lethality."

Jonathan stopped to think about the implications of what he was being told. This explained why the Ferox seemed so unstoppable: bullet proof skin, metal inner skeleton, seemingly impossible strength, innate combat aptitude, but worst of all, a non-negotiable motivator for violence.

Things just do what they can. Jonathan's father's words echoed in his thoughts.

The creature resulting from what Heyer described couldn't bother entertaining a moral argument about murder. There would be no conversation Jonathan could ever have with a Ferox that would convince it that violence wasn't the answer. For them, violence was in fact the only answer. What was worse, it wasn't even the Ferox's fault; their biology required it of them.

"Why Earth?" Jonathan asked. "Why target them to Earth?"

Heyer looked to the floor again, placing his fingers over his eyelids. Jonathan worried. The alien was about to tell him this was not so simple again.

"Perhaps it is fortunate for the time being, that it is not so simple a matter as Earth being targeted," Heyer said.

"Perhaps it is fortunate?" Jonathan asked.

"If Earth was simply under attack by a conqueror, this would be a diplomatic problem," Heyer said. "Earth would have no choice but to surrender, as a full onslaught of these creatures would cripple your way of life in a matter of days and your planet would be easily invaded afterwards. No, this is a unique circumstance, and conquering earth is not the immediate goal, at least not yet. You see…." Heyer delayed, and the pause worried Jonathan. "It was my species. They played God. My species turned the Ferox into the incarnation you now know."

"Your species made them into weapons?" Jonathan asked.

"Yes, but before you get upset, please try to understand the history," Heyer said. "My species is almost entirely extinct."

Until now, Jonathan had imagined Heyer came from some planet out amongst the stars, filled with enlightened beings, sending themselves out to help aide less civilized species. It was like a child making up a story to explain something he didn't understand, and forgetting he'd made it up.

"I'm sorry," Jonathan said.

Heyer waved him off as if to indicate that this was not an emotional confession, just a piece of the puzzle Jonathan would need to understand.

"I've only ever met one member of my species," Heyer said, "my older brother, Malkier. Jonathan, I've been alive for thousands of years. My earlier formative years I spent with my brother, traveling the stars and dimensions that we had knowledge of from the libraries of information that our species left behind. The only impression I have of my species comes from my brother and historical records.

"I could speak volumes about those times, but what is relevant to our current situation is this," Heyer began. "We eventually each chose a species to settle with, live among. We took on bodies that allowed us to blend in with that species and became a part of those worlds. I chose Earth because Malkier said that the people here were the most like the people I had never known, our own species. Malkier, who had been alive to see the self-destructive traits of our species end in our inevitable extinction, was loathe of living among a race with similar characteristics," Heyer explained. "He chose to live amongst the Ferox."

Heyer saw the look on Jonathan's face.

"I can tell you can't imagine what would lead him to make this decision. What you have to understand is that Malkier's choice is one of virtue. Or at least it started as such. He felt a responsibility to the Ferox to restore their biology to what it was before our species corrupted them. Though it may seem hard to believe, the Ferox possess a trait very inhuman that my brother prizes above any other," Heyer said.

"What's that?" Jonathan asked.

"They are incapable of hurting their own species," Heyer said. "They do not fight among themselves; violence is reserved only for their enemies and their mating requirements. They will never have a civil war or a squabble over resources; they have no countries. They live in tribe-like communities but if one member moves from one tribe to another, they are immediately accepted. My brother, having watched our civilization destroy itself, found comfort in integrating with such beings. After thousands of years with the Ferox, he has come to love them much the same way I've come to love mankind."

"I guess—" Jonathan paused. "I guess I can understand that."

"The current problem we now face is quite simply this, Jonathan," Heyer began. "The planet of the Ferox can no longer sustain their reproductive traits. My brother and I, though we come from an advanced civilization, are not scientists. What we know, we have learned from our libraries and years of study—but there was never a well-educated member of our species to teach us, so our knowledge is highly fragmented. We do not possess the means necessary to fix the Ferox."

Heyer let this information stew for a moment.

"Unfortunately, my brother will stop at nothing to save them. I have tried to negotiate with him; I've asked him to let the species run its course. Unfortunately, he is completely willing to sacrifice Earth to have the species with which he identifies survive."

Heyer was pacing now.

"I had to strike a bargain with my brother to preserve Earth as unharmed as possible. What we have now is a balance. A fair confrontation, as fair as we can make it, where certain humans are given the necessary enhancement to fight the Ferox for their lives. One at a time, in a controlled setting that does not disrupt the majority of life on Earth. He has agreed, only because I am his brother and this is my home, to maintain the Ferox population at a stable minimum. Only enough to ensure the species can persist. This is all to buy time as he searches for the solution to the mating problem. You have to understand—this was the best I could arrange for mankind."

Jonathan was thinking intensely. "Your bastard brother is playing cross-dimensional ecology? I am fighting for my life because he wants to save an endangered species of monsters that your civilization corrupted forever ago! I am just buying time, by giving them a damn combatant to fulfill their reproductive rituals."

"Malkier could have opened doors into this world and let the Ferox loose on the planet. Your way of life would have been destroyed. Your military would have been in constant combat with these creatures, thousands would have died, and that would only be the beginning. Mankind was to be enslaved, bred in camps, devices such as the one in your chest forced on the males so they could present a challenge to the Ferox in an arena. All so the Ferox could persist.

"This was the only solution I could come to with him to preserve both planets' existences. To ensure the fewest casualties on Earth for a fight that was never its responsibility."

Jonathan hated every word of what he was hearing. He was a sacrifice. He was fighting for no one but himself after all.

Things made sense now. This was why Heyer said the creature valued him, because he was a resource it needed for its species to survive. It was like a hunter thanking a deer he was about to eat for its meat. That was why it was instinctual to stack the bodies. They kept a count of their own kills. They worked themselves up into some type of combat-based mating frenzy and presented their kills to their females. Jonathan realized, then, that this still couldn't work. It didn't make sense; Heyer was leaving something out.

"Wait!" Jonathan said angrily. "Heyer, even if I died and the creature took my body to the Ferox planet, it would only allow for one male to mate. That couldn't possibly sustain the entire Ferox species. You'd need a lot more. Hundreds of people like me."

Heyer hung his head.

"Jonathan, there is a reason I am constantly moving all over the globe," Heyer paused and stopped pacing. "You are not the only combatant in play."

Jonathan's image of reality was shattered again.

"When a Ferox is allowed access to one of the gates to Earth," Heyer paused, "it hits a network of possible nodes where it will find a combatant, most in major cities. The nodes are targeted to those with the device implanted; the Ferox arrives in close proximity to the individual it will fight."

That explained why the beast would show up within a ten-mile radius of his house. It wasn't his house at all; it was him.

"How many of us are there?"

Heyer looked away. "The number fluctuates," he said. "Few men are the victors, and those that are, aren't for long. The nodes often need to be replenished."

Jonathan nodded angrily. "This is so much worse than I feared. I thought you knew what you were doing. I thought I was fighting for Earth. I knew you'd tell me the odds were against us, but I trusted that you had a plan!"

Heyer saw the look of betrayal on Jonathan's face. It clearly hurt him to see, and Jonathan didn't care.

"You're right, you know. I shouldn't have asked. What the hell is the point?" Jonathan said as he angrily paced the garage. "That's all I was that night you came looking for me, that night you put this thing into my chest. You were replenishing a node, refilling a damn bird feeder."

"No, Jonathan," Heyer said. "Please don't see it as such."

"How in the hell am I supposed to see it?" Jonathan asked. "It doesn't matter what I do, how prepared I am, how vicious I become. It's just a matter of time."

"If you were nothing more than a sacrifice to the Ferox, if you were nothing but a reinforcement, I never would have activated you!" Heyer said, raising his voice.

Jonathan, still looking for a string of hope in all this terrible news, tried to rein in his growing rage at the sound of Heyer's yelling.

"Jonathan," Heyer said, "I do have a plan. I just can't accomplish it on my own. I needed help."

Jonathan felt like he was on the park bench again, desperate for the alien to help him, desperate to know things weren't impossible, that he wouldn't leave him with nothing but a void of inevitability that couldn't be filled.

"You remember what you said, Jonathan?" Heyer asked. "That if man found themselves in a similar predicament, it would lead to the most violent rebellion in human-kind's history."

Jonathan stopped pacing.

"The Ferox are at the brink of extinction. My brother—he lives amongst them as one of their Alpha leaders. They do not know that he is not of their species. He is the only one who can allow them access to the gates they require to get to Earth and bring back their trophies. They saw him as the great leader, the one who found the way to spare them, but the tides are shifting and he doesn't want to see it. The youth of the species are beginning to challenge his leadership."

"They're going to turn on him," Jonathan said.

"The moment of rebellion is not far off. When that time comes, he will give them complete control of the gates to appease them. If they discover he is not of their species, they will kill him and take control of the gates in the process. Either way, mankind is in trouble, and we need—"

"You couldn't kill him," Jonathan interrupted. "You couldn't just dismantle the gates and do away with your brother."

It wasn't a question; it was a statement of comprehension. Insight into the alien had struck Jonathan so suddenly, he just blurted out the words as they came to him. He saw so clearly now what had led Heyer and mankind to this terrible point.

Heyer took a long breath. "My brother's madness was too sympathetic, Jonathan. I can't say what I would do to save man if they were going extinct. It all seems so easy, I know, but if your mother was about to commit some atrocity, and you were given the option of stalling her in the hopes that you could find a solution, don't you think you would have tried to save her life first?"

"I don't know what I would do, Heyer," Jonathan said. "I can admit that much."

Heyer seemed to relax at this. He was plainly defensive over the life of his brother and the decisions he'd made to preserve it. "I believe, now," Heyer said, "that it may not be my choice any longer."

"You had a chance once, didn't you?" Jonathan asked. "You sympathized with him, and you couldn't kill him. I spent all this time thinking that you kept me in the dark because you didn't want the government cell knowing what you were up to. That was really only half of it though, wasn't it? You didn't want me to know the truth about the Ferox. You were afraid I'd hesitate, like you did. You were afraid it would get me killed."

"It's painful to kill the enemy you understand, to make a villain of the desperate. I feared endangering your life if I gave you any sympathy for the Ferox. It only would have made it harder to do what you inevitably must."

They sat for a while then, Jonathan still trying to make all the pieces fit in his head, still trying to see what plan the alien could possibly have in the midst of such a complicated mess; Heyer, too, seemed caught up in his own thoughts. When they both seemed ready, Jonathan asked the question.

"Heyer," he said, "you said you had a plan. Please tell me there is a light at the end of this tunnel."

The alien nodded. "I activated you, Jonathan. I have had your name in the registry of compatible subjects for years. You could be the strongest combatant they've ever faced," Heyer said, "but physical reasons aside, strength alone does not make a General."

"What?" Jonathan asked.

"Many die in their first confrontation with the Ferox," Heyer said. "But some are like you, Jonathan. They refuse to lie down. I have been activating those amongst mankind with the higher compatibilities to their devices. The most likely to win. I have been increasing their numbers slowly as to not raise the Ferox loss rate too noticeably. I have done this because a war will soon be upon us. If we wish to contain it, we will need an army. That army will need a leader. That leader will have to be human."

"You want me to lead an army?" Jonathan asked. "I don't know the first thing about leading."

"I activated you now to give you the time to become the man we'll need you to be," Heyer said. "I told you I did my best to follow my moral compass, but I can't shoulder this alone. I need a voice from your species. I need someone who knows what we are up against and understands what will be required to stop extermination. I need someone who can tell me when I've lost my way. I chose you to be my compass, because I know you will not abandon mankind to fate, not at any cost."

Jonathan felt sick.

He found his legs wouldn't hold him. He sat on the bench, afraid to hear anything more the alien had to say. "There must be someone else, there must be someone who wants this, someone experienced in war. I've never led anyone; I'm twenty-two...." Jonathan trailed off. The number of reasons the alien had to be wrong about this decision were too numerous to bother listing.

Heyer nodded at Jonathan's reasoning. "I have not voted in a human presidential election for quite some time, Jonathan. Admittedly, it may not be my place. Still, do you know what really stops me from selecting a candidate?"

Jonathan listened but mostly focused on containing his nausea.

"It's a paradox, I know. It just seems that anyone smart enough to know the responsibility of such a seat of power would never be dumb enough to apply for it. I only trust a man with power when he is wise enough not to want it."

Jonathan felt like climbing into himself. "Dams the Gate," Jonathan whispered, "that was the name the Ferox gave. Seems like more than a name now—seems like a sick joke."

Heyer became so silent then. Jonathan, looking up to him, though perhaps he, too, needed to sit down. Instead, the alien seemed to be blinking at him like he was in shock, like he had just been hit with a tranquilizer dart and wasn't quite sure what was happening.

"Jonathan, are you absolutely sure that was the name the Ferox gave?" Heyer asked.

"I'll never forget that name," Jonathan said.

Heyer stepped forward, still seemingly caught up in his own thoughts, and placed a hand on Jonathan's shoulder. "I think we've discussed enough tonight, Jonathan," Heyer said. "I have to go. I will see you again, once you've had enough time to process all this. Stay diligent in your training."

"Heyer, why are you—"

The alien was gone before he finished.

CHAPTER FORTY-ONE

HOURS HAD PASSED in the garage before Jonathan had come to grips with enough of what he had been told to walk into the house. Until then, he'd just sat, thinking over every revelation, clinging to the small threads of hope the alien seemed to have. He was more afraid of the future than he'd ever been.

When he finally rose to his feet and walked into the living room, he was surprised to find that everyone was home. Collin and Paige sat at the table. Collin looked cheerful; he was studying of all things, which was odd. Hayden was on the couch, Leah and Jack beside him; he was watching Star Wars again. Jack waved when he entered. He hadn't expected his neighbors to just be hanging out in his home, but Leah and Paige were friends, so it was probably to be expected now. He was just glad she was there.

How Jonathan was to behave around her was unclear. That such a worry could even enter his consciousness, given what he now knew, was absurd to him. How could his mind so obviously prioritize the wrong concerns? As everyone was present, and Jack right beside her, it didn't seem like a question he needed to feel out just then, so he sat down on the couch. Just close enough to Leah as to betray no meaning. He liked the idea of watching a movie now. He'd done enough heavy lifting with his brain for the day.

"Jack's never seen Star Wars," Leah said as Jonathan sat. "Hayden couldn't let this be."

Jonathan nodded. This, of course, made perfect sense.

"Hayden?" Jack asked. "How many times have you seen this?"

"I don't know, kid," Hayden said. "Probably fifty."

"Wow," Jack said, "and you never get sick of it?"

Hayden shrugged.

"Just one of those things," Hayden said. "Every time I watch it, I get giddy with the same feeling I had the first time. I can't help wishing a wise old man would show up and train me to use the super powers I never knew I had."

A groan escaped Jonathan's lips. He hadn't expected it, or to sound like he found what Hayden said so silly as to be offensive.

"Oh yeah, Tibbs?" Hayden asked, wanting an explanation for the response he'd gotten.

It was Jonathan's turn to shrug. "Any old man ever shows up and offers to train me to use super powers, I'd assume he wants me to fight a war he can't fight for himself," Jonathan said. "Sometimes wanting something is better than having it."

Hayden looked like he was going to argue, launch into a long-winded rant. Instead, he seemed to get lost thinking about it.

"Might have a point," he said.

CHAPTER FORTY-TWO

WEDNESDAY | SEPTEMBER 7, 2005 | 8:00 PM

SHE BLAZED DOWN the freeway, the lights of the city fading behind her as she turned onto Interstate 280. She poured on the throttle dangerously, pulling herself down tight around the sports bike to cut the air.

Rylee, now committed to leaving, was making a conscious effort not to look in the rear view, not to even let the thought gain ground in her mind. The more distance she put between herself and Manhattan, the less likely she was to turn back when her resolve wavered.

She had little on her, just her gear and what she'd crammed into the knapsack strapped to her back. She wasn't leaving behind anything she couldn't replace. All she needed was the bike and her stuffed bank account. They gave her the freedom to go where she pleased, the freedom to run.

She'd planned it for weeks now. She didn't know if he could track her. Maybe it didn't matter where she was. Maybe he could find her anywhere. She wasn't letting herself worry about the consequences of rebellion. The chance had to outweigh the repercussions. To Rylee, what mattered was that she was doing something, anything, to take matters into her own hands, to control what she could.

If he wanted her, he was going to have to chase her down. If he didn't like what she was up to, he would have to find a way to stop her.

She had no idea how far he might take it. She supposed it would depend on how much it interfered with his schemes, but Rylee didn't believe he would kill her. He seemed to need her too much.

Seattle.

It had to be a city on the other side of the damn continent, but she knew it was the place to start. There was something important there, something he was trying to protect, something she could leverage.

She needed to know what that man valued. If she could take it away, she might be able to take her life back.

DEAR READER

I am an independent author and *word of mouth* is the most powerful form of marketing at my disposal. If you enjoyed The Never Hero, and know others would want to follow The Chronicles of Jonathan Tibbs, please tell your friends. Spread the word via Twitter, Facebook, Instagram, or any other social media at your disposal. Also, the more reviews posted to Amazon and Goodreads, the more likely it is for future readers to find their way to this and other works. Even a few short words is greatly appreciated.

COMING IN 2016

THE NEVER
PARADOX

CHRONICLES OF JONATHAN TIBBS

VOLUME 2

ABOUT THE AUTHOR

T. Ellery Hodges lives with his wife and son in Seattle, Washington. He is currently hard at work on the sequel to The Never Hero. If you'd like to know more about T. Ellery, visit his blog at www.telleryhodges.com, follow him on twitter @telleryhodges, or *like* The Never Hero page on Facebook! If you prefer e-mail, he'd love to hear from you at telleryhodges@gmail.com